CUT
ALL
TIES

JAMES DUNN

Paperback ISBN: 979-8-3628736-1-5

Cover design by BespokeBookCovers.com

For Mandi and Nya.

*The world is a brighter place for having you both in it...
most certainly stranger, but definitely brighter.
All my love.*

ACKNOWLEDGMENTS

My heartfelt thanks to two women, whose work helped the scatter-brained author of this book to focus:

Kat Etoe, for invaluable feedback and advice at an embarrassing early-stage; and to Shelley Routledge, editor extraordinaire.

Many thanks to Peter and Caroline O'Connor for their incredible work on designing the finished book.

I can't wait to work with you all again, if you'll have me.

The somewhat tired statement bears repeating here: while the above listed share in this book's strengths, its many faults are mine alone.

James Dunn

CHAPTER 1

The urgent call woke Gayle Stillwater from a sound sleep. She hurried into jeans, a red T-shirt and a lightweight suede jacket and made her way outside to wait. She had no socks on beneath her white canvas shoes but there was no time to go back inside for something warmer. She hunched her shoulders to protect her neck from the bitter October night.

It's got to be a mistake, she thought.

For the tenth time, she took her phone from her pocket and redialled Danny. She pressed it hard into the shell of her ear and turned her back on the whipping wind. After four rings, his terse voice instructed, *"Leave a message."*

She hadn't smoked in seven years, not since learning she was pregnant with Finn, but she wished she had a cigarette now.

"It's me again," she said, lips so numb that she had trouble pronouncing the words. "Call me back, please?" She hung up and checked to see if she had missed any calls or texts from him.

Nothing.

The cops got it wrong, she told herself. Danny had

simply drunk a few too many beers and passed out somewhere. In the morning, he would call to explain, then she
would rip him a new arsehole for worrying her.

But the police wouldn't have called if they weren't
already certain. A mistake of this magnitude seemed
unlikely.

No one could live as Danny did without a call of this
kind being inevitable. She'd warned him this day would
come. She pictured him now; slowly nodding as she spoke,
feigning interest as he stared into the middle-distance, until
his patience broke and he just walked away.

On the other side of the road, the River Soar flowed by,
dark and unhurried. Its rippling surface reflected the crescent wedge of moon hanging in the cloudless sky above a
phalanx of trees. The wind passing through their branches
issued a pained, lonely moan.

She looked over her shoulder, up at the dark windows of
her own flat and wanted to be there. Finn was sound asleep
under his Batman duvet, snoring gently, while her friend
and neighbour, Bobbi Okoye, lay curled in the armchair.

Gayle stepped down off the kerb to get a better look
around the bend in the lane, but saw no approaching car.
The police said they would be with her soon, but that was
ten minutes ago. "Come on," she mumbled, taking her place
on the pavement again. She shuffled her feet to keep the
blood circulating.

Halfway down the lane, a fox crept out from behind a
parked car. It looked her way, eyes made iridescent by the
humming streetlights. The scavenger watched her for a
moment before getting spooked, and it skittered across the
cracked and pocked road, disappearing into the shadowy
hedgerow at the river's edge.

A whip of wind blew her auburn hair into her face. She

reached for the scrunchie that she always kept in her jacket pocket. As she tied her hair into a ponytail, the cold found its way to her exposed belly and she shivered. She crossed her arms over her breasts and buried her hands in her armpits. Her exhalations plumed in the air like the smoke for which she yearned.

On the tail of those cravings came the others. Alcohol. OxyContin. She had been an addict by only nineteen. Though she had been clean and sober for years, her lips were cracked and dry with a sudden thirst. She wanted to fade away into the numb, warm chemical haze where she found safety in feeling nothing.

But she couldn't allow that. Her hard-won sobriety was precious, in no small part because both her parents had been hopelessly lost to their own addictions. Finn was the reason for her transformation: she owed it to him to be a better person; a better mother than she had known.

At the end of the tree-lined lane, she saw the approach of pale-blue strobes of light. The almost-silent police car cruised out of the shadows. The beacons stung her eyes and she looked down, squinting, until it stopped at the kerb beside her.

A female police officer – a young Asian woman with a long, straight nose and heavy-lidded eyes – got out of the passenger side.

"Ms Stillwater? I'm PC Chauhan," she said. "Come on, it'll be warmer inside." She opened the rear door and gestured Gayle over. The smell inside was a heady cocktail of pine air-freshener, burgers and piss.

As she put on her seatbelt, the driver looked at her over his shoulder. He was white, early-thirties, with a shaved head. A two-inch scar in the shape of an inverted V was carved into the flesh above his left ear. He set his jaw as his slate-grey eyes fixed on her in the rear-view mirror, though he neither greeted her nor introduced himself.

She turned away, watching the coruscating blue light play on the façade of the building and the cars parked along the lane.

Chauhan took her seat and the door thumped shut. "This is PC Rhodes," she added when her partner said nothing.

Rhodes did a three-point turn and drove towards the main road.

Gayle stared out the window, watching the river disappear behind a tangle of bushes and trees. In spite of the heaters, the cold she felt was bone-deep and would not be dispelled.

* * *

The drive to Leicester Royal Infirmary took little more than ten minutes.

In an easy-going tone, Chauhan asked, "What do you do for a living?", turning back to look at Gayle.

Behind the wheel, Rhodes made a show of clearing his throat.

Gayle stopped chewing her thumbnail for a moment. "I work in a bar," she managed, her voice croaky.

"Oh? Where at?"

"'*The Marquee*'."

"Yes," Chauhan said. "I know the place. I've never been inside though."

Again, Rhodes cleared his throat. "Picked up one or two troublemakers from there," he said. His eyes were once more fixed on Gayle. He only looked away to use his high-beams to flash through a red light.

Chauhan lowered her voice, leaning towards him. "Are you all right?"

He cast her a glance, shuffled in his seat and let out a sigh. "Almost there," he announced quietly.

Gayle looked out the window again as the city streets slid by, consciously trying to relax her tense shoulders.

When Rhodes stopped the car at the rear of the hospital, Gayle realised she tasted blood. There was a tear in the skin along the side of the thumbnail that she'd been chewing, almost to the cuticle.

She squeezed her thumb tight inside her fist until PC Chauhan let her out into the bracing wind. As she found her feet, that treacherous part of her mind reminded her that while most shops were closed at this hour, there was a petrol station a forty-minute walk away where she could buy a reliable bottle of booze.

"Forget it," she whispered to herself. If the officers heard her, they gave no sign.

Even at this hour, the hospital was busy, though foot traffic thinned as they led her through the labyrinthine hallways to the morgue. She wondered how often the two of them had made this same journey.

They went through a door marked *Viewing* – Chauhan first, then Gayle and Rhodes. The room was small, with a soft-looking leather-effect settee and a side-table, upon which sat a box of tissues and a scattering of magazines. A water-cooler bubbled in the corner. These details barely registered, however, as she was transfixed by the large window in the right-side wall, covered by closed horizontal blinds.

A greasy flutter of nausea passed through her and she felt momentarily light-headed. It must have shown on her face, because Chauhan laid a gentle hand on her shoulder.

Her half-closed eyes looked at Gayle with obvious concern.

"Would you like a cup of water?" she asked.

Gayle licked her dry lips and shook her head.

Rhodes stood by the window, beside the blind's pulley controls.

The door opened and a tall male doctor with tiny lozenge-shaped glasses entered. He was in his late-fifties, with baggy black trousers and a crumpled grey shirt that Gayle doubted had ever been near an iron. His wispy white hair was thin and he didn't offer his hand in greeting, but stood with his fingers interlaced, a frown wrinkling his forehead.

He launched into a well-rehearsed speech: "I'm Dr Ansell, the coroner. I'm very sorry to ask, but you're here to supply a formal identification, if you can. While the deceased was carrying ID, you should keep in mind that the person through that window may or may not be Mr Gowan."

Gayle nodded.

"My assistant will lower the top sheet to reveal the deceased's face. A nod of your head will verify that it is indeed Mr Gowan. A shake of your head would be to say that the deceased is somebody else. Okay?"

Again, she nodded. "I understand."

"Also, I must warn you, Ms Stillwater, that the deceased was very badly beaten. You may not be able to say yes or no definitively, in which case I assure you, that is perfectly fine. You're under no obligation."

"I'm ready."

Rhodes raised the blinds with a jarring metallic rattle.

Beyond the glass, the other room was pale blue and sterile. Less than three feet from the window, a young man stood beside a stainless-steel table. A body lay stretched out upon it, covered head-to-toe with a surgical sheet; its whiteness made more stark in the wash from the overhead fluorescents.

Standing beside her, Dr Ansell gave his assistant a discreet nod.

Moving slowly, the assistant folded the sheet back to the body's throat.

She bit her lip and choked down the urge to beg them for more time. *Not yet*, she thought. *I was wrong: I'm not ready.*

But she looked.

The face was lumpish and red, swollen and bruised almost beyond recognition. A deep tear in the skin of the forehead revealed blistering-white bone. His dark hair was cut short and in the lobe of his right ear, the corpse wore a gauge piercing. On his neck, he bore a tattoo: *Finn*.

Instead of screaming or bursting into tears, Gayle turned from the window and walked to the settee. She sat, catching her breath, icy hands on her knees, looking down at her pinched and bloodless knuckles. She flexed and rubbed them together, trying to dispel the chill. She cupped her hands and blew into them.

The blinds rattled down, hiding the body from view.

Dr Ansell remained in his place by the window. "Ms Stillwater?" he asked.

She gave a gentle nod. "It's Danny."

"You're certain?"

"The tattoo," she explained. "Finn's our son. It's his birthday next week."

"I'm very sorry."

Gayle gripped her knees with both hands, digging her

fingers in. She released a shuddery breath. "What happened?" she asked.

"Further investigation will reveal more, but it seems that he was beaten to death."

She looked from the coroner to Rhodes to Chauhan and back. "Can you tell me who did it?"

Rhodes pursed his lips, shifting his weight from one foot to the other. He looked down and, after a pause, said, "Enquiries are bein' made."

Gayle nodded. She knew what that meant: *No.*

"Do you need us to call someone for you?" Chauhan asked softly.

"Can you just take me home?"

Chauhan looked quickly at Rhodes, blinking her eyes. "Um, ready whenever you are."

But all the same, Gayle couldn't move her feet. She closed her dry eyes, but was unable to banish from her mind what had been done to Danny's once handsome face.

She made no effort to move, despite what she told the cops. She sat in silence for a moment, feeling suddenly exhausted, and all the while wondered how the hell she was going to tell Finn.

CHAPTER 2

It was after one a.m. by the time Rhodes parked at Soar-Bank Apartments. Gayle expected him to remain seated, but he got out to open her door then dropped back behind the wheel again.

Chauhan exited but stood with her forearms resting on the roof of the police car. She cupped the side of her face, squinting in the flash of the beacons. "Are you sure you don't need anything?" she asked. "There are services I can give you the numbers for. Websites too. They're quite good."

"We need to go," Rhodes told her, his arm lolling on the steering wheel. "This is taking too long."

Gayle bristled at his attitude but fought to keep her composure. She shook her head. "No, I'll be fine. Thanks for the lift back." She turned and headed for the entrance, feeling their eyes on her.

She found the key and let herself in, but not before hearing Chauhan ask softly but with urgency, "What's your problem?"

"Don't you know who she *is*?" Gayle heard him ask

before the door shut and the engine growled, taking them away down the lane.

She rode the rumbling lift to the third floor, watching the numbers change. The steel doors cast back her ashen reflection; even her usually-bright green eyes with their almost cat-like inward tilt looked empty and haunted. She tamed her hair and drew the jacket more tightly around her body. Although the common areas of the building were always warm, she didn't feel it.

Thinking back on the cop's comments, she thought, *Oh yeah, and who am I exactly? Just some violent tart from the council estate? A gangster's bitch? What the hell would you know about it?*

The doors slid open and Gayle stepped into the hall-way, turning left. The overhead lights were on their dimmest setting. The hard-wearing beige carpet absorbed the sound of her footsteps as she made her way to 4 D, keys in hand.

The entrance hall was not much bigger than a double-wardrobe. She hung her jacket beside Finn's and pushed through the door into the flat proper.

The open-plan room was a combined kitchen-diner and lounge, the two spaces only made separate by where the kitchen's laminate flooring met the lounge's beige carpet. By the light of a small lamp, she saw Bobbi curled on the settee. She dozed with her lips parted, covered to the waist by a crocheted throw.

Gayle eased the door shut and removed her shoes. She tiptoed barefoot across the lounge and turned off the lamp. Bobbi stirred but did not wake.

She pushed through the door into the small hallway leading to the bedrooms, passing first her own then the bathroom, stopping outside Finn's room. As she always left it ajar, she heard the boy's faint snoring from inside.

Peeking in, she saw him in the purple wash of his night-light, diagonally across the bed, covered to the waist by the duvet. His thick hair was brown like Danny's and stuck up as though he were an anime character. His pyjama top had hiked up to his mid-chest and she watched it rise and fall as he dreamed. On the pillow beside his head, his ten-inch stuffed Batman plushie kept guard.

She wanted to cross the little room and kiss his cheek, but was afraid she would wake him. She couldn't face looking into those guileless eyes of his – not yet.

Gayle pulled the door to and went to the bathroom. She washed her face, staring at her reflection in the medicine cabinet. In that moment, she looked older than twenty-seven. Her eyes were red and puffy; every little wrinkle and laugh-line looked like it had been etched with a knife.

She imagined she was looking not into a mirror at all, but a magical portal to some elderly, wiser version of herself. She wanted to ask this older Gayle how she was going to get through this. When all she received was a sorrowful sigh, she turned off the light.

In her own room, she stripped off her jeans and T-shirt and slipped naked beneath the covers. Some foolish part of her thought that if she could only sleep, the last hour would prove to have been a dream and things would be back to normal upon waking.

But sleep would not come. When she closed her eyes, she saw only Danny's ruined face. Even when she tried to conjure a memory of him alive and happy, she was tortured instead by the memory of the last words they spoke to one another. He was meant to take Finn to the cinema last week, but called to cancel. When she pressed him, he would not give a reason.

"*You can be a selfish bastard,*" she had said at last.

"*I've got something on that I can't get out of,*" he said. "*I tried.*"

"*I was able to walk away from those people for our son. Why can't you?*"

"*I thought you didn't want to talk about that stuff.*"

"*I don't.*"

"*Then what do you want me to say?*"

"*When are you going to grow up and stop letting him down?*"

"*I'll make it up to Finn.*"

"*Like last time?*"

"*And I'll make it up to you.*"

"*I've heard it all before, Danny. Just... do whatever,*" she had said and hung up.

At the time, she even thought that he might be seeing someone that he had not wanted to tell her about. Their own relationship had ended when Finn was just a toddler, and while Danny had sometimes shared her bed until as recently as a year ago, she was under no illusion that he was celibate. His secretiveness was – at least in part – her own doing, having insisted that gang-life ended at her front door.

She turned onto her side, adjusting the pillows over and over before flinging one to the other side of the room. Its passage through the air fluttered the curtains before landing in the corner.

She gripped the remaining pillow as if in a headlock and lay on her front, face buried into it to stifle a long groan.

"What did you do?" she asked, her voice muffled in the dark.

Gayle couldn't remember how many times she had

warned Danny that this would be his end. As a high-up member of the *West-End Crew*, his life on the street had been filled with brutality from a young age, and when she followed him into it, she had seen for herself that few if any gangsters made it out alive. Her own escape had been the exception and not the rule, a fact for which she was grateful every day.

She had begged him over and over to do the same. There was a good man inside Danny, buried very deep beneath his often cool, coarse and sometimes aggressive demeanour; a man to whom she had once been devoted. While she had seen him whip a bicycle chain into a rival's face, opening a deep laceration above the teenager's left ear, he had also been tender with her, protective and loving. In those early days, he might well have been the only person after her grandparents died to ever show her genuine kindness.

At last, reflecting on this tragic flaw in Danny's soul, the tears came. She squeezed her burning eyes shut, moaning into the pillow, weeping not only for his violent loss but that she had been unable to save him from it.

CHAPTER 3

"Dead?" Bobbi whispered, a frown knotting above her large, dark eyes. "How?"

Crouched on the settee in flannelette pyjama bottoms and a cream T-shirt, Gayle hugged her knees. "Somebody beat him to death." She rubbed her grainy eyes and checked her watch. It was almost half past six. Finn was going to be up soon.

Bobbi fidgeted with a strand of her cornrows. The coffees that Gayle had prepared sat on the table, going cold. "I'm so sorry," she said. "Do the police know who did it?"

Gayle shook her head. "I got the impression they think he got what he deserved."

With her dusky voice low, she said in her soft Nigerian accent, "You know, if you need anything, I can stay." She placed a hand on Gayle's wrist.

"I'll be okay," she said. "You go. I've got to call Danny's mum and... somehow, I've got to tell Finn." She ran her hands back through her hair, massaging her scalp. "I don't know how I'm going to do this."

"You know where I am if you need me."

Gayle forced a smile. "You're one in a million."

After she hugged Bobbi goodbye and was alone again, Gayle called Finn's school to explain that he wouldn't be in, then took a hot shower. Dressed in jeans and a lemon blouse with three-quarter sleeves, she made another coffee and sat in the armchair, readying herself to place the call she was dreading.

When the line connected, she heard sniffling and unsteady breathing on the other end. "Gayle," Lorraine whispered, her voice choked with emotion. "Does Finn know?"

"He's still asleep."

"What *happened*? Have the police said anything to you?"

"No, nothing."

"They said there'll be an inquest." Lorraine stuttered over and over, as if unsure on what to say next.

Gayle found a loose thread on her right knee and began picking at it. "I'm so sorry. I just don't know what to say."

"That boy," Lorraine said. "He was just so..."

"I know."

"...so... *stupid*. I'm going to Hell, I know, but he *was*. Why couldn't he be more like you and get away from those people?"

In truth, Gayle agreed about that last part, but couldn't bring herself to speak so plainly in light of his death. "I think he was trying, Rainey. It was really hard for him."

Lorraine sniffed. "I can't believe I'm so angry at him for dying. What kind of person am I? That can't be right, feeling that way about your own son."

Gayle knew that Lorraine was a good woman who had done her best after the death of her husband to raise a head-strong young boy with a violent temper. At that point in her life, Lorraine couldn't see that a lot of his acting-out came from that trauma, as well as his dyslexic and attention-deficit traits.

"You're in pain," she said. "Don't beat yourself up. I think even Danny would understand. He knew he was no angel. You can't help feeling mixed up."

Lorraine blew her nose and Gayle held the handset away from her ear. The two women took turns consoling one another for a few moments before Gayle said, "We'll come up to see you soon," she said.

"That'd be lovely. But don't rush. I'm not going anywhere. You just look after that handsome boy. He's your priority, sweetheart, not me. I'll take care of... you know, all the arrangements."

"Look after yourself, Rainey, okay? I love you," Gayle said. In many ways, Lorraine had been more of a mother than the sorry excuse of a woman that had given birth to her.

"I love you too." Lorraine sighed. "That boy of mine should have been better to you."

They said their goodbyes and hung up. Gayle dried her eyes and had almost collected herself when she heard Finn splashing water in the bathroom sink. A moment later, he padded into the living room barefoot, hair in disarray, still wearing his pyjamas. He mumbled a good-morning and went straight to the TV and turned it on. He flopped down on the settee, rubbing his eyes and yawning, waiting for the Sky box to boot up. He looked around the living room as though it were his first time seeing it.

Finn turned to her, frowning. She usually had his coat and shoes laying out by the small dining table, along with his bag and packed lunch.

"What time is it?" he asked, voice still froggy from sleep.

While the shape of his face was like hers, his eyes and that frown were all Danny.

She considered building up to it; reminding him about the talk they had after Lorraine's dad died of colon cancer. That appeared to be the kindest way, but burying the lede in that fashion seemed insensitive. She vacillated until she thought she was going insane with indecision.

In the end, she came and sat next to him and put her arms around him. She kissed the top of his head.

"I love you, Finn," she said.

"Yeah. I love you too."

"And you know your Dad loved you?"

"I know."

Gayle gnawed on her lower lip. "Last night, sweetheart, there was a really bad accident and..." Her hands trembled on Finn's shoulders. "He died last night. There wasn't anything anybody could do." Words failed her then as she watched him absorb the meaning of what she said.

His eyes welled up and started her crying again. He tried to say something, but a sob burst from his lips instead and she pulled him to her breast, smoothing his hair. She hugged him against her and felt his body shuddering as he wept. She pressed her cheek against the top of his head, rocking gently from side to side. His hot breath and tears soaked into the front of her blouse.

Beneath the pain, she felt the rise of a sudden anger. As she tried to soothe her little boy, she felt angry at Danny for never considering how his loss would impact their son.

After a while, Finn pulled back. He rubbed at his eyes with balled-up fists and wiped his face with his sleeve. To her surprise, he got to his feet and went back to his bedroom. She heard the door close and his quiet weeping continued.

She considered going after him, but decided he needed time on his own.

Feeling lost, she got up and washed the coffee mugs. She left them on the rack and turned off the flow of water, then bent at the waist, leaning with her elbows on the rim of the sink. She rubbed her eyes and pinched the bridge of her nose with her thumb and forefinger. "God damn it, Danny," she muttered.

Gayle hated him in that moment for the pain he had caused Finn. She tried to shame herself out of feeling that way, telling herself that Danny hadn't *wanted* to die, but it was also a tragic fact that he had never tried to take control of his own life as she had done.

Having been an isolated and resentful child growing up in a series of foster homes, Gayle had never taken her school exams. To better her earning potential, she'd enrolled in courses online to pass her GCSEs, scrimping to pay a child-minder who watched Finn a couple of times a week. Money was always tight and Danny offered to help, agreeing to come over to take care of Finn while she studied.

At first, he was on time and attentive, but little by little, he had wavered. He began to arrive late and sometimes wouldn't show up at all. Once she had returned from the local library with an armful of books to find Finn in a soiled nappy, crying in his playpen, and Danny passed out on the bathroom floor, a bottle of cheap vodka by his outstretched hand.

Gayle saw that trying to provide him a stable base to call home had in the end been only enabling Danny's lifestyle. She called an end to the relationship. She admitted to herself that she was no longer in love with him and that she hadn't been for a long time. Eventually almost a full month would go by without seeing him.

She continued to raise their son more or less as a single parent. She would not have admitted it to herself while he was alive, but the brutal truth was that Danny's relationship with Finn had become more that of a favourite uncle than a father.

She went back to the living room and dropped onto the settee. She reached for the remote and flicked through the TV channels for half an hour before the breakfast shows went to the local news.

Danny's murder was the top story. Although the news-caster didn't give his name, she said that a young man had been found dead in the city centre, over footage of Leicester Market quarantined by tape that fluttered in the wind. "Police," she said, "have not ruled out the possibility that the death might be gang-related. And next, local MP Mitchell Barrett has weighed in after a brutal armed-robbery last week left a victim—"

She turned off the TV then got to her feet and went to check on Finn. She found the boy sitting cross-legged on his bed, hugging his Batman plushie, drying his eyes with the sleeve of his pyjama top.

She sat beside him and he turned on his bottom, laying his head in her lap. She stroked his hair away from his fore-head. "Are you going to be okay, sweetie?"

He shrugged.

"Do you want to talk about it?" she asked.

His voice was monotone and not much more than a whisper when he said, "I think I'm too sad."

"You know you can tell me about it, don't you? If you want to tell me something or ask me something, now or later, it's okay. We can talk about anything you want. I don't want you to feel too sad or too scared to talk to me."

Finn didn't answer, but after a hesitation, he nodded his head. "I know."

She gave his shoulder a gentle pump. "Do you want to be alone for a little bit?"

At once, he shook his head and pushed himself upright. She drew him in against her, and he sat with his head bowed, hands together in his lap.

"I've got an idea," she said. "Let's go for a walk. Get some fresh air."

Again, he said nothing, but hopped down off the mattress and headed for the living room.

Gayle looked over at the little bedside cabinet, upon which was a photo set into an eight-by-five acrylic block, with herself, Finn and Danny smiling at the camera. It had been taken last summer at Twinlakes theme park during an all-too-brief good period between the two of them. They all looked happy.

* * *

The sky was fully overcast and grey, but the temperature was a good deal warmer than it had been last night. The wind too had eased and no longer dried out her eyes. The walk across the park to the playground at the western end took them across a bridge. Finn insisted on being lifted so he could look down into the River Soar, towards a small water-fall where there were a cluster of rushes and lily pads. Signs warned the public that swimming was forbidden.

Gayle walked with Finn past the café building and around the well-tended green, upon which people would play football or cricket in the summer months. Now dog-walkers ambled across, throwing sticks or tennis balls for those mutts who were off-lead.

Trying to lighten his mood, she said, "Hey, you know something? When they built the park in the eighteen hundreds," she said, "you know what they found buried in the ground? Elephant bones."

Finn looked up at her, trying to work out if she was being serious. "An *elephant*?"

"Yep. And a rhino."

"No way, that's silly. Was there, like, a monkey in there too?"

"There might have been. But definitely the rhino and the elephant."

He turned his gaze to his feet, scuffing his shoes along the path. A few moments later, he regarded her again with scepticism. "I thought elephants lived in Africa."

"India too."

"Then where are all the English elephants now?"

Gayle couldn't help imagining an elephant with a bowler hat, monocle and a walking cane. "Well, they weren't *English*. We had travelling zoos back then too, you know."

"Oh yeah." He let out a quiet laugh – just a small one, but it was good to hear.

At the play area, she relinquished Finn's hand and he rushed over the soft woodchips for the rope climbing frame. She told him to be careful and took a seat on one of the nearby benches.

She usually lived for the simple pleasures of just walking and talking with her son, but then she thought of Danny and adult life came crashing back in upon her.

In spite of playing dumb to the police, his death had not been quite the surprise she had allowed them to think.

She thought back on her younger days. Violence had not been an everyday occurrence, but it was certainly no rare thing. Her run with the *West-End Crew* had lasted only four years, but in that time, she had seen a number of large-scale fights, a few stabbings and two fatal shootings. Most clashes were with other gangs like the *Saffron Hill Mob*, the much smaller group called the *Braunstone Bangers* or the *East Side Boys*. It was an *East Side Boy* that she'd seen killed by a shotgun blast in Beaumont Leys. It had been revenge for the sexual assault of the sister of a *WEC* elder. Danny had been driving with Gayle and another girl, Sharon Stipe, in the back. Anthony Lyefeld, the shooter, got out on Heacham Drive and that was the last she ever saw of him.

From her coat pocket, her phone began to ring. She didn't recognise the number. She considered letting it go to voicemail, but thought it might be the police.

She swiped the screen and held the phone to her ear. "Hello?"

"Gayle?" a man's voice said. It was deep and, by his accent, sounded local.

"Who is it?" she asked.

"It's Jax."

Her spine stiffened. As if expecting him to be standing behind her, she looked back. She was alone with Finn in the play area; even the dog-walkers were more than a hundred yards away. Finn had moved on to the slide. He climbed the shiny steel chute before he dropped to his knees and slid down backwards. He paid her no attention.

Gayle tightened the scarf around her throat. "I didn't know you had my number."

"Yeah, I got it off'a Danny ages ago. Have you heard?" His voice was calm.

"Yeah, the police came to see me."

"I can't believe it, you know?" he told her. "I'm so fucked up about it. He was like my brother."

"I remember." She kicked a chunk of woodchip into the nearby bushes.

"I'm gonna find out who did it. Believe that. And when I do... well, you know, right? You, though. How are you doing?"

She wanted to hang up. "How do you think I'm doing? My son's dad is dead."

"God, I'm so fucked up about it. I don't know what to say." Neither of them spoke for a long time, but then finally Jax cleared his throat and continued. "Look, you said the feds talked to you, yeah? What'd you tell 'em?"

Gayle turned on the bench, sitting with her feet on either side of it. "What could I tell them? I don't know anything."

"Right. Right."

"What happened?"

"Some lads jumped him. Three or four of 'em, from what I hear. They just stomped him, mate – just fuckin' *stomped* him."

"I saw what they did."

"You *saw* it?" For the first time, his tone became lighter and lowered in volume. He sounded as though he had turned his face away from the phone's mic.

"I identified his body."

Jax groaned. "Fuckin' hell, babe. I'm sorry. Where are you?"

"I'm in town," she said and didn't offer to elaborate.

"We should get together, you know? You and me and a few of us from the crew. Kind of like a wake. Pay our respects and that."

"I don't think that's a good idea. I'm not part of that shit any more."

"Still. He was my bruv and that makes you my sister."

"No, you're wrong. I'm nothing to you. Remember?"

"You're *family*," he insisted, "no matter what, no matter how we left it. I'll look after you. Do you need money?"

His saccharine tone gave Gayle the creeps. "No, I don't need anything."

"Sweet. Look, you've got my number now, yeah? Just give us a call, any time."

"Uh-huh."

"When did you last see Danny?"

She sighed, losing patience. "He came to see Finn a couple of weeks ago. Why do you want to know?"

"Finn, yeah. How is he doing?" His concern sounded forced.

"Jax, I told you to your face that I'm done with all this, remember? My boy's dad was just killed. If he listened to me and got away from you lot, he'd still be alive."

"Did you talk on the phone since he came to see you?"

"I don't remember."

"Did Danny tell you what he was up to lately? Did he say anything?"

"About what?"

"About anything. About *anything*, Gayle."

"Listen. Danny loved you all more than me, all right? Probably more than Finn when it really comes down to it. And that's why he's dead, so don't call me again." She terminated the call, blocked his number and stuffed the phone into the deep pocket of her coat.

Finn was busy spinning a swing around, tangling its chains to make himself dizzy. She called him over, pushing herself up off the bench.

"Are we going, Mum?" he asked.

"Yeah. Come on."

Without argument, he climbed down and staggered

over. He wiped at his reddened nose with the sleeve of his coat and reached out for her hand.

Together, they walked back the way they had come. Finn chattered amiably but Gayle wasn't really listening. A chill licked up and down her spine. She didn't feel safe until she was inside and had locked the front door and engaged the security chain.

Finn retrieved some toys from his bedroom – Batman, the Joker and a Batmobile with a plastic torpedo launcher. He lay on his belly on the carpet, growling in a low voice that the Joker's days were numbered. He supplied the sound effects of punches and kicks as Batman and the Joker fought and tumbled over the bonnet of the Batmobile.

Gayle kept herself busy placing seven breaded fish fingers on the grill tray and putting a saucepan of water on to boil. The chore of peeling potatoes to mash was supposed to take her mind off the phone call, but it didn't work.

Jax.

She hadn't spoken to him in seven years – and in fact, struggled to remember the last time she even thought of him.

And he had her phone number.

CHAPTER 4

When Gayle first saw Danny Gowan, they were at the Clock Tower in the city centre. He sat on a bench without a back, eating chips from a polystyrene tray.

It was early April and already hot. Carly Anders was fifteen minutes late to meet Gayle and she was considering going to the cinema on her own when she and Danny caught sight of one another.

The wind blew his thick brown hair back from his forehead. Though not much taller than she herself, he could have been a model from a clothing catalogue. He popped a chip in his mouth and raised his hand in a wave. She liked his eyes and the forthright way he looked at her.

Embarrassed to have been caught staring, she looked away, but found that his eyes were still on her when she glanced back. He lifted the tray of chips, held out like an offering.

She looked around to see if Carly had turned up at last. When Gayle saw that she hadn't, Danny beckoned her over and patted the bench beside him.

It made her self-conscious at first, the way he openly

looked her up and down in her white leggings, pale denim jacket and colourful paisley blouse. She had dyed her hair with streaks of blonde and blood-red and it was cut in a choppy style that reached her shoulders.

She pushed away from the wall. He smiled as she came closer. She had the sense that he was searing the image of her into his memory. He didn't even blink.

She wore a nervous smile and said, "What's up?"

"Want a chip?"

As opening gambits went, it wasn't much, but she liked the sound of his voice: deep but smooth with a confident tone.

She reached for a small, crispy wedge and bit the end off.

Danny tapped the bench again. "Sit down."

She did, but faced back the way she had come. She felt his eyes on her again and her heart raced.

She gave her name when he asked it and, when she asked his, he said, "I'm Danny Gowan," as if it should mean something.

She went off with him before Carly Anders arrived and Gayle didn't miss her a bit. She found Danny funny, charming and really handsome in his boot-cut black jeans, black T-shirt and black bomber jacket.

He bought her a fruit cider at the first bar that didn't ask her for ID, since she was still sixteen. He didn't kiss her that day, though it wasn't for lack of trying.

She went out with him five or six times – mostly to the cinema, sometimes clubbing – before she found out he was with the *WEC*. She knew of the gang, of course, though never met any members. The introduction – or indoctrination – was a slow, steady process. Six weeks passed before she met Jackson Knox.

Though only fourteen – two years her junior and four years younger than Danny – Jax nonetheless carried himself with a man's confidence. Standing just five-eight, he was stocky, with a shaved head atop a bullish neck. He had fists like ham hocks and his nose was twisted to the right of centre, having never healed properly after a couple of breaks. His eyes were recessed deep behind his heavy brows into pools of perpetual shadow.

She learned that Jax was the nephew of the big man – Felix Knox, overall General of the *West-End Crew*. While Jax had only recently been made a full member, he swiftly crushed all charges of nepotism, as his temper was already legendary. He thought nothing of knocking down someone from an opposing set, no matter how senior they were, how many of them there were, or who was watching. His prowess as a fighter earned him the respect of even the more senior members of the gang.

Unlike a lot of the kids whose violence had its roots in acting-out or in peer pressure, Jax *enjoyed* inflicting pain.

From the moment she met him, Gayle had the impression that the Jax persona was a living, breathing mask that he wore. He knew how to mimic normal human emotions but they never seemed to reach his eyes. That telling absence of sincerity was hard for most to pick up on, but Gayle was always uncomfortable around him.

A lot of the gang in her estimation were mentally or emotionally troubled. Jax was the most extreme example. She was in no position to comment, of course, as she had enough self-awareness to see that she was emotionally troubled herself.

Her own interest in the gang was rebellion. With no living family members, save for her imprisoned father, she had come up through the system. It had hardened her;

made her bitter and cynical. She was angry at the normies for the way they seemed to have opportunities thrust upon them. There was comfort in being among other rejects and knowing that she wouldn't have to worry they would victimise her, ridicule her, or make her feel unwanted. She could stay out all night, run the streets, smoke and drink and do drugs, without concern for anyone. There was always a house-party going on somewhere. She could walk out of her foster parents' house without being worried where she would sleep, because there was always a spare bed or a settee in someone's house or flat.

Then one night it all became much too serious. She was hanging out with Danny and two *'youngers'*, junior gang-members, all drinking cheap cider on somebody's futon. Danny's phone rang and the moment he answered, he sat bolt upright, kicking over the wooden crate they'd been using for a table.

She sat up, about to ask what was happening, but Danny placed his hand over her shoulder, keeping her back. His face was turning red. *"What?"* he cried. "Is he alive? Well, where the fuck is he?"

Gayle looked to the other two, but they seemed just as baffled as she was.

"I'm on the way," Danny said, stuffing the phone into his jacket pocket. He turned to one of the youngers, whom she only knew as Bugs, and said, "Get your fucking car keys. Salvo's been shot." He headed for the door, pulling Gayle by the wrist.

The ride to Gallards Hill, deep in *WEC* territory, took only five minutes, with the engine of Bugs's Honda Civic screaming the whole way. When they arrived, she saw the Captain, Salvatore "Salvo" Cardini lying in a pool of blood on the dark pavement.

Danny leapt from the car. Beside her, Bugs too got out and rushed towards the prone body. "Is he alive?"

"I can't tell," Danny said. He bent down, grasping at Salvo's blood-stained jacket. He groaned, both legs twitching in a feeble cycling motion.

Bugs turned back to Gayle. "Call a fucking ambulance," he cried.

"No time," Danny said, grabbing Salvo by the armpits. "We'll get him to the hospital. Grab his fucking legs."

Together, the dragged him into the back of the Civic, his head on Gayle's legs. He had been shot four times; twice in the chest, once in the left leg, and one bullet caught his left hand, taking off his little finger.

"Put pressure on the bullet holes!" Danny screamed at her.

She did the best she could while being thrown around in the back seat. There was so much blood that her clothes were covered and the seat itself was saturated. The olive skin that Salvo had inherited from his Corsican parents was now pale and waxy. His eyes were half-closed and unfocused.

When they finally made it to the A&E, she watched Danny and Bugs carry him inside, but by then she knew it was too late: she had felt his chest when the breath left him for the last time. His eyes were like those of a terrified child. He was twenty years old.

The feeling was unanimous among the elders and OGs that nothing less than a death for a death would suffice. Most of the guys and a lot of the girls clamoured to be the trigger. She didn't know how many would actually have done it if they'd been asked. Even Danny talked about reaching out to an associate in Birmingham, Brummie Charlie, who could procure guns.

Jax took the lead on the inevitable revenge attack, along with Danny, Bugs and a handful of others. They worked out that a Captain known only as Nuke from the *South Side Squad* was responsible for the drive-by.

Danny never told her what they did that night; as far as she was aware, he never spoke of it to *anyone*. The rumours were that Jax had done better than gun Nuke down: he took a hatchet and cut off both of Nuke's hands, his feet and lastly his head.

From that point on, Jax was the new Captain, and he cultivated an unofficial inner circle, of which Danny was part. With this close-knit council, he secretly expanded into breaking and entering and small-scale heists, as had the infamous Birmingham gangster, Wyman Cross, who built up his own criminal empire out of a similar business model more than a decade earlier.

In the turf war that followed, several *WEC* members would be killed or injured. Bugs was stabbed to death in a city centre nightclub. Somebody dragged a younger called Ripley down a flight of concrete stairs, leaving him with permanent brain damage. Another guy called End-Zone was shot in the neck at a chip shop and placed on life-support. His family consented to shut it down and allow him to die four days later.

The *South Side Squad* was all but annihilated in a series of retaliatory stabbings and acid attacks lasting almost a month.

Jax's ruthlessness surprised no one, though he showed greater cunning than anyone credited him with. While the police turned up in force to take Jax in, they never charged him with anything more serious than brawling. Gayle suspected that his uncle had been busy behind the scenes, using his influence to pull a few strings. Thus-established as a Captain to be feared, things began to calm down. The season of peace that followed made it easy to forget the brutality which preceded it.

After that, it seemed to be business as usual; the gang operating like a kid's club whilst funnelling drug money to Felix.

Things felt different to Gayle. She wanted out and even told Danny, insisting that he should leave with her before they were both arrested or killed.

"And go where?" he asked. "This is our family, Gayle – the only one that ever *mattered* anyway. What do you think we're gonna be able to do?"

But things were harder for the girls in the gang. The boys talked a good game about unity and loyalty, but too many of the girls Gayle knew had turned to prostitution to make money. In many instances, their own 'boyfriends' had turned them out.

Then a girl she knew, Tina Pollard, died of an overdose. She hadn't been seen in two weeks. When she failed to pay the rent, the landlord let himself into her bedsit and found her decomposing body in the bath.

By then, Gayle's drinking had been out of hand for a long time, and she took Oxy every day to cope with the stress. She was able to wean herself off the pills, finding out only later how dangerous it could be to go cold-turkey from an addiction to Oxy and booze. She was lucky not to kill herself trying to get clean.

Shortly after they buried Tina, Gayle missed her period and two tests confirmed that she was pregnant with Danny's baby. This took the decision out of her hands. All that was left was to announce her plan to Jax.

Standing outside *The Barrel & Goose* pub that Jax used as an unofficial headquarters in the heart of the city's west-end, Gayle threw up in a gutter. She thought about earlier that morning, when she said to Danny, "I mean it, I'm done," as she buttoned up her jeans.

He sat on the edge of the bed. "It's just not as easy for me as it is for you," he said, shirtless, head bowed so low it almost hung between his knees.

She almost laughed. "It's not easy. I'm terrified. But I'm not gonna be like Libby or Maria and have my waters break all over the lino in a fucking crack-den." She finished dressing and left him sitting there, picking at the scabs on his knuckles.

To her surprise, Jax didn't forbid it. His face remained impassive. His dark eyes regarded her with what felt like cold disdain, but he nodded. "Well," he said around a cigarette. "You gotta do what you gotta do."

Gayle pushed up from her chair and stepped around it. "All right then," she said. She placed her left palm over her stomach though she had not yet started to show. Seeing his eyes following her hand, she smoothed her T-shirt, picking it away from her clammy skin.

She turned and walked to the door. The skin began to creep along the nape of her neck. She waited to feel his big hands snatch at her hair, but she made it to the exit untouched.

Over her shoulder, she heard him say, "See you around."

CHAPTER 5

Later that night, she ran Finn a bath and laid out a fresh pair of pyjamas. She sat with him on the settee after, trying to concentrate on her coursework while he watched *The Lego Batman Movie* and ate praline ice cream. She finally admitted defeat and put down her tablet, drew Finn close and buried her nose in his hair.

"You always smell good," she told him, "you know that?"

He said nothing.

"You've been very quiet."

Finn shrugged. "I'm getting sleepy," he said, putting down his ice cream.

"Okay," she said, giving him another squeeze. "Scoot."

He hopped down off the settee and went to the bathroom. As she washed up the ice cream bowl, she heard him brushing his teeth. With the crockery dried and put away, she went to check on him and found him already under the covers, facing the wall, his night-light off.

She switched it on, illuminating the room in a soft purple glow. She sat on the edge of his bed and stroked his hair back behind his exposed ear. His eye was squeezed tight.

She forced a small smile. "You faking sleep, matey?" She regretted the words as soon as she spoke them. His cheek was wet with tears.

"Mummy," he whined.

"Hey," she cooed, sinking down to put her arm around him. "Hey, it's all right."

"I wish it was all back to normal," he said, "like before." He wiped his nose with his palm.

"I know, darling. Me too. But it's gonna be okay."

Finn rolled over, rubbing at his eyes with the sleeve of his pyjamas. "You're not..." he started to say, but burst out in a sob again.

"It's all right," she said, drying his cheek with her thumb and kissing his forehead.

"Are you gonna die too?"

"No," she told him, looking him in the eye. "Definitely not. Don't even think that. We're going to be okay."

"I don't want to be on my own," he said, taking hold of her wrist with both of his hands.

"You won't be. All right? I promise."

"You mean it?"

"Cross my heart," she said, but left out the last part.

Gayle stayed with him for another twenty minutes, soothing him and listening to his shuddery breathing begin to deepen. When she was sure he was asleep, she got carefully to her feet. Her backside had gone numb. She crept to the door and pulled it gently to.

In the living room, she flopped back onto the settee and covered her face with the cushion.

Not for the first time that day, she felt the urge bubbling

up within her to take a short drive to the nearest off-licence.
Her mouth felt *so dry*.

Give it a rest, she told herself and sat up. She reached
for the remote and started channel-hopping. When nothing
could hold her attention, she powered it off and reached for
her phone. She browsed Facebook for a while before seeing
what she knew had been coming.

The *Leicester Mercury* had a post whose headline read,
"*Leicester man, 29, dies in vicious attack.*"

Gayle clicked on it.

The article confirmed that Daniel Gowan, originally
from the Beaumont Leys area, had been killed in a brutal
attack that left him with massive head trauma. His lifeless
body was found by two young women leaving a pub at last
orders around eleven-fifteen. The bio it gave of Danny was
cursory at best, but did make mention of his criminal
history. A police spokeswoman was quoted as saying,
"*While the investigation is still active, given the deceased's
prior history, we can't rule out the possibility that his murder
was gang-related.*" There was an open appeal for any
witnesses who might have been in the area after eight
o'clock that night and a number for them to call.

Against her better judgement, Gayle clicked on the
comments. Amidst the condolences and statements of
surprise, the *oh-my-God's* and the *what's-this-world-coming-
to's*, she saw too many comments that angered her. Some
posted *'Scum', 'Live by the sword, die by the sword'* and *'No
real loss to anyone'*.

"Bastards," she muttered.

She put the phone down and closed her eyes, laying her
head back, blowing air through her pursed lips. Had there
been any alcohol in the flat, she knew that she would have
poured herself a glass right then.

Now that Danny had been named to the public, she found herself imagining what might happen when Finn went back to school. Only this last April, she'd had a call from the principal, which had resulted in yet another fight with Danny.

She had arrived to find her son weeping in the back office with a teaching assistant trying to calm him. When he saw Gayle, he rushed into her arms, sobbing harder. She tried to get him to speak, but he was too upset to find his voice.

From across the desk, the officious bastard of a principal folded his arms. "Finn struck another child, I'm afraid. He used a toy telephone as a weapon and cut the other child right here," the principal said, drawing his right forefinger across his right eyebrow.

"No way," Gayle said. "That's not right. Finn wouldn't do that."

The assistant piped up then, with her hands in the pockets of her oversized trousers. "I saw it happen," she said.

"The other child's mother is... well, very upset, as you can imagine," the principal continued. "I think it's best that Finn takes a long weekend to realise that we use our words and not our hands, and comes back on Monday with an apology." He gave a smug smile. "How would that be, Finn?"

In her arms, Finn cried harder.

Later at home, he was calm enough to explain that the other kid, Spencer, had been teasing him all week that his daddy was a drug dealer. Finn had been holding the toy phone at play-time when Spencer started again.

"I said, 'You're lying,' but he said, 'No, my daddy says so,' and kept calling me names. Then he tried to take the phone away from me and I told him I had it first and then he pushed me." His lip wobbled. "So that's when I hit him. It wasn't hard though, Mummy, I promise."

Days after, Danny stood smiling in the kitchen when she told him. He slipped his sunglasses up onto his forehead and crouched to Finn's height, hugging him. "Good lad," he said. "That's how you're supposed to deal with bullies."

"Don't tell him that," she insisted, but Danny just gave her an amused smile.

"Oh really?" he asked. "Like you haven't—"

"Don't," she warned him. "He's just a kid."

"With his Dad's right arm," Danny enthused, and hugged Finn again. The poor boy just stood there, looking confused.

Now, looking at patterns in the ceiling plaster with sore, grainy eyes, Gayle worried about the days to follow. Taunting. Bullying. Not for the first time, she found herself wishing she had given Finn her surname instead of Danny's – though, of course, her birth name had not been Stillwater, but Jessica Gayle Slater, which she changed to disconnect forever from her parents, Daria Slater and Ryan Breach.

Too late now, she thought.

Gayle pushed up from the settee, poured a glass of water to slake her thirst, then refilled the glass and took it to the bedroom.

She stripped out of her clothes and wearing just boy-shorts, she climbed under the duvet. She closed her eyes, anticipating another night of sleeplessness and worry, but within minutes she dropped off.

There was no relief in sleep.

She dreamt of a long-ago night in Scarlet Bay, on the wind-whipped Lancashire coast.

The brutal thrust of a knife.

The blood-spattered face of her father, wild-eyed and smiling.

"Wasn't that something, Jessie?" he rasped, smearing a droplet of blood as he wiped his whiskered chin.

The night was cold, but Jax Knox was sweating in a long-sleeved T-shirt, a thick black hoodie and an Adidas jacket. He wore a baseball cap and navy jeans with a black pair of jogging pants over the top of them. He finished a cigarette as he walked. A fine drizzle hung in the air, seeming not so much to fall as to linger on the breeze like a spray from a fragrance bottle.

A black and white cat sat on a low brick wall, protected from the precipitation by the tangled limbs of a bush. Its eyes glimmered like jewels as it watched him pass. As he drew alongside it, the cat reared back and hissed.

Jax flicked the butt of his cigarette at it. The butt arced and hit the bush, bounced off and fell to the cold ground. The cat stood perfectly still, refusing to be intimidated. It growled low in its throat.

He ignored it and kept walking. He took his phone from his jeans pocket and searched for X-Ray's number.

Alex Raymond answered on the fifth ring. He sounded sleepy. "Jax? What's up, man?"

"I need a ride," he said.

X-Ray sighed. "Bro, what time is it?"

"Just after midnight."

"Fuck." X-Ray cleared his throat. "I'd just fallen asleep."

"I'm nearly at your place."

"Fuckin' hell, bro. I mean..."

Jax laughed. "Get outta bed, you lazy cunt. You're gonna love this, I promise."

X-Ray sniffed and cleared his throat again. Jax heard him spit something up. "I'll get dressed. Five minutes?"

"I'll be outside," Jax said and ended the call. He put the phone back in his pocket.

X-Ray lived with his mum on Bendbow Rise, by the underpass. Jax was there in two minutes, smoking another cigarette in the shadowy shelter. Overhead, he heard a car race down the road, its engine screaming.

In spite of the council's best efforts to clean up the area, the underpass had been tagged so much that little of the original white paint remained. He recognised most of the handles and could identify the scribes from the way they wrote *WEC* on the concrete.

Jax had a pen in his pocket. With a flourish, he wrote his name and the date in a small white square, smiling to himself. He felt like an artist, signing his work.

He smoked the cigarette to the filter and threw it into the road. He returned the pen to his pocket and walked up the incline to X-Ray's house. In the right pocket of his jacket he had a pair of leather gloves. He put them on.

X's black Volkswagen Golf was parked facing the other way, two wheels up on the kerb. In the house, Jax saw a light on in the hallway. It snapped off and the door opened. X-Ray spotted him at once, standing under the streetlight beside the car. He closed the door behind him, rolling an ache out of his shoulders and came over.

Jax fist-bumped his lanky friend hard then clapped him on the shoulder. "Feeling all right, bruv?" he asked.

"I'm getting a cold." X-Ray said, sniffing his hawkish nose, then turned and spat a wad of phlegm. "I feel like shit, bro."

"Let's get in the car," Jax said. "You'll feel better when it warms up."

X-Ray stepped around to the driver's side, unlocking it with a beep. "Where we going?"

Jax climbed in but didn't put on his seatbelt. When X-Ray was behind the wheel, he also eschewed the belt. He turned the engine over and pulled away, leaving the underpass behind them.

Jax turned the heater on full-blast. The little car was hot in no time. Wearing three layers, he was sweltering, but didn't complain. He played with the volume knob, lowering it so they could talk.

"Where are we going?" X-Ray asked.

"Boynton Road."

X-Ray took his eyes off the road and gave Jax a confused look. "The allotment?"

Jax nodded.

"What for?"

"I've gotta show you summut."

X-Ray spent the drive coughing or sneezing, even sometimes rolling down the window to spit out whatever choked him.

Jax couldn't help but laugh. "You should be in bed, bruv."

"Real funny."

"I'm not joking, you look like shit."

"I don't know why you're laughing – you're gonna get it now too."

Jax scoffed. "My immune system's top-notch, mate. I don't get colds."

In truth, he couldn't even remember the last time he came down with anything worse than a sore throat. He was blessed with a rapid metabolism. X-Ray on the other hand seemed to catch flu four of five times a year. Even at the height of summer, hay-fever kept him sniffling and gasping for air. His pockets always bulged with snotty tissues.

"It's fucked up, ain't it?" Jax asked.

"What is?"

"Danny gettin' himself merked."

"Proper fucked. You found out who did it yet?"

"Nah," Jax said. "But it's gonna be a war when I do."

X-Ray nodded. "I'm in."

"I can always count on you, bruv."

The car cruised down Winstanley Drive and turned left onto Rancliffe Crescent. Jax looked around, but there was nobody on the streets. The windows in the nearby houses were dark, their residents sleeping.

Jax's excitement was building. He had to force himself to breathe slowly, deeply. He glanced over his shoulder through the rear window. Theirs was the only moving car.

X-Ray turned left onto Boynton Road. On the right side of the street, he turned the Golf into the entrance to the allotments. They went over a small speed-bump and stopped, concealed by a high wooden fence on the left and thick bushes on their right. Behind them, a winking street-light fizzed and strobed.

In the silence, he turned to look at Jax. "We going in?" He reached into his pocket for a tissue and blew his nose as noisily as a horn-blast. He sniffled, probing his nostrils for anything clinging on.

"What makes you think we're going in?" Jax asked.

"Well... I mean, ain't we? Why else...?" The look of blank confusion on his face made Jax smile. "You got me out of bed for what? You said you had something to show me."

Jax laughed. "Don't be so mardy," he said. "*Of course* we're goin' in. Why else do you think I'm dressed this way?"

"Proper joker tonight, ain't ya?" X-Ray grumbled, frowning. He looked over Jax's attire. "I was starting to wonder. Should I have gloves?"

"Nah, you'll be all right."

Jax and X-Ray got out of the car and headed over to the fence. Jax scaled it with ease, making hardly a sound, then dropped to the concrete path on the other side. X-Ray was less agile and the steel rang and echoed through the night. He almost snagged the cuff of his jeans on the top, but finally made it over. He jumped, landed hard and dropped to one knee.

"Fucking hell," he hissed when he got to his feet. He rubbed his grazed kneecap.

Jax laughed. "Don't be a pussy. Follow me."

He led X-Ray across the unlit land to the plot on the far side where nothing grew but weeds. A cheap greenhouse stood in the shadows, its loose windows rattling in the wind.

Jax pointed inside and – confused – X-Ray poked his head in. He looked around, as if unsure what he was supposed to be looking at. His eyes wandered down to where a large ceramic plant pot stood, half-submerged into the hard-packed ground.

"That's what you want to show me?" X-Ray asked, wiping his nose on his sleeve.

Jax shook his head. "You need to lift it out."

"You're losing it, mate."

In spite of his grumbling, X-Ray did as he was told and hauled the large pot out of the hole with a grunt. He put it aside and squinted down into the blackness.

"See anything?" Jax asked.

After a moment, X-Ray said, "No. It's empty."

"Should there be summut in there?"

X-Ray looked at him, blinking stupidly. He sighed.

"How am I s'posed to know? Mate, what the *fuck* are we doin' here?"

Jax fixed him with a stare, searching his eyes. In all the years he'd known X, he'd proven himself to be a loyal soldier as well as a top-notch driver. He would follow Jax like an obedient old dog – complaining and grizzling, certainly, but wouldn't defy him. What X-Ray lacked in brain cells, he made up for in heart. He was telling the truth.

"So, you didn't know?" Jax asked.

"Know what?"

"Never mind," Jax said. "Put it back and let's fuck off, yeah?"

X-Ray dropped the pot back into the hole and, more confused now than ever, followed Jax back to the fence. He continued griping the entire way, kicking stones along the path. "A lift, you said, not fuckin' around pretending to be a gardener."

Jax said nothing. He climbed back over the gated entrance and waited by the car. When X-Ray finally made it over, they both got in.

He looked over at Jax. "You gonna tell me what that was about, bruv? I feel like shit and you're makin' no sense."

Jax reached into his left jacket pocket and pulled out an opaque plastic square, roughly the size of a cigarette packet.

"What's that?" X-Ray asked.

"See for yourself."

X-Ray took it from him, lifting it up to get a better look. "What is it?"

"Open it and see."

Still visibly baffled, X-Ray did as he was told and unfolded the plastic square.

Jax laughed as he watched his friend's deepening look of confusion.

Each time X-Ray unfolded the plastic into an ever-larger square, its crisp rustle covered the sound of him clearing his throat. Finally, when he had the thing stretched out to a three-foot square, he found the ends and shook out the folded plastic.

"It's a... why the fuck you givin' me a shower curtain?" he asked, struggling to hold it up in the confines of the car. The bottom of it draped his thighs and one corner laid over the steering wheel. "Are you losin' it, bruv?"

From his left jacket pocket, he took out a folding knife and snapped it open. "Not me," he said and drove it into X-Ray's chest. He whipped it out and slammed it in again.

X-Ray tried to raise his hands to ward off the attack, but Jax batted them away with ease.

He pounded the knife into his friend's skinny chest again and again, punching noisily through the plastic. The blood looked almost black as it spread across the opaque sheet. X-Ray wheezed, his strength having deserted him. His eyes fixed on Jax as he drove the knife home a further ten times, but the light in them had already faded and winked out.

Jax let go of the handle and looked at the knife poking from X-Ray's chest. He reached out his finger and tapped it, wanting to see if it would spring up and down with a *twang*. When it didn't, Jax laughed anyway.

He glanced over his shoulder. The street was empty, silent.

He withdrew the knife, its blade smeared with blood. The interior of the car was remarkably clean thanks to the shower curtain. Even the fingers of his glove were only minimally spotted with gore.

He got out and pushed against the door, shoving it

closed rather than slamming it and walked away without looking back.

Jax folded the blade into the handle of the knife and retraced the path the Golf had taken. On the way, he saw a sewer drain by the kerb and he stopped to drop the knife. It clattered on the iron bars but didn't slip down. For a moment, Jax wondered if the handle was too thick, but he nudged it with his toe and it disappeared into the blackness with a soft splash.

He continued on his way, shedding his clothes like a snake sloughing off a layer of dead skin. He peeled off the tight leather gloves and deposited them into another drain like a man posting a letter.

Around the corner, Jax saw a wheelie bin that a resident hadn't brought in off the street. He took off his cap and dropped it in. Further along the same street, he saw another bin in which to dispose of his jacket.

On Winstanley Drive, Jax looked around and when he was sure he wasn't being watched, leant against a wall and took off his shoes. The pavement was still wet though it had stopped raining and his socks soaked up water. He shucked out of the jogging pants, put his shoes back on and stuffed the unwanted garment into a nearby hedge.

Jax felt much better. The night had grown colder and now wearing fewer layers, he was no longer sweating. The stroll home took almost fifty minutes but the chilly air was invigorating. With every step, he felt lighter, as though an invisible weight were lifted from his shoulders.

He smiled when he reached the door to his flat.

Just one more loose end, he thought.

Inside, Jax undressed and climbed under the covers. He laid down and fell into a peaceful sleep.

CHAPTER 6

In the morning, Finn was up and about before Gayle opened her eyes. When she came fully awake, she heard cartoons playing in the living room.

She pushed herself into a sitting position and stretched the stiffness out of her neck. She felt as though she had slept on a flight of stairs.

She wrapped herself in a fluffy yellow dressing gown and pushed through into the living room. Finn had pulled back the curtains. She squinted until her eyes adjusted.

"Morning, Mummy," he said. He was on the settee with an enormous bowl of Coco Pops that had long since turned into lumpy chocolate milkshake.

To her surprise, he had taken his school uniform from his chest of drawers and put it on, although a closer inspection revealed that his red jumper was inside out. There was a splodge of chocolate milk on the left side of his chest.

"How are you feeling?" she asked him.

"I'm okay," he said.

Gayle went and put the kettle on, then sat beside Finn

while it boiled. She patted him on the knee, then put her arm around him and gave him a quick hug.

"So, you're feeling up to going to school, are you?" she asked.

He stopped munching on his cereal and looked at her then. His face become suddenly grave.

"I don't have to," he said. "I can stay off if you need me to keep you company."

She smiled and kissed his forehead.

"'Cause if you get, you know, lonely or sad a little bit, you can pick me up and we can go to McDonalds to cheer us up."

"Oh really?"

"Yeah. And 'cause Mrs Keane's with us today because Miss Lumley's having a baby, I won't mind."

"I'll try not to forget that," she said, heading to his room to fetch him a fresh jumper.

After showering and dressing in jeans, a white blouse and a lime-green jumper, Gayle checked her phone and saw she'd missed a call from an unknown number.

On the voicemail, a man identified himself as Police Constable Nash. His voice was cool when he said that Danny's belongings were available for her to collect. *"I'll be in the station all day,"* he added, giving her a number to contact him on, then terminated the call.

"Oh, God," she muttered.

* * *

At just after half past one, Gayle drove into a gravel car-park, paid for a two-hour stay and hurried down to Mansfield House police station. The wind blew her hair and wrapped its icy fingers around her throat. The temperature had dropped to below freezing and by the time she pushed open the entrance door, the fine hairs in her nose felt like they had frozen. She blew into her raw hands with little effect then flipped her hair out of her face.

She gave her name to the desk sergeant and said that she was expected. He directed her to sit at one of the uncomfortable-looking plastic chairs against the wall. She did, but was right in the draught from the glass door, which blew open a couple of inches in the hammering wind. She changed seats, but the chill found her anyway. She drew her coat tighter and stuffed her hands into the pockets of her jeans. She wished she had remembered her scarf and gloves.

After a fifteen-minute wait, a uniformed officer with a goatee and slicked-back blond hair approached. A fleeting look of surprise played across his lumpish features as he quickly looked her up and down. *"You're* Gayle Stillwater?" he asked, standing awkwardly for a moment.

She looked down at herself. "Am I not what you were expecting or something?"

After a hesitation, Nash held out his hand to shake. When she took it, he said, "Blimey, it's colder outside than it looks." He flexed the fingers of his hand when she relinquished it.

"I was told Danny's things were ready to collect," she said.

Nash nodded. "This way."

He led her out of the reception area and through a heavy door. The hallways were painted an institutional grey-blue and the floor was covered in coarse blue carpet tiles.

The place was such a maze, it was a wonder how anyone got where they were going. Perhaps, she decided, court cases only stretched out for so long because everybody struggled to get out of the police station.

Nash led her into a room decorated the same cool grey-blue as the hallways, but the carpet – while still blue – was the real deal instead of glued-down tiles. A plain generic table like those found in offices all over the world stood with three bucket seats around it. Unlike the reception, the room was sweltering. Against the right-hand wall were three white-painted radiators. After being half-frozen in the early-winter wind, she could feel their heat burning against her cheek.

Nash gestured her to the seats in front of the table. Gayle sat, unbuttoning her coat, while the cop stepped around the desk and took a seat opposite. He pulled open the top drawer of the desk and removed a sheaf of papers and a clear plastic evidence bag, upon which was scrawled a series of numbers in black marker.

"These are all the items that Mr Gowan had on his person," Nash said, dropping the bag instead of placing it onto the desk. "Everything was taken into evidence and logged. Our technicians performed a search on his phone."

"Do you know who killed him?" Gayle asked.

Nash looked at her for a long moment before shaking his head as if trying to dispel an unwanted thought. "Nope," he said. "The investigation's ongoing. As I understand, he was a known gangster," he said with a dismissive half-shrug, as if that were answer enough. "Is that how you two met?"

Gayle bristled. "What does that have to do with anything?"

"You might know who took him out better than I would."

"I beg your pardon."

"Your fella wasn't exactly a fan of the police, now, was

he? I suppose you could say the feeling's mutual." Nash drummed his fingers on the desk. "*Was* mutual," he corrected.

She huffed, shaking her head. "He should have tried being a cop. Seems like they'll hire anyone."

Nash laid out the papers for her to sign and tossed a biro to her side of the desk. He shook his wristwatch free of his shirtsleeve and gave it a meaningful look.

Without bothering to read the documents, Gayle scrawled out her signature.

When she was done, Nash read Danny's things out from an inventory form as he dropped everything into a padded jiffy bag. He sealed it and handed it to her.

"Sorry for your loss," Nash said.

"Yeah," she said, pushing up from the chair. "I'll bet."

She followed him out of the overwhelming heat and back into the dreary hallways. He pushed through door after door. Her eyes were beginning to hurt from the blazing fluorescent lights.

They came to the reception and Nash pulled the door open for her, holding it with one foot. An icy blast of cold air struck Gayle full in the face, momentarily taking her breath away.

Nash stuffed his hands into his trouser pockets. Without looking at her, he muttered, "Ta ta, love," as she passed him.

She heard the door slap shut as she descended the steps. She tucked the envelope under her arm, still annoyed by the cop's attitude. "Dickhead," she muttered.

Once she was back in the car, she turned the engine over and put the heaters on their maximum setting. She peeled back the envelope's sticky seal and upended it onto the passenger seat. She checked that there was nothing still inside, then dropped it to the floor.

On the seat were a set of keys, three pounds and fourteen pence in loose change, a Sharpie marker, a cracked brown leather wallet and Danny's Samsung S9.

She took up the phone and pressed the power button. The mobile started up and she saw a photo of Finn, smiling in a blue Foxes' football shirt, on the lock-screen. Gayle recognised her own hands on the boy's shoulders. Danny had cropped her out.

She remembered his password – his own name, lower-case, with the a's changed to ampersands – and unlocked the phone. Curious what the police had found, if anything, she checked his call log. There were a lot of random numbers that she didn't recognise. Danny had called someone named Mel at a quarter to eleven on Monday morning.

She wondered who Mel was.

She saw a missed call from Jax at two-thirty and a text a few minutes later:

where r u, mate?

There were other messages, more recent, but she told herself to be careful about reading too many. Sometimes there were things a person would be better off not knowing.

She saw that on the night he was killed, Danny was meeting someone called Scotty to collect some money. Scotty's final text was to say that he was running late.

Gayle didn't know anybody named Scotty and Danny had never mentioned him. In itself, that wasn't unusual: she probably wouldn't have wanted to hear it anyway.

She knew she should stop there and put the phone down, but it was no use. She checked his gallery.

There was one labelled *Finn*, with more than three-hundred photos in it. She knew some of the pictures, but there many that she had never seen from when Danny had the boy to himself. Here, Finn smiling on a swing. There, Finn riding a bicycle with training wheels. Another, with Finn and Danny on the bus, their faces made up like tigers after Danny had taken him to the rugby.

Amongst the galleries labelled *Camera* and *Screenshots* was one titled *Mel*.

Gayle couldn't help herself.

Mel, she found, was a podgy blonde with crystalline blue eyes and a life-loving smile. In one picture she wore a red dress, posing with a glass of white wine in a living room that Gayle didn't recognise. In another, she was a naked blur in the shower, turning towards the camera, her eyes made red by the flash. The most recent was a landscape shot of what she presumed was Danny's cock buried between a pair of stretch-marked arse cheeks.

She felt a sudden flush of anger and shame and shut the phone down: anger that Danny had been seeing this woman and shame that she had invaded his privacy. She put the phone in her bag.

She sighed and tussled her hair for a moment, thinking things through. She wasn't surprised that he had been seeing someone else but had to admit that it hurt her feel-ings. She hadn't realised consciously that she'd been holding onto a tiny spark of hope that he might work things out one day and they would get back together.

Gayle pushed the thoughts away. She lifted his wallet and saw what she expected to see: his debit card, National Insurance card and his provisional driver's licence. The wallet also contained cash. She pulled the notes out of the top of the wallet and counted twenty-five pounds in a ten and three fives. From between the plastic notes, a scrap of paper fluttered out, grazed her thigh and fell to the floor between her feet.

She put down the wallet and reached for the paper.

The handwriting wasn't Danny's.

QD00714283DS

Gayle read it again, puzzled, but the meaning of those twelve characters eluded her.

She turned the slip of lined notepad paper over, but it was blank on the reverse.

What the hell could it be?

Before she could work it out, she noticed the time on the dashboard clock. It was already twenty-five past two. She stuffed the slip of paper into her jeans, put the car in gear and rushed to pick up Finn from school.

CHAPTER 7

After dropping Finn off with Bobbi, Gayle made it to work by a quarter to seven that night. The queue at the bar inside *The Marquee* was six deep and even her boss, Ricky Dutton, had emerged from his office to pull pints and mix cocktails. She moved past the drinkers, pushed through the door marked *Staff Only* and headed into the small, windowless back room. She took off her coat and got to work right away.

As an addict, earning a living pulling pints should have been torment, but her lack of formal education limited her options. Things might be different when she passed her book-keeping course, but until that happened, Gayle chose to view the job as exposure-therapy. Each time she made it to the end of the night having resisted temptation, she felt a flush of pride at having proven her resolve. Seeing the state of the bar's patrons at the end of the night helped to keep her straight: she realised how she had looked and behaved while intoxicated. She remembered all too well how it felt to wake with a hangover so intense that she just wanted to die. With every cocktail she mixed and every pint she pulled, she thought, *Rather you than me.*

Most of the customers were students from the nearby university campuses. Fewer than a dozen of the people Gayle served were older than twenty-five.

Ricky Dutton was proud of *The Marquee*'s on-the-nose styling: brick walls painted a butterscotch hue with blood-red vinyl booths; bulb-ringed signage above all the doors; canvas prints of actors and actresses from Hollywood's golden years around the walls. The only concession to the approaching Hallowe'en was a plastic pumpkin used as a tip jar, a menu of four ghostly-themed cocktails, and a rubber bat that Gayle hung from a shelf behind the bar.

It was half past nine before things started to quieten down and Ricky rewarded Gayle's hard work by sending her to the cellar to change the barrels. Out of habit, she braced herself when she twisted the gas-fed coupling head into a fresh keg, but managed it without getting a face-full of lager.

Later, during a rare lull, Gayle sat on a bar stool beside the other barmaid, Ruth Simpson, who drank a half-pint of Fosters. Gayle fished a slice of lemon from her glass of water and took a bite of the bitter fruit.

Like her, Ruth wore a black tank top with *Marquee* emblazoned across the front. The straps of her red bra had slipped off her chubby shoulders. She made no move to push them back into place, but scratched at the face of the Geisha tattooed on her arm.

"You think I should get another?" she asked, tilting back her head to look through the thick-framed glasses that had slid down her nose.

"Another Geisha?" Gayle asked, dropping the rind back into the glass.

"I was thinking a samurai on the other arm. You know the ones? That scary face-mask and the helmet? Maybe a sword that comes up this way?" She traced along the front of her shoulder and across her collar bone.

"Definitely," Gayle said. "That'd be cool."

"Would you come with me? We could get one together."

"I don't know about that."

"Too scared?"

"I've got one," she said. "That's plenty."

"You never told me."

Gayle shrugged. "It's old," she said, taking another sip of water.

"Let me see."

Gayle took a furtive look around. She could feel her face begin to colour. "It's nowhere you'd call... *obvious*."

Ruth's mouth hung open. "You've got a puss tat?" she whispered.

Gayle laughed. *"No."* Looking around again, there seemed to be nobody paying them any attention. She slid off the stool, unbuttoned her black jeans and pushed down the lace of her hipster panties. On her right hip, just below the bone, was a dove in flight.

"Oh, that's beautiful," Ruth enthused.

There had been a time when Gayle thought so herself. She designed it, taking her carefully worked-out drawing to the tattooist. At a casual glance, the bird was girly, almost whimsical, but a closer look revealed that its wings formed a subtle *W* for *West-End,* with the word *Forever* hidden in the feathers of the near-side wing.

Gayle hastily buttoned up her jeans and hopped back onto the stool.

"That's proper sexy," Ruth said. "You should show it off. I know I would. Why would you cover it up?"

"I was young," she said. "It didn't come out the way I wanted."

"Are you gonna get another?"

Gayle shook her head.

"You should," Ruth insisted. "If I had a figure like yours, I'd be tattooed all over. I'd never cover them up." She rubbed her shoulders again, as if she caught a sudden chill. "I like my arms, but the rest of me is too podgy. You've got a great body."

"Not since having my son," Gayle said.

"You can't tell."

"My belly's not the same."

Ruth laughed. "Jesus, you seen *my* gut? It looks like a pensioner's tits."

Later, just after ten, Ruth hurried around with a dustpan and brush, treating the patrons to a look at her green thong, which her milk-white arse had all-but gobbled up, while Gayle cleared the tables. Each was littered with empty glasses, chewed straws and shreds of beer bottle labels. She carried a stack of seven pint glasses held against her left shoulder and a trio of pitchers in her right hand.

As she washed the glassware, Ricky came out briefly to collect the takings and stuff them into a canvas tote-bag, then rushed back to the office. Shift manager, Ewan Forrester, threw empty liquor bottles into the glass bin beneath the bar with a crash.

In a booth in the far corner, a young couple dressed in black were all over one another. Gayle supposed they would be dry-humping in another ten minutes. She smiled to herself and decided she would let Ewan deal with that.

A cluster of young guys huddled around a fruit machine

by the entrance, jostling one another and slapping at the buttons, infuriating the one playing. His face reddened by alcohol, he shoved one of his pals, who stumbled and dropped his pint. The glass shattered on the floor. Over the music, Gayle heard Ruth groan, *"Oh, for fuck's sake!"*

As Gayle carried a heavy crate of clean glassware over to Ewan, she caught the aniseed aroma of the white Sambuca he emptied. She refilled the shelves and wiped down the bar. Over at the fruit machine, its winning klaxon sounded as change dumped into the tray. A roar went up from the mob of lads, who all shoved and jostled for a fistful of coins.

She noticed another group in a booth near the toilets. Eight student-age guys and three girls with too much makeup all huddled together, having drawn up chairs from nearby tables. Unlike the rest of drinkers, they were quiet, grouped like conspirators.

She returned the blue plastic rack to the glass-washer, laying it on top of the hot metal lid as it rumbled and sloshed. She wiped her hands on the hips of her jeans and headed over to see what was going on.

From time to time, she'd caught people scrawling graffiti on the tables with marker pens. She even caught one group of lads gambling over a game of five-finger filet; a stack of five-pound notes waited for the one who could jab a penknife in the spaces between the fingers of one hand without bloodshed.

As she drew closer to the toilets, she caught the familiar smell of weed. She sighed, preparing herself to give the culprit a mouthful.

One of the girls – twentyish, with a gemstone piercing between her lower lip and chin – turned as Gayle approached. Sensing something, the others looked this way.

Moving as one, they all pulled their hands away from the table.

"I don't care what you *are* doing," Gayle said, "but I *know* you're not drinking."

One guy, also about twenty, with unruly black hair creeping out from under a woollen beanie, looked about to say something. He had a large nose that had been broken a couple of times.

She stopped him with a raised hand. "Before you argue, don't waste your breath. My boss is already calling the cops, so you've got ten seconds to just fuck off. I'm gonna tell your mates in the loo the same thing. When I get back, you need to be gone." She gave them all a look that said the conversation was over.

She turned on her heels and went straight to the lavatory labelled *Male*, pushing through the first door into a small vestibule. The smell hit her hard before she even opened the second. The weed was pungent and very poor-quality. Someone was going to have to smoke a lot of it for an even halfway decent high.

Experience taught her that the best way to handle these situations was with volume and bravado. Before she had one foot in the room, she had already raised her voice and started barking orders.

"Right, get the fuck out," she commanded, "before I flush that crap and you lose your money."

Four young men stood in the small room; two squeezed into the tiny stall and another two at the urinals along the left wall. The two in the stall passed a joint back and forth, half-obscured by a pall of grey smoke. Their eyes were glassy and half-shut. The one holding the joint – Asian, skinny, wearing a tight black T-shirt and frayed jeans – dropped it in surprise. The other was white; his chubby, greasy face littered with whiteheads. He looked at Gayle, barely comprehending.

The other guy wore glasses and swayed at the urinal with his dick in his hand. He jumped half out of his skin at the sudden intrusion. His hands let go and he sprayed his own trousers and feet. His face flushed red and he quickly zipped up, stumbling by her without washing his hands.

The last guy was younger, probably just eighteen, and his dark little eyes fixed on Gayle. He wore a black hoodie and his hands were stuffed into the front kangaroo pocket. His oversized navy jeans hung almost all the way off his arse, so he looked as though he were all torso with tiny legs. He was neither surprised nor scared – in fact, he looked irritated to have been interrupted.

This one, she decided, was the dealer. He was probably with the dark-haired guy in the beanie, meaning that this guy carried the gear whilst his buddy collected the cash.

The Asian lad in the stall tried to say something. He bent down to pick up the joint, but Gayle shook her head. "Don't bother," she said. "Just get lost. Go on."

He shouldered past his friend, who still looked as though he couldn't quite work out what was happening.

Gayle hooked a thumb at the door and stepped to the side. At last, both the smokers went back out into the bar, the vaguely-sweet stink of skunk clinging to their hair and clothes.

"Bitch, don't be fuckin' wit' my customers," the dealer said. "Go collect glasses, innit." The accent he affected was a weak imitation of the East-End London patois that movies had popularised. He spread his legs to shoulder-width and cocked his head to the side. He adjusted his crotch with his left hand and wiped at his nose with his right.

"Just clear off," Gayle told him.

He shifted his weight from one foot to the other and laughed, looking off to the side before turning back with a cocky grin. He looked her up and down and said, "What are you? Some undercover fed? Why don't you shut up before my mandem slap you?"

She moved her hands to her hips, not defiantly but so she could more easily reach the can of self-defence spray she kept in her pocket.

She said, "Look, dickhead, I know how this works. My boss is calling the cops. And your mate outside, your *mandem*, the one with everyone's money... Well, since he's not come in to help you out, I'll bet you he's already legged it. He's gonna fuck you for the dough and leave you to get nicked with the gear."

The dealer sneered, but didn't speak.

She continued: "Who are you with?"

"What you talkin' about?"

"I told you, I know how this works. Are you with someone, or are you just some middle-class smartarse pretending to be a gangster?"

In spite of her confident demeanour, Gayle's legs felt rubbery with a rush of adrenaline. She felt the urge to pee. Beads of sweat unravelled from her armpit and moistened the sideband of her bra.

The dealer continued to look her up and down. Unimpressed, he said, "Unless you come to suck my dick, sket, you can fuck off."

"Just do one," she said. "You've got five seconds. Five."

"Or what?"

"Four?"

"What you gonna do, you fuckin' bitch?"

"You're wasting time. Three."

"Two," he said, laughing.

"I told you—"

The dealer took a quick lunge forward, shoes squeaking on the tiles, and froze.

Gayle jumped back and collided with the wall, reaching into her pocket. She withdrew the spray – a can of semi-permanent paint that marked an attacker for identification.

The dealer didn't approach. He just laughed, rubbing at his nose.

Gayle regained her footing, holding the spray out, aiming for his face.

He kept laughing, feinting a lunge from time to time, little eyes dancing with amusement.

Gayle sidestepped towards the door, ready to turn and bolt. One more. Another.

The dealer's mocking laughter trilled in her ears.

Her heart hammered in her chest. Sweat prickled her forehead.

"Scared, ain't ya?" he said, straightening up. "You should see yourself." He made a scornful, dismissive noise by sucking on his teeth.

"Listen," she said, "why don't you—"

And he lunged again, rushing forwards, but Gayle squeezed off a blast with the spray. He dodged to the side and missed the sudden jet of red mist. Before she had time to swing her arm, he whipped out one foot and caught her in the left hip, slamming her back against the wall with a yelp. She crashed into the tile, hitting her head so hard that she saw sudden, bright pinpoints of light. She slipped down, knees buckling. She dropped her left hand to hold herself up, half-crouched on the wet tile floor, then brought her right hand around and released the rest of the spray, this time catching the bastard full in the face.

He cried out and backed off, but she launched herself

up, slamming her shoulder into his chest. He stumbled, blinded, flailing, grabbing at whatever he could find and twisted his fingers into her hair.

She squealed in pain but kept moving forwards, knocking the bastard back until he tripped over his own feet and slammed his right knee into the nearest urinal. He stumbled and, with her weight against him, crashed against the toilet stall and slid down it. She caught herself before she could topple onto him, but dropped her right knee into his stomach, knocking the wind from him in a rush of halitosis. He spluttered, wiping his face and his closed, sticky eyes.

"You bitch," he blurted, "what the fuck was that?"

Gayle got to her feet, wincing at the pain in her hip. "I told you to get out," she said through gritted teeth.

"You fucking *blinded me*," he cried.

"I wish. You'll be sore, but it's not permanent."

Spit dribbled over his chin and down his hoodie. He opened his eyes, groaning. She could see the whites were red-raw and tears streamed down his face. *"Fucking bitch,"* he wailed.

She pointed to the door. "Go."

As he scrambled to his feet, the contents of his pockets spilled onto the floor. He cursed and crouched onto one knee, flailing over the piss-stained tiles for his things.

"Leave it," Gayle said.

"Fuck you."

Gayle whipped out a kick of her own, catching him in the shin with the toe of her shoe. He squealed as the skin over his tibia tore open.

Behind her, the door opened and Ruth Simpson stood looking in. "Are you okay?"

Instead of answering, Gayle stepped over the dealer,

who hugged his injured leg with both hands. "Get out," she said.

He struggled to his feet, holding a red-stained hand out to steady himself. He limped to the door and Ruth shuffled aside, allowing him past without a word. In the threshold, the dealer stopped and turned back, glowering with his red-dappled face running with tears, snot and spit. He pointed to Gayle with one stained finger. "You're dead, you cunt. The *West-End*, they're gonna fuckin' rip this place apart. My boys are gonna cut off your fuckin' head."

Gayle said nothing.

The dealer turned and left. The door slammed shut behind him.

"What the hell was that?" Ruth asked.

"Just some idiot," Gayle said, looking down at the belongings scattered on the floor: a packet of Rizzla rolling papers, a few cling-film twists of weed, half a dozen rocks of crack, barely a pound in random change and a pearl-handled switchblade.

She pulled off a fat wad of toilet paper to fish the weed and crack wraps out of the puddles of piss and flush them down the toilet. She left the change and papers where they were, but took up the switchblade with another bunch of toilet paper, slipping it into her back pocket.

"What are you doing?" Ruth asked, but then the door opened.

Ewan stood, looking concerned. "What's going on?" he asked. "You both all right?"

"We're fine," Gayle said. She walked to the door, eager to get out of the stench. She wiped at her damp forehead with her forearm. The ache in her hip meant that she couldn't walk with her left leg fully stretched out.

In the bar, she saw that what had been a bluff turned

out to be right on the money: the little bastard in the beanie was gone, along with half the crowd he'd been dealing to. The rest of the patrons who weren't senselessly inebriated seemed amused, no doubt wondering what had happened to the red-faced idiot who came stumbling out of the toilet.

Gayle excused herself and left Ruth to explain things to Ewan. She headed into the small back room.

With the door closed, she reached into her rear pocket and pulled out the tissue-wrapped knife. She unbundled the wad of paper and held the smooth-handled weapon in her right hand. With her thumb, she pressed down on the little black button and, with a *snick*, a four-inch blade swung out of the handle and locked into place. Its edges were razor sharp and the end terminated in a wicked point.

Idiot, she thought. At least her spray was legal. A weapon like this would grant its owner prison time.

She pressed the button once more and – careful to be mindful of the cutting edges – folded the blade at the hilt, then pushed it into the handle where it clicked into place.

The adrenaline was still coursing through her. She slipped the knife back into her pocket, without the tissue this time, then looked at her trembling hands. The nail of her thumb was stained at the end with a spot of red paint.

First, someone had killed Danny.

Then, out of nowhere, she received a call from Jax.

Now, a younger from the *West-End Crew* was dealing at her workplace.

Danny, she thought, *what is all this about?*

CHAPTER 8

Gayle made it back by a quarter to one on Thursday morning. She parked her ten-year-old Fiat 500 in her space in the courtyard behind the building and made her way inside, dragging her sore feet. The last of the drinkers had finally moved on at ten to midnight and the clean-up was slow-going. Ewan took pity on her and let her go at half-past. In spite of her weariness, her mind was spinning as though she had been shooting double-espressos.

She didn't bother calling for the lift, instead pushing through the door for the stairwell, climbing up one level to Bobbi's first-floor flat. They each had a key to the other's place and Gayle let herself in.

In layout, each flat was a carbon copy of the other, but Bobbi's place could not have been more different. The place was decorated with colourful rugs, cushions and throws. Because the tenancy agreement forbade painting the walls, each was hung with paintings, wall-art and sheets of fabric that rippled in the cool breeze passing through the half-open balcony door. Bolts of fabric were stacked four-feet high beside a sewing machine and a comfortable padded stool.

Bobbi sat on the settee, which stood in the same place that Gayle had hers – albeit without the throws that her friend favoured. She wore colourful silk pyjamas with a matching scarf around her head, from the top of which sprang a cluster of black curls. Her face was shiny with a skin peel.

Without looking up from her book, Bobbi asked, "Rough night?"

"Definitely had better," Gayle said, dropping into the settee beside her.

Gayle spied the book's title when Bobbi folded down the corner and laid it on the coffee table. "'*The Secret Teachings of Mary Magdelene*'?" she asked. "I thought you were done with the church."

Bobbi shrugged. "Old habits." Her father was a Christian minister. After the deaths of her mother and older sister, he brought his remaining three children from Lagos when Bobbi was seven. At twenty-two, she came out to the family and was disowned by everyone but her older brother, Michael – an accountant in Birmingham. The next oldest, Zachary, had followed their father into the ministry. They hadn't talked in more than two years.

"Did Finn give you any trouble?" Gayle asked.

"That boy couldn't cause trouble if he tried. We read a story and he was asleep before we got to the end."

"I got lucky with that kid."

Bobbi nodded. "He's better behaved than me at his age. I was a tomboy." She pushed the sleeve up her right arm, past the elbow, revealing three pale scars on her right forearm. "I broke it falling out of a tree. They put metal pins inside. I still can't fully extend it. You look troubled."

Gayle forced a smile. "Abrupt change of topic."

"Want to talk about it?"

Gayle looked at the time on her phone. "It's late," she said. "I should grab Finn and get out of your hair."

Bobbi shook her head. "Why don't you join him?"

"You've only got one bed," Gayle reminded her. Bobbi's spare room was really more of a walk-in wardrobe and warehouse for half-finished designs.

"I'll sleep here," she said. "The settee is probably comfier anyway."

Gayle patted Bobbi's knee. "I can't lie," she said, "I'm knackered. I don't really fancy carrying a half-asleep kid to the lift."

"Good," Bobbi said with a smile. "Settled. Then once you get some rest, you can fill me in on what's got you looking so worried."

"Are you sure?" Gayle asked, unable to stifle a yawn.

"Go on."

Gayle hugged her goodnight and headed through the door, down the short hallway to the bathroom. She used the toilet, washed her hands and face, then rubbed her teeth with toothpaste squeezed onto her index finger.

In Bobbi's bedroom, Finn lay in the centre of the double-bed, one leg in and one leg out of the duvet. He murmured in his sleep. She covered him properly, then stripped to her underwear and got in beside him.

In spite of the stress of the evening, she was asleep almost immediately.

* * *

When Gayle woke, she was disoriented. She lay in the unfamiliar bed for long moments, blinking away the ghosts of sleep, adjusting her eyes to the light streaming through the parted curtains. It glinted on a delicate white-gold crucifix that hung from a brocaded chain around the bedside lamp.

It took her longer than it should have to recall she was at Bobbi's. Her head was sore and for a split-second, she was dismayed, thinking that she must have drank last night. Then she remembered the fight in the toilets and supposed the knock to her head might have been harder than she first thought. A quick inspection revealed no lump, but it was tender to the touch.

She got out of bed and felt a sore place on her hip where the bastard kicked her. She lowered the side of her undies to check but saw nothing, figuring it was unlikely to bruise.

Little arsehole, she thought, then almost laughed when she pictured him scrubbing in vain to wash the paint from his face.

She picked up her work tank-top and slipped it over her head. It reeked of booze and weed, as did her hair. She could do with a shower.

Wiping at the corners of her mouth, she walked bare-legged into the living room.

Finn was gone, but Bobbi stood in the kitchen, frying eggs in a pan. She listened to Prince's *'Little Red Corvette'* on her phone, volume turned down low, wearing black flared jeans and a white V-neck lace-up top. She had taken out her cornrows, now with a full afro with a black-and-white polka dot ribbon holding it away from her face.

She didn't turn, but said, "I thought I heard you getting up."

"What time is it?" Gayle asked.

"Eleven-thirty."

"Tell me you're joking."

"Nope. Don't worry." Bobbi laid four slices of bread under the grill. "I went up to get Finn some fresh clothes and got him off to school. You obviously needed the rest."

"I haven't had much sleep since…" she admitted, trailing off.

"Of course not." She slipped a spatula under the eggs and laid them on the plates. "Eggs and toast?"

Since Bobbi's only table was taken up by the sewing machine, they ate on the settee with their plates on their knees.

"What happened last night?" Bobbi asked, splitting one of her yolks.

Gayle groaned. "It's all happening at once. I have no connection to my life *before*. I worked hard to keep it that way. I cut *everyone* off. Danny was the only exception. I'm a different person. And then, the other day I get a phone call…"

She went on to explain about hearing from Jax and the altercation with the dealer last night. She left out having taken the switchblade, however, which still sat in the pocket of her jeans on the bedroom floor.

When they were finished, Bobbi cleared away their plates then rejoined Gayle on the settee.

"It's an occupational hazard," Gayle said, "coming across people smoking weed or doing lines. But what he said when he *left*…" Gayle shrugged. "He couldn't just be some random idiot talking shit."

"So, what are they doing? Trying to scare you?"

"It's working," Gayle said with a humourless laugh. "I should have known there's no way I could get away *clean*. But it's been almost seven years. Why now unless it means something?"

"Like something Danny was into?"

"Right. But I warned him to keep that shit away from me and Finn. I don't know the first thing about what he was up to."

"Do you know anyone who would?"

Gayle mulled it over for a moment. "Maybe," she said, remembering Danny's phone. "Whether they'll speak to me is another matter."

Bobbi sat back, arms folded. She crossed her legs at the knees, jabbing at the inside of one cheek with her tongue. She bounced her foot in the air while she thought over the problem. "What else can you do?"

"I'll need to try the police again." Gayle blew air up past her nose. "Not that they'll be any bloody use. You should have heard the way that bastard Nash spoke to me."

"I'd have reported him."

Gayle shrugged. "What's the point? To them, I'm no different than Danny or Jax or any of the others. I'm just some skank off the estate, aren't I? I'm just some junkie tart. I'm nobody."

"I can go with you if you like. See how they handle two bad bitches giving them a hard time," she said with a wink.

Gayle let out a small laugh. "If I see Nash again, I'll need you to stop me kicking him straight in the bollocks," she said.

After a coffee, she told Bobbi that she needed a shower and a change of clothes before driving back to Mansfield House. They rode the lift skyward and chitchatted about Bobbi's designs. She had been unable so far to come up with any label name more interesting than *Fashion by Bobbi*, which she said was pathetic. "I'm counting on you," she said.

"You'll have a long wait," Gayle said. "I'm not that imaginative."

"I was hoping for some kind of play on my name."

Gayle smiled. "*B.O. Fashions.*"

Bobbi laughed and thumped her playfully on the shoulder. "Bitch. My designs are *not* like a stinky armpit."

When the lift let them out on the third floor, Gayle circled around Bobbi and stood on the right side of the corridor. The flat they passed belonged to Carl; a greasy little pervert who liked to hang around the lift and try to strike up conversation, then would openly eye-fuck anybody foolish enough to stop and chat. He was probably harmless, but he gave Gayle the creeps nonetheless.

Noticing the wide berth that she gave 4 G, Bobbi's half-smile wrinkled her nose. "We should knock the door," she whispered, "give him a thrill."

"Heart-attack, more like," Gayle said, fishing her keys out of her handbag. She rattled through them and went to insert it into the lock.

But the door stood ajar, the white paint chipped and scratched around the lock. The frame of the door was also scratched around the striker plate.

"You're fucking joking," Gayle muttered to herself and pushed the door. It creaked open.

The vestibule was dark and appeared to be as she had left it.

Bobbi reached out and snatched Gayle's forearm. "Don't go in," she pleaded. "Let's call the police."

Gayle felt sick, but more than that, she felt angry. "I can't," she said. "I've got to *see*."

"Don't touch anything else with your bare hands," Bobbi told her. She reached up and untied the ribbon from around her hair. She handed it to Gayle.

She wrapped the strip of silk around her fingers,

holding it in place with her thumb. Her pulse raced and she felt it throb in the sore spot on the back of her head.

She reached for the door, hesitated, then lifted her hand to almost head-height. If there were any fingerprints left, they would be by the door handle and not so high up. With her other hand, Gayle patted the rear pocket of her jeans. The switchblade was still there, locked away. Not knowing what to expect, she considered taking it out and having it at the ready. Common sense told her that her intruders would not still be inside; she had simply been the victim of a robbery. Her TV would be gone and probably her iPad, but she was not in mortal danger.

Nonetheless, her skin broke out in a sour sweat.

With her ribbon-sheathed hand, she shoved at the door.

It swung slowly in.

The fridge door was wide open and its contents were all over the tile floor. Glasses and cups and plates had been pulled from the cupboards and smashed on the counter tops and floor, leaving jagged shards mixed with the milk, orange juice and unopened packets of chicken breasts, bacon and cheese. Everything had been stepped on.

The dining chairs were knocked over, laying on their backs, but were intact. In the living area, the TV was where she had left it, but the screen had been dented and smashed in three places. The settee was slashed open and the stuffing and foam was strewn all around the room. The drawers in her side tables had been pulled loose, upended and lay in pieces amongst their innocuous contents: utility bills, notepads, pens and Finn's scarred and dented Matchbox cars.

Careful not to step in the slippery remnants of food on the floor, Gayle moved deeper in.

Behind her, Bobbi had pulled out her phone and was

already talking to the police. "I want to report a break-in," she said.

Gayle stepped through the door to the bedrooms and bathroom. Bobbi's voice faded into the background.

In the bathroom, the medicine cabinet had been ripped from the wall and lay in splinters and spicules of glass in the bath. Medicine and beauty products were scattered all over the room. On the wall, in red lipstick, someone had scrawled SSS in block capitals. But she knew that the *South Side Squad* hadn't done this.

In the bedroom, her clothes had been pulled from the chest of drawers and lay on the floor. The wardrobe door had been wrenched off its top hinge and the wardrobe itself had been tipped sideways, now lying diagonally against the wall. Her mattress was slashed open and pulled off the bed. Beneath it, she had hidden a wrapped present for Finn's birthday: a Batman play-set. It had been stamped on and destroyed.

She hurried down the short hallway to Finn's room, eyes tingling and burning. She pushed the door and it caught on his damaged belongings. She shouldered it all the way open.

His toys lay all over the floor, some mangled and broken from having been stamped on. His stuffed animals were disembowelled, with their cottony viscera thrown about the bedroom. His posters were slashed and the shelves were pulled from the walls with sufficient force to rip out wall-plugs and leave a dusting of plaster on his chest of drawers, which itself had been thoroughly rifled through.

On his bedside table, the photograph of Gayle, Finn and Danny had been smashed. Beside it was a red tin box, about the same size as a shoebox. She lifted the lid and saw that it was empty. She wondered if Danny had given it to their son, for she had never seen it before. She closed the lid.

On the floor, half under the bed, she saw the photograph album amidst the wreckage. She sank to her knees and picked it up.

She didn't know if she would be able to bear the pain of seeing the photographs inside torn or defaced.

But she had to know.

She opened the first page, to where she had fixed Finn's ultrasound photo and the first pictures taken of him in hospital.

The photos all appeared to be present, each one untouched.

Gayle held the album to her chest, eyes misting with tears. She trembled not only with fear, but a bone-deep fury.

CHAPTER 9

As police investigated the scene, Gayle collected a change of clothes for herself and Finn, then returned with Bobbi to the downstairs flat. She put the photo album on the coffee table, took a hot shower, dried and dressed and had just about collected herself when the police came to speak to her.

While they walked her through exactly what had happened, Gayle caught sight of Bobbi in the kitchen, tapping her wrist. She saw that it was half past two.

"We might have to do this later," Gayle started to say.

"Don't worry," Bobbi said. "I'll go pick him up." She stood, slipped her bag over her shoulder and stooped over the coffee table to pick up the Fiat's key. She gave Gayle a small reassuring smile and left.

The cop – PC Paul Reid – was tall and heavily-tanned, with a thick moustache that hid most of his mouth from view. When he spoke, he seemed to be performing some kind of ventriloquist's act. "And did anything appear to be missing?" The blue biro in his left hand hovered above sheets of loose paper on a clipboard.

"It didn't look like it," Gayle said. "Everything was just... *destroyed*."

"And tagged by the *South-Side Squad*."

Gayle scoffed. "You know anything about them?"

"A little. They're bad news."

"They were. They're nothing now. The *West-End* almost wiped them out back in the day."

"I'm not very up on the gangs," Reid admitted. "Do you have any real reason to think the *WEC* are responsible?"

Gayle stood then, exhaling deeply. She ran her fingers through her hair. "Are you even listening?"

Reid set his jaw. "Listening," he said. "And annotating." He tapped his clipboard with his biro.

"Can't you just *do something*?" she asked, hating the pleading note that crept into her voice. She crossed the small room to the balcony, peering out at the car-park below. "Can't you just question him?"

"Who?"

"Jackson Knox," Gayle said, "who else?"

Reid clipped his pen to the board and leant forward with it resting on his knees. "Miss Stillwater," he said, "from what you said, break-ins and warnings aren't really Jax Knox's style. I don't know him as well as you, but to be honest, I'll be surprised if anything comes of it. Of course, we'll speak to as many gang members as we can, but given the tag, I'd expect that it was in fact someone from SSS with an old grudge you may not remember."

"For Christ's sake," Gayle said through clenched jaws. "What is it with you lot?"

Instead of responding, Reid continued: "Or one against Mr Gowan that you knew nothing about."

"I don't care what the bloody tag says," Gayle said, keeping her tone calm in spite of her frustration. "It *wasn't* the SSS. Are you going to check on Jax and see if he has an alibi or not? I mean, what if my little boy had been in the flat?"

Reid raised his hands in a placating gesture. "Maybe CSI will find a definitive print of someone we know. Failing that, if you're adamant Jax Knox was involved, we'll speak to him too. It's a safe bet he'll have an alibi if what you say about him is true, so with no convincing evidence, we'll be unable to charge him. The most I can suggest is you file for a restraining order, but without knowing for sure he was here or that he made a direct *threat* against you..."

The conversation continued in the same vein for another half hour, until Gayle wanted to scream.

Having grown up in a never-ending series of foster homes, she had none of Bobbi's faith in the police. She'd seen first-hand their ineptitude at almost every turn, aside from once, when they'd arrested her father for murder.

She took her seat again, no longer even listening to Reid prattle on. She tapped her foot on the floor, shaking out her hair. As time dragged on, she felt a headache beginning to bloom behind her right eye.

She looked again at the clock and saw that it would soon be a quarter past three.

"Are we almost done then?" Gayle asked, unable to hide the annoyance from her voice.

Reid put down his pen. "*You* called *us*," he reminded her.

"And I shouldn't have bothered. Like an idiot, I thought the police might take something like this seriously. I honestly thought you might want to do your job... you know, that thing you get paid to do? But if you've got bugger all to suggest that's worth anything," she said, slapping her knees and getting to her feet, "then maybe we should forget the whole damn thing before my son gets scared when he sees you. Kids do that, you see: get *scared*. Not that I expect the fucking cops to give a shit about that. You can leave now." She turned the handle and opened the door.

Slowly, Reid got to his feet. He pressed the control for his lapel radio and told someone that he was done. He slipped his pen back into his breast pocket and stopped beside her on his way to the door.

"No matter what you may think," he said, "we're not all bad, Miss Stillwater."

"You don't all *have* to be," she told him. "Thanks for nothing."

When she was alone again, she stalked over to the window once more. Beside it stood Bobbi's tailor's dummy, bedecked with swathes of fabric and a tape measure around its neck. She whipped an elbow into its guts and sent it back into the wall where it tottered before falling over.

Embarrassed for the petulant display of anger, she bent to pick it up and put it back as she had found it.

Another waste of time, she thought.

But the cop *was* right about one thing, however. She knew Jax Knox a hell of a lot better than he did.

*   *   *

There were five of them in the car that night: a black Volkswagen Golf with tinted windows belonging to Alex 'X-Ray' Raymond. He fancied himself the next Lewis Hamilton and as his idol had done as a kid, X-Ray competed in go-kart races on weekends. Unlike Lewis Hamilton, he was also a car thief.

In the passenger seat beside him, Jax puffed on a joint before passing it behind him to Chris Gorman. He took a

*couple of heavy drags and Gayle was grateful for the silence:
it was the first time he had shut up in almost ten minutes.
She sat in the middle, pressed between Gorman and Danny
on her right. They held hands, her knuckles against his left
thigh. She looked at Danny and he gave her a patient smile.*

*Blowing enough smoke to make it hard to see, Chris
passed the joint to Gayle. It was almost done, but she didn't
want any more. She didn't want to put her mouth to something that Chris and Jax had already slobbered over. She
handed it to Danny, who apparently didn't mind. He toked
on it and passed the roach to X-Ray, who finished it off.*

*Gayle shuffled her bum forwards in the seat so she could
relax back. She closed her eyes and laid her head against
Danny's shoulder. He gave her hand a squeeze.*

*Chris started talking again, but she tried to zone him out.
She brushed her lips against Danny's jaw, which was prickly
with stubble. She wished they were anywhere else in the
world right now, just so long as they were alone. Weed not
only relaxed her, but made her horny too. Or maybe it was
just being beside him, with the warm, clean smell of him.*

*She nibbled on his earlobe. He turned to her then and
kissed her, and for a few moments it was as though she had
gone deaf. She couldn't hear Chris Gorman's prattling or the
thrum of the engine; all she could feel was Danny.*

*She was almost seventeen and unlike a lot of the girls
with the gang, she had been a virgin until only two months
ago. While the setting had been the furthest thing from her
idea of romance – a wooden bench on Braunstone Park, with
only his jacket to protect her backside from splinters – he
himself was gentle. To her, if to no one else, he was kind. She
knew that she loved him, but hadn't said it yet. She was
loathe to reveal the depth of her feelings in case he laughed at
her. She didn't believe he was using her – after all, if he was*

only interested in sex, there were plenty of easier girls around – but she was afraid of rejection nonetheless.

Had they been alone, she thought she might have told him then. She wanted to tell him what he meant to her and how he was the only person in the whole world who had ever given a shit about her. Then she would beg him to undress her and make love to her. She ached to feel him thrust into her again. They had only done it four more times since that night on the park and for her, it had never been the cheap fuck or the casual sex the other girls described, but had been lovemaking each time.

Her girlishness in this one regard surprised and embarrassed her, adding to her reluctance. Still, she felt as though her feelings could be clearly read in every look she ever gave him.

By the way their hands were entwined on his thigh, she could feel his erection growing against her wrist. She smiled at the feel of it twitching, like a balloon being inflated. She laughed a little.

Danny turned to her again. "What?" he asked, smiling.

"Nothing," she said, burying her face in his neck.

That quiet little reprieve was not to last. Gradually, the sound of Chris Gorman's incessant mouth came back to her.

As he went on about who-knew-what, X-Ray started to nudge the volume of the stereo higher.

He was twenty, tall, with cruel little beady eyes. His short blond hair bristled against the ceiling of the car and his height forced him to hunch over the wheel no matter how far back he pushed his seat.

Chris Gorman was pudgy, with the kind of cherubic face and lips that would have better suited a woman. His hair was cropped short, but it was so thick that, in the darkness of the car, he seemed to be wearing a black swimming cap.

Even through the rolls of his neck, the veins stood out as he shouted above the thumping grime music. X-Ray had the stereo turned up so loud that it rattled the windows. Chris spoke so forcefully that he sprayed the front headrest with spit.

Jax rubbed the back of his shaved head and spun in the seat, glaring. "Oi, fat cunt! *Keep spitting on me, fam, and see what happens.*" Jax turned the volume dial, bringing it down a few decibels.

X-Ray piloted the Golf around residential streets as though they were at Donington racecourse. He stomped on the brakes to take a corner. Jax laughed, but Gayle had to brace herself to avoid being pitched through the window. X-Ray revved the engine and the tyres screeched as they struggled for purchase. They turned right and she pressed into Chris Gorman's cushiony right arm. He looked at her to smile – suggestively, she thought – and those Cupid-lips flattened to make a pale slash in his chubby face.

She pressed her knees together and wedged them between the front racing seats to keep from sliding around. Danny's hand tightened around hers.

Chris had begun chatting about football, but Jax cut him off. "Fuck that, mate," he said, his voice cool. "What I want to know, bruv, is what's with your fuckin' cousin?"

Chris's voice stuttered to a halt and he sat staring at the back of Jax's head with his jowls shuddering. As X-Ray worked the pedals, Gayle saw his dark little eyes staring at Chris in the rear-view mirror. In that moment, it seemed he had earned his name for his ability to stare through someone.

"Whatcha mean, Jax?" Chris asked.

"That fuckwit with the SSS, mate. That's what the fuck I mean."

The South Side Squad were based around the Saffron

Lane area. As far as gang numbers, they were nothing special, but there had been a number of serious beefs and scuffles over the years.

"He's my second-cousin," Chris explained.

"What's one of them?" Jax asked.

"A cousin you can fuck," X-Ray said and the guys broke up with laughter – even Chris, though he remained on guard.

"Is that it, you bender?" Jax asked. "Do you get down with him?"

"I ain't gay. Our great-Grandads are brothers or summut."

"That's third cousin, dickhead," Danny said.

"How would you know?"

Danny laughed. "That'd make him less of a relation. I'm helping you out, you prick."

"Well, there you are then," Chris whined. "I only met him once at my uncle's wedding."

Jax turned in his seat, glaring at Chris.

In the passing illumination of streetlights, Gayle saw the cold look in Jax's eyes. That lumpish nose flared. A spot was beginning to form in the crease of his left nostril. His face looked like a four-year-old had sculpted it from Play-Doh then kicked it across the playground.

"He's been coming into our fucking turf though, bruv," Jax said.

"I don't know – has he?"

Jax scoffed. "Mate, he's been visiting your yard."

"Who told you that?"

"Who gives a fuck? The point is, one of them SSS cunts has been in your house. Tell me I'm wrong."

"My mum helps out the family," Chris said. "She's a hairdresser, bro, you know that."

"I don't care if she gives happy massages, stupid, that's fucking out of line."

X-Ray chimed in. "He should know better than to go rolling into our turf. That's asking for a pasting."

Jax slammed his hand against the dashboard. "That's what I'm fucking saying. Chris, you've gotta deal with this."

"What do you mean?"

"Do you even have a brain in that head, or is it just fat in there too?"

"I just don't know what... I mean, look, my mum just makes a little bit of extra money and... I don't know, what do you want me to do, mate?"

Jax turned in his seat again. "Are you thick? Shank the cunt. That's what I want."

"What?" Chris's face had gone pale.

"You heard me. That's where we're going right now – innit, X?"

X-Ray turned the wheel, taking them down another residential street, screaming between the rows of parked cars.

Gayle's palms were sweating. She let go of Danny's hand and blotted them on her jeans. She looked at him and saw him with his right arm resting on the windowsill, gnawing on the pad of his thumb. He was clearly troubled, but said nothing.

"Now?" Chris said.

"Right fucking now," Jax told him. He reached into the glove compartment and came up with a Swiss Army knife. The blade was already out. It was rusty at the hinge and silver electrician's tape had been wrapped around the handle. He passed the knife over his shoulder by the blade tip.

Chris's hand shook as he took it by the handle. "What am I supposed to do?"

"You've gotta put your fucking work in, fam," Jax said. "This cunt disrespects your fuckin' turf, now you've gotta show him why he shouldn't. I don't give a fuck if he's your third cousin, tenth cousin, or your fuckin' great aunt's dog-walker. We're your brethren, innit. We're your fuckin' blood. So, step up. Be a fuckin' man and do this shit."

The knife glinted in the diffused light that reached them through the tinted windows.

Gayle could smell Chris's sweat. It was rank and sickly-sweet.

"Stop up here, fam," Jax told X-Ray, pointing to the pavement by a red pillar box.

X-Ray slowed the car and brought it to a stop with a jolt and a bark of rubber as the wheel grazed the kerb. Jax threw open the door and got out. He came around to Chris's door and yanked it open.

"Out," he said. "We're switching. You're gonna need to see clear."

Chris fumbled with the release button of his seatbelt. Slowly, he got out.

Gayle shuffled closer to Danny, who turned diagonally in his own seat and put an arm around her shoulder. He pulled her close. Jax hopped into the back beside her and slammed the door.

In the passenger seat, Chris reached for his seatbelt.

Jax shot out his meaty paw to stay his hand. "You'll get tangled in the belt, innit," he said. "You'll need to move fast, trust me. Leave it off."

Chris did as he was told.

X-Ray revved the engine and pulled away.

Gayle's throat was dry. She felt as though she could feel an inner fire blazing through Knox's skin.

Jax propped the elbow of his left arm on the back of the

front seat and looked past her through the window, then over his own shoulder to stare out the back. He tapped Chris on the right shoulder, and he visibly flinched.

Jax said, "Yo, give me that t'ing for a minute, bruv." He put out his hand.

Chris passed the knife back and Jax rolled it around in his palm.

She knew that a standard Swiss Army knife had a cutting edge on only one side, but this one had been ground down on the rounded edge too, honed to a point and fixed so that it could no longer be folded.

She felt Jax's eyes boring into her. He didn't have a face built for smiling, but he gave it a try. It looked wrong, like a Hallowe'en mask.

"Kiss it for me, babe," Jax said.

Gayle's voice was croaky. "I'm sorry?"

"The shank. Kiss it. For luck. Chris is gonna need luck, innit. Just a peck, that's all it needs."

Gayle reached to take the knife, but Jax pulled it back.

"Be careful," he said. "This fucker's sharp. I'll hold it for you so you don't cut off your lips." He laughed then. "Danny wouldn't like that, would ya, mate?"

Danny said nothing.

Jax held the knife closer to Gayle's mouth. The car jumped and shimmied over the potholes. His eyes were dark, hidden beneath a mantle of bone and bushy eyebrows, but seared into her.

Sweat rolled from her armpits. Gayle leant forwards, mouth inches from the knife. She planted a grazing kiss against the flat of the blade and hurriedly pulled her head back. She raised a hand to her mouth but there was no blood.

Jax smiled that predatory grin. "Good girl," he whispered with a wink.

He turned forwards once more and dropped the knife into the cup holder by the hand-brake. Jax tapped X-Ray on the left shoulder and, as though it were a cue, X-Ray reached for the volume knob. The music swelled and she winced at the sudden din.

As if he knew what was coming, Danny pulled Gayle tighter against him, wrapping her up in both arms.

Jax threw his body against the passenger seat, wrapped his right arm around Chris's thick neck and held him tight. Chris reached up, gasping, his hands finding fistfuls of Jax's hoodie sleeve, but Jax was powerful and did not loosen his grip. He grabbed his own right wrist with his left hand and pulled back.

Gayle cried out in shock. She could see the veins pulsing in Jax's temples. He bared his teeth and a thread of spit rolled down off his lower lip.

In the seat, Chris began to buck and kick, his arms flailing. His right arm whipped out and caught X-Ray in the side of the head and the car swerved to the right, towards a parked Nissan Vectra, but X-Ray whipped the wheel around to avoid a collision. Driving straight again, he threw out his own arm, awkwardly punching Chris in the side of his face, then hammering at his chest twice, three times, four.

Next to her, Jax was rocking back and forth, as though trying to tear Chris's head off. She heard him laughing, high-pitched and manic. She wanted to tell them to stop, but couldn't find her voice. Danny slinked down in his seat, pulling her with him, to protect her from the flailing arms.

Abruptly, Jax let go and Chris fell forwards, his head against the dashboard. He reached for his throat, his coughing and spluttering drowned out by the music.

X-Ray hit the brakes, pitching Gayle and Danny forwards. Her head connected with the back of the driver's seat before being thrown just as fiercely back when the car came to a stop.

Jax threw the door open and was on the pavement while the tortured brakes still squealed. He tore at the passenger door and snatched at Chris, snagging him by the collar, dragging the bigger man – squealing – from his seat.

Jax dragged Chris across the concrete and onto the grass leading to Braunstone Park, then thrust him down to the ground in the shadows of a copse of trees. He bent at the waist and rained down heavy fists into the back and side of Chris's head.

Gayle knew to keep her mouth shut.

Jax kicked and stomped at Chris's chest. With one savage kick to his throat, he flipped Chris over onto his back and began slamming his fist into his bloodied face. His pathetic cries turned to gurgles as he choked and gagged on his own blood. Jax threw one last kick, cruelly whipping his head to the side. "Traitor piece of shit," he hissed. Then he came back to the rear of the car and leant in. He beckoned at Gayle with his bloody right hand. "Get out," he said.

Gayle froze. Danny arm tightened around her.

"Jax, I don't—"

"Hurry up," he said, "we gotta get outta here. Get in the front."

Reluctantly, Gayle shuffled forwards, eyes on Jax, untrusting. Any moment, she expected him to snatch a handful of her hair and slam those heavy fists into her face.

Gayle got in beside X-Ray and the Golf took off, leaving the still and bloody body behind them before she had even shut the door. They rocketed around the roundabout, taking the third exit. Only then did X-Ray reach out and lower the volume to normal levels.

"What the hell was that?" Danny asked.

"Fuckin' rat," Jax said. "He didn't deserve to be in the fuckin' WEC, fam."

"Is he dead?" Gayle asked.

"Who cares? Fuck him. If he isn't dead, he best be moving out, 'cause he ain't welcome in the ends."

Gayle felt sick. She pressed the control button for her window and lowered it two inches. The inside of the car felt too hot, too oppressive. She glanced to her right and saw that the knife still lay in the cup holder. She felt Jax's presence behind her, like a coiled snake ready to strike.

Danny will protect me, she thought. He won't let Jax do anything.

Behind her, Jax started to laugh. "What you lookin' at that for, sis?" He reached for the knife, holding it up by the handle. "You think I'm gonna fuck you up too?"

X-Ray started to laugh.

Gayle turned sideways in her seat, bracing herself with one hand on the dashboard and the other on X-Ray's headrest. Danny's face was like stone. His eyes moved from the driver, to Jax and back again.

Jax turned the knife over in his hand and offered it to her by the blade.

"Go ahead," he said, "for real. Put it back in the what's-it."

She took it. She popped open the glove compartment and tucked the knife away amongst the rolling papers, lighter and the bag of weed.

Jax grabbed her by both shoulders and shook, shouting in her ear. Gayle cried out and pulled away, turning in her seat, left hand already curled into a fist.

Jax laughed. "Jesus, fam, your girl's a psycho, bruv," he said, slapping Danny in the chest. "Got your fuckin' hands full there, innit."

As he threw the car around another corner, X-Ray was also laughing, glancing up at the rear-view mirror to share the moment.

Danny wasn't laughing, but he forced a smile.

She lowered the sun visor, relieved the see a vanity mirror glued to the back of it. She wanted to be able to keep an eye on Jax.

"Where are we going?" Danny asked.

"Nearly there," Jax said. He leant forwards between the seats and pointed at a spot ahead on the street to the right. "X, behind that Renault, bruv."

X-Ray coasted the car to a stop. The car sat idling for long minutes with no one saying anything. Danny cast a look at Gayle and gave her a wink and a smile. It's all right, the wink said. Trust me.

And she did. She followed him into this gang: it gave her a sense of security; a family that she had never had. People had her back and there was comfort in knowing that she would be protected in times of trouble.

But she didn't trust Jax and doubted she ever would.

"What are we doing here?" Danny asked.

"Pickin' up my sket," Jax said. "Just taking her to a party."

Gayle looked at the red-brick semi on their right. The front door opened, shut, and a young girl in a braided pony-tail, white blouse and a too-short skirt breezily trotted down the path.

The door behind Gayle opened and Jax got out. He walked around the back of the car and, through the dark-tinted rear window, saw him grab her about the waist. The two of them were roughly the same height when they locked lips. Jax pawed at her breasts. After a moment, he guided her to the car and pushed her in between he and Danny.

Snapping chewing gum, she said, "Hiya. Everyone all right?" She had a soft Northern Irish accent.

Now that she was closer, Gayle could see that the girl wasn't as young as she had first thought; perhaps twenty-two. Her blue eyes were large and gave her a wild, frenzied look.

"This is Nikki," Jax said. "And you're a fuckin' freak, innit, babes?" He had his hands on her thigh.

Nikki giggled around the wad of gum in her mouth. Her lips were so thin that they almost weren't there at all. Her dark brown hair was lacquered and tightly braided, giving her a severe look that did nothing to soften her oblong face and bulging eyes.

"And where's your knickers?" Jax asked.

Nikki snapped her gum and gave him a wide grin. "In me bag," she said. "Like you wanted."

"Then, what you waitin' for?" Jax asked, lifting himself up off the seat to take down his joggers.

Gayle spun around in the seat before she caught a complete eyeful of what he had in his hand. Beside her, X-Ray started to chuckle.

In the vanity mirror, she saw the back of Nikki's head as she kicked her legs over Jax's waist to straddle him. She started to rock and moan.

"Fuckin' hell," Danny muttered, turning to look out the window.

In the slashes of light from passing cars, Gayle saw Jax's face, brows knotted and the tip of his tongue jutting between his teeth. His eyes whipped up, away from Nikki and fixed on Gayle's in the mirror. He winked.

She slapped the visor away.

In the seat behind, Nikki started to moan. Jax was laughing again.

CHAPTER 10

After dinner, the twenty-four-hour locksmith arrived and got to work on the door.

Bobbi handed over control of the TV to Finn and got to work at the sewing machine. To give he and Gayle privacy, she connected a pair of headphones to her mobile and sat before the sewing machine, working the pedal with one bare foot and feeding the fabric across the slide plate.

During episodes of Spongebob, Finn periodically sprang up in excitement and sometimes went to check on what Bobbi was doing.

Gayle was relieved to see some of the old Finn returning.

Bobbi dropped a few things into his hand and he came racing over to Gayle. He opened his palm, showing her half a dozen pound coins and two large, glittery plastic buttons. From his pocket, Finn produced his black Velcro wallet with the Batman logo on the front – a present from Danny – and dropped them in. Tucked inside was an expired X-box gift card and Gayle's old ID, which she had never cut up.

While of course no longer valid, as the name was the one she had been given at birth, it technically didn't expire for another six months. Finn liked the grown-up feeling of having the cards.

She chewed her lip, debating how to tell him what had happened to their home, but decided it better not to crush his good mood.

She excused herself to the bathroom for a moment to call work out of Finn's earshot. When Ricky Dutton answered, Gayle lied, saying, "My little boy's not well and I can't get a baby-sitter."

Unimpressed, he said, "All right. Let me know if you can make it in tomorrow, it's gonna be busy." Dutton hung up.

Later, Gayle sat beside Finn and reached into her bag for Danny's phone. She scrolled once more through his contacts. There were only a few names she recognised.

I wonder how many of the others are in prison or dead, she thought.

The most recent texts after those she'd already seen were from she herself. Gayle opened the thread and scrolled down. She had gone back in time less than two months before reaching the end.

She frowned, thinking about Mel.

Did she check his phone? Gayle thought. *Is that why he deleted my old messages? And cropped me out of his photos?*

She flicked her teeth with her thumbnail.

What difference does it make now? she asked herself.

A further search revealed nothing that could shed any light on what Danny had been doing in the days and weeks before his murder.

Just Scotty borrowing some money, she thought.

But who was Scotty? There were only a handful of texts between them spanning the last year and all were casual invites for drinks.

She opened up his web browser and checked Danny's history.

Nothing but unimportant emails and paid-for porn sites.

Except...

Gayle adjusted her position on the settee as she opened the National Rail website.

Her frown deepened. Danny hadn't mentioned planning a trip somewhere.

Not that he'd tell me anyway, she thought.

She opened up his mobile banking app, hoping to see some payment that might shed some light, but it was password protected. She tried the one he used for his email but with no luck.

The cops would have checked that out already, she told herself. *If there were any clues, even those bastards wouldn't ignore it if they thought it could get them an arrest... even if it meant arresting the wrong person.*

Another dead end.

After less than an hour, there was a knock at the door, startling Gayle. Bobbi went to check but it was only the locksmith. He handed Gayle the new key and left.

As late afternoon gave way to evening, Bobbi again offered up her bed to Gayle.

"No," she said, "it's all right. We'll just sleep here in the living room."

"Really?" Finn asked. "Like indoor camping."

"Yeah," Gayle said, forcing a smile for him, "it'll be fun, right?"

Bobbi fetched blankets from the spare room and Gayle arranged the settee into a makeshift bed for Finn. After getting him tucked in, Bobbi read him another story then placed a hand on Gayle's shoulder.

"Don't be up all night worrying," she whispered. "Things will work out."

But Gayle wasn't so sure about that. When Bobbi went into the bathroom, she squatted at the foot of the settee beside Finn.

"I like staying at Auntie Bobbi's," he said. "And I don't have to brush my teeth."

"Yeah, well, don't get used to that, mate," she told him, planting a kiss on his forehead. "Now get some rest."

"Are you still wide awake?"

"I'll be going to sleep too, soon," she said. "Sweet dreams, all right?"

"Okay. Night night." Finn wriggled until he was comfy then closed his eyes.

Gayle sat on a cushion at the foot of the settee, turning Danny's phone over in her palm. At midnight, she was still awake. The soft snores of her sleeping son were the only sounds in the flat.

She kept her eyes on the door.

Gayle reached into her pocket and withdrew the pearl-handled switchblade.

In the faint light that filtered through the curtains, she lifted the knife and turned it slowly around between her fingers. The razor-sharp blade caught the light, dripping down to the hilt like melted butter.

We're safe here, she tried to tell herself. *Nobody knows we're here with Bobbi.*

But her fear did not subside. There was no way to know what Danny's killer or killers did or didn't know about her.

If anyone breaks in, she thought, *they'll have a surprise*. She watched the light play on the steel blade and thought again of the knife in her father's hand, driving into another man's belly, and the sudden, hot spurt of blood.

'*Like father, like daughter*,' she imagined Ryan Breach saying.

Gayle shuddered and looked again at the door.

This is different, she told herself.

But the thought of actually using the knife made her guts somersault.

She pictured Jax Knox walking through the door, fixing her with those predatory, deep-set eyes of his. In her mind, he smiled at the sight of the knife, raising the front of his hoodie to expose his belly.

"Don't play pretend with me, bitch. You ain't got it in you," she imagined him saying. *"You don't. But* I *do."*

Gayle folded away the blade and tucked it back into her pocket. She leaned forwards on her knees, hands clasped to stop them shaking.

Just before seven on Friday morning, Gayle opened her eyes to the sound of the shower running. She had given in to sleep a little before three and had lain fully-dressed on the floor with a pillow beneath her head, a warm orange-and-green woollen blanket drawn up to her chest.

On the settee beside her, Finn sat up, rubbing his eyes and yawning so wide that it seemed he was going to dislocate his jaw. The hair on the left side of his head stood up in a cowlick.

She made him a breakfast of Corn Flakes and sat on the

arm of the settee while he ate, massaging the stiffness out of her neck.

Bobbi came into the living room, humming a tune Gayle didn't recognise.

"Good morning," she said and pulled the curtains back all the way. She wore a green tank top, grey-and-white camouflage leggings and a floral head-wrap. Tucked under her right arm, she had Finn's school uniform that she had washed and tumble-dried the night before. "Everything all right?" she asked Gayle.

She nodded. "Yeah. I think I have an idea. We can talk more about it after I get this little dude off to school."

Through a mouthful of Corn Flakes, Finn mumbled, *"Boring."*

When it was her turn under the hot spray, Gayle worked out the knot in her neck and washed her hair. Clean and dry, she dressed in her Nikes, navy-blue cargo pants, black T-shirt and a black Puma hoodie.

Finn was dressed and Bobbi had tried to tame his hair with a tub of styling mousse. He checked himself over in the mirror and after a moment of indecision, broke into a smile.

"Hey, Mummy, *look*. Don't I look cool?"

She nodded. "All you need now is an earring and a leather jacket."

He frowned. "Earrings are for girls."

Bobbi fetched her leather blouson, bug-eye sunglasses and her burgundy handbag. "Let's hit the road," she said.

The drive took twenty minutes in school-run traffic and parking was a bitch. Gayle was forced to put two wheels up on the kerb on the corner of the street. She snapped on her hazard warning lights and got out.

As Finn pushed the seat forward to climb out, Bobbi said, "Don't go kissing too many girls, Casanova."

"Casa-what?" he asked, hopping out onto the concrete.

Gayle walked him to the entrance, her hand wrapped tight around his. His little mitt was warm and soft. When they reached the open iron gates, she turned him to face her and squatted down to his eye-level.

"Be good, all right?"

"I'm always good."

"Yes, you are," she smiled. "And I'll pick you up later."

"Uh-huh." Finn was distracted, looking off to the playground, where squealing friends of his were racing around in circles, trying to tag one another with their lunchboxes. Some wore holiday jumpers with ghosts, pumpkins and skeletons on the front. She had forgotten all about the school's dress-down day.

"Finn," she said, "listen to me a minute. I want you to stay around the teachers today, okay?"

He frowned at her then, as if she had taken leave of her senses. "What, like, all day? Even when I'm playing and stuff?"

"Even then. Don't go wandering around on your own. Always stay with people you know."

"Oh," he said, drawing out the word. "You mean like stranger-danger stuff. I know," he said, looking back to where his friends were playing, "we did lessons on that."

"Good. Now, don't I get a kiss any more?"

He kissed her on the cheek and she held him close for a moment, then told herself she was being a fool and couldn't hold on to him all morning. If he hadn't suspected something was wrong already, he soon would if she didn't get a grip on herself.

"See you later," she said.

"Bye." Finn turned and ran after the other kids, calling out his friend's name: *"Callum! Wait, Callum!"*

Gayle watched him go, then headed back to the car. She got behind the wheel and shut the door. She took a deep breath to calm her nerves. She turned and saw Bobbi peering at her over the top of her bug-eye shades.

"So, if we're gonna talk," she said, "are you buying the coffee, or am I?"

CHAPTER 11

When Jax came to visit his mother, he brought a four-pint carton of milk, a jar of Nescafé and a loaf of bread. She made him coffee and two slices of toast with strawberry jam, then he asked if he could borrow ten pounds. As always, she gave it to him. He said he needed it for petrol, but the car was three-quarters full. He had thirty quid in his back pocket, but he stuffed in the tenner anyway.

He visited Sonia Knox perhaps once every two months, sometimes staying for an hour and other times the entire weekend. Since his dad died when Jax was thirteen, his mum didn't sleep much, so he was confident she would be awake when he knocked the door at a quarter past six.

Jax hadn't slept yet, but he wasn't tired. He still had a few pills and a couple lines of coke in his system, which would leave him virtually narcoleptic when they wore off, but that wouldn't be for hours yet.

When his lank-haired waif of a mother excused herself to get dressed, Jax went to the downstairs loo and laid out the last of his cocaine on the back of the toilet. He snorted through his mum's tenner, wiped away the remnants from the porcelain and cleaned his face. His heart felt like a jack-hammer in his chest.

Struck with the sudden need to be out in the elements, Jax made his way through the house for the back door. On his way, he noticed that the decor in the living room had changed again. This time, her interest-*du-jour* was an Indian aesthetic with incense on the mantelpiece, meditation statues and framed pictures that looked like they came from the least-graphic sections of the Karma Sutra. By her armchair was a well-thumbed book by some guy who called himself Krishnamurti.

Jax picked it up and opened to a random page. He read some shit about the description not being the described then lost interest. He dropped the book, not bothering to place it where he had found it.

He walked through the tidy kitchen and opened the back door.

The grass was not yet wild, but it certainly could do with being mown. Perhaps the wannabe-guru who was fucking his mother would be put to work outside soon.

Still wearing his black puffer jacket, Jax sat on the rocking chair on the patch of concrete in front of the garden. It was maybe twelve feet square, without bushes or plants or flowers, but the six-foot fence around it had been painted with sunflowers, azaleas, ivy, clematis, roses, poppies and even half a dozen gnomes with silly faces. It looked as though a team of kindergarteners had been employed to give the garden some character.

Jax rocked back and forth, his attention drawn to the lawn, where he had interred numerous boxes of bones in the clay and mud. He knew the precise locations of his little coffins and even remembered their contents.

In a tobacco tin in the far-left corner was his first find: a sparrow that he happened upon as a child of nine, injured and twitching on the pavement outside the house. He brought it home in his pocket and hurried to his bedroom to look over his little treasure in privacy.

The bird was barely moving. He didn't know what was wrong with it. Maybe, he thought, a mean cat had been toying with it, but had been scared off.

Either way, he sat cross-legged on the carpet and watched the sparrow die. When it was still, he played with its little legs, stretching them out and folding them in. He did the same with the wings, fascinated by their range of movement.

Jax had wanted to see inside, so he took a little penknife that he liberated from his dad's tool box and cut the bird up. He didn't know what he was doing, so made a real hatchet job of it, which annoyed him. He decided he would have to be more careful in the future, so placed the pieces of the sparrow in the tobacco tin and when his parents weren't watching – which was most of the time – he buried it in the garden.

Further experiments followed on field mice, a frog he found and even a rat carcass he saw one day by a drain in the playground at school. He waved it at some of the other kids at lunchtime, chasing them around, until one went and told an adult. Before his English teacher could get to him, Jax turned and fled for home so no one could take his lucky find.

The bastards suspended him for that incident, but it didn't matter: he only turned up when he felt like it, mostly for art class because he liked to paint, and total expulsion would follow a year or two later anyway.

His dead back-yard menagerie would grow over the years to include the body of a vixen he had found and bits of a rabbit that he'd stolen from a neighbour's hutch. The little bastard bit him, so Jax throttled it. It kicked and scratched with its hind legs, making a mess of Jax's left arm, so after it was dead and he cleaned himself up with some Savlon spray and a bandage from his mum's first-aid box, he ripped the fucking thing apart and left pieces out for scavengers.

When his dad saw the dish on the grass, he asked what Jax was doing with the meat, but Jax said it was chicken he had saved from dinner as part of an animal observation project for school. He was, he said, tasked with cataloguing foxes and hedgehogs drawn by the scent of free food, as well as whatever scavenging birds swooped down for a feast. Dad wasn't convinced and tanned Jax's hide, but he didn't give a shit. In truth, he hardly felt the hits any more and hadn't been able to repress his laughter.

There were more bones in the garden, of course, ranging from a magpie that he had caught in a home-made snare to a French Bulldog pup he lured from a neighbour's garden with peanut butter.

Jax didn't want to kill the puppy, because he liked the way it tickled his arm when it licked him. But he knew he couldn't keep it – its barking would alert his parents when they got home – so he poisoned it with slug pellets hidden inside pieces of turkey.

His eviscerations had become more skilful with practice and he taught himself a lot about how the creatures moved when they had been alive. Sometimes he would pose them – which he did with the bulldog pup – as if it had been sleeping and then create still-lifes in pencil, charcoal, acrylic paint or pen. Like his post-mortems, his art had improved, to the point where now Jax could create remarkable pieces on walls with cans of spray-paint if he so chose. His penmanship was excellent and unlike everyone in his social circle, when he put words to paper, his style was calligraphic – though his spelling was poor.

Lost in his reverie, Jax didn't notice the knocking at the door, until the voices were in the kitchen behind him.

"He didn't do anything," his mum said in her gentle tone, "he was here all night." In spite of all he had done to her over the years, his mum always spoke well of him – to the police if to no one else. That's how, without having to turn to see or to hear anyone call his name, he knew cops were in the house and he was about to be nicked.

Jax continued to rock in the chair, smiling to himself. He exhaled, watching his breath fog in the cold air.

* * *

They had him in the cell for an hour before someone came to interview him. The cop who sat across from him in the interview room – a tall streak of piss with a greying goatee – identified himself as DS Pierce.

Luckily, he had no more drugs on him when he was searched, so they couldn't charge him with possession.

Pierce explained that their interview was being recorded and Jax had the right to free legal representation, but Jax just shrugged and asked what he wanted.

"Where were you yesterday?" Pierce asked, hands folded on the table.

Jax leant back in his chair. "My mum's," he said, knowing she would give him an alibi.

"All day?"

"Yeah. All day. We were watching the telly. So what?"

Pierce maintained his composure. "You wouldn't know anything about a break-in at a private residence?"

"Nah, mate. You're thinking of someone else."

"How about Gayle Stillwater? When's the last time you spoke to her?"

Jax frowned. "Who?" he asked at first, then snapped his fingers. "Oh, you mean my mate's skank. That's been a while."

Jax was always calm when he lied. He never even thought about it. In fact, the more he stuck to his story, the more real it seemed. It wasn't that he *forgot* about destroying Gayle's place in a rage, but rather that the reality and his fabrication of watching the TV with his mum existed in parallel universes, while he in his omniscience recalled both at the same time. He could declare either thing, confident in knowing that both would be true. Were he to take a lie-detector test, he would pass with flying colours.

He knew they had nothing they could charge him with. If someone saw him breaking in, the cop would have said something by now. Jax didn't worry about fingerprints, since he had worn gloves and he kept his head shaved, so hair wasn't a problem. All he had to do was keep cool and wait.

The drugs in his system were wearing off and he started to feel sleepy. He almost laughed to himself when he imagined falling asleep mid-interview.

Across from him, the cop's shoulders sagged, though he tried to hide it. He cleared his throat. "Why did you tag her bathroom with SSS initials?"

Jax just looked at him. "Dunno what you're talkin' about, fam," he said.

"First, someone kills her old boyfriend, then she gets her place broken into? You expect me to think that's a coincidence, genius?"

"No," Jax said. "I don't think it's a coincidence at all. If anything, Sarge, you're probably doin' me a favour nickin' me."

"How do you work that out?" DS Pierce tried to keep his cool, but the tone of annoyance in his voice betrayed him.

"Friends of mine are gettin' killed. People's homes are gettin' broken into. Who knows? I could be next. Maybe you should do your job and check out that SSS lot, innit?" he said, starting to yawn. He stifled it with his fist.

The muscles in Pierce's jaw bunched.

Jax half-smiled, almost able to *feel* the cop's desire to reach across the table and grab him.

Instead, Pierce smoothed the cuffs of his shirt, folded his hands together again and said, "Let's start again from the beginning."

Jax relaxed into his chair as much as it allowed. He closed his eyes, rubbing his forehead, resisting the urge to nod off. The door squeaked and footsteps strode into the room. He opened one eye, regarding the tall, serious man with the close-cropped brown hair with amusement.

Speaking for the recorder, DS Pierce said, "DI Graff has entered the interview room," and gave the time. He switched off the tape. "What is it, Miles?"

Detective-Inspector Graff was in his early forties and his broad shoulders blocked the door, which he held open with his heel. He raised one hand and gave a twitch of his forefinger in a *come-here* motion to Jax.

"Let's go, shit-stain," he said, "your brief's been on the phone. You're free to go."

Pierce sat back in his chair, sucking in his lips.

Jax smiled. "Shame," he said, "I was just gettin' comfy."

To Pierce, Graff said, "Sorry about this, Nick."

"Not to worry, boss," Pierce said, getting to his feet. He

slipped his hands into his pockets. "I'm sure we'll be seeing each other again, won't we, Mr Knox?"

"Not likely, bruv," Jax said, "I don't go to gay bars." He strode past Graff, giving him a beaming, toothy smile.

Graff escorted him through the hallways, holding open doors, refusing to be drawn by any of Jax's snide comments or questions. At last, they reached the rear exit and Graff held open the fire-door.

Jax descended the two concrete steps into the courtyard behind the police station. Against the high brick wall opposite were two police cars and an unmarked black BMW, all empty. The door behind him sighed shut.

"Well," Jax said, reaching into his pocket for his Marlboros and shaking one out, "that was a lot of fun." He placed the cigarette between his teeth and waved it at Graff, who stood with his arms folded across his chest. "Got a light?"

The muscles in Graff's jaw bunched. "You want a thick ear, sunshine?"

Jax laughed. "You ain't big enough." He plucked a disposable lighter out of his pocket and lit the Marlboro.

"Get this through your head, you little twat," Graff warned, nostrils flaring, "if I wanted to build a case on you—"

Jax snorted smoke through his nostrils. "You'll *what*? Get this through *your* head, you *big* twat... You do what the fuck *I* say. Got it?"

Graff snatched a handful of Jax's jacket with his right hand, slapping away the cigarette with the left and slammed him against the wall. He clamped his hand over Jax's mouth and nose. He leaned in close, hissing through gritted teeth, "Who do you think you are? I don't work for *you*, you jumped-up little cunt. You can't use me to clean up your shit forever. You're getting sloppy, boy. If it wasn't for your uncle, I'd put you in the fucking ground right now. You got that?"

Jax raised both his palms, smiling beneath the big hand.

Letting go with obvious reluctance, Graff took a step back. His face was turning red and his eyes, so dark brown that they were almost black, narrowed in a fierce scowl.

Jax could taste blood. He felt the pain of a split lip when he smiled, but ignored it and smiled even wider. With the back of his hand, he swept away a thread of blood that trickled down his chin. He took his eyes away from Graff, found his cigarette on the floor and picked it up. He took another drag, inhaling the hot smoke deep into his lungs, then craned his head and opened his mouth to blow a series of smoke rings into the bigger man's face.

"No," Jax said. "You won't."

Graff's hands fisted at his sides so tightly that Jax could see the knuckles turning white. The big man almost shook with rage.

Jax laughed, plucked the cigarette from his mouth and flicked it away. He turned on his heels, laughing even harder, and left the big dumb bastard seething in silence.

CHAPTER 12

They sat by the window in a corner of Costa on St George's Retail Park, where Gayle sipped at a cappuccino and Bobbi stirred some brown sugar into a macchiato. They each had a cinnamon and raisin swirl, but Gayle hadn't yet touched hers.

"So," Bobbi said, after a sip of coffee, "what are we going to do?"

"It has to be Jax," she said, "or someone doing his bidding."

"Okay, but why? I thought they might have smashed up your place to, like, send a message or something."

Gayle shook her head. "I think they were looking for something. Not valuables. They *smashed* my TV, but they didn't take it. They left the DVD player and Finn's Xbox. No. I think Jax – or whoever – wrecked the place to, yes, leave a message, but only out of frustration when he couldn't find what he *really* came for. That's when he went ballistic and destroyed everything."

Bobbi pulled her swirl apart and popped a chunk in her

mouth. "So, what were they after?" she asked, chewing. "Drugs?"

"No. Even at his worst, Danny wouldn't have tried to hide drugs in the flat."

"Money then?"

"Possibly. But when Jax didn't find it, he wrote 'SSS' on my wall so police wouldn't suspect him."

Bobbi took a sip before returning it to the saucer and wiping some moisture from the corner of her mouth with her thumb. "Or," she said, "maybe he *did* find it. Maybe this is all over."

Gayle shrugged. "How can I take that chance?"

"Well, what do the police think?"

"I don't think they give a shit. By the time they do realise that this is serious, someone could get hurt. All they suggested was filing for a restraining order."

"Well, what would have happened if you *had* been home?" Bobbi asked, crossing her arms over her bosom in disgust. "Or Finn, for that matter?"

Gayle shrugged. "I suppose Jax would have questioned me and probably slapped me around. I don't think he's crazy enough to hurt a six-year-old boy."

"You don't sound like you believe that."

Gayle hesitated. She wasn't sure if she really believed it either. "I don't know," she said. "Either way, he didn't come for me at your place, so I don't think he's watching, but I can't risk putting you in danger. I'll take Finn and stay at a hotel tonight."

Bobbi started to protest.

"It's the way it has to be," Gayle said. "I've involved you too much already."

"But then what? You're going to go on the *run*, alone? Until when?"

Gayle almost laughed. "I don't have enough money to run for a *week*."

"Then I'll lend you some, whatever you need – even though my dad always says, *'Lending is the first-born of poverty.'*" Bobbi leant forwards on her elbows once more. She put both hands around her half-empty macchiato. "I've got almost five-thousand put away."

Gayle shook her head and laid her hand on Bobbi's wrist. "Thank you, but that's out of the question. You've saved that for your shop."

"You're a stubborn fool."

The two women sat in silence for a moment. Bobbi picked off another chunk of her cinnamon swirl, chewed up a bite and sucked her sticky thumb.

Gayle stared out the window. She watched the cars driving up the incline, looking for spaces. Even at this hour, the car-park was busy and nobody was following the one-way arrows.

"So," Bobbi said, "where do you go from here?"

"I cut ties with everybody when I left," Gayle said. "But I think there's *someone* I can talk to."

"Who?" When Gayle hesitated, Bobbi said, "Oh, come on, you're not endangering me by telling me *this*."

Gayle kept her voice low. The café was two-thirds empty and the staff were on the other side of the room, but she decided to be as discreet as she could be. "There's a guy that used to supply us with things. He'd feed us tips for robberies the guys were planning or chemicals to cut down drugs. I don't know if he's still connected, but he might be able to fill in a few blanks for me."

Bobbi raised her eyebrows. "This was a friend of yours?"

"Not exactly," Gayle said, thoughtfully turning her mug

around on its saucer, "and he probably won't help anyway, but I need to try."

Bobbi placed her hands together, almost prayer-like, inflated her cheeks and blew between her palms. "You know, in three years of knowing you," she said, "this is the most we've talked about your time with those people."

"I thought I'd moved on from it all."

"There must be something I can do."

Gayle took a moment to mull things over, then said, "All right. If you want to help, keep an eye on the time, okay? If I don't call you by two at the *latest*, you go and pick Finn up from school and go straight to the cops."

Bobbi leaned in closer. "This guy's *that* dangerous?"

"Babe, that's what I've been saying. They're *all* dangerous. The gang was fucked up when I was with them and I'm certain things are worse now. *Jax* is worse now."

"Maybe I should wait in the car," Bobbi said. "When you go to see this guy, I mean. You might need back-up."

"No," Gayle said. "You'll be more help staying local to pick up Finn for me. But, there is one more thing you might be able to help me figure out."

Bobbi drained the last of her macchiato and pushed the little cup and saucer to the side of the table. She seemed happy to be needed. She leant forwards with interest.

Gayle reached into the pocket of her cargo pants and came up with her mobile phone and the slip of paper that had been in Danny's wallet. She laid it out on the table and turned it around so Bobbi could see.

"Danny was carrying this," she said, "the night he died. I can't make sense of it. I thought it might be a password."

Bobbi held the scrap of paper in her fingers, a barely perceptible frown creasing her forehead. "A password for what?"

"That's what I can't work out."

After a moment, she said, "You know, this doesn't look like a password to me."

"No?"

Bobbi shook her head. "Too random. Who'd remember it? I'll bet you it's a tracking number."

"For what?"

"Not sure. Perhaps a delivery he was expecting."

"Or," Gayle said, "how about a package that *he sent*?"

Bobbi licked her lips, nodding. "Something he knew Jax would come looking for."

"And he sent it somewhere Jax wouldn't know about."

"If you're right," she said, fluttering the scrap of paper, "then this will tell you where it is."

Gayle went onto Royal Mail's website and typed the number into their tracker, but the code was unrecognised. She tried again, using both upper- and lower-case letters, but to no avail. Wherever Danny had sent the letter or package, he hadn't used Royal Mail.

"What other services are there?" Bobbi asked, thinking out loud.

They tried Hermes with the same result. Gayle checked for postal services on Google, and followed a link to the Courier-Ace website. She selected their tracker facility and as she waited for the page to open up, finished her cappuccino.

Bobbi's dark-chocolate eyes sparkled with curiosity as she stared out of the window. She tapped the fingernails of her left hand on her teeth, lost in thought.

Gayle checked her phone. The page opened. She took the slip of paper from Bobbi, breaking her out of her reverie. She typed in the code. The page took a moment, then finally opened.

Bobbi slid back her chair with a loud scrape and stood behind Gayle. She leant over her shoulder, peering at the screen.

Whatever Danny had shipped off was in a sorting station in Cardiff, Wales, awaiting final delivery.

"Cardiff?" Bobbi asked. "Does Danny know anyone in Cardiff?"

In spite of having drunk a large cappuccino, Gayle's throat felt dry. She shook her head, looking up at Bobbi. "Not in Cardiff. But just outside of Pontypridd. He has an uncle there."

Aled, Lorraine Gowan's brother.

Gayle had spoken to the man only two or three times on the phone and to the best of her knowledge, he and Danny had not been in regular contact. Each Christmas without fail, uncle Aled sent Finn a new grotesque jumper that would be too big for the boy until the following yuletide. It had become a joke between them who was going to take the present to the charity shop. She always sent back postcards to thank Aled for his gift and to wish him well, but beyond that, she knew very little about him.

"Are they close?" Bobbi asked.

"Not really. But the only other family he has is his mother. She's local. He wouldn't risk putting her in danger."

"But would Jax know about the uncle?"

"I doubt Danny would've brought it up. Even if he did, he must have figured Jax would never travel all the way to Pontypridd."

Still staring at the little map on the screen, Bobbi asked, "What do *you* think?"

She was silent for a moment, then said, "I think he might have underestimated Jax."

CHAPTER 13

Gayle dropped Bobbi off in the city centre to pass a little time window-shopping. It was, she said, a good way to get a leg-up on the competition and check out changing trends in fashion.

With her hazard lights on, Gayle opened up her glove compartment and took out Danny's phone. It would soon need to be charged.

She found Melanie's number, psyching herself up to dial the girl with her own phone and say... Well, say what exactly?

Hey, honey, you don't know me, but we kinda-sorta shared a boyfriend and he's dead now, and the people that did it are after me, so you should keep a look out over your shoulder too. Friendly warning.

Gayle played the scenario through her mind a number of times and couldn't come up with an approach that would work.

Of course, that assumed that Melanie would answer a call from an unknown number in the first place.

On the other hand, Gayle could call with Danny's phone, but she rejected that idea almost immediately.

She opened up the text message thread between he and Melanie and, trying not to read them, scrolled to the very first one.

She moved one message at a time from the beginning of their acquaintance, gleaning in spite of herself that they met in a club. They passed flirtatious texts until Danny asked her out for drinks.

Although Gayle knew her intentions were good, she couldn't help feeling like a psycho ex-girlfriend. She tried to banish those thoughts from her mind.

After one more date, Gayle found the text that she had been looking for.

Melanie invited him to her place two days before Christmas last year. She gave her address.

Gayle arrived at the house on Grasmere Street a little before eleven in the morning. She was certain that she had seen the name of the street before and when she arrived by following the sat nav on her phone, she understood why: Leicester Royal Infirmary was less than a ten-minute walk away.

She parked opposite the mid-terrace. Now that she was here, her assertion that doing this would be easier face-to-face seemed naïve. Each time she played the scenario in her mind, she could see it ending in some stupid cat fight.

Grow up, she told herself. *Stop stalling and get it over with.*

Gayle got out and crossed the road.

The house was indistinguishable from its neighbours, as

indeed it was from any of the other samey houses on the nearby streets. The numbers on the doors seemed to be there as much for the residents themselves as for the post-man. She reached out and gave four brisk knocks.

She fussed with her hair for a moment, wondering what she was supposed to say.

Gayle was about to knock again when a light, sing-song voice called out, "Just a minute." She heard the security chain rattle back. The door swung inwards. Since each of the houses had a raised step at the entrance, Melanie was used to looking down automatically. She had bright blue eyes and lipstick on her teeth.

When she saw Gayle, the smile dropped from her face and a look of quiet alarm overtook those sapphire eyes.

"You," she said. "What do you want?"

"You know me," Gayle said, more to herself than to Melanie.

"Danny's ex. Oh, *fuck*. Look, I don't want any trouble."

Gayle raised her hands in a placating gesture, but she was prepared to reach out and hold the door open if Melanie should suddenly try to slam it in her face.

"It's not like that," she said, "I promise you. We need to talk, just for a minute and then I'll go. Please, can I come in? I swear, I don't care about your relationship."

She didn't look convinced, but after a beat, Melanie took a step back, gesturing Gayle in, sizing her up with her eyes.

She gave the girl an uncomfortable smile, trying to signal that this was awkward for both of them. Melanie appeared to be three or four years younger than she herself; chubby, with curly blonde hair that Gayle thought better suited a poodle than a person. She wore a flower-print tank top and a thick jade-green bra to hold up her gargantuan breasts. She was barefoot in a pair of white shorts that, thirty or forty pounds ago would have been fine, but now bordered on scandalous.

"What do you want?" Melanie asked, closing the door.

"Is there somewhere we can sit for a moment? Please?"

Huffing, Melanie led them through the front room and into the living area at the back. She allowed her heels to thump on the floorboards.

Gayle imagined the internal monologue in which the girl was engaged: *If she thinks she's going to cause a scene in my own home, she's got another thing coming. Bloody cheek, expecting to be invited to sit like an old friend.*

"Have a seat," Melanie said, gesturing to the flower-print settee. She took her own seat in the armchair, scratching at a red-ringed whitehead on her right knee.

Gayle sat perched on the edge, hoping not to have to stay too long. "I know this is weird," she said. "Trust me. There's no bad blood here, okay?"

"All right," Melanie said, nodding, clearly hoping that Gayle would hurry and get to the point.

"It's about Danny," she said. "He was killed. Three nights ago."

Melanie didn't say anything. She stared at Gayle for so long that she wondered if the girl had heard her at all. She considered repeating before Melanie finally said, "Are you serious?"

She nodded. "I'm afraid so. He was beaten to death in the city centre."

Melanie raised a hand to her mouth and began to chew on her thumbnail. From around that chubby digit, she said, "Are you... are you sure?"

"I identified him."

"Oh, Jesus, I heard about *somebody* on the news, but I didn't think... That was *Danny*?"

"I'm sorry you had to find out from me," Gayle said. "But I thought it was only fair since you were seeing each other."

That shook her out of her apparent trance and she looked at Gayle as though shocked. "Well, yeah, but I mean... we were sort of a casual thing," she said. "He was a good bloke and everything, but we weren't serious. Actually, I think he was more serious than me. Wow," she said, returning to chew on her thumb. "That's crazy."

Gayle's sudden annoyance surprised her. She wanted to slap the girl and scream in her face, *"My son's lost his father, you idiot! He may have just been a side-piece to you, but he was still a person, for God's sake!"*

She maintained her composure and said, "Did you know Danny was with the *West-End*?"

The girl nodded but didn't speak. She looked down at her toes, wiggling them.

"I think the gang killed him, though I'm not completely sure why. Since then, I've had phone calls and my flat was broken into and trashed. That's why I'm here. They were looking for whatever Danny took, but I don't have it. If Danny ever told them about you, they might think he gave *you* whatever it is they're looking for."

"What?"

"Money, or drugs perhaps. I really don't know, not yet."

"He didn't give me anything."

"Either way, they might come looking. I think you should take precautions. Call the police. Or just get away for a while. I know how it sounds, but this is serious."

Melanie was silent again. Below her knotted brow, her eyes flicked this way and that, as if looking for some sign as to what to say written on the carpet. She drew a shuddery breath that made her breasts heave, then slowly let it out through her pursed lips.

"I know it's a lot to take in," Gayle sympathised.

Just then, she heard creaking on the enclosed stairs leading down between the front room and this one. The door pushed open and a sleepy, tall man dressed only in grey Calvin Klein briefs stepped into the room. His thick black hair was in disarray and he needed a shave. His bony chest sprouted a thin line of hair that ran over a paunch that was out of place on his otherwise spindly frame. The outline of his morning glory was clearly visible in his briefs and he yawned a greeting to Gayle, as if he had known she was here all along. He muttered, "Hey, babe," to Melanie and staggered off into the kitchen and the downstairs bathroom beyond.

Gayle didn't know what to say.

"I think you should go," Melanie said, looking at her at last.

"Yeah," she said, getting to her feet. She didn't wait for Melanie to lead the way. She heard a creak of chair springs behind her and, irrationally, Gayle expected to have her hair suddenly pulled, or to feel a kick in the base of her spine, but made it to the front door without incident. She opened it and stepped down onto the street. She turned and Melanie was at the door.

"Look," she said. "I'm, like, sorry for your loss and everything. And it's sad, for real. But we weren't a proper item or whatever and he wasn't that good... well, you know what I mean. Rest in peace and everything, but like I said... I'm sure it'll be all right. Take care." She gave a commiserating smile and closed the door.

Gayle stood in the street, not expecting to feel as angry as she did right now.

That stupid, uncaring, self-centred...

"Slag," she muttered, then crossed the road and got into the car.

She put the key in the ignition, but didn't start the engine.

She had done her best, had done the right thing. It wasn't her job or responsibility to take care of the peroxide dope, any more than she had the right to vet his girlfriends after he and Gayle had decided to call it a day. She couldn't blame Melanie for not caring about Danny any more than she could blame him for taking up with the bimbo in the first place.

I'm the one who gave Danny a lifelong pass to breeze in and out of my life, she thought. *I'm the one who never let go that there might be hope for us.*

"What a mess," she said to herself.

She looked through the window at the house with the blue door.

"Oh, fuck it," she said aloud.

She reached into her pocket for her phone. The battery was at twenty-one percent and would need charging soon, and she had left the charger at home.

Gayle turned on her mobile data and opened the Google Earth app.

She took a few minutes to survey the streets and the houses in which she was interested. When she was confident that she could pull it off, she started the car.

CHAPTER 14

Like many of the city's older streets, Danbury Road was so narrow that cars struggled to pass one another, managing to do so only by mounting the kerb to some degree. Even then, Gayle reckoned it would only take an extra coat or two of paint to cause a fender-bender.

The street was nestled in a maze-like estate between Birstall and Beaumont Leys and each of the houses had seen better days. All had small front gardens with hedges, some with low brick walls, some with ramshackle wooden fences, and many without property boundaries at all. Those often had a car parked where the garden should have been. A lot of those dilapidated vehicles were missing their wheels and were held aloft by house bricks.

Weeds reached up through cracks in the pavement and the road surface too had seen better days. A couple of times, she was forced to crawl along in first gear to avoid obliterating her tyres on gaping potholes.

Nonetheless, there were children's toys left out in the open house-fronts – sandpits, blackboard easels, a pushchair and a naked doll, a toddler-sized ride-along car with a domed roof – and the residents didn't seem to fear that these things might be stolen. A passer-by might wonder who would *want* to steal them, but Gayle understood that while the residents of the estate knew how to keep to themselves, everybody still knew one another's business.

One house at the far end of the street was the neighbourhood outlier: it wasn't in disrepair; there were no toys in the garden or run-down cars parked at the kerb. Its waist-high boundary wall was well-maintained and had a working latch-operated gate.

She cruised by slowly, then brought the Fiat back up to speed and went around the block. In the next street over, Mulberry Road, there was a van outside number fifty-eight, but outside sixty-two, there was enough space for her to park in.

She checked herself in the mirror. She wore only a little makeup and in spite of her troubled sleep, it didn't show on her face.

She got out of the car, locked it and walked down the street, around the block towards seventy-seven Danbury Road. The wind brought the temperature to only a little above freezing. She raised her hoodie's zip to half-mast and stuffed her right hand in its deep pocket, not to keep warm but to feel reassurance from the switchblade inside it.

She had no intention of hurting anybody, but she was prepared to do so if it came to that.

Tony Henry was in his forties when she knew him, which placed him around fifty-three now. She hadn't seen him in almost eight years and even back when she was active in the *WEC*, she hadn't been a core member and so had little to do with Henry personally.

He had been a gruff-voiced portly man with thin hair and a ruddy complexion. She remembered him wearing long-sleeved shirts always rolled up to his elbows. His arms and hands looked like fatty legs of pork that had been dropped on a barber's floor. His chubby, hairy-sausage fingers used to gross her out.

Tony made his living by all manner of illicit means and although not part of any gang as far as Gayle was aware, he was a respected associate. No one knew quite how much money he'd managed to hide away, but despite rumours that he could live anywhere he wanted, he chose to stay where he had grown up. Rather than move to a better area, he embarked on endless home improvements, and as a result, number seventy-seven stood out like a castle in a slum.

The ground-floor bay-windows of the semi-detached house were double-glazed and spotless, as was the front door, which itself was framed by hanging planters containing colourful perennials. As Gayle approached the iron gate, she spotted the camera ensconced in the doorway arch.

Other houses had damaged brickwork and cladding, but seventy-seven was in good repair. Even the guttering looked new and from what she could see of the roof, it had been re-laid for a loft conversion.

She made her way down the short garden path. The grass either side was immaculate.

At the front door, she rang the doorbell. Gayle didn't look directly at the camera, but didn't face away from it either.

At head-height, the door had a semi-circle of bevelled stained-glass. Through it, Gayle made out movement. A figure too small in height and girth to be Tony Henry drew nearer.

The door opened inwards and she was greeted by a slim woman in her fifties. Her hair was black and streaked with grey, but it looked as though it were more by design than a quirk of genetics. She had on a pair of salmon-coloured straight-line trousers and a silk baby-blue blouse that revealed a tanned, liver-spotted chest. She wore a wedding ring that was worth more than Gayle's car. Cat-eye glasses finished the look but when she spoke, her accent was local and her tone suggested that she was a lifelong chain-smoker.

"Can I help you?" she asked.

"Morning," Gayle said. "I was looking for Tony Henry. Is he home?"

The woman frowned; only a little but it was unmistakeable.

"No," she said, "he popped out for a paper. I'm sorry, what's your name?"

"Gayle," she said, "Gayle Stillwater. I don't think we've ever met, but I knew your husband quite a while ago."

"Oh, really?"

From somewhere in the depths of her memory, Gayle grasped at a name and hoped for the best. "Well, I know Kenny more than Tony."

The slight, almost imperceptible frown faded from the Botox brow. Her eyes, which Gayle saw now were slate-grey with pale green striations, widened a little.

She wondered if she had said the wrong thing. Her palms had begun to sweat.

The woman at the door smiled little white veneered teeth. "How do you know my Kenny?"

* * *

Tony was going to buy a greyhound and Cassie was just going to have to lump it.

They had argued about it over the last couple of weeks.

Typically, she thought it was a waste of money, but Tony knew she would change her tune once the two-and-a-half-year-old bitch started piling up the trophies.

Jilly's Hope had already made her debut race and finished second. Tony knew that if he wanted to buy the dog, now was the time. Three, or perhaps even two more races and the competition would be too fierce.

Of course, Tony didn't have room or time – or frankly the inclination – to house and run a greyhound. He didn't want to care for or train the dog, he just wanted to *own* it and make money.

The paper with the odds on the dog races lay beside him in the two-year-old Land Rover. Tony knew a guy who could put him in touch with the owners and give him the inside information on what the dog was worth. He would offer low first, but he was prepared to pay a few thousand above the value. He considered it a good investment.

Tony pulled onto Danbury Road, guiding the big car between the neighbour's sacks of shit and parked outside his house. By now, the old bag at seventy-nine had to be in her nineties; she was half-blind and carried a cylinder of oxygen with her at all times. The bitch wouldn't sell to him, but she couldn't have long left now. Tony planned to make her inheritors an offer on the house when she finally popped her clogs. Then he could build a garage between the buildings. He didn't know what he would do with the house, not yet, but no doubt the missus would think of something – which, like as not, would mean new windows and turning the south-facing room into a studio for her watercolours.

"Happy wife, happy life," he muttered, getting out of the Land Rover. He locked it and walked down the path with his paper tucked under his arm. He let himself in, called out to Cass and stepped through the glass-paned doorway into the living room.

Cassie was sitting on the settee with a younger woman, both drinking tea from the good china.

Tony knew her – he was certain of that – but from where, he couldn't be sure.

"There you are, Tone," Cass said, smiling. "This is Kenny's friend. What did you say your name was, love?"

"Gayle," she said.

"That's it. Well, say hello, you big lump. I swear, Tone, your manners…"

He couldn't place her, not yet, but despite the unassuming half-smile on her face, there was definitely *something* about her…

How did he know her?

* * *

Tony Henry had put on a good forty or fifty pounds. His hair was almost white and in full-retreat, and the ruddy skin of his cheeks and nose were now a blazing red. His dark little eyes were confused and suspicious. Gayle could see that she had caught him off-guard and bought time by having won over his wife, but she needed to hurry.

Cassie said, "She's lost touch with Kenny since he went to Sheffield and she was… where did you say you'd moved to?"

"I took a year out after studies to go backpacking in Vietnam and Cambodia. We fell out of touch, but a mutual friend mentioned he was studying at Sheffield and I thought it would be nice to say hi."

"You look older than Kenny," Tony Henry said.

"Tone," Cassie said, admonishing him for his social *faux pas*.

Gayle smiled. "I was in the year above," she said, nodding. "It's all right."

"I've got his number," Cassie said. "Unless, you'd like his address? It's student housing, you know how they live." She rolled her eyes. "Four boys in one house, it doesn't bear thinking about."

"To be fair," Gayle said, "I've talked your ear off for ages and you made tea and everything. Tony, do you mind if I have a word for a minute? It's not too cold out and Kenny told us all what a beautiful garden you have."

"Tone always had a green thumb – haven't you, love?"

"I can't wait," Gayle said, standing.

"Come on, Tone, don't be so rude."

"Yeah," he muttered. He dropped the newspaper onto the glass-topped coffee table. "Follow me."

She kept a few steps behind as he led the way. A pair of French doors opened into the dining-room and patio extension. They rounded the dining table and he slid open the patio doors. She stepped out first and moved to the right, out of Cassie's view.

Tony shut the door and followed.

"Where do I know you from?" he asked.

Gayle undid the top button of her combats, lowered the zip halfway and folded down the right side. She thumbed down the elastic of her bikini briefs and revealed the tattoo of the dove on her right hip.

She saw Tony's face flush red and he glanced back at the patio doors with a fleeting look of panic. When he saw that Cassie was not watching the display, he turned back.

With the tip of her finger, Gayle outlined the letters

hidden in the feathering of the dove. "See?" she asked. "I'm with the *WEC*. I need your help."

Whether by instinct or lechery or both, Tony reached out his fat fingers to touch. While his hand was still inches away, Gayle let go of her waistband and slapped the back of his wrist.

"Do you mind?"

Like a naughty schoolboy that had been caught out, Tony said, "Sorry."

Gayle buttoned herself up. "We've got a job on," she whispered, "but we're in a hurry. I need something to cut down half a key. I don't know who we're selling to, and they could be cowboys, so the Captain wants a gun."

"Jesus *Christ*," Tony said, taking Gayle by the shoulder and urging her to the path that led across his lawn. "Keep your voice down."

"That's what I am doing," she said, lower still.

"Who fucking sent you here?" he asked.

"I told you."

"But which Captain?"

Although she remembered some of the names of the leaders of the other smaller *WEC* factions – Davey, Macca, Aztec – there was no way to know which of them still held that position. Leaning closer, she said, "Who do you think? Jax."

Tony frowned. "For fuck's sake," he said, covering his mouth. "What's he playing at? He knows I've got rules about this. What if you're being fucking watched?" He glanced around above his high fences, as if trying to spot signs of covert surveillance.

"No time," Gayle said, "I need it now. The meet's on, it's happening *right now*."

"Fucking hell," Tony said, hands on his hips. He

stopped walking, looking down at his feet, scuffing the toe of one shoe in annoyance. "This is fucking above and beyond. You tell him, right, you tell him I expect looking after for this. And he still owes me for sourcing that fuckin' motor for him."

What motor? she thought but didn't say. Instead, she nodded. "Usual fees," she said. "Plus five percent."

"Fuck that. Fifteen."

"Ten's all he authorised me to deal."

Tony snorted, shaking his head, but Gayle could see through the mock disbelief. Tony was seeing pound signs. "All right," he said. "Ten." He gestured to the far end of the path and the large shed at the other end of the property.

The path wound in a serpentine fashion across a garden that was not as stylish as the interior of the house, to which she credited Cassie's tasteful eye. Tony's domain did not seem to know what it wanted to be. The pond was ringed by a mix of black and brown slate, decorated with miniature ferns, ivy, plastic bull-rushes, a stone Eiffel tower beside a ceramic gnome with a fishing rod and a small babbling waterfall powered by an electric pump. The grass was mown and neatly trimmed around the perimeter and there was a Japanese-inspired meditation garden on the far-left. The right side had a series of flowerbeds on platforms of various heights.

"I knew you weren't a friend of Kenny's," Tony said.

"No, you didn't," Gayle said. "Come on."

They rounded the seven-foot pond, in which were five large fish cutting paths and figure-eights in the murky water. Gayle was careful to stay out of arm's reach and slipped her hand into the pocket of her hoodie, holding onto the switch-blade. The babbling water made her want to pee. She hadn't realised until then that she hadn't gone all morning.

The large shed at the end of the garden was dwarfed between two large conifers and its window could just be seen through a tangle of climbing ivy. A heavy padlock secured the door.

Tony found his keys and unlocked the door.

It was surprisingly pokey inside and the air was stuffy with sawdust, compost and a faint odour of turpentine. A table to the right of the door was covered in gardening supplies: tiny plastic planting pots and trays, gardening gloves, pruning shears, secateurs and cable ties with which to secure ivy or trellises.

Tony stepped in first and Gayle followed close behind. She gripped the edge of the door and swung it shut behind her. Below the window on the left were stacks of flower pots in different sizes.

"Look, just give me a minute, all right?" he said, reaching into his pocket again. His meaty hand came up with a phone. "I don't know about this price. Let me get it confirmed with Jax first. Business is business."

Without speaking, Gayle snatched at the nearest of the smaller pots in her left hand and swung it full-force. It shattered against his right ear and Tony went down to his hands and knees amidst shards and fragments of ceramic.

He reached for his head. His fingers were red with blood.

"Don't move," Gayle told him, drawing the switchblade. "You stay right there."

"You fucking *bitch*," he whined.

She was too close to him for comfort. She side-stepped around him, between his meaty left flank and the splintery wooden table behind her. When she had a little space, she looked the table over once more. There was a dirty rag inside a plastic pot and she plucked it out and threw it at him as he knelt prostrate.

"You'll live," she told him. "Use that."

He snatched at the rag from the back of his neck and held it against his bleeding scalp. He hissed in pain. "What the fuck is going on?" he blurted, raising up his left leg to plant his foot.

Moving fast, Gayle booted him hard, high between his meaty buttocks. Whimpering in pain, he fell forwards, arresting his fall with one hand on the dusty floor.

"Don't you move," she told him. "You try to get up and I'll use this knife, Tony, I swear to God I will."

"Who the fuck are you?"

"We'll get to that," she said. "Right now, put your hands behind your back."

"What for?"

"Because I don't trust you." She reached for a pair of black cable ties.

He put his hands behind his back and Gayle looped the first tie around one wrist but left it with a little slack. She fed the second through it then made a loop around his other wrist. She pulled both tight until the skin of his ham-like wrists went white against the plastic.

"Now what? You gonna steal my fucking compost?"

Gayle looked around. There was a good reason that the large shed seemed so small on the inside. The rear wall was unadorned by gardening equipment and the only thing in front of it was a stiff-bristled yard brush. She moved it out of the way, checked to see that Tony had not gotten up, then ran her hands over the wall. She found a grip in the shadows and cobwebs an inch from the roof. She pulled the wooden panel and it came away with a creak. Gayle

stepped to the side, shoving at the six-foot long fake wall. It
scraped against the concrete floor.

Tony looked at her over his shoulder, clearly furious
that she knew about his stash somehow. He must be
wondering which of his contacts had betrayed him. She
almost wanted to put him out of his misery and remind him
that he had loose lips after a few lines of coke.

Behind her, he said, "I fucking know you."

"Oh?" she said, trying to sound uninterested.

He started to laugh. "That's right. You're that gormless
cunt Gowan's bint, ain't ya?"

"Used to be," she said, peeking out the window. Cassie
didn't seem to be watching, but all the same, Gayle needed
to hurry.

"I heard he got himself shanked. Maybe you should
think about that."

"Do you know who killed him?"

"Fuck off."

She was close enough to slam her foot again into his fat
coccyx.

He yelped in pain. "Rumours," he said, voice close to a
sob. "I just heard rumours."

"It was Jax, wasn't it?"

"Maybe. I mean, probably – how the fuck would I
know?"

She rummaged around behind the fake wall as they
spoke. There were two steel shelving units, one of which
contained a variety of plastic tubs and bottles; some filled
with innocuous powders like bicarbonate of soda and
creatine, others filled with potentially dangerous chemicals. She supposed the place was a bomb waiting to
explode.

"Why would he do it?" Gayle asked, poring over the

contents of the second shelving unit, looking for anything she could use. "Danny was Jax's right-hand for years."

"What else comes between men?" he scoffed. "Women... or money."

"What money?"

"Jax never told me. I just know he was looking into a robbery."

"And this motor you say you sourced," she said, "that was the getaway car?"

"You're not as thick as you look."

Ignoring the jibe, Gayle said, "How much did you charge him?"

"A grand. Mates-rates. But he hasn't paid me yet."

"You call a thousand pounds 'mates-rates'? Jax must have been expecting a decent take. What other equipment did you get for him?"

"Nothing, just the Beamer."

"And who were they robbing?"

"I didn't fucking ask and I definitely don't wanna know now, 'cause whoever it was, something obviously went tits-up. Why else would Jax take out his own crew? That little prick Gowan must have had it coming if you ask me."

"It's not a good idea to antagonise me."

"And fuck you too."

Tony Henry knew better than to be caught with anything as serious as a gun, but she found weapons of other kinds: an aluminium baseball bat, two hunting knives, a balisong, a small axe, two wrecking bars and a wicker basket containing four knuckledusters. On the middle shelf was a telescopic baton. She took hold of the hard rubber grip and tested its weight.

She turned, whipping out her hand. Three steel columns, each marginally smaller in diameter and the same length as the handle, slid out and locked into place, forming a steel pole eighteen inches in length. Gayle slammed the end into the wall of the shed, sliding the steel poles back into the shaft of the handle and locking it in with a *click*. She slipped the baton into the deep side pocket of her cargo pants.

Also on the shelving unit was a grey metal tin, half the size of a shoebox. Inside was loose change and a dusty roll of money secured by an elastic band. She took it off and rifled through the notes.

"Yeah," Tony said, "fucking rob me too. Go on, put your other foot in shit."

"And what are you gonna do, Tony? Call the police?"

"I fucking *know* people, you cunt."

"So what? The people you know are already after me, so what do I have to lose?"

Tony started to laugh. "I get it now," he said. "Danny ripped Jax off and now he reckons *you've* got the dough." The chuckle rattled in his throat. "Stupid slag. I feel better knowing it's just a matter of time until he finds you and cuts out your tongue. That's if you're *lucky*."

She flicked through the notes and stuffed them into her left rear pocket. "I might make it a little longer than that now. Thanks to you, I've got four-hundred pounds for petrol."

Tony coughed again. "What are you going to do with me?" he whined, apparently no longer seeing the funny side of things.

Gayle left the panel of wood where it was and stepped closer to him. "I don't have to do anything with you. You won't go to the cops and I'm gonna be gone by the time you break out of those ties."

"I'll tell Jax you've got his money."

Gayle crouched down in front of him until they were more or less eye-to-eye. She gave him a sweet smile and pressed her left hand against his cheek. He winced and glared at her with a look of utter loathing. She said, "So what? He already thinks I have it. You can't do anything to me. But that's not as important as what he could do to *you*."

"What?" he whined. "He wouldn't do anything to me."

"Why – because you're so important? You stay here in this street like you're some kind of man of the people, but you're not as well-liked as you think you are. I know Jax a lot better than you do. You're a *worm*. He always said so. Don't forget, I spent a lot of time around him. All of us *'slags'* did. How do you think I knew about your hiding spot? Danny and him used to joke about you all the time. I think Jax hates everybody, but he hates leeches like you most of all. You sourced him a car, right? When he's got no use for you, he'll see that you're a loose end, just like me. So, tell him whatever you want, or maybe you should be thinking about your wife. And Kenny." She smiled again, cocking her head to the side as she dug her thumb into the still-weeping gash under his thin, blood-stained hair. Tony cried out and Gayle pulled away her hand, but only to slap him with it.

"You fucking bitch," he cried, a sheen of tears coming to his eyes.

Gayle got to her feet and looked out the window again. She didn't expect to see anyone watching and nobody was. She backed to the door and pulled it open.

"You'll fucking get yours, you stupid cunt," Tony said. "You'll wish you were dead, like that gormless idiot fella of yours."

She ignored him and left him to bellow to himself down in the muck and dust. She hurried around the side of the shed to the rear wall of the property. She sized it up, took a step back, planted her feet and launched forwards. She seized the top of the wall and scrambled and kicked her way up. She threw her right leg up and over, then the other, twisted and came down on the other side of it in a paved yard with a cobweb-laced barbecue and an empty sagging washing line.

She wiped the dust and splinters off the front of her hoodie and raced for the gate between the side of the neighbour's house and the perimeter fence. She pulled back the bolt lock, then tore open the gate and hurried across the cracked and sprouting paving slabs to the street beyond. She was already reaching into her pocket for the car keys and for a second, couldn't seem to find them. Her heart caught in her chest, but then she grasped the familiar keyring and pressed the button to unlock the car.

Adrenaline and the exertion of getting over the property wall almost caused Gayle to drop the key, but she held on tight and hurried behind the wheel. She fumbled with the ignition for a moment, then got the key in, turned it and threw the car into first gear.

She hurried down the road, turned left and then almost immediately right again, getting the hell out of there before she remembered to put on her seatbelt.

Ten minutes later, Gayle pulled over on a non-descript side-street and got out of the car. She was shaking all over.

She walked around to the front of the car, resting her backside on the bonnet and leant forwards. She closed her eyes and took a few deep breaths. Her hands wouldn't stop shaking.

"It's okay," Gayle told herself aloud. "You're fine. You did what you had to do. And you're *fine*."

CHAPTER 15

Jax sat behind the wheel of his dark red Ford Focus, on the other side of the terraced street from the corner shop. He hung his arm out the open window in the bracing cold, his cigarette half-smoked.

Beside him, Steph Doughty hugged herself, the lapels of her leather jacket turned up. "Fuck's sakes, Jax," she moaned, "can't you at least put the heaters on?"

"Don't work," he said, staring past her. Jax sucked in a lungful of smoke, letting it stream through his nostrils.

"It's Baltic in here."

"You didn't have to come," he reminded her.

"*'Just a quick stop'*, that's what you said. *'Won't be a minute.'* Been bloody ten already."

"If it's a problem, get the bus." Jax finished the cigarette and flicked the butt. He wound the window halfway up.

"You know I ain't got no money," she said, blowing into her hands. "Jesus, they're turning blue."

He shot her a look that she had enough sense not to challenge. She turned her head to follow Jax's stare.

"Where *is* this bitch?" Steph asked. "She didn't leave already, did she?"

"No," he said, beginning to wish he hadn't offered to give her a lift home. If he didn't need the cash that she was holding for him at her place, he might have cut his losses and told her to fuck off.

While she was only an associate instead of a fully-fledged member of the *WEC*, Steph Doughty had her uses. For one thing, she let them cut up drugs at her place, and sometimes stashed stolen goods and even weapons for them. She was also good for a quick jump when the fancy took him, but was too common and plain to be anything worth bragging about.

"So, anyway," Steph said, turning back to him, "how bad are we talking?"

"Look under the seat," Jax said.

She bent forwards over her budding beer gut and reached between her ankles. After fumbling around for a few seconds, she came up with the thicker half of a broken pool cue. "Nice," she said, getting a feel for it.

"Whack her a few times if you have to," Jax said. "Let her know you ain't fuckin' around. But don't kill her. And don't mention my name."

"I know," she said. "I wouldn't do that."

"Scare the shit out of her and get her to tell you the truth. But *quick*."

Through the half-open window, Jax heard the jangle of an old-style bell. Melanie Welles stepped down off the step leading to the shop, holding a carrier bag in one hand and a four-pint bottle of milk in the other. She flicked her head to the side to clear her platinum-blonde curls out of her face. She wore her long royal-blue overcoat unbuttoned and her breasts bounced around in her floral top as she walked along the street.

Beside him, Steph turned and gave Jax a smile. "You gonna give us a kiss before I go?"

"Don't be daft," he said, leaning across her and opening the door. "Get a move on."

Steph stepped out onto the pavement.

As she closed the door, Jax said, "Remember, don't fuck her up too bad."

Steph jogged across the road, looking both ways as she went, looking for witnesses. She held the cue tight against the thigh of her jeans.

Jax turned over the engine and crept after them in first gear. Even in the middle of the day, cars were parked along both sides of the terraced street, narrowing the road to a single lane.

At the corner, the two women took a left. When Jax also made it around, he saw Steph had let the distance between she and Melanie to stretch to about fifty yards.

The street terminated in a quiet cul-de-sac with only three parked cars and a gated entrance to a small, empty park at the end. A pair of swings had their chains knotted together and a spring rocker in the shape of a horse was chipped and covered in graffiti.

Jax pulled over and waited. Above the whistle of the wind, he heard Steph say, "Hey, Melanie," as she broke into a run again.

The girl looked back over her shoulder, her mass of hair once again blown into her face.

Steph swung the cue hard and cracked the silly bitch in the meat of her left thigh. She squealed and dropped her shopping, backing away. She turned and took off, heading for the other side of the park, but Steph was too quick. She whipped the cue around again and brought Melanie down to the ground, where Jax couldn't see beyond the leafless bushes behind the painted iron fence.

He made a U-turn and backed up. Through the half-open window, he could hear shouting but could make out none of the words.

He glanced at the surrounding houses, looking for peeping neighbours, but saw no tell-tale fluttering of curtains. This end of town saw its share of trouble, but all the same, Jax didn't want to dawdle.

In the cup-holder, his phone began to ring.

"Perfect fuckin' timing," he said, snatching it up. He frowned, looking at the screen: *T. H.*

Jax hadn't talked to Tony Henry in ages. Though curious, he didn't have time for a chat, so declined the call. A moment later, Tony rang again, but Jax cut it off once more.

He turned in his seat, bracing his arm on the passenger headrest, looking out the back window. The shouting had subsided.

Jax checked his watch. Steph had been on the fat tart for close to two minutes.

He balled his fist and slammed the side of it into the horn, issuing two short, impatient bursts.

Thirty seconds later, Jax was about to hit the horn again when he saw Steph hurrying out from the park's entrance. She flung her arm out to the right, sending the cue flying through the air behind her, striking the fence and clattering to the concrete. She yanked open the passenger door and jumped in. Jax floored it and the burning tyres stuttered on the tarmac.

He hurried right and left and right again through the maze of terraced streets before he found Infirmary Road and followed the traffic into the city centre.

Beside him, Steph was twitchy with adrenaline. Without being asked, he reached for his packet of Marlboros and held it out for her. She plucked out a cigarette, put it between her lips and lit it. She drew in the first drag, held it, and released it in a sigh. "Fucking hell," she whispered.

Jax made it through a light as it turned red, following the road for Steph's place in Beaumont Leys. He looked over at her as she sat with her eyes closed, holding the cigarette in her right hand, which he could now see was dotted with blood. She took another drag and blew the smoke at the glowing cherry.

"Are you gonna fucking talk to me or what?" Jax said.

As though she had been released from a trance, she looked at him again, her bright blue eyes wide. "Oh," she said, "right. Sorry, that was fucking intense."

"What happened?"

"Well, I dropped her with a crack on the back of her head. You shoulda seen it. She went down like a sack of spuds. I thought I'd killed her or summut, but when I got closer, she had a broken beer bottle. She must have landed near it. She fuckin' *went for me*, so I smashed it out of her hand with the cue. Must've broke a few fingers."

"Who gives a fuck about her fingers?" Jax asked. "What did she *say*?"

"Oh. Yeah. She reckons she hadn't seen Danny for a few days. I asked her if she has your money and she's like, *'No, no, I don't know nothin' about it'*, so I bang her one again, and she's still like, *'I ain't got owt, I promise.'*" Steph was smiling as she spoke, turning in her seat like an excited kid. The cigarette wobbled in her hand. "It was mental. All this side of her face was just pouring," she said, drawing the fingers of her free hand down the left side of her face.

"Fuck," Jax said. "And you definitely believed her?"

"She wouldn't've lied, babe, not after that. You know, forget the fingers, I might've broke her *wrist*: it was dangling like this," she said, imitating with the hand that still held the cigarette. Ash dropped onto the console between their seats. "But that's not the best bit. You'll love this."

"What?"

"Guess who she saw earlier?"

Jax gripped the wheel so hard that his knuckles were white. *"Steph."*

She reached over and, with her thumb, wiped away a bead of sweat that popped up above his left eyebrow. She kissed his jaw and whispered, "Gayle Stillwater."

"She *what*? She says that cunt came to see her?"

"Yep. Just this morning, trying to warn her. Fat lot of fucking good that did."

Jax frowned. "And... what else? What did she say? Think."

Steph's smile faded as she said, "Not much. Fatty says that she came to warn her about you and to ask about if Danny gave her your money. Fatty kicked her out and that was it."

Jax took the cigarette from Steph and drew on it as he drove. "Then if that's true, Danny *definitely* didn't give it to her."

"Suppose not. But I've gotta be honest, babe, I wouldn't be bothered about it."

"What?"

"You can always make more money. Fuck it." She stroked the back of his neck.

Jax pushed her hand away. "It's not *just* the fucking money," he said.

"Well, what else?"

Jax didn't speak.

Then he remembered the phone. He snatched it up out of the cup-holder, glancing away from the road while he searched his call log. He clicked on Tony's number and held it to his ear.

After three rings, the fat bastard answered. "Jax, I want her fuckin' *dead*, mate. You get me? Fuckin' dead. She almost caved my fuckin' head in."

"Who?" he asked as a reflex, but the realisation came to him quickly. "Oh, let me fuckin' guess. Gayle."

Tony Henry was quiet for a beat, then said, "Uh, yeah. How'd you know already?"

"Don't worry about that, Tone," Jax said. "Tell me everything." After letting Tony Henry go on for almost ten minutes, he said, "I need a favour."

"Name it."

"I need a strap. Summut fuckin' reliable. Untraceable. And I need it tonight."

"I'll call up Brummie Charlie."

"No," Jax said too sharply, "not him. I want it kept quiet, yeah? Get it from someone else, someone unconnected."

Tony hesitated. "Yeah, if that's what you want. I'll make a call. I'll run it round to your place myself."

"No, call me first, I'm not sure where I'll be."

"All right," Tony said, "no problem. Talk to you later."

Jax disconnected the call then scrolled through his contacts once more at a red light.

Beside him, Steph's earlier excitement had become quiet concern. "Are you okay? This sounds serious."

"You better fuckin' believe it. And I need the cash you've got stashed for me," he said, putting the ringing phone on speaker and dropping it into his lap.

The light turned green and Jax took off, changing quickly up through the gears.

"Now who you ringin'?" Steph asked.

The line opened. *"Jax, mate. What's going on?"*

"Vince," he said, "drop whatever you're doing 'cause I've got a job for ya..."

CHAPTER 16

Gayle made it back to the city to pick Bobbi up on Humberstone Gate, outside the Subway. She trotted over to the Fiat and got in, taking a small paper bag from her handbag and passing it to Gayle.

"Here," she said. "I got you a present. Oatmeal and raisin."

"You're a godsend."

Gayle took a bite of the soft cookie and pulled out into traffic. She finished it before they made it halfway down Charles Street, then gave Bobbi a quick run-down on the morning's events.

"You know," Bobbi said, "if I was hearing this from somebody else, I wouldn't believe a word of it. So, what's our next move?"

"I've got to get out of here," Gayle said, turning onto St George's Way.

"You mean, we."

"What I said still stands, Bobbi. The fact is, I don't know if I can keep Finn and myself safe, let alone you. I appreciate everything you've done, God knows I do, but I just couldn't live with myself if I pull you any deeper into this."

"God, you smell of cat piss," Bobbi said, wrinkling her nose.

"Don't change the subject."

"What have you been doing?"

"I mean it, Bobbi."

"I know you do," she allowed, lowering the window to let in a little fresh air. "And it's touching you're so concerned about me. But tell me this... where were you just now?"

Gayle glanced away from the road to look in Bobbi's face. She saw that the other woman was every bit as serious.

Not wanting to reveal too much, Gayle said, "I surprised an old gang associate and I... well, I stole some things. This guy, he seems to think that Jax pulled a robbery and Danny double-crossed him for the money."

"Well, I definitely want to circle back to that, but first tell me this... Could you have done that with Finn beside you?"

"No," she said.

"Admit it, girl. You need help. You're my best friend, probably my *only* friend. How am I supposed to abandon you when you need help the most?"

"I just don't—"

"Did I ever tell you, my dad has a saying he likes. He says, *'Only a fool tests the depth of water with both feet.'*"

In spite of herself, Gayle smiled. "I think you missed the meaning of that one."

"Not at all, because I'm obviously a fool, so what else is there to do but jump right in?" Bobbi gave her a broad smile.

Gayle didn't know what to say. "Okay," she relented. "You can come with us to see Aled. But as soon as I get things worked out, you come home and keep your head down. Better yet, it'd be a good time to visit your brother."

Bobbi crossed her heart.

"We're probably gonna die," Gayle muttered.

Bobbi put on her sunglasses. "You're so negative. How much did they rob?"

"I don't know, but this guy was in it for a grand and it's enough for Jax to kill for."

At the St George's Way roundabout, Gayle came off on Humberstone Road before taking a left on Dysart Way. Traffic was moderate for a quarter to two in the afternoon and she figured she'd be at Soar-Bank Apartments in less than ten minutes.

"How long will it take to get to Pontypridd?" Bobbi asked.

"Around three hours," Gayle said, "if we get lucky. But we're gonna catch rush-hour traffic."

"And school traffic when we pick up Finn."

Gayle nodded. "So, I think we should stop somewhere for the night instead of heading straight for the farm. If nothing else, we're gonna need to eat and Finn will be exhausted."

"Sounds good. You had anywhere in mind?"

"The route takes us through Bristol. That's as good a place as any."

"I've never been. But if you need to take a rest," Bobbi said, "I'll get us there. You can try to catch some shut-eye in the back with Finn."

"It might come to that."

At the turn-off, Gayle hit her indicator and waited for another motorist to take pity on her. When one did, she waved her thanks and threw the little Fiat down the bumpy road. They came to a stop at the kerb and Gayle took off her seatbelt but left the engine running and the heater turned up.

"I'll just be a minute," she said and hopped out. She trotted to the entrance and let herself in.

On the third floor, she walked down the hallway until she reached her flat. She was impressed with the speed with which the landlords had reacted: the doorframe had been repaired, the door replaced and the whole thing had been given a lick of paint.

She took it now from her keyring and slotted it into the lock. The new mechanism was stiff but she managed to turn it. The door needed a couple of millimetres planed off the edge that met the doorframe as it was stiff and creaked as she pulled it open.

The little vestibule was as she had left it and gave her a peculiar sense that she had imagined the last twenty-four hours, but when she pushed open the door to the flat proper, she was greeted by the destruction she remembered all too clearly.

She pulled the entrance door and it groaned on its new hinges. She tugged on it to get it closed, but it caught on the frame and would not sit flush.

No wonder they got it done so quick, Gayle thought. *Cowboys.*

She left it as it was. She needed only a few things and then would be back on the road.

She stepped over the detritus in the kitchen and went to the bedroom. In the top shelf of the tipped-over wardrobe, she had a small Nike holdall. She took it out and searched amongst the clothes on the floor for anything that didn't look ruined. She packed two changes of underwear, thick socks, a pair of jeans, two T-shirts and a heavy black jumper and took the bag to Finn's room. She collected some clothes for her son, being sure to pack enough to keep him warm if the weather turned bad and laid it on the bed.

She looked around at the devastation, pausing for a moment, remembering how it had been, as though she could mentally rehang the broken shelves, stitch together his ruined toys and mend the posters torn from his walls. Just looking at what Jax had done to her son's room, to the symbol of his innocence, was almost enough to make her want to cry.

No more, she told herself. She had shed enough tears because of that son of a bitch.

She looked at the smashed picture-frame on Finn's bedside cabinet and realised something was different. The red tin box was gone. Gayle supposed the police must have taken it for fingerprint analysis. She realised then that she hadn't asked Finn where he had gotten it after all – with everything else, it had slipped her mind entirely. She made a mental note to ask him about it when she picked the boy up from school.

At last, she caught a sour smell that made her wrinkle her nose. She even looked around, wondering for a moment if she had missed something foul that had been left behind in the debris. She realised, however, that she reeked of sweat and compost. She brought the front of her T-shirt to her nose.

Bobbi had been right: she did indeed stink like cat piss.

Gayle shucked out of her hoodie and peeled off the T-shirt, carrying both items and the holdall back to her room. She started to look for her washing hamper, then realised how stupid that was and dropped her smelly clothes to the floor. She laid the holdall on the bed and remembered that she still had the switchblade in the pocket of her hoodie.

She retrieved the knife and dropped it into her back

pocket with her wallet, but it felt too bulky back there. She took the wallet and threw it into the open holdall. All she wanted to have to hand were things she would need in a hurry, like the knife and the baton.

After a few minutes of looking, she found her phone charger near the socket beside the bed. She dropped that in the holdall too, then zipped it closed and searched the floor for something else to wear. She picked up a canary-yellow V-neck T-shirt and threw it over her shoulder. From the pile of beauty products by her chest of drawers, she picked up a can of deodorant and applied some liberally, then slipped into the T-shirt.

Gayle took a last look around at the remnants of her life and carried the holdall to the front door. She dropped the bag to put her arms through her suede jacket and checked her watch. After the stress of the last couple of hours and the coffee she had drunk earlier, she needed to pee.

The second door in the small vestibule was for the tiny water closet, comprised of a toilet with a perpetually cold plastic seat and a small sink. Gayle shut herself in, dropped her pants and sat down.

She started to pee and out of habit, pulled her phone out and began to check out Facebook. She checked Danny's profile. The RIP messages had come flooding in, many from members of the *WEC* that she knew and a lot she didn't. She even saw one from Melanie and almost laughed when she read it.

RIP, angel.
You're in a better place now.
xxx
Mel

Then, Gayle heard voices.

She had finished urinating and the instant she heard them, she stopped breathing.

Oh, shit.

She heard a heavy, woody creak.

The voices were louder now. Right outside the door.

"—you sure?"

"Shut up. I'll check the bedroom."

Now, both voices were whispering. *"Are you even sure you saw her?"*

"That's her car outside, bruv."

"I thought we were just following her."

"Will you shut the fuck up?"

She couldn't be sure, but she thought one of the voices was familiar.

Gayle held her breath. She realised she had left the lavatory door unlocked.

Moving slowly, silently, she stood up in a crouch and reached for the door. The lock was a tiny sliding bolt. She had her fingers on it before she remembered it creaked and made a high-pitched metallic whine when it engaged.

She reached to the roll of toilet paper, carefully pulled off a single sheet, wiped herself and pulled up her cargo pants.

The voices were deeper in the flat now, but she could still make them out.

"—not here."

"Well, the door didn't fuckin' unlock itself, did it?"

From the sound of things, they were in the living room.

She buttoned up her trousers. Every move she made sounded like the hit of a snare drum. A fine sheath of perspiration coated her face. Her palms were slippery and she blotted them on her legs.

She pulled the switchblade from her pocket.

Got to move, she thought. *Now!*

But nerves had rooted her feet to the spot. She looked down at her feet, willing them to move, but they were stuck fast.

"...The lads are on the way and she can't have gone far," the more familiar of the two voices said.

Gayle blinked sweat from her eyes.

"Hold on a second... what's this?"

If she didn't move now, she was cornered. If they caught her, she was dead; if she was dead, Finn was an orphan; and if Finn was an orphan...

The horror of that thought was enough to unstick her feet. She gripped the doorknob in a slick hand, twisted and threw it open with all her weight.

The door slammed into the shoulder of one of the two men, knocking the air from his lungs with a deep, heavy grunt. She heard the door connect with his skull, filling the small room with a sickening *smack*. Even as she was aware of the impact, she fell forwards under her own momentum, scrambling with her hands and feet over the man's tumbling body.

She hit the floor hard, her legs over the prone body of one of her would-be assailants. She had no sooner landed than she climbed to her knees and from her knees to her feet.

Behind her came a guttural cry and she turned to see the second man lunge at her. It was the same red-faced son of a bitch she had sprayed in *The Marquee*. He got a grip on her jacket, lost it, stumbled over the other guy, and snatched at her again, catching her around the waist like a rugby tackle.

Gayle slammed her left shoulder into the doorframe.

She cried out in pain and fell to her knees. The knife flew from her grasp and skittered to a halt on the carpet in the middle of the hallway.

Winded, she heaved herself forwards, kicking with both legs. She turned and saw Red-Face trying to get to his feet. She wriggled like an eel and shook free of his grip. She was over the tangle of bodies, almost past the threshold, but the red-faced bastard caught her by the cuff of her cargo pants and tripped her.

She landed hard, but was right beside the knife. She snatched for it and thumbed the button – *snick!* – and she swung behind her in a fast, looping arc.

Red-Face saw it coming, but it was too late. He managed to get his arm up to protect his face, but the razor-sharp edge did its work, slicing open the back of his hand – so sharp that at first there was no blood. He kept reaching for her, even as she kicked and twitched and hauled herself away from him, but then the open mouth of his wound began to seep. Seeing the blood, he stopped flailing and collapsed onto his side, clasping his injured hand with the other.

Gayle hurried to her feet and raced down the hallway before they could give chase. She made it to the lift but the door was closed. She jabbed the button over and over but the doors would not open. She looked back and saw that Red-Face was still on the floor. The other one staggered out of the flat, blood dripping from a gash above his left eyebrow.

She hammered the button again and again.

Over her shoulder, the other one started towards her. He was slender, shaven-headed, his skin the colour of caramel. His almost feminine features twisted into a snarl. He braced himself against the wall for balance, coming fast.

She slapped the call button and the lift finally opened. It was empty. She all-but dove inside before the doors could open all the way, pounding the ground-floor button over and over with her palm. In the hallway, she heard him getting close; heavy footfalls pounding on the carpet, calling out her name. She heard the red-faced one screaming. The doors at last began to close, but too slow, too slow. He was almost upon her. She saw his face, the fury in his eyes, then the doors slid shut and the lift began to move.

Alone, she breathed hard and fast – *too* fast: she was going to hyperventilate.

She forced herself to breathe more slowly. Easy. Easy.

Gayle reached into her pocket for her phone. Her hand was still slippery, but she got the handset and unlocked it. She called Bobbi.

The phone rang. Rang. Rang.

"Hello?"

"Get out of here," Gayle screamed, "go, get Finn!"

"Gayle, what—"

"No time! Two men! Get Finn! Go where we said! I'll get away and I'll meet you, just get Finn! Don't let anything happen to him!"

"But, Gayle, I can—"

"There's more coming! *Go!*" she shrieked.

The call disconnected and she prayed that Bobbi had listened; that she wasn't coming to try to help.

The lift rumbled and rattled slowly downwards.

Before she reached the ground floor, Gayle heard the sound of an engine revving, then the tortured scream of rubber on tarmac, before fading into the distance.

Please, God, Gayle thought, *let her get away.*

With a bump, the lift stopped on the ground floor. Slowly, the doors slid open. The hallway was empty.

She took a tentative step out, looking up and down the hall for anyone watching her. Nobody was. To her right and behind a fire-door, she could hear heavy feet rushing down the stairwell.

Quickly, Gayle took a step back and hit the 4 button for the top floor.

The caramel-skinned man almost slipped on the last two steps, his arms spinning like the sails of a windmill, before he caught the handrail and steadied himself. He grasped the steel rail and yanked the door open, barrelling through it and towards Gayle.

The doors slid shut and, with a rumble and whine, the lift began to ferry her skywards once more. She heard the two men shouting after her, until their voices faded into the mechanical grumbling.

She couldn't do this forever. Sooner or later, they were going to catch her.

The roof offered neither sanctuary nor escape. Soar-Bank had only one stairwell and no fire-escape. She couldn't climb through a window because they were all double-paned and had stoppers on their hinges to dissuade suicides.

The buttons on the panel ignited with a faint amber glow when they reached a given floor level. 1 lit, faded and went out, and 2 began to glow, stayed constant, then began to fade. There was no digital read-out on any of the floors to tell her attackers where the lift carriage was currently.

She jabbed out a finger and hit 3. The lift stopped and the doors sighed open. She slapped the number 4 again and jumped out of the lift before the doors began to close.

The hallway was empty, but down the stairwell, she could hear the thumping of feet and the slap and squeak of hands on the handrails.

Hurry.

Gayle rushed down the hallway towards her own flat.
Surely they wouldn't expect her to go back there.

She stepped over the puddle of blood coagulating into
the hardy hallway carpet, pressing her back against the
doorframe, facing away from the stairwell and the lift.

She strained her ears, listening.

Dimly, she could make out the ruckus on the stairs, but
growing louder and louder still.

The fire-door banged open, loud enough to make her
jump. She could hear their ragged breath.

"Up," one said, his voice husky. "Still going up."

"I'm knackered, Vince," the other whined. "And my
fucking *hand*."

"Come *on*."

She heard the fire-door open again and the sound of feet
slapping on the stairs. It grew dimmer... dimmer... gone.

Moving as quietly as possible, Gayle went for the fire-
door.

When she reached it, she could hear the lift clatter to a
stop on the floor above.

Hurry, she thought.

As carefully as she could manage, she pulled the door
open, slipped through and eased it shut behind her. Open-
mouthed, she held her breath.

She heard them in the hallway above; voices muted
behind the upper door.

Sacrificing speed for stealth, she crept down the stairs,
taking them one at a time despite the impulse to rush. The
seconds ticked by like minutes and each of her footfalls
sounded deafening in the echoing stairwell. Her heartbeat
was thunderous. The rush of blood in her ears was like the
fury of some massive waterfall.

When she reached the first floor, she stopped with her

hands against the cold steel of the fire-door. She wanted to shove it open and run, but she had to be clever, had to be careful...

Just wait, she told herself. *Any minute... easy...*

Up above, she heard the door on the fourth-floor push open with a metallic scrape and sigh of its pneumatic hinge.

Even as she heard it, Gayle eased open the door for the first floor and squeezed through. She carefully shut it without a sound. The two men's footsteps grew louder, louder.

With the door shut, Gayle turned on her heels and hurried down the hallway for Bobbi's place. She reached into her pocket for her keys, half-certain that she wouldn't find them, but then had them in hand and opened the door, easing it shut behind her.

Unlike her flat, which had a view of the river and the street, Bobbi's faced the back of the apartment complex and looked out on only the courtyard and resident's car-park. Also unlike her own, Bobbi's window had a shallow balcony and a patio door that could be fully opened.

She drew back the curtains and hastily unlatched the door. She pulled it open and stepped out into a sudden and unexpectedly cold wind. It froze her face, her hands, threatening to chill her to the bone. She realised then that she was soaked through with sweat.

Gayle kicked her foot up over the iron railings, swung her other leg over and balanced with her ankles between the bars. The metal was like ice under her palms. She looked down, some ten or so feet above the concrete.

I can't do this, she thought, but knew that she had no choice. They were making their way down the stairs now. Perhaps they had split up and if they had, she had no time to waste.

Below the balcony and a little off to the left, a silver Vauxhall Zafira was parked against the wall. From here to its roof would only be a drop of four or five feet and if she got enough momentum, she could make it.

Gayle saw herself going for it, over-shooting the roof and slamming into the concrete, shattering both legs. And she'd be lying there, helpless. And Finn would be alone.

No choice, she thought.

Gayle sucked in a lungful of cold air, held it, then jumped.

CHAPTER 17

She landed on the roof of the Zafira and automatically dropped to her hands and knees so as not to slip off. In a movie, she would have deftly jumped down and made for the populated roads of the city, but instead the roof of the car bowed inwards and the alarm began to blare.

The noise was strident in the frigid afternoon air.

The alarms would bring her pursuers in a hurry.

Gayle slipped off the side of the car, stumbled, righted herself and ran as fast as she could for the scrub-land behind the Soar-Bank car-park.

If she took the road in front of the flat, she would be caught before she had a hope of getting to safety if either of her pursuers had a car. She angled to the right, towards Abbey Park Lane, trying to get out of the open. She risked a look over her shoulder. She couldn't see either of her pursuers yet, but the alarm was sure to bring them.

Gayle pushed hard, pumping her legs for all they were worth, trying to build some distance. The cold air brought tears to her eyes and made her lungs ache, as though breathing fine fragments of ground glass. Her shoes pounded on the cracked and uneven concrete.

Steadily, the surface grew worse and Gayle was forced to slow her pace. Divots and potholes were everywhere, with clusters of wiry weeds poking through, as if the wild earth were trying to reclaim the industrialised land. She misjudged her footing and her left came down in a greasy-looking puddle, soaking her to the ankle. She tried to halt the trip by hopping on her right, but it was too late and she pitched forwards.

She went down, hard, slapping her hands painfully on the ground, but she tucked her head in and rolled over on her right shoulder. Her left thigh struck the cold and damp ground. Rattled, Gayle hissed at the pain she felt in her stinging hands. She got to her feet, praying she hadn't broken her ankle, but it seemed to just be soaked and cold.

Behind her, she heard shouting.

She looked and saw both men giving chase. The caramel-skinned one – Vince – was in the lead. In his hand, he held what appeared to be a box-cutter. The other one stumbled after, clutching his slashed hand to his chest. They were almost three-hundred yards away, but coming fast.

Gayle bolted. Ahead and to her right, the scrub-land gave way to housing developments and the skeletons of these buildings were hidden behind plywood fences. There was no way through, so she raced past them, hoping to not find her path blocked.

She glanced at her watch. It was after three already.

Bobbi should be with Finn by now, heading through traffic for the motorway.

Gayle kicked her legs out in front of her in long strides wherever possible; sidestepping or jumping over potholes, scrags of heavy brush, or discarded brick piles when it was not.

Ahead of her, growing closer, larger, was a red-brick building and Gayle knew where she was. The building sat on the Grand Union Canal, which paralleled the River Soar and cut under Abbey Park Road and flowed through the park itself.

A path ran beside the canal and Gayle headed for it, checking her speed as late as she could to avoid pitching headfirst into the ice-cold water. She turned right, keeping the canal on her left and started pushing hard once more.

Ahead was a zigzagging ramp leading up to the street. She reached for the steel handrail, spinning herself around with enough force that it pulled her shoulders. She raced up the ramp.

The two men were still a good distance away, but were strong, fast and getting closer with every second.

Ahead, she saw the large, busy roundabout, clogged with lanes of traffic.

The train, she thought.

Leicester Railway Station was a five- or fifteen-minute drive from here depending on the traffic on St Matthew's Way and St George's Way. If she took the same route at a steady pace, she could do it in thirty minutes. She checked her watch again and began to run once more.

Her sodden shoe slapped and squelched on the pavement as she ran. The discomfort that she first took to be the cold was worse than that. With every footfall, she felt a tiny burst of pain in her ankle. She hadn't suffered a break but a nasty sprain, which she could tell was going to get worse.

She pushed the pain away and whipped her head, looking from side to side. Seeing no fast-moving cars, she cut across the road between the idling traffic. Horns began to honk.

She made it across the first three lanes without incident. She jumped onto the kerb at the roundabout, where a light turned green and three more lanes of vehicles began to move.

"Oh, Jesus," she said aloud, breathless.

She couldn't wait. She burst into the first lane, where the driver of a blue Honda Civic had spotted her and braked. He rolled down his window to shout something, but then she was past him, into the second of the lanes, cutting behind a white van. She looked for a big enough gap, picked her spot and rushed for it. A blue Nissan Qashqai slammed its brakes on and slid a few feet on the wet tarmac. A cold rush of adrenaline shot through her stomach and she expected to feel the sharp, sudden collision, but darted out of its path and up onto the grassy roundabout with inches to spare. A furious chorus of horns filled the air.

Gayle poured on another burst of speed, enduring the agony of the ice-cold air stabbing her lungs. She raced across the grass for the opposite side of the roundabout and another river of traffic.

She looked over her shoulder. The men were both at the other side of the roundabout, but the traffic was moving steadily now and they were stuck – at least for the time being.

Fearing her luck wouldn't hold if she tried to rush through another stream of cars, she hurried for the crossing, where a couple pushed a baby-buggy to the opposite side. The light was just starting to blink as she reached it, but she made it to the opposite side before being stranded.

The pain in her ankle was worsening, starting now to

move through her foot and into her calf, but she pressed on regardless.

With the busy junction behind her, Gayle ran along the street, dodging oblivious pedestrians and a cyclist. A double-decker bus idled at a bus-stop, where a queue of passengers waited to get on.

Panting, her breath coming in ragged wheezes now, Gayle pressed close to the wall to avoid colliding with people. By the time she reached the corner of Belgrave Gate and St Matthews Way, she could no longer run. She had to drop back to a quick walk with intermittent jogging until she caught her breath.

She checked her watch. Almost a quarter past three.

She reached into her pocket for her phone. She unlocked it and saw it was down to seventeen percent.

"Oh *fuck*," she said aloud. The charger. It was in the holdall. And the holdall was still in the flat, along with her wallet.

She couldn't go back. It was too dangerous. No matter what, the only thing she could do was push on. The money she had taken from Tony Henry wouldn't last long, but at least it would get her to Bristol.

She found Bobbi's name in her contacts and dialled.

The phone immediately dropped two percent and the charge-warning flashed on the screen. Gayle dismissed it and held the phone to her ear.

"Come on," she muttered, jogging once more.

The phone rang again and again.

After six rings, she heard Bobbi's voice. "Gayle, are you okay?"

"Fine," she said, still trying to catch her breath. "How are you? Have you got Finn?"

"He's here," she said, "we're fine."

"Where are you?" she asked.

Bobbi took a second, then said, "Just got on Braunstone Way. We're about five minutes from the M69."

"Is Finn okay?"

"He's fine, don't worry. What happened? Are you all right?"

"Yeah," she said, looking over her shoulder. There was no sign of her pursuers, but she couldn't let that slow her down. "I think I got away. I'm heading for the train."

"I could turn around and come and get you."

"No," she said, "I'll be all right." She couldn't afford to wait in case the two men caught up to her. If Finn and Bobbi were moving, they were also safe. "I'll meet you in Bristol. I've gotta go, Bobbi, the phone's dying. Please keep him safe."

"I will. *You* take care, okay?"

"I'll talk to you when I'm on the train." Gayle disconnected the call and put the phone in her pocket. "Thank God," she said aloud.

Groaning, she poured on a little more speed, running uphill along St Matthews Way. She was now less than a mile from the station.

CHAPTER 18

In spite of her best efforts, it was almost twenty to four by the time Gayle reached the station on London Road. The sky above was darkening.

The pain in her ankle was excruciating now and forced her to limp. Still afraid that she was being followed, she nonetheless had to take a moment to recuperate outside the station. She leant against the wall, bent at the waist, sucking cold air into her ice-lined lungs. The furious pounding of her heart felt like it shook her entire body. Her face and hands were numb from the cold, but her armpits and back were soaked through and blazing.

Afraid to wait any longer, she limped up the ramp and into the building. She moved as quickly as she could through a second set of doors and into the station.

To her left was a WHSmith, while on the right, she saw a café with both indoor and outdoor seating. People sat and enjoyed paninis and hot drinks while they waited for their train. On the wall, high above them, was a large digital read-out of destinations, the platforms from which they were scheduled to depart and at what times.

Ahead of her was a bank of automatic ticket machines, with a couple of manned kiosks behind Plexiglass. When her turn came, she spoke to a neatly-dressed young man in a crisp white shirt with the sleeves rolled up. He smiled politely when he saw her, although she knew that she must look a wreck.

"I've got to get to Bristol," she said.

He began to type into his computer. "Leaving today?"

"As soon as possible."

"Fewest number of changes?" he asked, but appeared to be speaking to himself at this point. "I think... *Ah*," he said, "I've got one leaving in ten minutes, platform three. Changes at Derby, then you board the sixteen-thirty-five for Bristol Temple Mead."

"How much?"

"Open-return?"

"One way," she said, "cash."

He gave her the price and Gayle peeled off three twenties and waited for her change. He slid it and her ticket under the Plexiglass screen and wished her a good journey.

She hurried for the covered walkway leading down to the platforms. She slotted her ticket into the steel body of the automated turnstile, pushed through and collected her ticket when it was spat out the other side. She followed the arrows and carefully descended to the platform.

Her reprieve from the wind was short-lived and the force of it found her now as it barrelled down the tunnels and beneath the awnings. It froze her damp clothes to her wet skin and she shivered. She felt as though all the blood had been bleached from her face.

The platform shop, beside which her train sat idling, was hardly bigger than Tony Henry's shed. She quickly looked around inside, praying to find a phone charger. Her luck was in for once and she picked it up, along with a wide-toothed comb, a Snickers bar, a bottle of Evian and a can of antiperspirant.

With her supplies, she limped along the platform to the last carriage and got in. The entire train was more than three-quarters full, but she managed to find an open pair of seats on the platform-side, just back from the window. She sank into it, relieved to be off her injured foot. She closed her eyes for a couple of minutes, until her heartbeat had returned to normal and she stopped sweating.

Gayle turned so she was sitting sideways across the seat and lifted her foot onto the one beside her. She took off her shoe and her moist sock. Her foot was almost bone-white and her toes were pruned. She massaged her ankle and felt an electric stab of pain when she turned her foot inwards. She left her sock and shoe on the seat and continued to massage feeling back into it. She reached into the bag for the chocolate bar. The first bite reignited her appetite. She finished it and threw the wrapper into the bag.

She took the USB cable out of its small cardboard box. She plugged the end into the phone and unwound the metallic clip holding the cord in a tidy loop. She leant down and plugged the USB into the wall.

The phone was at twelve percent. It dropped to eleven.

"Fucking hell," she muttered, unplugging the cable. She disconnected the handset, then plugged it in again. As before, the battery would not charge.

"Piece of shit," she said, pulling it from the wall again.

She thought for a moment that the wall ports would only work when the train was in motion, but in short order the whistle blew and the train began to chug along the track. Still no power went to the phone. She tried the second available slot with the same result.

The train picked up speed and ferried her away into a pitch-black tunnel. The announcement came over the public address system, listing the scheduled stops. As Derby was the first of these, Gayle stopped listening and looked around. The seats opposite hers were unoccupied and also had USB ports built into the wall. She tried the cable there. No good.

Of course, she could ask another passenger to borrow their charger, but she couldn't imagine anyone wanting to lend their property to someone who looked and smelled the way she did right now.

She unlocked her phone and selected Bobbi's number. She read it over and over again, trying to commit it to memory. She turned it onto power-saving mode and locked the screen, then took a moment to peer along the carriage between the rows of seats to see if she had been followed. She recognised no one.

Twenty minutes later, the train came to a stop at Derby. In her shoes and socks once more, she disembarked and looked up and down the platform, hoping to see a payphone, but there were none.

By her watch, she had almost ten minutes before the scheduled departure of the train bound for Bristol. Part way down the platform, Gayle spotted the women's toilet and limped inside. The ache in her thigh muscles had faded, but her ankle was still in bad shape.

The small room had a row of sinks on the left and an L-shaped set up of stalls in front of and to her right. She laid a couple of sheets of paper over the cold toilet seat of the nearest stall, then sat down and peed. She checked her phone. Eight percent battery life.

When she was done, Gayle flushed and washed her hands,

looking up at her reflection. Her cold cheeks were rosy-pink but the rest of her face was as white as chalk. She had a smudge of dirt on her forehead above her left eyebrow. She rubbed it off. Her damp T-shirt had mostly dried now, but the smell of her sweat lingered and her skin felt sticky. She ran her wet fingers through her hair, taming it into something approaching order. She washed and dried her hands again and left.

Out in the cold once more, Gayle looked at the digital display box, trying to find her destination. At last, she saw that her train was on time, scheduled to leave platform two shortly. She limped that way between the commuters and stood gazing up and down the track.

At the far end, a striding pigeon scoured the concrete, inspecting the leavings of the last mob of travellers. It pecked at discarded crisps and sandwich crumbs, then marched along again in an ungainly waddle, in search of another treat.

On her left, a middle-aged man in a grey suit stood, idly swiping at the screen of his smartphone with his thumb and repeatedly checking his wristwatch. He rocked back and forth on the balls of his feet, his bad comb-over lifting from his liver-spotted skull by the gusting wind.

Gayle took a breath and walked towards him, smoothing her hair back from her face.

"Excuse me?" she said, playing up the girlish tone in her voice.

The man glanced at her, then checked around before his eyes settled on her again. "Can I help you?" he asked, his tone less helpful than annoyed at the intrusion.

She gave an awkward smile. "My phone's about to die and I have to get in touch with a friend. I wouldn't ask if it weren't serious. I have money," she said, withdrawing the bundle of notes she'd liberated from Tony Henry's shed. "Two, three minutes at the most."

When he looked up from the cash she held out, his brow was deeply furrowed. He looked behind him again, no doubt wondering if this was a scam of some kind. His errant strip of greying hair blew away from his scalp again. He smoothed it down and said, "Well, I *am* quite busy..."

"Please," she said. "I know this is strange but I'm desperate. Name your price. I'll give you the cash first."

He looked again at the notes in her hands, sucking on his lower lip. "Two minutes?" he asked, narrowing his eyes.

"I swear."

"Fifty quid."

She peeled off the notes without complaint and held them out. The man took the cash and with clear reluctance, handed over his iPhone. He stayed close by, presumably in case she made a run for it with his property.

Gayle found the keypad and got half the number entered before her memory gave up. She took out her own device – six percent – and copied the remaining digits. She held the man's phone to her ear and put her own away.

The line rang and rang, then at last connected. *"Hi, it's Bobbi. Leave a message. Bye,"* her recorded voice sang, drawing out the farewell.

When the tone beeped in her ear, she said, "Bobbi, it's me. I'm okay. I'm in Derby right now. My phone's dying. I hope everything's okay. Please message me or call as soon as you can – I'm freaking out."

The man in the suit had his hand out for his phone.

Biting her lip, Gayle said, "Okay. Talk soon. Please call me." She disconnected and held out the iPhone.

He snatched it from her fingers, giving the device a look

as though she had left it smeared with dirt, and shuffled away along the platform.

Fifty pounds lighter and no better off, she wrapped her jacket tighter around her body.

They'll be okay, she told herself. *Just got to get a grip*.

Above her head, the PA system binged and bonged and a man's tinny voice announced the train bound for Bristol Temple Mead was inbound. He advised passengers to stay back from the edge.

The train arrived in a hiss of air and a screech of brakes. Gayle saw it was much older than the one that brought her here. She was unlikely to find any way of charging her phone on board.

For a moment, she was afraid it wasn't going to stop and would leave her stranded in Derby, with the miles between her and Finn increasing with every passing second. Eventually, the long train came to a halt, its last carriage having overshot where she stood waiting. Commuters crowded in front of the doors instead of waiting for those inside to disembark.

She walked past them all and found a carriage in the middle. She got lucky again with the seating arrangement and found a pair of unoccupied seats facing the direction in which they would be heading.

She glanced at her phone. No calls. No messages. And the battery level had dropped again; five percent now, with an exclamation mark beside the icon.

She groaned and put it in her pocket.

She could try to find a payphone when she arrived at Bristol Temple Mead. There may even be a phone-charging station.

She looked out the window at the dark scenery rushing

by. The rattle and clatter of the train was soothing and the movement made her eyes feel heavy.

Something – perhaps a noise, perhaps a sudden jolt on the tracks – made Gayle jump before she realised she had fallen asleep. She checked her wristwatch and found that she had nodded off for nearly half an hour.

Before she could fall asleep again, she got to her feet. She held onto the headrest as the carriage swayed and reached into her plastic bag for the antiperspirant. She could take the smell of her own sweat no longer.

The train had no signs to indicate that the toilet was occupied, so would have to check the old-fashioned way. She got to her feet and headed for the door to the next carriage.

In the corridor connection, as she passed the heavy concertina-style rubber, she saw those passengers travelling behind her. There were businessmen tapping away at laptops, students sipping cans of beer and families noisily talking. Nearest to the door was a blind man in a soft cap. He had a golden retriever lounging by his feet. As if sensing Gayle's gaze, it lifted its blocky head and regarded her with its gentle brown eyes. The dog opened its mouth and its pink tongue rolled out. As the mutt panted, it seemed to be smiling at her.

She let herself into the small lavatory and engaged the bolt on the door. It stank of shit and forced her to breathe through her mouth. She shucked out of her jacket and hung it on the hook behind the door. The carriage rocked too much for her antiperspirant to stay standing on the counter beside the sink, so she slipped it into the pocket of her cargo pants. She peeled off her T-shirt and hung it from the door handle.

Pushing down the sink tap freed a weak trickle of water

that she used to wet her hands, but it cut off automatically after five seconds. She pressed it again and cupped a little water in each hand. She washed her face and her neck. She rubbed water over her shoulders, arms, under her armpits, between her breasts, over her stomach and the small of her back. She dabbed herself dry with a handful of toilet tissue and dropped it into the water-less toilet bowl. When was dry, Gayle sprayed herself and her T-shirt with a blast of antiperspirant, then aimed a five-second burst into the lavatory.

She looked in the scarred mirror, satisfied that she was as clean as she was going to get. She turned her T-shirt the right way out once more and slipped it back on with her jacket. She sprayed again, returned the can to her pocket, then flushed the toilet and disengaged the lock.

Feeling marginally better, she stepped out, bracing herself against the movement of the train with one hand on the wall. She looked to the rear carriage again, wanting to see the dog.

But Gayle saw something that she wasn't expecting.

Behind the blind man, in the space between the head-rests, she saw a shaved head, looking down. A man's face, half-obscured by a hand held over his nose, as if scratching an itch, his flesh the colour of caramel.

From between the rocking seats, she saw one eye open and look straight at her.

Shit, she thought, turning at once and heading back the way she had come. At the door to the carriage, she looked back over her shoulder.

No longer sitting, Vince stood over his seat, still looking at her. He reached across the aisle for the seat opposite to brace himself.

Gayle almost walked into the doors before they could

slide open. She thought about throwing herself into her seat, taking off her jacket and covering up with it as though she were asleep, but if he recognised it, she would be trapped.

She considered heading back into the toilet and riding out the journey there, but he was getting closer.

She had to keep moving.

She abandoned her things and kept walking. She kept her head down, wincing at the pain flaring in her ankle. She reached the end of the carriage, hands shaking as though she were afflicted with delirium tremens again.

As she moved into the next carriage, she remembered the other man. Her guts lurched. Where was *he*? What if he were in front of her and the two of them were working in tandem, moving through the train to meet in the middle?

No, she thought. The cut to his hand had been too bad for that. He was losing too much blood and must be in too much pain to continue the chase. No, he must have left his friend to follow Gayle alone, while he went to Leicester's A&E department.

With another door between them, she risked a look back. She saw him through the glass, still coming forwards, but he didn't seem to be looking at her.

In the next of the corridors, a couple in heavy winter parkas shared a bag of chips. They stood next to a pair of large suitcases, their handles still bound by white tags from East Midlands Airport. They paid her no attention and the woman – a waif-like blonde in heavy glasses – got up on her tiptoes to kiss her partner's jaw.

Gayle stepped around their luggage, excusing herself as she went. She hoped for another toilet stall that she could duck into, but there was none.

The train jumped and jostled and she lost her balance. She put her left foot out to steady herself and another burst of pain went off in her ankle. She fell into the doorframe, banging her shoulder even as she pushed it open. She caught herself on the wall before she could go down to her knees.

"Are you all right, love?" the guy behind her asked.

She turned to say that she was fine before hurrying on, but caught sight of her pursuer through the glass.

He had stepped into the carriage, less than thirty feet away from her. He stood still, clinging to the overhead luggage racks as though crucified.

He was staring straight at her. His fine features split open in a smile.

CHAPTER 19

Jax locked the car and followed Steph Doughty to the common entrance to the block of flats, passing three kids taking it in turns to kick a football against the wall. They knew better than to stare.

They exited the lift on the top floor, where the stink of piss and bleach hit Jax full-force. The white paint was peeling and colourful graffiti tags covered most of the walls. Overhead, the strip lights had been broken and never replaced. Amidst the strewn crisp packets and cigarette butts, were discarded syringes, tiny balls of tin-foil and a couple of used condoms.

Steph let them in and Jax headed straight for the living room. On the settee, Steph's younger sister, Sharelle, was painting her toenails and watching a game-show on TV.

"Where's Dream?" Steph asked, laying her keys on the TV cabinet.

"In the bedroom," Sharelle said without looking up. "I put her down about half an hour ago."

Although the building was a shithole in an area only a couple of steps removed from a slum, the flat was at least warmly-decorated if without much flair. Most of the cheap furniture was new and those older pieces were in good repair.

Jax crossed to where Sharelle sat, blowing on her toes. "Move your leg," he said, tapping her knee before dropping into the seat.

She threw her leg up before he crushed it against the cushion. "Charming," she said.

Steph shucked out of her leather jacket and threw it over the back of the settee. "You staying for summut to eat, Relle?"

"Nah," she said, getting to her feet and casting a look at Jax. "I think I lost my appetite."

Jax gave her a sweet smile and his middle finger. She scoffed and headed for the door, slipping into her shoes and jacket.

When they were alone, Steph went into the bedroom to change and check on the baby. When she came back, she was barefoot in jean shorts with more rips than fabric and a black Lycra work-out top. "Sleeping like a log," she announced.

"You got enough milk and stuff?" Jax asked.

"Yeah, ta."

Jax was pretty sure that Dream wasn't his – the kid was blonde, for one thing, although Jax's mother was a white woman with blonde hair – but regardless, he tried to look after Steph. A lot of the guys did the same, some out of loyalty and others because they were also unsure whether or not they had fathered the baby.

Steph was twenty-one, with dirty-blonde hair in a perpetual ponytail. When they fucked, Jax was pretty good about making sure to use a condom, since she wasn't the discerning type and he didn't want his dick turning green.

On the other hand, there had that time when he and four of the older lads – X-Ray among them – had all gone at her right here in the living room. Steph was okay about that kind of thing. She didn't even mind if you came on her face, which they all did, apart from Robbo, who was too drunk. Jax recorded that night on his phone and uploaded it to an amateur site. Of course, he kept that part to himself.

"You got anythin' to drink?" he asked.

"Couple beers in the fridge."

"Bring us one, yeah?"

Steph got up and headed for the kitchen, the cigarette hanging from her lip. When she returned, she carried a can of Foster's in one hand, dripping condensation onto the carpet, and a silver canister that read *Coffee*. She handed him both.

Jax popped open the tab of the beer first and took a long swallow. He drained half before he lowered the can from his lips. He held up the coffee tin and said, "How much is here?"

"Five or six hundred."

"Like you haven't counted it."

"Fine, five hundred and forty-five. Better?" She shook a Marlboro out of the pack that he had given her and lit it. She took a deep drag and then caught herself. She offered it filter-first to Jax, but he shook his head and she went on smoking. Through a hazy cloud, she said, "It's nice when you come 'round."

He knew she liked him – even loved him, perhaps – but he didn't feel the same. He could have told her that she was wasting her time, but why mess up a good thing? She would do anything he asked, and he wanted to keep it that way.

He noticed a cluster of red spots on her left cheek. There were three of them that formed a perfect isosceles triangle. If he made a slice from one to the next with the knife in his pocket, the wound would point straight to her left ear, from which dangled a large silver hoop. Jax liked her ears. Her face was nothing special, but her ears – although quite large – were delicate, smooth and well-shaped. Both her tits had the same stretch-marks as her belly, but they were big and he saw the outline of her nipples as vague shadows in the black Lycra. The right one was pierced. He couldn't see the piercing, but remembered it well enough.

He wondered if he could connect the two piercings with dental floss and pull them tight so that her tongue lolled out of her mouth and her large tit was yanked up in defiance of gravity. He supposed that dental floss would be too flimsy. Fishing wire would be better, that way he could connect both piercings to her ears and pull them tight too. He smiled to himself.

Steph caught his gaze and looked him over. She pointed at his waist with the lit end of the cigarette. "In the mood, eh?"

Jax looked down. His erection poked against his jogging pants. He slapped it with one hand and it barely jiggled. "I dunno what you're talking about," he said.

Steph rolled her eyes. "Oh, go on then." She stubbed out the cigarette and slipped off the armchair. She crawled over to him and ran her hands up his legs, over his knees, to the waistband of his joggers. She pulled them down and Jax lifted his backside. Steph pulled his Calvin Klein hipsters down and freed his penis, taking it at once into her mouth. She started to bob her head up and down, sucking sloppily, stroking the shaft with her hand.

He looked at her ear while she fellated him, imagining slipping his fingers through the loops of her earrings and yanking them out. He could almost hear her cries of pain and surprise.

He reached for the Lycra top and pulled it. Steph lifted her arms and the garment slid up and off. Her tits slapped against his knees. She wiped her face and reached down for her heaving breasts, mashing them around the shaft of his dick. She spat on the head – a long, white and warm thread of moisture – and began to slide them both over and around him.

The familiar sensation began to build in him, but each time he felt close, Steph changed her stroke and he lost the feeling.

He tried to concentrate on the thought of pulling a hoop out of her ears and finally, after five more minutes, he felt close again. Steph had given up on the tit-wank and was back to sucking his dick. Then his phone rang and he lost the feeling altogether.

He grit his teeth in anger. He wanted to punch something and thought quite seriously about slapping Steph across the face, but instead, he reached into his pocket for the phone.

"Yeah?" he asked when the line connected.

Steph carried on regardless.

"It's Dom."

Jax could barely hear him over the sound of rushing traffic. "Who?" he asked.

"Dom."

And Jax understood. "Well, where is she? It's been hours, you prick."

"She fucking slashed me, Jax. I just got out the hospital. I'm walkin' in to town. It took twenty stitches."

"I just told you to *follow* her."

"We did. Vince still is. But I ain't heard from him."

Jax glanced at his watch. "When was this?"

"About three o'clock."

"And you're only *now* telling me, you fuckin' idiot?"

"I was gettin' my hand sewn up, mate. She nearly cut off my fuckin' fingers."

"I'll do more than that when I get my hands on you, you useless prick." Jax hung up. He searched for Vince's number. It went immediately to voicemail.

Jax turned on his mobile data and the phone buzzed with a dozen notifications. Amongst the nonsense updates, he had a message on WhatsApp.

> still following her like u said
>
> she ain't seen me
>
> shes on a train to bristol
>
> will txt wen i no where she's going

"What the *fuck*?" he said, slamming the phone onto the seat beside him.

He had turned flaccid in Steph's mouth. She pulled away, wiping slobber from her lower lip. "Dream's sleeping, Jax," she reminded him from her place between his legs.

He got up and pulled up the waist of his pants. He strode around the small flat, furious, thinking.

Why Bristol?

But he knew there was only one real explanation: either she had his money after all or it was waiting for her at her destination.

Jax tried calling Vince but the line only rang.

"Fuck," he muttered.

"What is it?" Steph asked. Deeper in the flat, Dream was stirring, babbling softly to herself.

Jax stopped pacing and looked out the window at the

black clouds that hung like smoke above the hazy fire-like glow of streetlights around the estate.

"Jax?" Steph said.

Without looking at her, he said, "I've got to go." He went to the kitchen and pulled the cash from the coffee can, stuffing the notes into his pocket. Still holding the can of beer, he drained what was left and dropped it into the bin.

Back in the living room, Steph was starting to get dressed.

Without another word, Jax went for the door.

Gayle hurtled through one more carriage, expecting to come to a dead-end any moment, while her pursuer closed the distance.

Buffeted by the train's violent jerks, she crashed hard into the shoulder of a portly man in a navy-blue peacoat and over-sized glasses. He cried, *"Oi!"* in pain and surprise. Gayle pushed away from him, apologising, but continued forwards.

She looked and saw Vince at the door behind her. He pulled it open and came through, but didn't run: he had as much trouble staying upright as she did, though was careful to grab hand-holds on seat backs, headrests and luggage racks. That strange, creepy smile still curled his lips.

She rushed through another partition in the carriages, her breath coming in frantic pants, sweat streaming from her forehead, stinging her eyes. She wiped her face with the sleeve of her jacket. She must have looked as terrified as she felt, because now passengers had started to ask her if she was all right.

Gayle didn't stop. *Couldn't* stop.

One more carriage.

Vince was still coming.

Pretty soon, she knew she was going to find herself with nowhere to go.

And then what?

She could beg a passenger for help, but remembered the box-cutter she'd seen Vince carrying. She couldn't endanger anyone like that. Even if she called out for a train conductor who could subdue her pursuer, her safety would be short-lived: the situation would have to be handed over to the police and she herself carried not one but *two* illegal weapons, none of which she was prepared to ditch.

She could hide in a corner between train carriages and if she was quick, she might have a chance to overpower him before he knew what was happening. The train was busy, however; if a member of the public witnessed the assault, police would be waiting for *her* at the next station and not Vince.

Another hard rattle of the wheels on uneven iron rails and the carriage was rocked once more. Gayle reached for a vacant seat-back, missed and collapsed to the right, slamming her right hip into it. This time, she fell.

As she hit the floor, she realised she could hear the first opening bars of the Goo Goo Dolls's 'Iris'. She felt her phone vibrating.

Behind her, the door was yanked open. Gayle looked and there he was. Fifteen feet behind her. He started to laugh softly to himself.

In front of her, a man – good-looking, early forties, curly brown hair – got out of his seat and bent down to help her up. He took Gayle by the right wrist, his other hand on her right elbow.

"Are you okay?" he asked.

But Gayle was already getting to her feet. "Please," she said, "I got to—"

"*Hey,*" another passenger – a woman this time – called out.

Gayle looked back. A large middle-aged woman in a Christmas jumper and multi-coloured leggings was shoving at her pursuer. Vince tried to shove past her, but she was having none of it: "Who the hell do you think you are?" she railed at him, as all the while, his eyes were fixed only on Gayle.

She broke free of the curly-haired man's grip, turning on her good heel and stumbling forwards once more. In her pocket, her phone went abruptly silent. Amidst the commotion behind her, she heard voices exclaiming, *"What's going on?"* and *"Hey, leave her alone,"* and *"Shouldn't we call someone?"* She barrelled through the door ahead, through the corridor connection and into the next carriage. She made it through without further incident, but after the next pair of doors, she saw that she had come to the end of the line. Ahead was a locked door without windows; the driver's cabin.

She considered pounding on it and begging for help, but even if the driver let her in, she knew Vince would get to her first. He would think nothing of slashing her with the box-cutter.

She glanced over her shoulder even as she backed against the side of the corridor. Vince entered the carriage, forty feet away, the door clattering shut behind him. He stalked towards her.

She saw there was no lavatory here, only a large shelf built into the body of the train, cluttered with suitcases. The exit featured a large glass window, reflecting back her pale face. Above it was a red handle inside a yellow box marked

Emergency Brake. A placard to its left warned of the penalties for using it without reason.

Nowhere to hide.

She reached into her cargo pants and closed her hand around the telescopic baton. She drew it and with a snap of her wrist, she racked the weapon out to its full length. She pressed into the wall beside the shelf, as hidden as she could be, knees bent.

Her pulse pounded in her dry throat. The train's fierce clattering and the wind-noise filled her ears. Although her palm was slick with sweat, she grasped the baton's grip so hard that her hand ached. She kept it down by her right calf, out of sight.

The door opened with a metallic screech.

She pushed herself hard into the corner between the luggage shelf and the wall.

The noise covered his approach, but a couple of seconds later, she saw Vince creeping forwards. His almond-shaped eyes fell on her and he smiled, licking the corner of his mouth. The cut by his eyebrow had dried. He stopped his approach and straightened up. He had his right hand in the pocket of his bomber jacket. He removed the plastic yellow box-cutter and thumbed out the razor-sharp blade.

"Nowhere left to go, bitch," he said.

"Who are you?" she asked.

"No one you know. The Captain told me you was gonna be trouble, but he didn't say you're fit an' all. It'll be a proper shame to have to slice you up, so shut up and come with me."

"Where to?"

"My bruv wants to see you, innit. He'll give me *bare* money to bring you in after this."

She scoffed. "Then you don't know Jax as well as I do. He won't pay you a penny."

"Shows what you know, sket. He wants you big-time. He'll make me boss of my own crew for this." Vince's smooth, unlined face frowned suddenly. He took a step towards her as he said, "Hey, what've you got—?"

She swung the baton up hard. It connected with a sickening *crack* to the left side of Vince's face, blasting his head back. Even as he tried to raise his hands to block, his knees buckled and the box-cutter flew from his grip. He performed a half-pirouette on his rubber-band legs and even before the baton had finished its arc, he was on his way down. He hit the floor with his knees first, then his forehead and lay in a heap at her feet.

She didn't wait to see if he would stay down. She turned towards the door, reached high and pulled on the emergency brake.

At once, the corridor was filled with the screech and squeal of brakes. The momentum propelled her into the wall, hard. Her shoulder slammed into it and the telescopic baton fell from her grip. As she regained her footing, holding onto the wall for balance, she heard an alarm sound, almost loud enough to drown out the harsh rasp of the brakes.

Vince still lay face-down, hurt, but not unconscious. She watched his hand open and close, as if trying to work out a case of pins and needles. In the centre of his palm, he had the initials *WEC* tattooed on the barrel of a smoking pistol. The box-cutter lay only a foot away from his flexing hand.

Gayle reached out for it, but Vince started to move. He rolled to a crouch and snatched at her T-shirt or hair. She gasped and jumped back, hesitated, then threw out a kick that caught Vince in the ear. Even as it connected, her left ankle twisted, exploded with pain, then buckled. She fell with a yelp, pin-wheeling her arms as she went down, landing hard on her tailbone.

Vince lay on his side, hands covering his injured ear. The blow had reopened the gash by his eyebrow and blood poured down his face, stained his fingers and formed a small puddle beneath him.

While he was disoriented, Gayle fought her way to her feet again, struggling for balance. She braced herself against the door with one hand and reached for the fallen baton with the other. She snatched it up, aimed at the window and threw herself into the swing. The emergency glass turned instantly opaque on impact; shattered into an intricate web of a million tiny cracks. She swung the baton twice more to smash out the glass and the cold wind rushed in, stinging her eyes and freezing her sweaty flesh. She rained down half a dozen more blows to clear away all the glass.

She looked out at the darkness, trying to discern something of the landscape. She attempted to use passing wooden posts beside the tracks to gauge their current speed, but whatever it was, it was too fast.

To her right, Vince struggled to his knees again.

Gayle slammed the head of the baton into the wall of the carriage, collapsing it into the handle. She slipped it into the pocket of her cargo pants again and gripped the windowsill with both hands. She kicked her right foot up onto it and pulled, hauling herself into a crouch, teetering precariously half-in and half-out of the moving train. Eyes adjusting to the dark, she saw they were passing farmland. Off in the distance, perhaps half a mile or more, she saw a string of lights that seemed to indicate a major road or perhaps a motorway. She saw nothing else but fields and armies of trees and bushes, standing sentinel in the cold, black night.

She risked a look behind her. Vince groaned. He was on his knees, holding his bloody brow with his left hand and scrambling for the box-cutter with his right. He blinked the gore out of his eyes and saw her.

Gayle looked out at the ground rushing past and for the second time, jumped out into the unknown.

CHAPTER 20

When she hit the ground, the air blasted from her lungs as she tumbled along the mushy, weed-tangled verge, trying to tuck her legs in and protect her head with her arms. As she rolled, the snagging weeds and dozens of sharp stones scratched and bit, jabbing her through her clothes. She tried to cry out when she struck something hard in her left side – perhaps her own elbow – but there was still no breath within her.

When at last she came to a stop and lay on her back, gazing up at the ink-black clouds and the faint crescent of moon beyond, her vision continued to tilt and roll. Above her own feeble gasps for breath, she heard the screech of the train's brakes.

She sucked in a breath that didn't want to come, telling herself she needed to move. Spread-eagled in the mud, she felt certain that she had broken her neck somehow, but found that she could wriggle her toes. Her ankle still sang with pain, troubling her worse than the dizziness, or the cuts and bruises that she felt all over.

She reminded herself that pain was good; pain meant she was alive.

But she wasn't going stay that way for long if she didn't get up.

Ignoring the dizziness and the pain crackling along the right side of her head, she got to her feet. She reached for her temple and winced at the contact. Her fingers came away tacky with blood. The cut seeped but didn't pump or gush. Holding out her arms for balance, she attempted to put her weight on her left foot, but the pain was too great.

She looked to her right, following the sound of the alarm. The train was coming to a squealing halt some eighty or ninety feet down the track.

Got to hurry, she thought. She turned and limped up the slippery verge. She used her hands to maintain balance until she made it to the top. On the other side, she was faced with a large expanse of black, boggy earth with patches of dense grass. A thick cluster of trees lay two-hundred yards further and in the distance, she saw a string of lights disappearing over the dark horizon. She rushed towards it as quickly as she was able.

As soon as she laid a foot on the tilled earth, the cold mud sucked her down almost to the ankle. With every hard-won step, the bitter cold bit deeper. A glance over her shoulder confirmed that she had gone no more than fifty feet, but she felt frozen to the marrow. She blinked blood or mud or sweat from her eyes, then wiped it away with her forearm.

Behind her, half-lost in the wind and the more distant ululation of the train's alarm, she heard a bellow. She paused to glance back, rather than risk slipping and falling face-first into the muck.

In the shadows, she saw movement. Vince had crested

the verge. He plunged after her, but the ground was hard-going for him too. He slipped, almost fell, but righted himself and forged on.

Gayle pressed on, quickening her pace as much as she dared.

Vince shouted again, but she couldn't make out his words.

Further and further she went, hurrying towards the trees, hoping to lose him there. With every yard travelled, the chill radiated through her feet and legs, until her toes felt numb, but that lack of feeling didn't spare her the agony in her twisted ankle. She sucked in the cold air and hissed with each breath, until her lungs felt as though they were crusted with a billion tiny ice crystals. Tears streamed from her eyes, blurring her vision, brought on by the pain and the cold.

Mingled with the threnody of wind blowing across the power-lines and over the open land, she heard quiet laughter, growing closer.

She struggled on, trying to block out the pain. When she made it to the stand of trees, she kicked her way through a thicket of tangling bushes. The ground had hardened and the going was easier. She looked back, breathless, and saw that in spite of the boggy earth, Vince was less than forty feet back. No longer laughing, she heard his heavy, animal-like pants and gasps. She badly needed to rest, but there was no protection even amongst the phalanx of trees.

She fell against the rough trunk of a horse chestnut, shielded from the wind by its shedding boughs. She took the weight off her left foot for a fleeting moment of relief. She reached into her back pocket, afraid that she had lost the switchblade in the fall from the train, but found it at once. She pushed away from the tree and stumbled on.

Her eyes had adjusted to the gloom, but the shadowy interior of the large copse meant that she had to be careful to avoid hurtling into sharp branches. Many times, snare-like bushes tugged at her feet, threatening to trip her. Skeletal hands of tree branches grabbed at her hair and jacket. Her feet were soaked through and her legs were muddy almost to the knees. She slipped in the rotting leaves that the trees had shed so far, but forced herself to get back up and power forwards.

She could hear Vince still thrashing his way through thickets of bushes behind her, but he no longer jeered. She prayed he had lost her in the almost-total blackness.

Gayle angled to the left, going for where she had seen the lights, although they were now hidden from view. She hoped that her numerous slips and stumbles hadn't taken her too far off course.

Though it felt longer, she thought she had been lost in the copse for no more than twenty minutes. She began to doubt how near the lights had been, or even whether she had actually seen them at all. As every muscle in her body burned and trembled, she thought she would collapse with exhaustion.

Gayle forced more from her limp-noodle legs, but stumbled over a thick tree root. Her shoulder slammed into the trunk and she spun and went to her knees. She felt a layer of skin graze away, but that was just one more in a legion of pain. She clambered to her feet, out of breath and continued on.

As if bursting through a curtain, suddenly Gayle was out of the copse and once more in open land. She looked to the left and right, seeing nothing but long, black blades of shivering grass and distant hedgerows. Ahead of her, above a rise in the dark land, she saw the familiar T-shaped lights that meant only one thing.

Motorway, she thought. Over the howling wind, she heard the faint sound of traffic.

She limped from the treeline and the cold wind found her at once. It sank fangs of ice deep into the wet, itchy flesh of her neck and brought her out in violent shivers. Her eyes began to blur with tears again and she sniffed, rubbing her nose with the sleeve of her jacket.

As she closed the distance between her and the rise, she heard the sound of passing vehicles grow louder. With every step, the earth became softer and harder to traverse. Her feet were so numb that she only registered the wetness when she heard the sounds of splashing. Looking down, she saw that the earth wasn't merely muddy but harboured puddles. Some were larger than others, but as she progressed, they grew not only bigger but deeper.

Gayle stopped. She breathed heavily and her tongue stuck to the roof of her mouth, burned dry by the frigid air. She squinted her eyes in the darkness to look at the black stretch of land in front of her.

Only, she saw now that it wasn't land at all. Separating her from the verge leading to the motorway was a twenty or twenty-five-foot-wide body of black, dirty water, running the length of the entire field. It wasn't a river or a stream, since it appeared to be standing water, likely left since the most recent downpour. As she risked two steps further, her feet sank to the ankles. There was no way to determine how deep it would become.

She turned to the left, splashing through the edge of the water, as though it were a moat keeping her from the safety of the castle on the other side.

Behind her, she heard a sudden roar. She had no time to

turn before something slammed hard into her back, taking her completely off her feet. She fell, smashing face-first into the muddy water. Submerged, she scrambled with her hands and thrust and kicked, finally breaking the surface and sucking in a painful breath. She felt hands grasping at her jeans, her jacket, her hair.

She twisted around, flailing with her own arms and saw Vince half on top of her. His face was spotted with splashes of mud and beads of water dripped from his hawkish nose. He grabbed at her face, but she slapped away his hands and got her right foot between them and drove a kick into his guts. He grunted, spraying her with his foul breath and spittle. He staggered back.

Gayle twisted around and hitched and stumbled into the water, splashing with both hands, kicking her feet into the sodden earth. Progress was slow and her feet threatened to suck down into the muck. The freezing water climbed her legs, submerging her to mid-thigh. She slipped and went down again, gagging and spitting as the foul water ran into her mouth.

Vince splashed after her, crying out, "Fucking bitch!"

He snagged a handful of her hair and she screamed as he pulled her back off her feet. She reached up for his wrists and dug her fingernails in. When his grip didn't loosen, she went for his face and scratched at his jaw and neck. He thrust her down into the water and it ran up her nose, into her mouth. She panicked, kicking and flailing once more, managing to twist free. She came up for air, choking and retching, rubbing at her eyes to clear them. Vince's bleats of laughter came between ragged pants for air.

He staggered after her. She felt his fingers grazing her back, her shoulder, then her sleeve. When he at last grabbed her shoulder, Gayle swung her arm and drove her elbow into his face. Vince grunted and fell back, nose pouring blood. He splashed into the water.

She wasted no time and made for the opposite bank again, slipping and sliding as the water rose over her hips, belly and over her breasts. She thrashed and lunged forwards, splashing her face with water. She coughed and spat. She felt her left shoe suck into the quicksand-like earth and come loose. She pushed on regardless and looked back over her shoulder. Vince, face streaked with grime and blood, was still coming, almost ten feet away. He bellowed again, screaming one curse after another.

When she clambered up the far bank, the water receded to her thigh, calf and finally her ankles. The ground rose sharply and she was forced to climb up on her hands and knees. At the crest, she saw what she hadn't noticed before: a barbed-wire fence stapled to three-foot high posts.

"I'm gonna slice the skin from your fucking face!" Vince screamed after her.

She grabbed handfuls of grass, hauling herself up, kicking with her feet. She was so close. She didn't dare look back.

"Get back here, you fucking bitch!"

"Get away from me!"

At the top at last, she found the fence was too high to climb over. It had ribbons of rubbish and strips of plastic tangled on some of the barbs and clots of sheep's wool like summer dandelion heads stuck to others.

Five feet to the right, the posts had buckled and the fence sagged, but was still too high to scale without tangling herself. Then she remembered the switchblade.

She reached for it and popped out the blade – *snick!* – and went to work on the fence post. She glanced back and

Vince had not quite made it to the hill. He splashed through the fetid water.

Gayle located a staple and slipped the blade between it and the wood. She tried to pry it loose and gripped the top of the post in her other hand, pulling and shoving on it in desperation. The wood was old and rotten half-through. She got one end of the staple free and with a metallic jangle, the barbed wire fell away. It caught on the left cuff of her jacket sleeve and she pulled her arm away, tearing the fabric.

"I'll kill you, bitch!" Vince roared. He was starting to clamber up the hill.

She pulled furiously at the post, until splinters bit into her fingers and threads of wood slipped under her finger-nails. She cried in pain, but continued to yank on the post. With a brittle snap, the post tore in two, leaving a jutting stalagmite poking up from the grass.

"Bitch!" Vince screamed again, almost in her ear.

Gayle twisted at the waist and threw the upper part of the post at him. It trailed a strip of barbed wire behind it, ringing like a tuneless violin string.

Vince tried to raise his hands to protect himself, but was too late. The post missed his head by inches, but the trail of wire snagged him across the lower lip, chin and throat. He cried out and slipped, landing with a wet *smack* on the grass. He let out the gurgled squeal of an injured animal. He struggled to his knees and reached for his throat.

She saw sprays of crimson blood jetting from his savaged neck. It flowed between his fingers, pooled in his mouth and ran down his chin, staining his entire chest in seconds.

Gayle retched. She could do nothing but watch as Vince slumped to one side and slipped and rolled back down the hill, finally ending up face down in the water. He floated, unmoving, with his arms out to his sides. His dark blood mixed with the black water.

She sat down, resting, getting back her breath. She shivered violently against the cold, wanting nothing more in that moment than to fall asleep.

No, she told herself. *Got to move.*

She looked down at her hand. She still gripped the knife.

She closed the switchblade and returned it to her rear pocket. She got carefully to her feet: she didn't want to lose her footing and fall into the water beside Vince.

She turned and looked down the other side of the hill. It ran down fifteen feet or so to the steel barrier and the motorway beyond. On her backside, she shuffled down the incline and kicked her legs over the steel rail.

Frozen and missing one shoe, Gayle turned left and hobbled along the hard shoulder. She reached for her phone. It was dead and dripped water. She removed the cover and battery and tried to shake it dry. She put it together again, but it would not turn on. She held it under her armpit in a futile attempt to dry it out.

She looked around but saw no road signs by which to orient herself. There were no emergency phones in sight.

The gravel pinched her toes as she limped along. On the other side of the central reservation, two cars sped past, their headlights dazzling her. She hitched along for almost a mile before she heard an engine behind her.

She turned, waving her arms above her head. She cried out for the driver to stop. Her voice was fried and hoarse.

She saw a curtain-sided lorry with a fitted bank of lights on its roof and red neon in the cabin. When it was two or three-hundred yards away, it blasted its horn.

"Please! *Stop!*" she begged.

The lorry blew past her in a rush of wind and a hiss from the air-braking system. She turned, expecting to see it disappear into the distance, but saw the blinking light of its indicator. The lorry slowed and pulled onto the hard shoulder, coming to a stop another hundred and twenty yards away.

She rushed towards it. The way her luck was running, she expected it to rumble to life and take off, but the large vehicle didn't move. A beer-bellied man in jeans, a dark green peacoat and a black watch cap climbed down from the cabin. He started towards her, hoisting his jeans up. "Are you all right, love?" he asked in a deep, Bradford accent.

She tried to talk; to thank him; to explain that she had to get to her little boy. As hard as she tried, however, her voice was lost. Less than twenty feet from the big man, Gayle stopped, unable to go another step. She shook all over. She covered her face with her hands and choked down the urge to weep. When she could at last speak, she muttered, *"God, help me."*

She felt a warm, gentle arm on her shoulder. "Bloody hell, love," he said. "You're perishing. Look, let us get you inside, in the warm, eh? Come on." Up close, he had a broad nose, a dark bristly beard greying at the cheeks and cocoa-brown eyes. He led her along the hard shoulder and she leant against him. Although not much taller than Gayle herself, he was solidly-built and his clothes smelled of cherry tobacco and Brut aftershave.

He helped her climb the ladder to the passenger seat, then came around the front and hoisted himself in next to her. He thumbed the controls on the dashboard and turned the heaters up full-blast.

"Thank you," she croaked, looking down at her chalk-white hands. She rubbed them together to bring back some feeling.

"You're soaked through, love."

"It's a long story."

"What's your name?"

"Gayle."

"I'm Barry. Hold on a second." With that, he turned his back on the windscreen and climbed up into the roof of the cabin.

Glancing up, she saw a hidden compartment behind a curtain, where he kept his belongings on a small travel-bed. He rustled around for a moment and pulled down a thick woollen blanket. He sat again and offered it to her.

"Listen," he said, "don't take this the wrong way or anything. I know people get funny these days, but I mean no harm. You should take off your jacket and get wrapped up in this." He had a warm, almost fatherly manner, that she had seen in others but had never experienced herself.

After a few minutes in the wash of the heaters, she shucked out of her jacket, setting off fireworks from the million little aches and pains that seemed to have blended into one. Underneath, her T-shirt was torn and bloody in places.

"Jesus," Barry said. "Let's get you to a hospital." He indicated, put the rig in gear and pulled out onto the empty motorway.

"No," she said. "I'll be okay." She wrapped the blanket around herself.

"Really, love, I think it's best—"

"I have to get to my son. Something really bad happened, Barry. It's best not to tell you what exactly, but I have to get to him tonight."

He was quiet for a moment, building up the speed, before he said, "Well, where is he?"

"Bristol." She pulled out her phone again and tried to revive it. The screen remained black. "Somewhere."

"I'm on my way to Taunton," he said. "Bristol's on the way, if you're *sure* you don't need a doctor."

"I'll be fine." On the floor by her feet, Gayle noticed a large thermos.

Following her gaze, Barry tutted. "Sorry, darling. The coffee's all gone, I'm afraid. I can't drink it after five in the afternoon or I don't sleep."

"That's okay," she said, tucking her chin into the blanket.

"Not to worry. I have just the thing." He reached past her and opened up the large glove compartment. He began to rustle around inside, came up with what he was looking for and handed it to her.

She looked down. In both hands, she held a half-bottle of Imperial Stag Scotch Whisky.

"I never drink and drive," he said, "but a little nip before bed and I'm out like a light. You look like you could use it."

CHAPTER 21

I don't drink. But thank you.

Gayle had spoken these words many times over the years, but couldn't remember ever having as much difficulty as she had now.

She should smile politely and shake her head.

But she wanted a taste; just one to help calm her nerves. If anybody else had experienced all that she had since Danny's murder, they would be *recommended* a little drink; and one didn't mean two and two didn't mean she had to get drunk.

But those were just the bullshit justifications of an addict. Whether by poor choices in her youth or some fatal flaw in her DNA caused by developing in a drug-addled womb, it all amounted to the same thing.

Swallowing to soothe her cold-parched throat, she watched the burnt-gold liquid slosh inside the bottle with every bump in the road. The thirty-five-centilitre bottle wouldn't have had much impact in the old days, but now was probably enough to send her into peaceful oblivion.

She thought about Vince's frightened-rabbit eyes as his

throat sprayed arterial blood. She remembered the sound of him choking, how quickly he had bled out and that it was her doing. She hadn't *intended* it, but she had killed him nonetheless. The enormity of that fact was overwhelming.

She laid her hand on the phone in her pocket, wishing she could talk to Bobbi but couldn't remember if her number ended in two-one-two or two-two-one. Visions of Vince's slack, open mouth rushed through her mind.

Gayle uncapped the bottle of Imperial Stag and held it to her nose. She breathed in the potent scent of whisky.

She put the neck to her lips and knocked it back. The whisky burned in her throat. She hissed as its heat seared her insides. She barely gave herself enough time to take a breath before taking the second – the glass in her shaking hand ringing against her teeth. She wiped away a dribble from her chin before taking the third gulp and capping the bottle at last. She had drunk almost a third in less than a minute.

Wrapped in the blanket, Gayle hugged her knees. She squeezed her eyes tight and buried her face into them.

In her mind, she saw Danny lying pale and still beneath a white cotton sheet... then Vince, with his petrified expression of disbelief, as the life-blood gushed from the wound in his throat... then Ryan Breach's hate-filled face as he thrust his knife over and over again into the guts of some unknown man...

To still the relentless slideshow, Gayle removed the cap and raised the bottle once more. It shook in her hand as she wrapped her lips around the neck. Whisky spilled down her throat. A sob began to build and she coughed, spluttering, covering her face with her tingling hand.

Barry reached over and took the bottle from her and screwed on the cap.

When she could speak, she muttered, "What the hell am I going to do?", unsure herself as to whom the question was directed.

Barry patted her shoulder. "You can tell me what's going on, you know," he said. "I may not look like it, love, but the missus says I'm a good listener."

Gayle raised her head, resting against the back of the bench seat. Tears wobbled in her eyes and she wiped them away with the back of her hand. "Oh, I'm in such a mess, Barry," she said. "And everything I do is making it worse."

"With your little boy, you mean?" he asked. "Is this about some... you know, custody thing?"

"No. It's nothing like that. I'm..." She hesitated, not wanting to tell him anything that would endanger him... or give him cause to kick her out. "I'm in some trouble and I sent him with my friend to keep him safe. They're in Bristol but I don't know where. I've got no money, my phone's dead and I'm just about out of places to run. I spent my whole life going from one kind of nightmare to another. I tried to change, I swear to God I did, but with the things I've done, even if I get out of this, I'll probably end up having my son taken from me. That scares me more than anything. So, here I am now – scared shitless, exhausted and with a belly full of whisky. I guess nobody ever really changes, do they? Not *really*... not who they are, deep down." She let out a bitter laugh. "Now I'm whining. Jesus, I'm pathetic."

"I doubt that very much," he said.

"You don't know me, Barry."

"Oh, I can tell things about people," he said. "It takes a lot to fool me. I may not be able to help with everything, but there is one thing I can do. Here," he said, reaching into the pocket of his jeans. He held up his Huawei P40 handset. "If your phone's not working, use mine."

"Thanks," she said, "but it's no help. I don't remember her number."

"But do you know her email? I've got all the messaging apps too. Maybe you can reach her that way?"

He was right. In her exhaustion and despondency, that hadn't occurred to her.

She took the handset from him. She logged in to his Facebook and found Bobbi's profile. Clicking the messenger tab, she quickly tapped out a message and hit *send*.

"How soon before we're there?" she asked.

"About half an hour, I'd say."

She looked down at the phone cradled in her lap, but Bobbi was not yet online.

By the time Barry exited the motorway and headed towards the centre, the whisky Gayle had drunk was starting to make her head swim. She had warmed up at last and the feeling came back to her bare and sore feet.

At a red-light, Barry stopped the rig and set the handbrake. He raised his arms above his shoulders, stretching out the stiffness.

"How long have you been on the road?" she asked.

"Since half-six this morning," he said, stifling a yawn with the back of one hand, "give or take. There's rules about that sort of thing, but what can you do?" The clock on the dashboard said that it was almost nine.

"And I'm slowing you down."

"Don't worry about it," he said. "I'd call it a minor detour."

"I'm sorry about everything. I don't want you getting into an accident because you're tired." She didn't like the way she slurred *'accident'*, though her thinking felt clear.

"Not to worry," he told her. "You sleep less when you

get to my age. Besides, I'm not going to let you out to wander the streets with nowhere to go."

In Gayle's hands, Barry's phone buzzed and rang with a notification. It had done so twice before as they made their way through the city centre, but it had only been notifications from Barry's Netflix watch-list. She glanced at it now, expecting more of the same, but it wasn't. Bobbi had responded.

> Thank God, are you all right??? Finn's okay, just missing you. We're at Bristol Central Travelodge on Anchor Street. Room 108. Be careful. See you soon! xx

She gave the address to Barry and returned his phone. He set the sat nav and told her that he would have her there in eight minutes.

When he pulled over into the bus lane outside the building, he turned and said, "Are you sure you're going to be okay?"

"I am now," she said. "I really can't thank you enough. I've got a little cash left."

He waved off the offer with a large hand. "I don't want a penny. It was my pleasure. I'll help you down." He got out and she watched him walk around the front of the lorry, hitching up his jeans as he went.

She checked that she had her meagre possessions in place. Her damp socks lay on the floor of the cabin beside her one remaining Nike. She balled up the socks and stuffed them into the pocket of her tattered jacket and slipped it on. Her cargo pants and T-shirt had mostly dried, but the jacket was still moist and reeked. She folded up the blanket and covered over the half-bottle of whisky, resisting the temptation to take it with her.

Barry opened the door and she climbed down. The agony in her left ankle had become a deep throb but she was careful to not put her full weight on it. The discomfort she felt in her scratched feet was dulled by the whisky, but she knew she was going to be sore in the morning.

In spite of her stink, Barry gave her a chaste hug. "Take care of yourself, all right, love?"

She was moved by his concern, but had no more tears left. She patted his wrist. "Thanks for everything," she said.

"I hope it all works out, love. Maybe look me up one day and let me know, eh? Barry Randall."

She smiled. "Take care, Barry."

Gayle wanted to see him off, but he wouldn't hear of it. He insisted that she head inside so that he knew she was safe. As she hobbled along the pavement, she passed a bin and left her Nike sitting on top of it. From the doorway, she waved and went inside.

Aware that she looked homeless – which she supposed was true – Gayle was grateful to see nobody currently manning the front desk. She pushed through the fire-door and summoned the lift, working out on which floor she would find room 108. She stepped into the carriage and pressed 5.

There was no mirror in the lift's interior, which was probably for the best. She wasn't sure she wanted to see what she really looked like. Feeling self-conscious, she breathed into her palm and sniffed, but could smell only the stench of dried sweat and foul water.

The lift shook as it arrived on the fifth floor. She stepped out, looking at the directions on the wall. She stepped through a fire-door, but with every limping step, felt more uneasy than excited. She thought she might be uncon-sciously expecting to encounter more members of the *West-*

End Crew, hell-bent on impressing Jax Knox, but she pushed that thought aside as soon as it came. Nobody knew she was here.

Gayle knew the real problem. She was embarrassed. Although not fall-down drunk, she was drunk nonetheless. Her emotions seesawed from excitement to see Finn, to shame and embarrassment for the state that he would see her in. She had never been drunk in his presence before.

The shame burned on her face as she stood outside room 108, with her hand raised, ready to knock.

From inside the room, she heard Finn chattering over the sound of the TV.

She knocked three times and immediately heard footsteps.

The door opened a crack. Bobbi stood in the doorway, a cautious look on her face, which fell quickly away and she beamed from ear to ear. She threw the door open and grabbed Gayle in a fierce bear-hug. With her face pulled into Bobbi's neck, Gayle was almost smothered. Nonetheless, she hugged back every bit as tightly.

"Mummy!" Finn cried.

Bobbi pulled away and Gayle saw him bouncing on one of the double beds in excitement. He raced over and crashed into Gayle with enough force to almost knock her over. She scooped him up and he wrapped his arms and legs around her.

She kissed his neck, absorbing the warm, clean smell of him. She felt the bumps of his spine against her hands and held him tight.

"I love you so much," she said. "Are you all right?"

"Just squished."

Gayle put him down, though couldn't bring herself to let go of him. She looked him over with a lump in her throat, wanting to kiss him all over but too ashamed to breathe on him.

"You seen the room, Mummy?" he chattered, oblivious. "Isn't it great? We get a TV and a bath and *everything*. Although we should have three beds, not two. Can you call the hotel people and see if they have an Xbox? You should probably get changed too, Mummy, you're a bit smelly."

"Finn," Bobbi admonished, though couldn't suppress a laugh.

"We've got pizza," he said, running off to the bed, where two Dominos boxes sat piled up on the bedside cabinet.

"Thank God you're okay," Bobbi told her. She guided Gayle out of the doorway and closed it behind her, then pulled her in for another hug. "What happened to you?"

"Not in front of Finn," she said in a whisper. "But can we talk later?"

Bobbi agreed.

Gayle limped forwards and laid back on the big double bed. She told herself that she was safe; that there was no way she could have failed to notice someone following her here. Nonetheless, she lay facing the door, certain that at any moment, it would be kicked off its hinges and she would once again be fighting for her life.

CHAPTER 22

Later, after forcing down the last cold slices of ham and pepperoni pizza and a strong cup of coffee, Gayle sat beside Finn on the double bed. She stroked his hair, kissed his forehead and told him she loved him. He smiled and within minutes, fell into a deep sleep.

Whispering to Bobbi, Gayle said, "I'm gonna take a shower." She rose to her feet, muscles stiff, groaning.

From her place on top of the single bed, Bobbi looked up from the mobile game she had been playing. "We stopped at a services on the way," she said, "and I got a few toiletries. I wish I'd thought to get a first-aid kit and some clothes."

"You've done too much already," she said with a weary smile.

"You'd do it for me."

"Too right," Gayle said, nodding, then limped to the bathroom.

On the sink, she found Colgate, a bottle of Listerine, three toothbrushes, shampoo, shower gel, a bath sponge, an exfoliating body-polisher, a can of hairspray, deodorant, moisturiser, a hairbrush, a sealed packet of hairbands, fingernail clippers and a travel-size bottle of talcum powder.

Gayle let out a *humph* of quiet laughter. "A few toiletries," she said to herself.

She stripped, throwing her soiled clothes into a pile on the floor, then inspected the damage in the mirror.

Her hair was dirty and matted. She had a graze on her right temple, but the blood had dried to form ruby crystals. Her hands and forearms were scratched and bruised. Both elbows were skinned but didn't bleed. She twisted to see as much as she could of her back. Her right shoulder was raw and crusted with dried blood. Her ribs were sore by the crease of her left breast, but nothing seemed to be broken. She had a plum-coloured bruise the size of her fist on the side of her left buttock, that she hadn't even noticed was tender until now, and another on the outside of her left thigh. She assumed that came from impacting the can of deodorant in her pocket when she jumped from the train. She didn't realise until now that she had lost it somewhere, though thankfully nothing else had gone missing. Both knees were abraded, her left ankle was swollen and the sole of her foot had a dozen or more tiny nicks and cuts from the sharp stones on the motorway's hard shoulder. In every crevice and fold of her body, she found streaks of dried dirt and God-only-knew-what. She tried not to think about that.

She started up the shower and stood under streams of blazing water. She bore the pain from her numerous cuts and grazes until the discomfort finally subsided, then soaped up with shower gel, being careful around the tender areas. After washing her hair, she turned off the water and patted herself dry with a towel and wrapped a fresh one around herself.

She stooped and reached into the pocket of her cargo

pants, retrieving the switchblade, and took it with her into the room, where the only light came from the bedside lamp, dimmed by Finn's school polo shirt.

Bobbi lay under the covers now, propped up on one arm, the strap of her tank top having fallen off her shoulder, swiping at the screen of her phone. She had eschewed the head-wrap and tied her hair into two large bunches. Without looking up, she said, "I keep looking for a report of what happened at Soar-Bank. Nothing yet."

"It won't be long," Gayle said, easing herself to sit on the edge of the double bed. Behind her, Finn didn't even stir. She pulled the end of the duvet up over his collar, then laid the switchblade on the bedside cabinet within easy reach.

"He thinks we're taking a weekend away," Bobbi said. "I didn't know what I should say."

"I'm not sure even *I* know what to tell him." She smoothed her still-damp hair away from her face, then leaned forwards, elbows on her knees.

"What's the plan?" Bobbi asked. "Do we go to the cops?"

Gayle shook her head. The very thought of doing so brought on a wave of nausea. "Not yet," she said. "Actually, I don't know if I ever will."

"What happened?"

Gayle looked back again to check on Finn, but he was still asleep. Turning back to Bobbi, she said in a shuddery whisper, "Because I killed somebody."

"What? *When?*"

"Those two guys from the flat," she said, "one of them followed me onto the train. He was trying to stay out of sight, but I saw him and ran. I got off the train but he chased after me, and that's when I..." She sighed. "I don't know how anyone will believe me, but it was an accident."

"Of *course* it was," Bobbi said, reaching out to take her hand. Her reassuring touch was warm, but in spite of the heat from the shower, Gayle's fingers were cold.

She looked down at her bare toes on the blue carpet. "I feel sick," she whispered. "It was just... I can't get it out of my head."

"Did anybody else see it happen?" Her forehead was lined with a deep frown but her large eyes showed not a hint of judgement, only concern.

"I doubt it," Gayle said. "We were in some field out in the middle of nowhere. I *know* he would have killed me without a second thought. But... it was awful."

"How did you get away?"

Gayle explained about flagging down Barry's lorry. "And he had a bottle of whisky in the glove compartment. With everything, I..." She tutted, shaking her head at her own lack of will-power. "You know what that was? That was six years down the toilet."

"You're not superhuman, Gayle," Bobbi said. "And a mistake isn't the end of the world."

"It might as well be. I've got nothing left, Bobbi. We've got no money. We've got no home. Danny's dead. If Jax finds me, he'll kill me – and probably you and Finn too. Even if I get away from him, I'll still end up in prison for what I did to Vince, and I'll lose Finn." Her lower lip began to wobble and she bit it. "He'll go into care, and then what life is he gonna have? He'll be just like Danny, just like *me*."

Bobbi slipped out from under the covers and came to Gayle's right, wrapping an arm around her left shoulder. "It won't come to that. And being like you is no bad thing," she assured her.

Through the tears, Gayle almost laughed. "You don't

know who I used to be, Bobbi. I still haven't told you half the shit I did or that I've seen."

"No," she admitted, "but I know you *now*. I know you've never been like this Jax and you're not even like Danny was – not deep down. That's the part of people that never changes. You're stronger than he was."

She sighed, wiping away a quiet tear with the ball of her fist. "I don't feel strong right now. I'm terrified. *Look*," she said, holding up her right hand. It trembled as though the temperature of the room had plummeted.

"I'm not surprised," Bobbi said. "I'd be a blubbering mess if I was you right now. But you're wrong about having nothing left. You've got Finn and you've got *me*. Don't forget, I've had to start again with nothing too, and you stood by me and never asked for a thing. You and Finn, you're like my family. One way or another, we're gonna work this all out together, so don't come apart on me now, okay?" She shook Gayle gently by the shoulder.

"I hope you're right about me," Gayle said.

Bobbi leaned in and planted a gentle kiss on her temple, to the side of the graze. "I've got faith in you."

"Thanks, Bobbi," she said, but those words felt too shallow to truly express the depth of her gratitude.

"Things will seem better after some rest."

When Bobbi returned to the single bed, Gayle eased back the duvet and got in beside Finn, who lay on his side, facing away from her, groaning at the painful protests of her every muscle.

She laid her left palm softly against Finn's warm back, feeling his ribcage expand and contract with each peaceful breath.

I won't let anything happen to you, she promised.

As she drifted off to a troubled sleep, she wondered if it was a promise that she had the power to keep.

* * *

Jax sketched by lamplight beside the open window of his first floor flat. Below him, Hinckley Road was as busy as always. Within minutes from his door was a pub, a couple of newsagents, a Pizza Hut, a Chinese take-out and even a solarium and a travel agent. The voices and the constant rush and growl of traffic faded into a background noise that he was barely aware of.

When he began with his pencil and A4 pad, he wrote *WEC* over and over in a range of improvised styles. He couldn't settle on one he liked and soon he gave up and drew an outline around his own left hand. He moved the pencil quickly, adding detail and shading to make it appear real. He sketched the web of veins visible in the back of his hand, then the tendons and even the small scar over his first two knuckles. He hastily sketched in the fingernails, then added a shadow to give mass and weight to the disembodied hand.

Pleased with the ten-minute sketch, Jax tore the page out and set it aside. He sharpened the pencil, dusting his desk with shavings that he swiped into a small bin. In front of him was half a can of Heineken. He drained it then discarded it too.

His pencil hovered above the blank page. He stared at the sheet of white paper and cleared his mind, all the better to allow inspiration to strike.

A moment or two later, his pencil was moving again. His touch light, barely contacting the paper at all, he drew a small oval, unsure what he was even doing until he added a mass of curled, windswept hair with heavier lines.

As he worked, Jax was relaxed, feeling none of trauma of the last few days.

He had the face sketched in with hair and a well-shaped torso – a woman's body – before he realised he was sketching a likeness of Gayle Stillwater. When that comprehension hit him, he wanted to scratch over the sketch, scribble and cross it from existence, then tear up the paper. But he didn't. Jax kept working. He drew her nude, reclined on a bed, chair or chaise-longue, which he quickly implied with a couple of curves to denote the compression in the fabric.

He was working on the legs, her left up and bent at the knee to protect her modesty, when his phone rang.

Jax picked it up, expecting it to be Vince, whom he'd called countless times with no response. But the number was withheld and the voice in his ear was a stranger. "A mate of yours said to give you a call. You needed a delivery?"

"That's right."

The caller read out the address and Jax confirmed. "See you in ten," the voice said, then hung up.

While they'd been talking, he saw that he'd received a text. A rush of excitement faded to disappointment when he saw that it was not from Vince but rather his uncle.

"Fuck me," he muttered. The old fart rarely sent him messages apart from birthdays and Christmas, so this was unlikely to be good news.

The message was curt and to the point.

Come see me.
My place. Tomorrow. 8 a.m.

Don't be late.

"Fuck," he said, slamming down his pencil.

He considered pretending not to have seen the message, but dismissed the thought almost as soon as it had come. Only the suicidal would disobey a direct order from the General.

Annoyed at the unexpected summons, Jax went to the fridge for another beer. He popped the tab and took a large swallow.

After pondering for a moment, he decided he had it. The doddery cunt had heard about Danny and X-Ray, that's all. Most likely, he'd figure some rival set was taking out the *WEC* elders and would want to know what Jax planned to do about it... that, or Jax was going to get a bollocking for not keeping things quiet, if not both. The old fart preferred things discrete.

Jax scoffed as he took another swallow. "Running a mob on the down-low," he muttered. "Yeah. *Right.*"

He returned to his sketch. Over time, the tension began to drain from his neck, shoulders and stomach; his grip on the pencil lightened.

Jax picked his light-source, then began adding shadow to Gayle's face, neck, collar and under her breasts. He had never had a good look at them in real life, but decided they were about medium size and he gave them a sensuous upwards tilt that they probably lacked in reality. After all, was not the purpose of art to enrich and improve upon the mundane? He didn't know how to express that sentiment verbally, but armed with a pencil or brushes or pastels, he could represent it with something visual.

Shortly, his phone rang again and as before the number was withheld.

"Downstairs," the voice said and hung up.

He poked his head out the window. Below him was a man in a baseball cap, dark jeans and a Deliveroo backpack with a matching sports jacket. A bicycle was left on its side by the wall of the building.

Jax descended by the back stairs and crossed the narrow hallway with the dim bulb glowing overhead. He unlatched the door and the stranger looked at him, nodding his head in greeting. Saying nothing, Jax pushed open the door and backed up.

The stranger came in and shut the door behind him. When he followed Jax upstairs, he said, "I'm Rick."

Jax let them, closed the door and gestured towards the shabby leather settee.

"Tony gave me a bell," the Deliveroo cyclist said. "He told me you needed a strap."

"And ammo," Jax said.

"Of course." Rick took his large cube-shaped backpack off and laid it on the floor. He took a seat and unzipped it.

Jax had to give it to whoever procured guns for Tony Henry these days: posing as a Deliveroo guy was pretty smart. He watched the guy push aside bags of empty plastic containers and pull out a red-and-white checked tea-towel. He unwrapped it to reveal a silver snub-nosed revolver.

"Smith & Wesson .38 Special," Rick said. "Holds five rounds. Totally clean. Imported from Ireland. Serial number's filed off," he said, pointing at the stubby barrel. "Otherwise, fresh out the box, never used."

Jax nodded his approval. "Loaded?"

"Not yet. Here, try it for size," Rick said, picking it up with his little finger through the trigger guard. The gun tipped upside down as he held it out.

Jax took the revolver. The gun was small in his hand,

but the grip was comfortable and the weight of it felt reassuring. He turned his wrist, surveying the well-balanced weapon from every angle.

Rick went through the gun's features in just a couple of minutes. The .38 was as uncomplicated as could be.

Jax liked it. "How much?"

"Five," Rick said.

"Tone told you it's for me, right?"

Rick frowned, unsure what he meant.

"*Four*-fifty," Jax said.

"Come on, mate, I'm discounting it already. I can get five and a half for it anywhere."

"Then you should've, 'cause you'll only get four and a half from me."

Rick was quiet for a moment, sizing Jax up with a quick, furtive glance. He took a breath and released it, his shoulders sagging. "All right, all right. 'Cause Tony vouched for you."

He smiled. "Good to know he *vouched for me.* Bullets?"

"You got the money?"

Still holding the gun, Jax reached into his pocket for the cash he'd taken from Steph Doughty. He peeled off the money and put the remaining ninety-five back.

He gave the cash to Rick, who was reaching into his jacket pocket for a cardboard box of shells. He set the ammunition on the coffee table and shuffled quickly through the notes before stuffing the wad of cash into his back pocket.

"I'll let myself out," Rick said, putting his backpack on again. He opened the door and stepped over the threshold. "Happy hunting," he said, pulling the door closed.

Jax listened to the footsteps descend the stairs. At the

window, he watched Rick pick up his bicycle, pedal it to the end of the street and turn the corner.

He checked the ammo. The box contained twenty brass-jacketed lead rounds. The bullets were beautiful and lethal-looking. He loaded the revolver as he had been shown, taking care to keep his finger off the trigger. He pulled and locked the hammer back, watching the trigger move as if pulled by an invisible finger.

The gun felt like a living thing in his hand; like a coiled snake ready to strike.

He carefully lowered the hammer with his thumb, then took the gun over to the desk and laid it down. He took his seat and drank another swallow of the cold, refreshing beer. Jax resumed sketching, but from time to time, found himself looking up at the shiny, silver revolver.

He wanted to shoot something. He wanted to shoot *someone*.

Once he got hold of Gayle Stillwater, he wouldn't need all twenty bullets. He may not even need one, since he had no intention of killing her so quickly – unless it was absolutely unavoidable. The gun was to keep her under control.

All the same, he hoped he would have time and opportunity to try out the weapon. He could imagine the feel of it in his hand, bucking and sending a powerful shudder down the length of his arm.

He finished the beer and the sketch thirty minutes later. He blew away the eraser crumbs and leant back from the paper, looking at his work.

He admired his art for a moment or two before realising that he wasn't finished.

He sharpened the pencil again and began to sketch a slit into the fine and slender throat of the naked image under his hand. He followed the contours of her collar and breasts, belly and flanks, creating ribbons of blood that painted most of her chest. He was careful not to overdo the gore and ruin the detail underneath.

"There," he said aloud, setting down the pencil.

Jax was satisfied. His jacket hung on the back of his chair and he reached for the inside pocket now. He pulled out the photograph that he had taken from Gayle's photo album.

It had been taken in the summer. She and her boy were smiling, cheek to cheek, their eyes squinted against the sun. Ribbons of her auburn hair fluttered across Finn's forehead. The boy's smile was beaming. Gayle's was beatific.

Jax smiled too, remembering that all-too-brief feeling of excitement he had felt when breaking into her flat. It felt good to wander around her home, looking through her things. It gave him a sense of the domesticity that he had never really known and in fact had never really wanted before. But seeing the way that Gayle lived – among pictures that Finn had painted at school, family-friendly DVDs, even her simple but attractive underwear drying in the bathroom – he imagined it would be a good life to come home to. Of course, the bourgeoning fantasy didn't last long before he had to get down to business and try to find his money. He had even taken the red tin box to transport the cash home, but when he hadn't found his money or the gun – and after he had gone ballistic – he realised he no longer needed the cash box. And then, he had seen the photo album.

He remembered sitting on the bed for a while, looking through the pictures at the life that Danny had tried but failed to properly live.

He laid the snapshot beside his sketch. He compared it

to her real-life face and was pleased at how well he had captured her.

Jax took up the revolver with his index finger over the trigger guard. He tracked the muzzle of the .38 from the boy's face, to Gayle's, then to his slit-throated impression and back again.

Jax began to fantasise about what he was going to do to them when he finally caught up to them both.

If Vince ever picks up his fucking phone, Jax thought. He tried the useless prick again, but as every time before, he didn't answer.

Jax slammed the phone down. "All right," he muttered to himself. "Think."

Bristol, the message had said. But why Bristol? To the best of his memory, Danny had never mentioned the place.

He tried to remember everything he knew about Gayle, hoping to recall something useful – like perhaps she'd been born there or maybe had family or friends from that region. But that couldn't be it. Gayle was a Leicester girl, born and bred, and she had no family after being orphaned when her nutter of an old man was sent down for life.

Then it *had* to be Danny. And if not family, then friends. Danny's home life hadn't been much better than Gayle's. At least Gayle knew who her father was, whereas Danny – to the best of Jax's knowledge – had never met his own. And his relationship with his mother had always been rocky and—

Jax smiled.

That was it.

His *mother*. It was possible that Danny gave her the money, not because they themselves were close, but because she would have a relationship with the kid and would make sure he was provided for. Even if that wasn't the case and that lying bitch Gayle had his money, which Jax thought most likely, Danny's mum might know why she was running to Bristol of all places. The way women talked, he wouldn't put it past the pair of scheming bitches to cook up some way to keep the cash that Jax had worked so hard for.

And he knew where the old bag lived.

He checked his watch. It was late. Lorraine Gowan would probably be in bed already, sleeping beside her husband.

Jax thought about going there now, but the husband complicated things. Even with the gun, he didn't relish the thought of breaking in and trying to subdue two people. True, he could call on a couple of the lads to help out, but he dismissed that notion almost as soon as he thought of it: things would look too suspicious if they learned that their victim was Danny Gowan's mum. Of course, his early-morning summons to see the General meant that he couldn't make any immediate moves. Jax knew better than to risk being late or not turning up at all.

But *afterwards*, he would get straight on her trail.

Jax looked down the stubby barrel of the revolver, the muzzle aimed at the photograph. He squinted one eye and tracked the gun from the centre of her forehead to his drawing of her.

"I'll see you tomorrow," he said.

CHAPTER 23

When Bobbi rose from sleep early on Saturday morning, Gayle was already awake. She sat at the desk beside the TV, which was tuned to the BBC news but with the volume turned down. So far, national news carried nothing relating to her. The clock beside the crawler said it was 7:24 a.m.

"Is everything all right?" Bobbi whispered, rubbing her face.

"Writing a list," she said. "I'm sorry, I borrowed the little notepad from your handbag."

"Snoop," she yawned and kicked her legs free of the duvet. "How are you feeling?"

"Like shit. Everything hurts."

"I'll bet." Bobbi came over and bent down to get a closer look at the bruised scrape on Gayle's shoulder. "Jesus, did you get mauled by a tiger on top of everything else?"

"You should see the other guy," she said reflexively, regretting saying the words at once. The image of Vince's dying face was never far from her mind.

"What's on the list?"

Grateful for the change in subject, Gayle turned in the seat. "I need a favour. Finn and I are gonna need some clothes, maybe enough for a week or so, and I'll need some shoes. I've written down everything I can think of, if you don't mind picking it up for me?"

"No problem."

"And a bag of rice to put this in," she said, plucking her mobile off the desk. "And a compatible charger. I just hope it can be saved."

"I'll have a quick shower and head straight out."

"I think I've got enough cash left," Gayle said, but Bobbi waved off her concerns.

"Don't worry," she said, "I'll get everything. You never know – we might need cash in a hurry."

Gayle wanted to argue, but knew that Bobbi might have a good point. There was no way she could know for how long they might be running, and the meagre sum of cash that she carried would not last long as it was.

"Okay," she said. "I'll pay you back, somehow. And I wrote down our sizes on the back—"

Again, Bobbi waved her hands. "Don't need them," she said. "What kind of tailor do you think I'd be if I couldn't tell your size?"

With that, she took her bag to the bathroom and closed the door softly behind her. Moments later, Gayle heard water splashing into the sink.

As well as borrowing Bobbi's pen and notepad, she found packets of paracetamol and ibuprofen, which she always carried to combat the occasional pain in her elbow. Gayle took two of each with a glass of water, trying to knock down the headache with which she had awakened. She gingerly probed the graze on her temple, where a small lump had formed.

When Bobbi returned to the room, she was fresh-faced, dressed in yesterday's clothes but fully made-up with her hair untied. She took the list when Gayle held it out for her.

"One more thing," Gayle said, stopping Bobbi before she could turn. She had collected her soiled clothes from the bathroom already, and reached into her cargo pants for the collapsible baton. She held it out to Bobbi. "Put this in your bag where you can get to it, just in case."

"Where the hell did you get this?" Bobbi asked too loud, then looked to Finn. He grumbled in his sleep, rolled over, but didn't open his eyes.

"I'll feel better knowing you've got some kind of protection," Gayle said. "Don't be gone too long, okay?"

Bobbi searched her eyes for a moment, then nodded. "I'll be quick as I can."

Less than an hour and half later, she returned, weighed down by a large plastic carrier bag and three branded paper bags from Primark. She dropped everything on the carpet, bumping the door shut with her backside.

Finn was already awake, sitting in his pants and vest on the double bed, drinking a glass of lukewarm Coke from the litre bottle that had come with the pizzas. "What did you buy me, Auntie Bobbi?" he asked.

"A big tube of glue," she said, "so your crazy hair won't keep sticking up."

"My hair isn't crazy. *Yours* is."

Gayle made two mugs of coffee while Bobbi unpacked the plastic bag. Inside was a pair of plain black Skechers and an ankle support strap, both in Gayle's size. She produced a kilogram back of long-grain rice, tipped a cupful into the small waste-bin by the desk, and handed it to Gayle.

She picked up her malfunctioning mobile and slipped it

inside, pushing it all the way inside until it was completely covered, then secured the bag with its sticky label.

Once the coffees were done, Gayle took her bag of clothes into the bathroom. Bobbi had picked out half a dozen T-shirts, two pairs of jeans, leggings, a bulky jumper, plain underwear, a pair of gloves and a scarf, as per the list.

She put on the underwear, black jeans, a grey T-shirt and royal-blue jumper. As she had been assured it would be, everything was a perfect fit. She slipped on the ankle support and shoes, wincing when she moved the tender joint.

When she returned to the living room, Finn was dressed in jeans and a red T-shirt with a cartoon dog on the front. He picked up his Batman wallet and stuffed it into the front pocket.

When Bobbi went to change, Gayle sat beside her son on the settee. She kissed the crown of his head.

"Did Bobbi tell you where we're going?" she asked.

"Nope. Where?"

"We're going to see Uncle Aled on his farm."

Finn cocked an eyebrow. "Uncle Aled?" he said, as if he had never heard of the man. "He sends me those gross jumpers but you make me tell him I wear them all the time."

Gayle just smiled. "That's him."

Finn shrugged. "All right."

When Bobbi returned in a black blouse and cropped jeans, Gayle had already packed their things into the Primark bags. "All set?" she asked.

"We are now," Gayle said, slipping the switchblade into her right rear pocket.

She followed Bobbi and Finn, limping along the hallway with one of the bags. As Finn walked, he ran his fingers along the wall, thumping off the doorframes he passed. Even with the ankle support, Gayle found the walk taxing. By the time they boarded the lift for the ground floor, she explained that Bobbi was going to have to do the driving because working the clutch would be too painful.

A fierce, biting wind swept across the Travelodge car-park, buffeting Gayle's back and chilling her thighs and backside, even threatening to rip the bag she carried.

Once inside, she gave Bobbi the address for Aled's farm, which she keyed into her phone's sat nav.

"We'll be there by eleven," Bobbi said. She started the engine and backed out of the parking space.

Jax piloted the Ford Focus between the eight-foot-tall pillars at the roadside and drove down the long, white spar-gravel drive. The lawns either side were immaculately tended, as if gardeners armed with rulers and scissors checked it each morning.

Hedges and flowerbeds surrounded the massive main house, set within with picturesque countryside near Leicestershire's Swithland Woods. Ivy climbed a trellis that reached the third floor's wrap-around panoramic windows. The dawning sunlight glinted off the glass, obscuring the inside from view. The front door was a large oak panel between a pair of two-storey windows, through which Jax could see the grand entrance foyer and the stairs leading to the second floor.

To the left of the building was a large conservatory, almost as wide as the house itself, where the pool and racquetball court were located. To Jax's right, set away from the house, was a five-bay garage, clad in the same polished limestone panels as the façade of the house itself. Half a dozen cars and four horse-boxes were parked outside it on the spar-gravel, along with a white Mercedes Sprinter, modified to allow for wheelchair access at the side and the rear.

A staff of four adults in high-vis vests with blue lanyards tended to six children, none of whom looked older than twelve, helping to get them astride a group of Cleveland Bays. Each of the horses wore blinkers over their eyes and their silky black manes shone in the morning sun.

Jax stopped the car beside one of the empty horse-boxes and got out. From atop his mount, a sandy-haired kid with Down's Syndrome spotted Jax and gave him a wave. He didn't wave back, but crunched over the gravel, ignoring the smell of horseshit, heading for the front door when a voice stopped him.

He turned and saw his uncle climb out from a Land Rover hitched to one of the horse-boxes. Uncle Felix wore black loafers without socks, cream chinos and a white V-neck sweatshirt, the sleeves of which were rolled up to his elbows. He closed one eye against the sun, his butterscotch skin wrinkling almost to his ear, showing his perfect veneers in a wide smile. His receding hair was cropped close, almost bald, and the white of the one eye regarding Jax was yellowing. His lower lip wobbled when he spoke, which aside from a slight shuffle in his walk was the only sign of Parkinson's.

"Good to see you, young man," Felix said, taking Jax's hand in both of his. "How was the drive?"

Jax tried not to look down at the old man's soft hands. On his right, he had six fingers; a vestigial digit without bone jutted out from the meat beside the little finger.

"Fine," he said. "You wanted to talk to me?"

Felix clapped him on the shoulder. "Of course, of course, but that can wait. Come say 'hello'."

Jax let himself be led back to the horses. Two were saddled but were without riders. For a moment, he was afraid the old fart would insist on a trot around the property, but Felix reached out a gentle hand and stroked the horse's neck. The horse issued a soft snort.

Through the gap in its blinkers, Jax saw the long-lashed eyes watching him. The Bay took a step back, but Felix took hold of its bridle and shushed it. The horse whinnied but began to relax under the old man's touch.

"There, there," he cooed in his soft Antiguan lilt. "Isn't she beautiful?"

Jax had no particular interest in horses, aside from seeing a pony-show video that one of the lads had sent him, which he found equal parts hilarious and horrifying. Deciding not to comment, he just shrugged.

Uncle Felix stroked the mare's nose and it lowered its big head, pushing into his hand. The animal seemed not to care about the old man's gross deformity. Felix fussed and complimented the horse, then leant forward and kissed it on what Jax assumed was the thing's cheek.

He shuffled his feet and dug his hands deeper into his pockets.

"I like to organise these rides a couple times a week," Felix said. "The horses are such good therapy for the kids."

One of the adults – a mannish blonde in her forties with a mole on the side of her nose – looked over from where she stood, guiding a child's foot into the stirrup. "And it's very much appreciated, Mr Knox," she said, her voice surprisingly girly. "The help you've given to the school after all these years... I don't know where we'd be without you, truly."

"Not at all," the old man assured her. "It's a pleasure. The only t'ing I love more than horses are children. My wife and I couldn't have any – bless her soul. Breast cancer. Almost five years ago now."

"How's the new one working out?" Jax asked, hiding his smile.

Ignoring the jab, Felix said, "Oh, Belinda's doing just fine. She's handling my meetings wit' the foundation today. We'll tell her 'hello' before you leave." To the blonde, Felix said, "I guess I'll leave you to it. You all know the route to my stables?"

Jax knew about the horse farm on the other side of Woodhouse Eaves, though had never been there himself.

The blonde nodded. "Yes, thank you."

"Well," he said to the kids, "I hope you all have a lovely day. There's sandwiches and refreshments waitin' for you. Take care now."

He took a step back and took Jax by the elbow. "Walk wit' me, boy."

They crunched over the gravel, though not towards the house but to the conservatory. The chatter of voices behind them faded as they walked.

"How's your mother?" Felix asked.

"She's all right," Jax said.

"Good. I always liked that woman. You give her my best."

The large conservatory had tinted windows and a sliding door. Jax found that it was almost completely sound-proof when Felix slid the door aside and loud pop music washed over them. They stepped inside and closed the door.

The warm air inside the conservatory was heavy. To his left, Jax saw the sixty-foot pool gently ripple with sparks of sunlight. Ahead and to the right was a well-equipped home gym, where Belinda Knox stood in a baby-blue sports-bra and Lycra shorts, doing curtsy lunges while holding a pair of four kilo kettlebells. He tried not to stare at her well-built arse.

Felix walked up beside her before she noticed him. Belinda lowered the weights and turned off the music with a small remote control. She bent at the waist and, with her duck-lips, planted a soft kiss on his mouth.

Your Skype meetings got cancelled, obviously, Jax thought but didn't say.

"My nephew's here," Felix said, gesturing towards Jax.

She turned and gave him a wave and a broad smile. "Nice to see you, sweetheart," she said with the voice of a Disney fairy. At only twenty-five, she had a face loaded with filler.

"Be a darlin' and fetch me a cup of tea," Felix said. "Drink, Jax?"

"You have a Coke?"

"With ice?" she asked.

Jax nodded.

"Coming right up," Belinda said and headed for the door leading to the main house.

Felix watched her go, licking his lips. When they were alone, he said, "Let me tell you, boy, you wanna know the secret to eternal youth? Twenty-five-year-old pussy, four times a week."

"I'll remember that."

"You got a woman yet?"

Jax thought of Steph, but said, "No, no one serious."

"Get one. Fuck hard, fuck fast, fuck often."

"I'll remember that."

Felix led them around the pool to a wicker patio set in the shade of a cluster of potted palms. He eased into the love-seat, crossing his legs at the knees, right over left. Jax perched on the edge of the armchair, looking back over his shoulder. From here, he could see that all the riders were now astride their mounts, crunching along the driveway to the country lane.

"You haven't been to see me in a while," Felix said.

"I've been busy," Jax said, thinking to himself, *Not like I have a fuckin' open-invite anyway, do I, Uncle Felix?*

"You're filling out," the old man said. "You were skinnier when I saw you last."

Again, Jax shrugged. In general, he was untroubled by nerves, but the insipid small-talk made him uncomfortable. The old fart's pretentions of civility, manners and familial concern were draining. They both knew there was a reason for the summons, and Jax would rather they just get to it.

"How's things with you?" Jax asked, cracking his fingers with the thumb of the same hand.

"No complaints. We're thinkin' of goin' back to Antigua for Christmas. Couple of weeks in the sun."

"Sounds nice."

"Belinda's never been. Thought it might be nice to show her where all this started, you know?"

"Why did you want to see me?"

Felix sucked in his wobbling lower lip, cocked his head and tutted. "You're an ill-mannered young brute, you know it? Business," he said, planting both feet, "waits for drinks."

"I thought business waits for no man."

"That's *time*."

"And time is money."

Felix smiled. "Funny you should say that."

"Why?"

"Patience, boy." Felix rolled his neck as if working out some stiffness.

Jax was not dressed for the warmth in the conservatory. He unzipped his black bomber jacket and blotted his forehead with the back of his hand. Like a lizard, his uncle sat in quiet contentment, soaking up the heat. His six fingers splayed out across his right knee.

Neither of them spoke for close to five minutes until Belinda returned with their drinks on a silver tray. She had dressed in a silver silk blouse, form-fitting black trousers and kitten heels that revealed her pink-painted toes. Her perky tits strained against the silk and her curled hair bounced as she walked.

She laid the tray down on the table between them, sliding an iced glass of cola towards Jax and placing a teacup with saucer before Felix, followed by a small teapot and a small jug of milk.

"I can make sandwiches," she said, looking to Jax. "Or we have bacon."

"That stuff isn't bacon," Felix insisted, face twisted with disgust.

"It's bacon *substitute*. It's better for you and it tastes just as good."

He dismissed the notion with a wave of his hand, then reached for the teapot.

"Nothing for me, thanks," Jax said.

"All rightee," she smiled, then kissed Felix on the butterscotch dome of his head.

Jax watched his uncle trace his hand up the inside of Belinda's thigh before she turned away and carried the tray back to the house. Her trousers could have been painted onto the firm rounds of her buttocks as she swished away.

Jax lifted his glass and drained half the coke. The fizzy stuff was ice-cold and good on his parched throat.

As Felix lightened his tea and stirred the brew, he said, "What you remember 'bout what I always told you?"

"About what, Uncle Felix?"

"'Bout keeping t'ings *low-key*. 'Bout keeping t'ings *quiet*."

"I'm trying."

"Two of our boys are dead. Does that sound low-key to you?" He sat back and raised the cup to his lip.

"No," Jax admitted. "But I'm on top of that."

Felix eyed him carefully. "Who did it?" His smoky voice had hardened, become cold.

Jax scratched his left cheek, repressing the smirk that tickled that corner of his mouth. "I got my ear to the ground," he said, "and it looks like it might've been *South Siders*."

Felix's eyes narrowed. "There's not many of them left."

"Most of the original elders have been put away, but immigrants have moved in and taken the name as their own."

"Who's their General now?"

"A Polish lad, Stefan Sokolik. They call him 'Solo'. His yard's out Knighton way."

Felix turned away, eyes closed, facing up at the ceiling. He was quiet for so long that he seemed to have nodded off.

Jax waited him out.

When Felix at last opened his eyes, he said, "Polish, eh? I don't know much about those Polish boys. What you hear about this Solo?"

"He's serious. He's done time, here and in Warsaw."

"This is bad news, Jackson. You understand me? I can't have this."

"I'm on it, Uncle Felix."

"No," he said, raising his voice for the first time. His right hand was fisted on his knee, the vestigial digit almost pointing at Jax. "No, you ain't *'on it'*, boy. If you was *'on it'*, you'd have buried this bloodclot by now." His accent grew more pronounced with his anger. He opened his fist and held up his fingers in a V. "Two of our boys, Jax. *Two* of them. Ain't you learned *not'in'*? I didn't build up this business to just let no Polish bumbaclot outfit fuck wit' me."

Jax stayed quiet.

Felix tutted. *"I'm on it,"* he whined. "Who you t'ink you are? You're just a *Captain*, boy. Remember who started this organisation. Before me, this city just had a bunch of kids all rippin' one another off, stabbin' each other in the ass. I built the *conglomerate*. No one else had the ambition. No one else dared. People warned me not to make my own nephew a Captain. God knows, your father would be rollin' in his grave. Did I make a mistake? Are you goin' soft?"

"I never traded off my name, Uncle Felix," Jax said, keeping his tone even. "And I've made a lot of money for you over the years."

Felix sighed. "But when you let this kind of fuckery go on, it makes me look weak, and I *won't* have that. On your watch, I've had my businesses attacked and now someone t'inks they can just kill two of your soldiers. And you – my *captain* – ain't got it handled."

"You're wrong about that, Uncle Felix. I know who knocked over Fat Joe's. Or, at least, I know who has his money now."

"Who?" Felix asked, leaning forwards, his elbows on his knees. He steepled his fingers – all except the gummy sixth digit of his right hand.

"Gayle Stillwater."

He thought for a moment before saying, "I don't know the name. Who is she?"

"She used to run with us. She was Danny Gowan's sket back in the day, but the way I figure it, she got shacked up with Solo, hit Fat Joe's, and pointed out Danny and X-Ray to get merked. She always was a devious cunt."

"And *she's* got my money?"

Jax nodded.

"Where is she now?"

"She's running. But I've got some of the boys following her," Jax lied. "And as soon as I leave here, I'm gonna catch up with that bitch. I'll make her pay, Uncle Felix. You can count on it."

Felix reached for his teacup and eased back into his seat. He raised the brew to his mouth and took a sip, wiping his moist lip on the back of the same hand. He rested the cup on his knee. "I want this dealt with now, *today*, or else it don't matter how much I loved your father, *you're* gonna have to pay the price."

As a rule, Jax didn't feel fear. He didn't have a death-wish, of course, and didn't enjoy pain in spite of having a high tolerance for it. His reluctance to be beaten up or to die didn't exactly equate to a fear of either, but he supposed that this right now was as close to terror as he could experience.

As the seconds stretched between them and Felix stared with unblinking eyes, it occurred to Jax for the first time that someone might not believe his lies. On the heels of that thought, he realised that if he was unable to convince his uncle, he was a dead man. Blood or no blood, Felix would have him killed – not here, not now, but soon, as surely as night followed day.

He knew he should be shaking; knew he should feel the

cold sweat of fear; knew that others in his position would be losing bladder control, or dropping to their knees to beg for forgiveness. But Jax felt none of that. All he felt was an iron-hard determination to be believed, so that he could go and do what he had set his mind to do.

At last, Felix broke eye contact. "You know, you got the devil in you, boy."

Jax didn't say anything. The glass had gone warm in his hand.

"Okay. You go get my money from this Gayle Stillwater. Then we deal with Solo. You got two days."

Taking that as his cue to leave, Jax nodded and stood. He turned and headed for the sliding door, feeling his uncle's eyes on him the whole way.

"One thing else," the voice said behind him.

Jax stopped. He turned.

"I want her alive. You bring her to me with the money."

Jax nodded and turned back to the door. With every step, he expected to feel a bullet slamming into his back, knocking him to the floor, but he gripped the handle and slid the door aside. He stepped into the cold morning air and got behind the wheel.

On the road again, he fired up a cigarette and blew a lungful of smoke out the half-open window.

Reflecting back on their conversation, he was unconvinced that Felix had believed his lies, either about Gayle having the money or Solo executing Gowan and X-Ray. That there was any doubt at all accounted for his giving Jax the benefit of the doubt.

Two days, he thought.

But bringing Gayle back alive was not an option: if Felix questioned her instead of killing her outright, he might believe the bitch over his own nephew. In that instance, Jax couldn't count on familial loyalty being enough to save him from a bullet in the head.

To Jax, that meant only one thing: when he was done with Gayle, he was going to have to take out his uncle as well.

CHAPTER 24

Bobbi drove out of Bristol on the M4 and along the Prince of Wales bridge across the River Severn. The rippling water reflected the cold grey of the cloud-choked sky. In the distance, Gayle saw the snow-white sail of a small boat, its dark maroon hull breaking the calm surface.

A short while later, they left the bridge and the M4 opened up to three lanes. They passed a sign welcoming them to Wales.

"Someone wrote that funny," Finn said, frowning through the window.

Smiling in spite of the headache that had not yet faded, Gayle said, "It's Welsh."

"People here can't speak English?"

"They do, but they have their own language too."

Finn was quiet for a moment, pondering this.

North of Cardiff, they left the M4 for the A470. They passed signs for places named Castle Coch, Merthyr Tydfil and Ffynnon Taf.

Bobbi said, "And people say Yoruba is a strange language."

"What's that?" Finn piped up from the back.

"It's a Nigerian language," she said. "I haven't spoken it much since I was your age."

Traffic began to slow as they approached Pontypridd. All along the left side of the road, houses were set into the hillside and on their right, sloping green valleys swept down and away into the distance.

Bobbi followed the directions through the centre of town, along residential streets which gave way to narrow country lanes that wound through the Welsh hillside, over-hung with bare tree limbs and snarls of high hedges.

Gayle's headache had not faded and she took two more paracetamol with the remnants of a lukewarm bottle of water Bobbi had left in the cup-holder. She lowered the window a crack to let in a little fresh air, which although clean and refreshing nonetheless felt heavy with impending rainfall.

"Are you okay?" Bobbi asked.

"I feel a little sick," Gayle said, leaning back against the headrest.

"We're almost there. You want me to stop anyway?"

"No," she said. "It's just nerves. I keep wondering, what if I'm wrong? What if there's nothing here? Even if Danny did send a package, what if it's nothing important?"

Bobbi patted her knee. "We'll find out pretty soon."

Gayle looked back over her shoulder. The drive was making Finn yawn.

Ten minutes later, she leaned forwards to re-centre Google Maps on Bobbi's phone, which was pinned to the heater vents. "This is it," she said. "Next right."

Bobbi slowed the Fiat. The lane was empty in both directions. She indicated and slowed to a crawl.

The farm had a wide D-shaped entrance to allow for

the turning circles of farm vehicles entering or exiting the property. The large wooden gate was open. Bobbi pulled off the road and the tyres crunched on the long gravel driveway.

Two-hundred yards away, the old grey stone farmhouse stood out from the green fields and bare, tilled earth, reminding Gayle of the ancient vertical columns at Stonehenge. Beside the front door was a slope-roofed wood-store the size of a three-seat settee, filled with chopped logs and kindling, and on the left flank stood a diesel generator. An old, gnarled tree stood at a crooked angle fifteen feet from there, at whose foot lay a pile of discarded machine and engine parts.

To the far left was a barn. It too stood at odd angles, though did not look as solidly-constructed as the house. It had been painted with bright red wood-stain at one point, but that had faded to a dark maroon. A tractor stood vacant in the bare earth between the two buildings, as if it had died on the way and would not be moved.

The Fiat rocked along the uneven path. As winter began to tighten its hold on the countryside, the otherwise picturesque landscape was turning cold and stark.

A shiver wormed its way through Gayle's guts and her trepidation grew.

Bobbi leaned over the steering wheel. "It's pretty," she said, "in a... *barren* kinda way."

When she reached the end of the gravel path, Bobbi angled the nose of the car towards the old tree. She set the handbrake and killed the engine.

"*This* is where uncle Aled lives?" Finn asked.

"Yeah, this is it," Gayle said, taking off her seatbelt.

Finn rubbed at his nose with the back of his wrist, unimpressed.

"Give me a second," Gayle said and opened the door. She got out and tested her footing on the gravel, before limping slowly towards the front door.

When she was ten feet away, it opened inwards with a groan of old wood. Dressed in a thick green jumper and well-worn jeans, Aled stood in the threshold. Although he had to be sixty by now, it was difficult to tell simply by looking at him: with his weathered face, thick mop of silver hair and wiry, greying beard, he could have been a decade younger or a decade older than his true age. In the doorway, he was tall enough that he had to stoop at the shoulders.

His expression was not as she had expected. She anticipated surprise or shock or worry – even anger – but his countenance was more blank than anything. In his right hand, he held a shotgun by the barrel at chest-height.

"How are you, Aled?" she asked.

Aled nodded slowly. "Gayle," he said by way of a greeting.

"Do you usually answer the door with a gun?"

"I do now," he said. He looked past her, at the lane from which they had come, then lowered the gun, storing it out of sight behind the doorframe. "I was expecting you, but not so soon."

She turned back to the Fiat. Bobbi had wound down her window, but neither she nor Finn had gotten out yet.

Turning back to Aled, she saw that he still surveyed the farm's entrance and the hedgerows between his land and the country lane with suspicion.

In a much stronger Welsh accent than Lorraine's, he said, "I think you'd better come in."

* * *

The houses on Highfield Road were mostly detached and semi-detached properties with three or four bedrooms. Some had lawns or small flower-gardens, but few if any were gated.

It had been a couple of years since Danny told Jax about his mother remarrying, but he found the place with little trouble. He smiled to himself as he remembered roasting the bastard about his new step-dad.

The detached house was on a corner plot with a well-kept triangular garden shaded by a large tree, which was bare now in the cold afternoon air. The cars parked on the pavements were mostly estates and SUVs. A silver Nissan X-Trail sat in Lorraine's driveway.

He chewed on his thumbnail, looking the place over. She seemed to be doing pretty well for herself now; not living the high life, but a long way from the council houses of Braunstone.

He turned off the engine and plucked the revolver from his jacket pocket, tucking it away in the glove compartment. He got out of the dark red Ford Focus and headed up the path.

To his right was a white garage door with a carriage lantern between it and the glass-paned front door. On his left was a large window with flowers on the sill. The wall was partially stone-clad from the ground to the bottom of the first-floor window. A tabby cat sat dozing behind the glass.

At the door, Jax checked his breath and rang the bell. He shuffled his feet, returning his hands to his pockets. He peeked at the window, looking for the tell-tale flutter of a curtain, but saw nothing.

After a moment, he rang the bell again. Through the bevelled glass, he saw a figure approach. The door opened inwards and a woman in her fifties regarded Jax with a half-smile.

"Can I help you?" she asked. She had a faint accent that he couldn't quite place. Her dark hair was dyed with reddish highlights and tied in a loose ponytail. She wore straight-cut jeans and green gardening Crocs. She had on a white tank top with dirt stains on the front and no bra over her small, drooping breasts.

"I'm sorry to bother you," Jax said, "but my car died and my little boy's crying. I don't suppose your husband's got jump leads?"

The woman shook her head. "No, my husband's at work—"

Jax shoved her hard and she stumbled, tripping over her own feet. She fell back in a heap on the carpet. He closed the door and, before she could react, Jax was on her, one hand covering her mouth, his other gripping her ponytail. "Hello?" he called out. "Anyone home?" He hoisted her to her feet, waiting, listening.

He heard nothing; not even the television or radio.

To his left, he saw the living room. Ahead was the kitchen and the conservatory extension. The door was open to the back garden, where he supposed she had been pottering around with plants when he rang the bell. On the right was a staircase with a dark-stained wooden balustrade. The cream carpet was clean and soft.

Jax spun her around, keeping his hand clamped tightly over her mouth, but wrapping his free arm around her neck. He held her tight. Against his chest, he could feel her trembling. Her warm breath blasted against his thumb.

He tried again. "Hello? We need help."

No voices. No movement.

"You're alone?" Jax asked, whispering anyway.

The woman nodded.

"If you scream, I'm gonna hurt you. If you're quiet, I'll ask you a few questions and leave. Understand?"

She nodded.

"What's your name?" Jax asked, lowering his hand to her slim throat. He felt the pulse pounding against his palm.

"Lorraine," she said.

"Lorraine Gowan?"

"Not anymore. Who are you?"

Jax slapped his hand over her mouth again and at the same time, let go of her with his left arm, slamming a punch into her kidney. She squealed, bending at the waist, trying to fall, but Jax yanked her upright again.

"Danny was your fuckin' son, yeah?"

She nodded.

"Who's your new husband?"

When Jax moved his hand, she said, "Jason Church. He's doing half a day, so you need to—"

He covered her mouth again. "I'm Jax. Danny's friend. Well, we *were* friends. Do you know my name?"

After a hesitation, Lorraine nodded.

Jax smiled. "Where's the living room?"

Lorraine pointed to the door immediately to the left of them.

"I think we should sit down, don't you? Have a chat."

He pushed her through the doorway into the cosy living room. A TV was bolted to the wall above the fireplace, in front of which was a round glass-topped coffee table with a pair of two-seat settees either side of it. Jax pushed her into the farthest one so he could see the front window and the street beyond. He saw no one watching, but knew he couldn't dawdle.

Jax sat beside Lorraine, his knee on the seat cushion,

pushing her against the armrest. She tried not to meet his eyes. They were darting around the room, no doubt looking for something that she could use to defend herself. She still had the shakes and the muscles in her jaw bunched together.

"Danny stole my money," he said. "I want it back. If you tell me where it is, I'll leave. But if you lie or fuck me about, I'll hurt you."

She licked the corner of her dry mouth and said, "I understand. He didn't give me anything, but you can—"

Jax slapped both hands over her mouth, grinding the back of her head into the armrest. He pushed up on his feet for more leverage and dropped a knee into her stomach. Under his hands, she squealed, but quickly grew silent again. He felt her straining to suck in a breath through his fingers.

"You heard me say *'don't lie'*, didn't you?"

He loosened his grip. "I'm not lying. The last time I saw him, it was August."

Jax drilled her with his eyes.

She matched his stare. Hers was forthright, her eyes very wide and with no trace of tears.

"He didn't give you my money?" Jax asked.

"No. I promise."

"What about Gayle? Does she have it?"

"Gayle?" Lorraine asked, frowning. "No. Of course not."

"How do you know?"

"Well, I... I just *know*."

"You two talk much?" he asked, still driving into her stomach with his knee. He braced himself with his left hand on the settee's armrest, the other held loose around her throat.

"A few times a month," Lorraine said, the pain evident in her voice. She tried to adjust herself, but Jax kept her still with a hard slap across the face.

He leant in, hissing, "Then why's she going to Bristol?"

"What? I don't—"

"Where's my fuckin' *money*?"

"I don't know," she whispered, "I swear to God, I don't."

Jax shoved her deeper into the settee. Lorraine's eyes bulged, face starting to go red. He wanted to drive his thumbs into her wide, defiant, staring eyes and blind her. He wanted to tear the house apart and burn it to cinders. He wanted, more than anything, for Danny Gowan to still be alive so that he could break every bone in his body, twist off his stupid head and crush it beneath his foot.

With unbelievable willpower, he forced himself to loosen his grip on Lorraine's throat. His handprint was visible in the wrinkled flesh of her neck. Her lower lip was split and oozed blood.

"Please," she managed to say.

Jax took a few deep breaths, his hands hovering in the air above her face, unsure whether to choke her or punch her or gouge out her eyes.

"I gotta think this through," Jax said, forcing his voice level. He inhaled. Exhaled. Inhaled again. "You're not lying, are you?"

Lorraine shook her head. Those large, staring eyes of hers were bulging, pleading wordlessly with him, but were not weeping. In a strange way, he admired her for that.

"He didn't give you my money. He didn't *give* it to anyone, did he? I know all the same people he knows and none of them would cross me for him." As Jax spoke, he ran his hands over Lorraine's face. He smoothed out the wrinkles in her forehead with his thumbs, then lifted up her eyelids, pulling back her lips from her teeth. He tapped her cheek with his palm in an almost friendly manner.

At last, a solitary tear formed in the corner of her left eye, shimmered there for a moment, then spilled down her cheek.

Jax thumbed the sudden wetness, running it back towards her ear, then brought his hand to his mouth and tasted the salty moisture on the pad of his thumb.

He said, "So, he didn't *give* the money to anyone. What do you do with money you can't hide and when you can't trust anyone to hold it for you?" Jax started to laugh. "You know what he did? That little cunt fucking *posted* it, didn't he? But not to Gayle, 'cause that's obvious. He knew I'd check her out and she didn't have it. He didn't trust that fat little whore he was bangin' either. And if he sent it to you, you'd have told me, wouldn't you?"

Lorraine didn't say anything. She didn't move.

Jax moved his hands over Lorraine's shoulders, squeezing, then brought his left back up to cup over her mouth as his right roamed over her small, sagging breasts. He kneaded the right one hard, twisting it and pushing down against her mouth to suppress the scream. She tried to fight him off, but he slapped her again, hard. She stopped resisting.

"So," Jax continued, "there's someone *else* Danny trusts who I don't know about. Any ideas?"

Beneath him, Lorraine cast a glance at the fireplace, then – as if catching herself – squinted her eyes shut. When she opened them, she stared at Jax. Her proud, defiant eyes were at last bejewelled with fat tears.

He glanced over at the fireplace. He hadn't noticed the framed photographs on the mantelpiece before, but his eyesight was perfect and he made out the faces with ease.

In one photo, a child of around three or four was cuddling a floppy-eared beagle pup. Jax recognised at once the younger Finn Gowan.

The second picture was much older by perhaps twenty years. In front of a non-descript brick wall, Lorraine was bleach-blonde, wrinkle-free and smiling behind a pair of sunglasses. In front of her, Jax saw Danny at age seven or eight, also smiling at the camera, eyes squinted in the sun. On the other side of him was a tall man, lean-faced, with a head of thick brown hair and a mole above his left eyebrow. All three wore rugby jerseys with the Welsh dragon on the chest.

Jax frowned. "Fucking Rugby League," he muttered. "Danny loved that shit. Had to twist his arm to watch football. And he supported the Tigers, but every time the Five Nations came around, he always put money on Wales. I never thought to ask why."

He looked down at Lorraine, who was still looking off to the side. He struck her once more to bring her eyes back to his.

"Who's that guy?" Jax said. "Danny never met his dad, you cheap slapper, so who is it?"

The eyes, he thought, as he gazed down at Lorraine. He knew those eyes and he knew that stare. They were like Danny's. They regarded Jax with the same look in them, that same pride and self-confidence.

He looked over at the photo of the boy and the beagle. The fucking son had inherited those same dark brown eyes. The man with the Welsh rugby jersey... his eyes were also large, direct and precisely the same shade of brown.

And it all clicked into place.

Jax smiled and lowered his face to Lorraine. He turned her face to the side and whispered in her ear, "Well, that makes sense now. He wouldn't send my money somewhere local where I could find it, not when he could send it to some sheep-shagging *uncle*, right? And isn't Bristol near Wales? So, why don't you tell me where uncle Gareth lives?"

Lorraine shoved against Jax, knocking him off balance, whipping out a hand and scratched his face. He stumbled until the back of his knee struck the coffee table. He squatted down, splaying his hands out behind him. He caught himself on the glass top, but it didn't shatter.

She was on her feet, already running past him, dodging around the settee and making for the door.

Jax shoved himself up and raced after her. She was quick, already at the exit, but Jax was faster and slammed into her, throwing her face-first into the wood. She fell in a heap and he grabbed her by the hair, wrapping his hand around her mouth before she could scream. She bit at his palm, whipping her head back and forth to get at him. He sidestepped, throwing her back over his outstretched leg. She crashed down onto the floor, striking her head with a sickening *smack*. He started to laugh as he saw her eyes swimming, straining to focus, then she went still. He watched her chest gently rise and fall. Out cold.

Jax dragged her by her wrists down the hallway and into the large kitchen. It was designed in a U-shape with white and black tiles, stainless-steel appliances and a huge American-style fridge-freezer. The view into the kitchen from the nearest house was obscured by a patio canopy over the window above the sink.

After a quick look around, Jax found a tea-towel hanging by a hook on the wall by the oven. He pulled it down and selected a four-inch knife from the block beside the kettle. He made an incision in one and then tore it lengthwise, stopping three inches short of the end, nearly doubling its length. He did the same to another tea-towel that he found in a drawer by the sink. He stepped over to Lorraine, rolled her onto her belly and tied her hands behind her back with one, leaving the other on the floor in case he needed to gag her.

He squatted on the floor to her right, feeling his face where she had scratched him. He checked his reflection in the polished side of the blade in his hand. He had a red mark above his eyebrow, a smaller one on his cheek and a cut on his lower lip. He licked at it and although it was sore, it was barely weeping when he pressed the back of his hand to it.

He shook her by the shoulder in an effort to bring her round, but it was no use.

Jax got to his feet and went to the sink. He took a mug from the mug-tree against the wall and ran the cold tap. Filling it with water, he drank some on his way back to the unconscious woman. He got to his knees by Lorraine's head. Her eyelashes fluttered but did not open.

Jax threw the water into her face.

She didn't splutter and come round at once, as he had seen people do in movies, but instead frowned and groaned as she tried to turn onto her back.

Jax put down the mug and held her in place. The knife lay within reach but he left it where it was.

He tapped Lorraine's cheek, slowly bringing her back to her senses. By the time her eyes steadied and could focus again, Jax had all but run out of patience.

"Wakey wakey," he said. "It's nearly over. What's your brother's name? Where does he live?"

Lorraine groaned again. She started to strain at the tea-towel binding her wrists.

He watched the muscles in her upper arms flutter and pull taut. His eyes followed the curve of her flexing triceps, wondering where the tendon was located and what would happen to the muscle if he sliced through it. He could imagine it snapping back up her arm like a spring, bunching under the skin below her shoulder.

"Tell me your brother's name," Jax said in as reasonable a tone as he could muster. "And where he lives. And then I'll go. Really, I'm gettin' annoyed now."

"Go fuck yourself," she said, her voice croaky.

Jax almost laughed. He reached for the second tea-towel, gagging her mouth, then picked up the knife. He cut off the little finger of her right hand. Blood squirted from the wound, staining the back of her white tank top and oozing over the floor between them. Jax plopped the slim digit on the tiles in front of her face. He waited until she stopped screaming through the gag, then pried her slippery hand open and cut off the next finger in line.

A moment or two later, he lowered the gag and – through sobs and groans of agony – she told him that Aled Gowan lived on a farm some fifteen miles or so south-east of Pontypridd. Jax removed a third finger, but Lorraine didn't change her story.

He stood over her writhing body, weighing up his options. He wanted to take the knife and cut out her eyes, but didn't have time for that.

He told her to face him and she was in too much pain to defy him again. She turned her head, eyes cast up to look at him.

"I just want you to know," Jax told her, "that I'm gonna kill all of 'em."

Those fucking eyes, he thought. *They're crying now.*

Jax spread his feet, placed his balance on the ball of his

left foot and slammed his right into her face. Her head snapped back and the force half-turned her onto her side. He kicked her until she was silent and unmoving, then washed his hands, dried them on the backs of his jeans and went back to the car.

"Ponty-fuckin'-pridd," he muttered, shaking his head. He checked Google Maps and confirmed his suspicion: Bristol was right there, just across the river from Wales.

Jax pocketed the revolver again and took off. He made a quick call to one of the boys on the way, and twenty minutes later, was doing a hundred on the motorway. He was barely able to suppress a smile for much of the drive, as he fantasised about doing the kid in front of Gayle. He could cut out the boy's eyes and make her watch when he did it.

Whatever cruelty he acted out would be nothing compared to what he did to Gayle Stillwater when she was his at last.

CHAPTER 25

The interior of the farmhouse was cosier than Gayle imagined from the outside. The living room had an old-fashioned rug with diamond-shaped swirls of yellow, green and blue, but time had homogenised it to a dark, dingy green. The floorboards were treated with faded lacquer and the magnolia wallpaper had vertical stripes of pale baby-blue. The furniture was old, mismatched, but looked comfortable. A rocking chair sat by the fireplace, in which a wood-burning stove blazed away. The kindling cracked and popped. It put out heat that Gayle could feel on her face like the touch of a warm hand. On the floor lay an old Irish setter, dozing in the heat. Though still mostly red, the fur around the dog's muzzle was white and a peppering of grey ringed his eyes.

"That's Max," Aled told them. "He's deaf as a post. Just let him sniff you when he's ready, young Finn, all right? Best not surprise him."

Finn didn't say anything, but nodded.

Aled went to make coffee with an old-fashioned kettle he boiled on the stove. They followed and he gestured to the dining table. It was old and weathered, but the chairs had comfortable padded seats. He placed the shotgun far back on the kitchen counter, out of Finn's reach.

"No coffee for you, young 'un?" Aled asked. "What's your poison?"

"Huh?" Finn frowned, looking quickly at Gayle with a concerned look on his little face.

"It's an expression," she told him. "What would you like to drink?"

"Oh." He leant to Gayle and whispered too loudly, "Why not just *say* that?"

Mortified, Gayle raised a finger to her lips, but she heard Aled chuckling softly with his back to them. "I think I have some Ribena around here somewhere. How's that?"

Just then, Max padded into the kitchen, mouth open in a wide yawn. He smacked his chops, then looked around for a moment as if surprised to have company. Then his fluffy tail wagged from side to side, thumping on the doorframe. He made a beeline for Finn, planting his paws on the boy's thighs and licking his face. Finn squealed, but stroked the dog's neck.

Bobbi sat in the chair beside Finn and, when Max noticed her, he hurried over and climbed up on her legs, panting with excitement.

The kettle began to whistle and Aled turned off the gas. He took three mismatched mugs from the cupboard and set about making the drinks, as well as a glass of diluted Ribena squash for Finn. With the drinks made, he joined them at the table and called to Max, but of course, the dog couldn't hear him.

Aled gave him a gentle poke in the back of the head. "Traitor," he said, sitting at the head of the table. Gayle sat to his left, and Bobbi and Finn were on his right.

"We should talk soon, I think," Gayle said. "But it's not all for little ears."

Aled nodded, then turned to Finn. "You know what? I reckon I still have a Scalextric around here somewhere. It's old, but I think it works."

"What's a skull-ex-ick?"

"I'll show you in a minute. You'll like it."

Finn didn't look convinced. He took a drink of Ribena, then went back to stroking the dog.

A little later, Gayle limped out to the car to retrieve her phone, which still sat in the bag of rice. The phone had to be restarted twice over, but the screen no longer flickered in shades of green. She used Bobbi's charger to replenish the battery.

When Finn tired of playing with the dog, Aled brought out a dusty, tattered box from the sloped cupboard that ran underneath the stairs on the other side of the living room wall. He got down on the floor with Finn to inspect it.

Gayle sat on the settee and kicked her left leg up onto her right knee, massaging her ankle. Bobbi took a seat on the other side of the settee. Max jumped between them both, begging Bobbi for affection that she was only too happy to provide.

On the floor, Aled cleared a large enough space to open the box.

Looking at it, Gayle was suddenly reminded of the red tin box in his bedroom. She got Finn's attention for a moment and asked him about it, but Finn just frowned.

"What box?" he asked.

"Did your daddy give it to you? Just, I never saw it before."

Finn shrugged. "I dunno," he said, then went back to

watching Aled, who opened a small plastic bag and pulled out a pair of Scalextric racers.

"It's *cars*," Finn said with surprise. "Do they work?"

"Let's hope so," Aled said and began clicking together the figure-eight track. He explained how the set worked, then plugged the track into the wall outlet and placed the cars in their grooves. "Ready?"

"Yeah."

"Set."

"What?"

"Go." Aled thumbed the button and his red car fired up, whizzing around the track with a whine.

"I wasn't *ready*," Finn said, slamming the joystick forwards in an effort to catch up.

"You should take a few practice laps," Aled told him, "while I talk to your mum and Bobbi. Then we'll have a *real* race."

"What do I get if I win?" Finn asked, smiling.

"I might have a Mars bar in the fridge."

"Deal. Only, I think the red car's faster, can we swap?"

"Why not?" Aled said, getting to his feet. His knees popped and he groaned. "Go for it, young Finn." He settled into the armchair, which was close enough to the settee that his feet were almost touching Gayle's.

Max jumped down off the settee and went to lie at his master's feet. Aled reached down and stroked the dog's floppy ears.

"So," he said. "It was addressed to me, of course, but it's really for you." He reached down the side of the armchair and picked up a box that Gayle hadn't noticed lying there. He held it out. "Postman brought it a couple of hours ago."

It was a Nike shoebox that had been taped all over with

brown parcel tape. On the lid, etched in black marker was Aled's address in Danny's handwriting.

She reached for it. The tape had been sliced with a knife around the lid and she hesitated before opening it. Her heart had begun to beat fast.

A glance over at Finn reassured her that the boy was content, racing the cars one at a time with his back to her.

She lifted the lid. Inside, was a note; a sheet of lined A4 paper, folded over on top of something in a plastic grocery bag.

"I'm sorry to say," Aled told her, "but I read it."

She picked up the note. It was clearly written in a hurry, as Danny's already-poor handwriting was considerably worse. The words were scratched deeply into the lined notepad paper and in places a faint pen-line connected separate words where he hadn't lifted away the blue biro.

She read it to herself.

Aled – It's Danny. Something serious has happened and I need you to get in touch with Gayle. You have to get her to come and see you RIGHT NOW. Don't take no for an answer. This is life and death.
Her number is 07742553155.
Remember – DON'T TAKE NO FOR AN ANSWER!

There was a second sheet of paper below it. Gayle shuffled the pages, glancing at Finn, who paid her no attention, then went back to Danny's letters.

The second page had been dated: Friday, three days before he was killed.

She took a breath and started to read.

CHAPTER 26

Danny rode in the back of the maroon BMW 3 Series. It was ten past six on Saturday morning, but he had been up since four.

Behind the wheel, X-Ray stuck to the speed limit and obeyed the traffic lights. He was dressed in all black, as was Danny, in black jeans and a thick black jumper with faux-leather shoulders. He wore black Nikes with the swoosh coloured over with marker pen.

Danny also wore black jeans but had a black long-sleeve T-shirt and a black hoodie on top.

They didn't talk much on the way to pick up Jax. X-Ray listened to the local morning radio instead of Spotify. He kept the volume low until the news reports and – most particularly – the traffic updates came on. There didn't appear to be any problems on the city's roads.

X-Ray stopped at Jax's place, but he was already waiting for them at the kerb, smoking a cigarette. He carried a black holdall. He threw it into the middle of the rear seat and got in behind it.

"You guys ready for this?" he asked, but he was being

only half sincere. Jax had told them both the bare minimum so far, which wasn't that unusual. There was some method to his madness: one couldn't reveal secrets if one never knew them in the first place.

It wasn't only that, however. Jax enjoyed being the one in the know. He got off on doling out information on a need-to-know basis.

Both Danny and X-Ray knew they were going to rob a bookmaker and had worked out what their parts were likely to be. X-Ray had switched over the licence plates with ones he picked up at a scrap-yard. Of course, that wouldn't fool a detailed police search, but at a cursory glance everything would appear normal. The car was in good condition and had a full tank of petrol.

Danny figured that he would be going in with Jax and, since only Jax knew the details, it was a solid assumption that they were going in when the place was trading, meaning that Danny was on crowd-control.

That part, he didn't like. Danny's preference was always late-night or early-morning burglaries rather than brazen stick-up jobs. The ever-present likelihood of having to hurt someone didn't sit easily: the fewer civilians or employees that might suddenly be moved to be a have-a-go hero, the better.

He and Jax held up a petrol station last summer. They managed to get away, but not before Danny had to slam the end of a baseball bat into the nose of the lone employee. He didn't feel bad about it, not exactly; Danny had told him to stay away from the alarm. If the guy had done as he was told, Danny wouldn't have had to break his nose. But it was a risky thing, slamming a bat into someone's face. He was acutely aware that if he struck too hard, he could have killed the guy. He checked the blow so it was enough to bloody his *nose but not seriously injure him, but with adrenaline flooding his body, he might have lost control of that situation.*

The money had been scarcely worth the risk. They made off with only three-hundred apiece, but Jax was bursting with excitement. He didn't care about the money or even the rush of the score, but went on all night over drinks about Danny busting open the cashier's nose.

"Bam! Oh, that was beautiful!"

Danny preferred to avoid that kind of trouble. This time, however, it didn't seem that he was going to get that chance.

Jax gave X-Ray directions until they pulled over on a residential street in in the Stonygate area of the city. "Kill the engine, bruv. Just wait a minute," *Jax said.*

X-Ray did as he was told. He relaxed, tapping his thumb on the wheel to the pop music playing quietly on the radio. He apparently felt none of the anxiousness that sat like a stone in the pit of Danny's stomach.

After a couple of minutes of doing nothing, Danny checked his watch and sighed. "What are we doing here, Jax?" *he asked.*

"You'll see. You'll love this." *Jax had a smug, self-satisfied grin on his face.*

A few moments later, Danny saw a girl walking down the leaf-blown street towards them. Her blonde hair whipped about her face in the wind. She was bundled up in a long black coat and a pink scarf.

"Here we go," *Jax said and got out of the car. He walked towards her and, through the windscreen, Danny saw her smiling. They talked for a moment, then Jax gestured to the car and ushered her to it.*

"You know her?" *X-Ray whispered.*

"No," *Danny said.* "You?"

"Never seen her before."

"What's Jax playing at?"

X-Ray gave a little laugh. "Fucked if I know, bro."

Jax opened the door for her and she got in next to Danny. "Morning," she said, breezily. She smoothed back her hair from her face. She was pretty, well made-up and her perfume was both delicate and fruity. Her nose had been made red by the cold.

Jax got in and closed the door.

X-Ray started the engine, but Jax put a hand on his shoulder. "Just chill here another minute, bruv. We've gotta talk."

The girl's name was Rebecca. As it turned out, she worked at the bookmakers. The plan was simple: she was going to open up as she would any other day, and as she raised the shutters, Jax and Danny would rush her. Once inside, she was to show them into the back and get them access to the safe. She wouldn't be able to get them into the main drop-safe, the key to which was held off-site by the company making cash collections, Royal Mail in this instance. But she could get them into the top safe, where there would be a few thousand pounds for their troubles.

"Also," Jax said, "there's a little cherry on top. But I don't want to ruin that surprise."

"And you'll settle up with me after?" Rebecca said. "You remember?"

"I won't forget, babe," Jax said, laying his hand on her thigh. She wore a skirt with black stockings. He leant in and kissed her on the mouth.

This fucking guy, *Danny thought.* I don't know how he does it.

Only, that wasn't quite true. A lot of girls had a thing for bad boys. And a surprising amount of them would go along with a robbery to fleece their arsehole boss out of a few hundred.

Jax got out and Rebecca followed. He kissed her again at the kerb and sent her on her way. He got back in the car and told X-Ray to drive. "I'll tell you when to turn."

He opened the holdall and emptied the contents. There were two black ski masks, two cheap sunglasses, half a dozen cable ties, a spray can of carpet adhesive, a folding knife, a box of latex gloves, a kid's wooden bat and a Glock 17 pistol.

"Jesus," Danny muttered. He picked up a mask and a pair of sunglasses.

"The bat's yours. And the knife. Take a couple pairs of gloves. The rest is mine."

"What about the gun, Jax? What the fuck you need that for?"

"It's got to look real for the cameras," he said.

"This will do for that," Danny said, hefting the small bat.

"She's a decent actress, if you get me, bruv. But anyone can get stage fright."

X-Ray started to laugh. "Good thinking."

Danny understood why Jax had only decided to fill them in on the details at the last minute. There wasn't a chance that Danny would have wanted to go along with this.

"In and out, mate, in and fuckin' out. No mess, no fuss. Follow my lead and do what I tell you."

Jax slapped X-Ray's shoulder lightly again and started pointing through the windscreen. He called out the turns and in short order, they were parked on the street with two wheels up on the kerb. X-Ray hit his hazard lights. It was twenty minutes to seven.

Ten feet ahead on the tree-lined street, Danny could see the bookies and his heart sank.

"Oh, Jax, what the fuck is this, man? You can't be serious. This is Fat Joe's place, and you know who Fat Joe works for."

"Relax, bruv. It's cool, I promise."

The sign above the building behind the cold steel shutters read Slattery & Co. Book-Makers. Danny wasn't privy to all the business dealings of Felix Knox, but he knew the names of some of the businesses that cleaned money for his drug income.

"I don't know, mate," Danny said, *"we shouldn't be fucking with the big man."*

"I said it's cool. I've got this. Besides, he'll never know it was us."

"Jesus Christ, Jax."

X-Ray decided to pipe up too. *"Danny might be right, bro. This is fuckin' risky. We're shitting where we live."*

"I told you, all right? It's cool. Stop acting like a pair of pussy-'oles and get my back. We're doing it."

Danny understood now why Jax had the gun. It wasn't just for the cameras: Danny knew then that he would turn it on he or X-Ray if they gave him any trouble.

Danny shook his head in disbelief. *"This is so fucked up, bro."*

"Shut up. Game faces, lads. She's coming."

Danny looked out of the window and saw Rebecca walking past them to the control box. She unlocked it with a key and raised the shutters with a clatter.

"Come on," Jax said, pulling on his ski mask. He put his sunglasses on, making sure that most of his face was covered. He slipped on a pair of latex gloves, then a second pair.

Danny was starting to feel sick. But he got prepared. He put the spray adhesive and cable ties back in the open hold all, slipped the knife in his pocket and kept hold of the bat in his left hand.

"Wait until the shutter's up," Jax said. "X, you stay cool, mate. Keep a fuckin' eye out. Any trouble, blast your horn, okay? Three, four minutes and we're out, so get the engine running once we're in."

Danny's heart thundered in his chest.

The raucous clatter of the shutter stopped abruptly and Rebecca fumbled with the keys, searching for the one to unlock the front door.

"Now," Jax said and went for the door.

Danny did likewise, slamming it behind him and running around the car.

Jax already had Rebecca by the hair, one hand over her mouth. He pushed her roughly into the door, but didn't say anything to her: he didn't have to. Rebecca didn't scream. She put the key in the lock and opened the door.

They got in off the street, fast. Danny shut the door behind him. The alarm by the door chirped. Jax shoved Rebecca towards the panel. She silenced the alarm with the fob on her keychain.

"In the back," he told her, spinning her around by her shoulder and shoving her again.

This time, Rebecca lost her balance and went down on her hands and knees. Her palms slapped on the thin blue carpet. "Fuckin' hell," she cried out, "easy."

"Look scared," Jax said, grabbing her again by her collar. He shook her.

Danny looked around. The main room had four circular tables with slots for betting slips and another for a cluster of blue biros. All around the walls were stencils of horses midgallop, rugby players in a scrum and footballers stopping a football with their chest. A bank of desks stood behind Plexiglass at the far end, where there was a door marked Staff Only.

Jax shoved Rebecca towards it. She dropped her keys and bent at the waist to pick them up.

"Hurry the fuck up," Jax said, "move it."

"Do the cameras have audio?" Danny asked, thinking aloud.

"No," Rebecca said. Her voice was terse and Danny could see her hands shaking. She got the key in the lock and pulled open the door. She led them into a hallway with four doors, two on either side. The two on the left were both toilets and the first one on the right was a small staff room. The last door was the manager's office, which they hurried towards. Jax stayed right on Rebecca's heels, his hand still on her collar.

Danny saw a camera in the centre of the hallway, pointed directly at them.

Any moment, he expected a cry of, "Armed police, get on the fucking floor!"

Rebecca got the door open and Jax ushered her in. He followed and Danny closed the door behind them.

"Brace yourself, babe, and go down," Jax whispered and slapped Rebecca across the face. Danny could see that he had checked the blow, letting his arm go limp, but Rebecca went down in a heap anyway. She landed on her backside, her hand already up at her face. Through the dark glasses, Danny saw that her eyes shone with tears.

"Let's move it," Danny said. "We're wasting time."

"Open the safe, Becks," Jax told her. He pulled the Glock out of the waistband of his black trousers. He kept his finger away from the trigger, but he jabbed the muzzle of the gun at her, threateningly.

"Jesus Christ," she managed to say, but Jax was on her then, grabbing at her with his free hand and hoisting her to his feet.

"You're fucking terrified of us, remember?" he said through gritted teeth. "You'll do whatever I say. I've got a gun so you do what the fuck you're told. Open it."

Rebecca did as she was instructed. She stepped over to the safe, but the shake in her hands was almost debilitating now. She struggled to keep hold of her keychain.

As she worked on the digital panel, Jax said to Danny, "The computer, under the desk." He pointed.

Danny looked and saw the black Hewlett-Packard tower.

"Spray it," Jax said. "Through the fan, the vents, everything."

Danny reached into the holdall and took out the can of carpet adhesive. He checked his watch as he pulled off the lid. Just over a minute had passed since they got off the street. His sense of time was wildly distorted, seeming as though it were rushing by and still somehow dragging simultaneously.

He dropped the holdall and hurried over to the PC tower. He shook the can and let loose a blast of aerosolised glue into the front and back of the computer, until he thought he could smell burning.

"That'll fuck it up," Jax said. "Look up, up there—"

Danny looked above the desk and saw what Jax was referring to. There was a glass-fronted cabinet full of wires, another computer tower and a stack of horizontal devices that might almost have been old-school VCRs were it not for the cluster of cables that connected them.

Jax said, "That'll be for the CCTV and the computers."

Danny didn't wait, but blasted the tower with the adhesive and started pulling at cables. Some of them came free from their ports, but others were held fast. He yanked and one of the drives came free of its moorings. It clattered to the floor and Danny stamped on it.

The safe was built into the wall. Rebecca unlocked it

with her fob and access code. Jax swung it open, then – still holding the gun on her – directed her to kneel. Jax took a cable tie from the holdall and bound her at the wrists.

"Gotta do it tight, babe," he said. The tie buzzed as he ratcheted it securely around her wrists.

She hissed in pain and Jax pushed her onto her belly.

"Danny," Jax said, "check the cupboards and the drawers."

"What for?"

"A bag or a lock box, something for petty cash." As he spoke, Jax rummaged around in the safe, pulling out banded stacks of five, ten and twenty-pound notes. He threw them all into the holdall. There were bags of change in the safe too, but he left those: they were too heavy for too little reward. Danny knew they were going to have to move fast.

He checked his watch. Two minutes gone.

"Someone's gonna come in," Danny said.

"The boss won't be in 'til eight. There's time, just find it."

"I'm looking, I'm looking," Danny told him.

Inside the cupboards were stacks of betting slips, boxes of biros and piles of envelopes. He pored over everything, pushing things aside and pulling others out of the cupboards, spilling the contents on the floor.

"There's nothing here," Danny said.

"There has to be. Keep looking." Jax threw the last of the notes into the holdall.

Beside Danny, Rebecca lay on the floor. She turned her face to the carpet and whispered through her grit teeth, "Hurry up."

Jax stood over her. "On your feet," he told her, pulling at her elbow.

Rebecca cried out in discomfort. "Watch it," she said, "you'll pull my fucking arm out."

"Where is it?" Jax asked, pushing her back against the wall. "This has got to look real. Don't worry." He lifted the gun, pointing it at the ceiling. "The box, where is it?"

"Next cupboard along," she said "There's a hidden drawer inside."

Jax pointed the gun at Rebecca's head.

"What the fuck?" she cried. "Don't! What are you doing?"

"You're scared, right?" Jax hissed. "Fuckin' petrified! Are you gonna piss your pants? Tell my boy where the fuckin' box is!"

"At the bottom, Jesus Christ, it's at the fucking bottom!"

Danny slammed shut the cupboard door and moved on to the next. Behind the stacks of till receipts and odd scraps of paper, he finally saw it. In the back of the lowest part of the cupboard was a drawer with a wooden knob for a handle. Danny slid it open, sending a pot of paperclips spilling onto the floor.

Inside the drawer was a red tin box. "I think I got it," Danny said, plucking it out of the drawer. He lifted the lid.

The tin was full of twenty-pound notes, all bound in stacks of a thousand.

"Jesus Christ."

At a glance, there had to be thirty or forty bundles. He snapped the lid back down and threw the tin into the holdall. "Let's get the fuck out of here, man," he said.

Jax still held the gun pointed at Rebecca. The tears in her eyes were real. "Listen to me," he said, "we're leaving now. Don't do anything. Just stay in this room until someone comes for you." He grabbed her by her upper arm and pulled her away from the wall. He turned her on unsteady feet until

*she was in the centre of the small office. "Face the other way,"
he said.*

Rebecca did as she was told.

*Danny grabbed the holdall and zipped it closed. He
stepped past Jax and put his hand on the office door.*

"Let's fucking go, man," he said.

*Jax pushed Rebecca forwards a little more. "On your
knees, babe," he said. "You're doing great. You'll do good out
of this, I promise. On your knees."*

She did as she was told.

*Danny could see that her hands were almost bone-white
beneath the cable tie.*

*"I'm gonna give you a kick," Jax said. "Just a little one to
get you on your belly. I'll see you later tonight, babe, okay?
It's got to look real."*

*"Okay," Rebecca said, trying to calm her breathing.
"Okay, okay, just don't fuck up and—"*

*Jax pressed the gun to the back of her skull and blew her
face all over the wall. The shot was deafening in the small
office.*

*Danny jumped back, his shoulder crashing against the
doorframe. "What the fuck?" he shouted. "You out of your
fuckin' mind?"*

*"Looks real to me," Jax said, snatching the holdall from
Danny.*

"So, what now – you shoot me too?"

*"As if, bruv. No cameras, no audio, no fuckin' witnesses
or big-gob accomplices to stitch us up." From the sound of his
voice, Danny could tell that Jax was grinning beneath the
ski-mask. "Let's go."*

*Jax threw the door open and bolted. Danny turned to
look down at the blasted-open shell that had once been
Rebecca's head. Her blonde hair was matted with blood and*

tufts of it clung to pieces of her scalp. There were fragments of chalk-white bone on the carpet.

Danny felt the gorge rise, but he choked it down and hurried after Jax.

They raced through the main room, out onto the street and into the waiting car. Jax got in the front and Danny barely had his foot off the pavement before X-Ray stamped on the accelerator, rocketing the BMW down the road.

With an expert hand, he threw the car around one turn after another, right then left and right again, putting distance between them and the scene of the robbery and murder. Soon, they came to a main road and X-Ray slowed to forty miles per hour. Traffic was still light and he moved around slower-moving cars where he could.

In the front, Jax peeled off his ski-mask. His eyes were electrified. His smile beamed.

"Good fuckin' job well done, lads," he said, dropping the pistol into the holdall at his feet. "Fuck me, that was beautiful."

Danny shook his head, unable to believe what he had witnessed.

"Shit," Jax continued. "Anyone else feel like havin' a fuckin' beer?"

CHAPTER 27

Gayle,

Something really fucked up happened, and I see now how rite you were all them times you told me to get out. You said I'm only alive cos of luck and it has to run out some day. Looks like that day has been and gone.

Jax has proper lost it. He ripped off Fat Joe last week and took the big man's money. X-Ray and me went along but I swear I didn't know what was happening till we were already there. He got some girl to get us in the door, then he blew her away. I can't get it out of my mind. She had no face left.

There's no way the big man lets us live, no way. There's only 1 chance, and I've gotta take it. I'm getting out of the city. If I make it, this letter won't matter, but if you're reading this, then it's too late and I'm gone. Don't feel bad. I got what I deserve, I guess. I want you to take the money. You'll do something good with it. You'll make a home for you and Finn. With me, it's only a matter of time before it ends up in my nose or something.

You were right about me, Gayle. You knew me better than I did. You knew I couldn't leave, just like you knew I couldn't do right by you or our son. It's not that I didn't love you. You both are the only people I ever really did love. But that just wasn't enough to stop me ruining it all somehow. That's why I know deep down that you're better off without me. I don't no why I'm that way. Some of us must just be built to self-destruct.

I try to be a better man but I think we both know that's beyond me. I've done so many terrible things, things I'm too ashamed to even admit to myself, that it actually hurts to look Finn in the eyes. That's not a good man, is it? Still, if I get through this, I'll keep you and Finn in my thoughts, and who knows? Maybe I'll look up one day and you'll be there, and I'll try to never let you down again. Gotta dream, right?

Until then, look after our boy. Look after yourself. Live a good, long life, Gayle.

All my worthless love,
–Danny

Gayle read the note twice over, but was still unable to work out her own emotions: the sadness of it all was overwhelming.

To her right, Bobbi was looking at her with concern.

She tried to speak, but couldn't find her voice. After a moment, she simply handed Bobbi the note to read for herself.

She hesitated, as if not wanting to invade Gayle's privacy, but then began to read.

Gayle looked down into the box. Inside, there was a plain, dark green plastic carrier bag. She lifted it by the handles and the bag rustled. It was surprisingly light and when she looked inside, she saw money. The cash was banded in stacks, mostly twenties, but there were two stacks of ten-pound notes. She shook her head in disbelief.

Gayle took one of the banded stacks of twenties and counted it. As she suspected, the stack contained a thousand pounds. A quick check showed forty stacks.

The box on her knee still felt heavy. She put the bag of money aside and checked on Finn once more. He was operating both controllers at the same time, easing the cars in tandem around the track.

Gayle peeked into the box for the last time. There was another slip of lined notepad paper on top of a second plastic bag.

This is proof, Gayle. He wore gloves when he used it, but maybe not when he loaded it.
Be careful.
–Danny.

The bag was opaque, with the word Tesco emblazoned on the front.

In it, Gayle saw a black pistol.

CHAPTER 28

The allotments were laid out in a grid. Two long paths – each wide enough for a car – ran the length of the land, parallel to one another and bisected by three others which ran across.

Most were owned, it seemed, by older men who either lacked the space to grow plants and vegetables at home, or just kept the patch to have a quiet place in which to be alone for a while.

Jax's mum rented a small plot from the council. At one point, she and his dad spent a lot of time here, growing tomatoes and colourful pansies, that she sold to friends for a little extra cash. After her breakdown, Jax said he would take it over.

It was a joke amongst the guys that he was going to start growing weed and poppies. "Everyone starts out small," Jax joked.

Danny had never dared come here alone before. He hurried along the path, passing by the old guys tending to their vegetables and one other who sat on a collapsible stool, drinking tea from his thermos, watching him closely.

He knew these old farts tended to form cliques and it wouldn't be out of the question for someone to approach and ask what the hell he was doing out here. He needed to be quick.

Jax's plot was at the far corner, last but one and was mostly weeds. His, like some of the others, had a greenhouse, though nothing grew inside.

Jax had to have stashed the money somewhere and the allotment was a logical place: the land was locked at night and there were witnesses around during the day. Few people even knew about it and the only reason that Danny did was when – high one night – he and Jax climbed the fence to smoke weed in peace.

He'd seen the large hole excavated in the earth, covered with a ceramic pot. Then, it had contained a bottle of tequila that Jax had shoplifted, a tobacco tin filled with skunk, as well as a wallet and mobile phone. Those Jax had taken from a London dealer whom the gang had caught up with the week before. From time to time, new gangs would try their luck like that: they would send out a younger over county lines to try shifting drugs in a high-demand area, with an eye towards setting up a permanent base of operations. The word was out that the city was WEC territory, but that didn't stop cowboys from giving it a try.

Jax almost killed the kid and no doubt would have had Danny not pulled him away. Jax took his money, phone and return train ticket, telling him to walk back to London. They'd shared a couple of joints and drank some tequila. It felt like the old days, before Jax had gone off the deep end.

Danny made it to the allotment and approached the greenhouse. The metal frame was rusted and the hinges squeaked when he pulled the door open. The motion disturbed the condensation on the glass, which began *running down the opaque panes like tears. The air inside was musty and still smelled vaguely of weed.*

He dropped to his knees and gripped the large ceramic pot. It was cold beneath his fingers and must have weighed ten or twelve kilos. He lifted it with his forearms, pulling it out of the hole in the mud and set it aside.

He expected to find the hole empty. That would be just Danny's luck.

Down there, smeared with mud, was a Nike shoebox. For a second, his heart sank. He thought, I should have known... More crap he shoplifted.

Nonetheless, he pulled the shoebox out of the hole. There was nothing else. Even before he opened the lid, Danny could tell by the shifting weight that the box didn't contain trainers.

He lifted off the lid and saw the Glock wrapped in one shopping bag, the money in another. Jax had apparently discarded the red tin in which the cash had been stored.

Danny slapped the lid back on the box, replaced the ceramic pot and got to his feet, brushing dirt off his hands and his knees. He grabbed the shoebox and shut the greenhouse door behind him.

He started back the way he had come, hurrying up the path. He was nervous before, but terrified now. He didn't see Jax or anyone he recognised, but he told himself to hurry anyway.

His nose had started to run in the cold. He sniffed and rubbed at it with the sleeve of his hoodie.

Up ahead, the old guy with the thermos was off his stool. He stood at the edge of the path, arms folded across his chest, openly watching Danny.

Rather than risk a confrontation, although he was certain the old man was no match for him, Danny cut right on a bisecting path. He quickened his pace and when he glanced back, the man was following him with his eyes.

At the corner that connected to the main path, he started to jog for the entrance. His trainers slapped on the concrete and the cold air made his lungs ache.

He made it to the end without anyone stopping him. He wanted to take it easy now, telling himself that he was safe; that by running he only made himself look more suspicious. Nonetheless, the gnawing fear hadn't diminished and he poured on the speed. He ran through the streets, making for Gooding Avenue and Braunstone Park beyond it.

There was no going back now. He was done with the gang, for better or worse. Jax was already looking for him because he'd been lying low after the robbery, and when he found out what Danny had done, he would be a marked man. His only option was to get out of the city, right now.

In the back pocket of his jeans was the letter he wrote for Gayle last night. He had gone through three drafts, screwing up the paper and starting over, before getting everything out.

He hoped she hadn't given up on him completely. Forty grand wasn't going to last forever, but if she agreed to meet him, he figured it was a decent down-payment on a mortgage. He himself had no credit history, but with Gayle's looking a little better, they might be able to find a place. He could get a job. They could start again.

By the time he made it to the park, Danny felt marginally safer. He stopped running. The muscles in his legs felt like they were pumping battery acid and his throat was burned raw by the cold. He waited for a moment, leaning on a tree and getting his breath back. The bitter wind froze the sweat on his forehead. After a few moments, he carried on.

He had it figured out.

He decided not to use a regular post office because he

wasn't sure if Royal Mail used metal detectors or X-ray machines on the stuff people sent. He told himself it was unlikely, but he decided there was less chance of Courier-Ace having that kind of technology. He did an online search and found a Courier-Ace collection point on Raven Road, just the other side of Braunstone Park.

Danny worried about running into someone he knew, perhaps even Jax, so close to home. The next nearest was on the other side of Hinckley Road in the Park Rise area. He didn't know it well, so decided that he was probably safer there.

He memorised the route and hurried through the park, figuring it was better to stay away from the streets as much as possible.

The walk along Hinckley Road and New Parks Way took more than twenty minutes. Danny held the shoebox under his arm, his bare hands dug into the pockets of his hoodie to keep warm.

Cars rushed by on his left as he passed the car wash on his right. He kept looking over his shoulder to check he wasn't being followed. He half expected a passing car to pull suddenly over in the bus lane, and that it would be Jax.

Danny didn't even feel safe when he finally made it to the shop in Park Rise. The jingling bell sounded as he stepped in. He blew into his cupped hands to get some feeling back.

The place didn't sell brown paper, so he bought some brown tape, a biro and a small spiral-bound notepad. He wrote out a quick note to Aled, another to Gayle and put them both inside with Gayle's letter. He hastily wrapped the shoebox secure with the tape and wrote Aled's address on the box with the marker pen he always carried.

The guy at the counter was a tall Asian man in a crisp

white shirt with the sleeves rolled up, a wiry beard and an orange turban. He glanced at Danny under bushy eyebrows. He looked tired.

Danny paid for the postage with cash and the shopkeeper slapped a sticker on the box, putting it beneath the counter to await collection. Then he pointed at the notepad in Danny's hand and said, "Give, please."

Confused, Danny handed it to him. With his own blue pen, the man started to write something on the pad. "No receipt, my friend," he said as he scribbled. "No new roll." He tore the page and handed Danny a slip with the code he had written on it. "You track with this," he said.

Danny looked down at the slip of paper. He thought about taking the package elsewhere, but he had already paid and didn't want trouble. The guy hadn't asked any questions about what was in the box, which was just as well.

Danny thanked him and left. He looked at his watch and saw that it was almost four. It was starting to get dark.

He called a local taxi company and booked a ride into the city centre. Sitting on the kerb while he waited, he went onto the Courier-Ace website and booked his collection.

He had a text from Scotty, writing to say that he would be in the High Cross pub at six with Danny's money. Danny replied with a thumbs-up emoji.

Scotty was a younger who had been with the WEC for only six months. He was a decent enough kid – only seventeen – and Danny lent him a hundred pounds earlier in the month to keep the electricity on at his mum's house.

Danny had forty pounds in his pocket and when he got his money back from Scotty, that would be plenty for a train to Pontypridd and a cab out to the farm. He could have taken some money from the bag before sending it, but he superstitiously felt that spending any of it before hearing *from Gayle would be tempting fate. That money was for their future.*

When the taxi arrived, he had it drop him off outside the High Cross. He went in the main entrance in the side of the building rather than the smaller set of doors on the corner, then ordered a Guinness and looked at the menu. He made sure to pick a seat near the double-doors. He glanced over the others in the pub to see if he recognised anyone. They were all strangers.

The sun had set now and Danny was famished. He went to the bar, ordered steak, chips and peas, savoured another Guinness, then tried to settle down to wait for Scotty. He bounced the heel of his right foot up and down. When he was done with his meal, he reached into his pocket and withdrew the foil packet of Oxy. He took out one of the little blue pills and swallowed it with a swig to settle his nerves.

Danny checked the train times and did some quick calculations. He could have a couple of drinks with Scotty, make the half-seven train and be in Pontypridd by eleven.

At a quarter past six, Scotty still hadn't turned up. Danny text him to ask where he was. Ten minutes later and Scotty messaged back to say he'd been held up, but was on his way and would get there by seven.

That didn't leave a lot of time, but it was doable. Danny wouldn't have time for pleasantries, but if he hurried, he could be at the train station in fifteen minutes – twenty at worst.

The Oxy pill wasn't doing much for his anxiousness, so he went to the bar for another Guinness with which to wash down a second. A white guy around his own age, sat beside him in a wheelchair. He ordered two Coronas. Danny checked out the barmaid's arse when she ducked into the fridge for the drinks.

Not bad, *he thought*, but Gayle's is better.

He watched the disabled guy wedge the bottles between his thigh and the side of his chair and take them over to a table ten feet away, where a good-looking Asian girl in a white blouse sat, talking on the phone. She winked when he gave her the bottle, sipped it, then carried on chatting.

Seven o'clock came and went, and Scotty still hadn't arrived. Danny slammed his empty pint glass down and checked the train times again. He could get a later train, but that would mean he wouldn't get into Pontypridd until twenty past midnight.

"Fucking idiot," *he mumbled.*

He dialled Scotty. The phone rang for a long time before finally going to voicemail.

Danny hung up.

Okay, *he thought*, it's not the end of the world. *He would be there late, but it wasn't unreasonable.*

Still, *he thought*, he's gonna get a fucking ear-bashing.

As the minutes continued to tick by and in spite of the Oxy, Danny's annoyance became worry. Scotty had always been a decent enough lad, and sure, he wasn't the brightest spark, but he'd never messed Danny around like this before. He'd known that Danny was second-in-command of the biggest of the WEC sets and had always been eager to please. He knew that his future with the gang depended on keeping the OGs happy.

Danny called again. This time, the line went straight to voicemail.

He slipped the phone back into his pocket.

Keep the OGs happy, *he thought*. Like me. And like Jax.

"Oh shit," *he said*. What if Scotty had told Jax that they were meeting here?

Danny got to his feet and took a step back on unsteady

legs. He collided with another man, reached out to try to arrest his fall, but went down on his arse anyway. The stranger helped him to his feet, taking him for a piss-head.

"Get off me," Danny said, pulling away.

"Easy, mate."

At the other end of the building, the corner door opened and banged shut. Even over the music, Danny heard the sound of a woman crying out and a glass smashing on the floor.

He saw Jax shoving his way past a couple standing by the door, his heavy brow knotted above his narrowed eyes and his clenched jaw. They exchanged a look and Danny knew he was fucked.

He glanced to his left, but saw none of the gang. Jax didn't want anyone else to know anything. He bolted, racing for the double doors.

Jax dropped low and gave chase.

Danny hit the doors hard, shoving them out. The bouncer shouted at him as he almost collided with a group of girls heading into the pub, but dodged them at the last minute. He tore off down the High Street.

Hearing more cries, he glanced over his shoulder to see that Jax hadn't been so lucky: a blonde in a white coat was sprawled on her back, with Jax rolling on the pavement, but then he was already getting to his feet, screaming Danny's name. The large bouncer went to grab him, but was too slow.

"Fuck," Danny hissed, looking forwards again, just in time to avoid a collision of his own. His feet slapped hard on the pavement. In his belly, four pints of Guinness were sloshing around and he could already feel a stitch growing in his right side.

Behind him, Jax bellowed.

He rocketed down the High Street as fast as he could.

Danny was taller, with longer legs, but Jax was gaining.

He cut right onto Carts Lane, barrelling along the pavement, then left onto Silver Street. A group of lads stood outside the pub on the corner, smoking. They jeered at Danny as Jax gave chase, still screaming. One of the lads snickered, "Run, Forrest, run," as he raced by.

Coming up fast was a right into St. Martin's Square. He darted in, slamming his shoulder into the wall and shoved off it. He ducked his head down, willing away the pain in his side as it grew more intense.

Jax wasn't far behind. Twenty feet at most.

He rushed past the closed shops and the gawking people, most of whom saw him coming and took a step back. One lairy bastard stuck out his foot to trip him, but Danny dodged, shouting "Cunt!" at the same time.

He ran through the arch on the other side, onto Hotel Street, which was busier with people milling around making their way to and from the pubs dotted everywhere on this side of town. He gripped his side, which was now in agony, and he grit his teeth against the pain. He was winded and slowing considerably. He forged on, his chest heaving with exertion. Sweat flowed down his back and from his armpits in cold rivers.

"Get back here!" Jax bellowed.

He was closer. Danny could almost feel his breath on the back of his neck.

At the corner with Market Place, he cut left once more, onto the cobbled road that led down to the Food Hall and the open-air market, both of which were now closed.

His footfalls were hard slaps that echoed off the walls and shop fronts. The stitch in his side was crippling and he could barely draw breath at all; it came in ragged pants. He hitched along down the road, praying for a miracle.

He neared the end of the Food Hall. He darted to his right, towards the empty stalls of the market and The Corn Exchange *pub sitting in the centre of it. He hoped he could lose Jax if not in the maze of wooden stalls, then in the crowd of smokers forever congregated outside of the pub.*

Danny's heart dropped when he saw not a single person in the marketplace. The pub was closed for remodelling. He had known that; how could he forget?

No time now, *he thought. He hurried as fast as he could, hitching along now, into the abandoned market, where foxes and pigeons were clearing up the edible leavings that the refuse workers had not.*

With a deep, furious yell, Jax slammed into Danny with the power of a steamroller, crashing him into the nearest rectangular market stall. He struck his right hip and razor-sharp agony exploded all through him. Danny shrieked in pain, collapsing on top of the counter. His legs wouldn't hold him and he slipped down, with Jax's grasping hands all over him.

"Where the fuck's my money?" he shouted, spit spraying Danny's face.

He raised his hands, trying to shove at Jax, but the bastard held him tight by his hoodie. He tried to wriggle free, but couldn't.

Jax slammed a heavy fist into Danny's face. It went numb instantly and he tasted blood. He tried to speak, but he couldn't even suck in a breath.

"Where is it?" Jax punched him again and again.

The numbness in his face faded and he knew his nose was broken. When he forced himself to cry, "I haven't got it," he spat bloody tooth chips.

"Don't lie to me, you cunt!" Jax drove a kick into Danny's guts, blasting the air from his lungs in a rush. He

couldn't inhale. Raising his hands to ward off the punches, he gasped in desperation, but Jax batted them aside, then slammed another fist into his face. The blow closed Danny's right eye and bounced his skull off the concrete.

Jax refused to let up, kicking and stomping, until Danny blacked out. When he rose from the darkness, he could barely see at all through the tears and the blood. He felt like he was choking. He raised his hands to his neck, feeling Jax grip his throat.

Sounding far away now, Jax continued to scream, "Where is it? Where's my money?" When Jax let go of Danny's throat, he sucked in a shuddery breath. "Tell me, you bastard!"

Danny was propped against the side of a stall, his ears ringing, brain foggy with a terrible pain and pressure in his chest. He slumped down, unable to use his legs. He tried to speak, but the breath he had taken now wouldn't be expelled. He gasped, feeling as though his lungs were on fire.

After a moment, it felt like all he could really see was Finn's smiling face in his mind's eye – and Gayle, but Gayle as she was when they first met, back when she loved him, before he had let her down, before he failed her, failed them both.

There was no pain now. Even Jax's voice seemed to be more a thought than a sound, as it continued to bellow from far away, "Where is it? Where? Where?"

Danny had stopped caring. He was weary. Things would be all right in the morning.

He didn't know if he thought it or said it, but as cold blackness swallowed him, there was only one word on his lips.

"Gayle."

CHAPTER 29

In stunned silence, Gayle opened the Tesco bag. The pistol inside had a matte finish, a textured grip and no visible hammer. The insignia on the barrel identified it as a Glock. On the trigger guard, she saw a tiny rust-red fleck.

That girl's blood, she thought with a shudder.

She glanced at Finn but he didn't look up from his game; now driving both Scalextric racers with a controller in each hand.

Bobbi sat on the edge of her seat, hunched with her elbows on her knees. She shook her head. "I wouldn't have imagined..." she started to say, but could not finish the thought.

"This is what Tony Henry told me about," Gayle said, breaking her silence. "And Jax is probably looking for the gun as much as the money. It's proof of armed robbery and murder."

Bobbi handed back the note, which Gayle folded and slipped back into the box.

"He must know or at least suspect that he can be linked

to it," she continued. "He's not going to give up, not when this could put him away for life."

Aled leaned to the side, resting his chin on his upturned palm. "Now you see why I dusted off the old shotgun."

"Listen," she said, frowning, "we should all get out of here. Jax had someone follow me on the train part of the way here. If he knows about this place and was told the direction I was travelling in, he might figure that Danny sent the gun and the money here."

"Would Danny have given him my address?" he asked.

Gayle shrugged. "I doubt it. Or at least, not *willingly*. But he could have said anything when Jax was beating him."

"No," Bobbi said, "he *couldn't* have. Jax would have had no reason to break into your flat if he knew Danny had sent this stuff here."

"You're probably both right," Gayle said, "but I'd feel safer on the move."

Aled smoothed out his beard, thinking it over. "I don't know. The fact you made it here and this Jax fella didn't is encouraging. We're pretty well isolated out this way. And to tell you the truth, Gayle, you don't look like you've got much running left in you."

"I'll be fine."

"I noticed that limp of yours. You could do with keeping off your foot for a while."

"He's right about that part," Bobbi said.

"And it'll give us time to figure out what to do," he continued.

"My ankle's sprained," Gayle insisted, "not broken. But I still don't want us to stay. I don't see my luck changing now that we're here."

"Well," Aled said, "if you won't rest, I won't try to

change your mind. But the least I can do is get you all fed properly before you go on your way. I've got sausage and bacon, plenty of eggs too. I haven't eaten yet... and Max wouldn't say no either, would you, lad?" He reached down to stroke the setter's neck. The dog licked Aled's forearm.

From his place on the floor, Finn let go of the triggers and the whirring race cars slowed to a halt. He turned to look at her. "And we haven't had no breakfast yet, did we?" he asked.

Gayle checked her watch. It was already half past one. In spite of the nervous, crawly feeling in her stomach, she had to admit that she was hungry.

She looked down again at the Glock, then covered it with the lid of the shoebox.

"All right," she said. "Just until I work out where we go from here."

In the kitchen, Gayle and Bobbi sat around the dining table again while Aled pulled out a large black frying pan and set to work frying sausages in lard. Finn stayed in the living room, content to play with the racers.

Gayle explained in broad strokes about the chase that led her to the farm, checking on her mobile as she did so. It had charged to eighty percent and while the device was slow to respond, it worked. The reception however alternated between one bar and no service at all.

She laid the shoebox on the table, afraid to let it out of her sight, while she chewed at a thread of dry skin on her lower lip.

"Okay," she said, thinking aloud, "so what are my options? One, I can drop this stuff off with the police anonymously. A few days from now, maybe by the middle of next week, they'll have Jax in custody."

"It could be longer," Aled said, laying out streaks of

bacon in the sizzling pan. Fat popped and burned his fore-finger, which he stuck in his mouth. "Locals will probably have to forward it to Cardiff," he said around the burned digit.

"And I haven't got enough money to stay on the move for more than a few days. So, option two, I drop off the gun but not the money. Only then I'm in receipt of stolen goods and the cops will be looking for *me*."

"What if you include a statement?" Bobbi asked. "Explaining you're in fear for your life."

Gayle let out a bitter laugh. "I wouldn't have to exaggerate much."

"Or option three," Aled said, "keep the money like Danny wanted."

"And what about Jax?"

"I'll drive the gun down to Cardiff myself and turn it in. I'll give a statement leaving out how you three showed up here. Take the cash and keep your heads down for a few days."

"But the note mentions the money," Gayle said.

"Then I won't hand over the notes. I'll say that I talked to Danny on the phone the other day. Simple."

"Why not just do what Danny said?" Bobbi asked, getting to her feet. "Start again somewhere new." She started to pace the kitchen, working off nervous energy.

"And look over my shoulder for the rest of my life?"

"Well, maybe there's something I can do," she said, leaning against the kitchen counter, opposite Aled. "What if I take the gun and instead of handing it in to the police, I go to the newspaper back home? I'll tell them the whole story, including the cops not taking you seriously."

Aled retrieved a carton of eggs from the fridge. "Not a bad idea."

"Right?" she asked, looking pleased with her solution. "That way, you've got them all. If we make a big enough scene, nobody will dare touch you – or me for that matter – because too many people will be watching."

"I'm not so sure," Gayle said. "Jax's uncle is Felix Knox."

"Who?" Aled asked, cracking eggs into the pan.

"The General. He runs everything. Danny used to say he'd made millions out of the drugs the gang sells and he's never done time for it – which is basically impossible, unless he has protection. Even back in my day, it was an open secret that he had *'friends'* in the police."

"But not everybody, surely," Bobbi said.

"He only needs some to do what he wants and others that will look the other way. We'll end up dead."

"Supposing he's that well-connected," Aled said, "he must have journalists on the payroll too."

"I'd bet on it," Gayle said. "He's never been publically linked to the *West-End*."

Bobbi sighed and took her seat again at the table. "God, this is a nightmare."

Aled plated up the food and Gayle called Finn in from the living room. Hopping onto the chair, he said, "Mum, you think I can get some skull-ex-ick cars for my birthday?"

"I'm not sure if they still make those any more," Gayle said, peeling the fat off the bacon with her knife and fork. The rest of the food was perfect: the sausage was lightly spiced and the thick toast was smothered with real butter. Aled seemed to have lost much of his appetite, feeding Max pieces of his leftovers before making another round of coffees.

When Finn went off again to play, Gayle breathed in

the steam emanating from her mug, holding it in both hands.

After a moment, she said, "There might only be two options, and neither one of them is particularly good."

"What are they?" Bobbi asked, sipping her own coffee.

"Like you say, I go into hiding. And I mean from everyone. Finn and I will never be able to see you again."

An expression of pain flickered across Bobbi's face before she regained her composure. She put her knife and fork together and slid the plate away from her, everything eaten but the egg yolks. "Or?" she asked.

"The other idea is pretty bloody risky, but I don't see another way. It means, Bobbi, you take Finn and the money and keep your head down somewhere. Don't tell me where you're going, but keep your phone handy. Aled, you take the gun to the police in Cardiff. Tell them Danny called you to confess about the robbery, but don't mention that he sent the money. Tell them that Jax is coming here to the farm to kill me."

"What?"

"When he called me the other day, I deleted his number, but if I can restore it, I'll arrange to meet him. I'll tell him I've got his money."

"You think he'll believe you?" Aled asked.

"Whether he does or not, he'll come. He wants his revenge. When you get to Cardiff, let me know and I'll make the call. You need to convince the police to hurry to me here because he could make it from Leicester in three or four hours."

"You want them lying in wait?" Bobbi said.

"Yeah. He'll never expect me to go to the police, not after everything."

"But would an arrest even stick? Won't his uncle be able to pull some strings to get him released?"

"If we were still in the Midlands, maybe. He could pressure a cop he has on the inside to conveniently lose the gun somehow, but I'm counting on Wales being too far from his influence. On the other hand, if I'm really lucky, his uncle will do our job for us and take Jax out while in custody."

"You think Felix would do that to his own nephew?"

She nodded. "Better that than risk going down himself."

Shaking her head, Bobbi said, "But, Gayle, what if they arrest you?"

"Why would they do that?" Aled asked.

"For being in receipt of stolen goods," she said.

"Not really," Gayle said. "If it came to it, I think I could work out a deal; my immunity for getting them the money. I'll have that to fall back on, which is why I say not to mention the money in the first place. That way I've got something to bargain with. No, my biggest worry is that Vince's body has turned up. Plenty of witnesses saw the chase, and there's probably CCTV too. If I'm linked to him, it won't matter much what I tell the cops, because I'll be taken back to Leicester and Felix will have me killed right alongside Jax. I'll overdose in my cell or find some unlikely way to hang myself."

Bobbi rubbed her face with both hands and leaned back in her chair. "'*Risky*' was underselling this one, babe."

"But that guy," Aled interjected, "Vince. That was self-defence. You're not guilty of anything."

Gayle shook her head. "The cops back home won't see it that way. They couldn't have been happier when Danny turned up dead and they could give less than a shit about me." She ran her fingers through her hair then sat back with sagging shoulders. "I don't think there's any way for me to get out of this clean. Whatever happens to me, I can't have Finn taken into care." She fought to keep her voice from breaking. "Bobbi, I need you to promise me you won't let that happen."

She reached out and laid her hand on Gayle's wrist. "I swear I'll keep him safe. But there *has* to be another way."

Gayle shrugged. "I'm open to suggestions. But I think we're out of moves to make... and almost out of time to make them."

The three of them sat without saying another word.

Her coffee forgotten about, Gayle opened up her phone and checked the recycle bin in her call history.

Jax's number was right there, as she expected.

She added it to her contacts.

"If you're sure about this, when do you want to get started?" Aled asked. "It's a quarter to three already. It'll be pitch black in just over an hour."

Gayle looked down. Bobbi's hand still laid on her wrist. She gave it a gentle pat. "No time like the present," she said.

CHAPTER 30

Twice a day, Aled took the dog for a walk around the farm to let him burn off some energy, as well as dust away some of his own cobwebs.

"The air's clean out here," he told Gayle. "It's like medicine you never knew you needed until you get it. Is your ankle up to it?"

She sat on the settee with her left leg on top of her right knee, her foot left bare, letting it breathe. The flesh was as white as the belly of a fish. Slipping the ankle support back on, she shook her head. "I'd better finish packing everything."

"I'll give you a hand," Bobbi said.

Aled looked to Finn, who crouched on his knees, trying to get Max to let go of his slobbery tennis ball. "You feel like a walk, young Finn?"

"Can I, Mum?" he asked.

"I don't know about that," she said. "It might not be safe."

"We won't be far. And I'll have this," Aled said, holding

the shotgun in the crook of his elbow, pointed down at the floor.

"*Please*, Mummy."

Gayle looked through the living room window. The sun had lowered beyond the hills though not sunk entirely. Long shadows stretched across the fields but enough light remained in the sky that she was able to see the end of the driveway and the turn-out to the country lane.

"Fifteen minutes," she said. "No longer. It's gonna be cold out."

Finn raced to the hallway and slipped on his coat, followed by Aled, who already wore a down-lined green jacket, a flat cap and Wellington boots. Max hurried after, tail swishing and barking in excitement.

"If this is a farm, uncle Aled," Finn said, "where's all the cows and stuff?"

"I had sheep once," he said, patting the boy's head. "A couple of goats. But it got to be too much work on my own. I mostly grow things now. This season, it's been potatoes. I've got a couple of young lads from Pontypridd coming out to help me dig 'em up. I don't make a fortune, but I own the land, so it's not like I need much."

When Aled opened the front door a crack, the dog shoved through and took off.

Gayle limped to the window, craning her neck to watch them go. "I'm regretting saying yes."

"They'll be okay," Bobbi said, getting up from the settee. She put her arm around Gayle's waist and gave her a reassuring hug. "And I'll take care of him too. I won't let anything happen to him."

Gayle sighed. "I know." Her heart ached to watch Finn move out of her line of sight beyond the side of the farmhouse, but she forced herself to not dwell on that now. She needed to stay focused on the plan, because if she faltered at being apart from Finn for ten minutes, the next few days without contact would break her.

Bobbi retrieved their things from the Fiat and brought them back to the living room. Before leaving to walk the dog, Aled had fetched two suitcases on wheels from the attic and a black Nike backpack.

Gayle dusted them off and helped transfer their new clothes into the suitcases, leaving only a single change of clothes for herself, which she left in the Primark bag. She put the shoebox containing the gun and the money into the Nike backpack and handed it to Bobbi, then counted out the remaining cash that she had liberated from Tony Henry, slipping it back into her pocket.

Limping to Aled's Land Rover, which he had brought around to the front of the house, Gayle dragged one of the suitcases while Bobbi took the other. They loaded their things in the boot and laid the backpack on the rear seat. That done, Gayle turned the Fiat around to face the entrance to the farm, then joined Bobbi at the front door.

Out on the field to her left, she saw the distant figures of Aled and her son. Max's swift shadow raced out in front of them, chasing his tennis ball.

Even through the thick jumper, the cold, sucking wind leeched her body heat. She drew her shoulders up and shivered.

"That everything?" Bobbi asked.

Gayle nodded.

"Let's get back in the warm and wait."

Inside, Gayle sat on the edge of the settee, craning her neck to see out the window. Although she couldn't see them, she heard Max's barking in the distance and periodic whistles from Aled.

Bobbi was too keyed up to sit. She stood in the doorway, shifting her weight from one foot to the other, hands buried in her armpits. Nonetheless, she cocked her head to the side and said, "Are you gonna be okay?"

Gayle shrugged. "I'm more worried about you and Finn."

"I won't let him out of my sight, I *promise*."

"What a fucking mess, huh?" Gayle said, forcing a weary laugh. "You know what I feel? Mostly, I'm angry with Danny."

Bobbi nodded.

"I *told* him to leave them," she continued. "We fought about it all the time. He'd sulk and disappear for a week, then he'd be back and we'd go round again, until I just fell out of love with him. Why the hell did it have to get this bad before he wised up?" She shook her head.

"You were all just kids," Bobbi told her. "But Danny was with them from an even younger age. He was... brainwashed, I guess."

"I feel guilty because he might still be alive if I'd gotten through to him."

"It's not your fault. You lived that life too, don't forget. He just didn't have it in him to change the way you did."

Gayle scratched her scalp, tousling her hair. "Maybe I haven't changed as much as I thought," she said. "Maybe it's not possible. I mean, look at what I've done. Look at what I'm *still* doing."

"All I see is you're protecting yourself. That doesn't change who you are inside."

"Jax and I have both killed people. When it comes down to it, Bobbi, do different intentions really matter? I don't know about that," she said, answering her own question. "But I suppose I can at least make some of this right if I can get Jax behind bars."

Bobbi was about to say something more when the sound of approaching footsteps brought both their attention to the door. Muffled but audible, Gayle heard Aled calling for Max.

He opened the big, creaking door and Finn stepped in, his nose and cheeks a ruddy red.

Coming in last, stamping the mud off his Wellingtons, Aled had the shotgun slung over his shoulder. "All right," he said. "Do you need a little longer?"

"No," Gayle said, getting to her feet. "Let's just get this started before I lose my courage."

She drew Finn close and hugged him tight, kissing his cheek and breathing in the scent of him. All he knew was that she had to talk to the police and would see him in three days at the most. She couldn't bear to have told him the truth and see the pain and fear in his eyes.

Gayle choked back the sob that built in her throat and carried him out to the Land Rover. The ache in her ankle was nothing compared to the agony in her heart.

She helped him into the backseat and buckled him in.

"I love you, Finn," she said.

"I love you too," he said. "I'll see you soon?"

"Promise."

He bit his lip and nodded, wiping his nose with the back of his right hand.

Gayle forced a smile and eased the door shut. She felt Aled's hand on her shoulder as he passed, heading around to the driver's-side door, shotgun held in the crook of his elbow. He gave her a parting nod and got behind the wheel, turning the engine over.

At her side, Bobbi placed her hand on the small of

Gayle's back. "Are you sure you don't want me to call you when me and Finn get situated?"

She nodded. "If things go to plan, *I'll* call *you*, in a day or two if not right away."

The cold wind moaned across the wide-open fields, rattling the bare boughs and twigs of the tree beside the Fiat. It buffeted her back, bringing her out in a shiver and whipping her hair into her face. She tucked it away behind her ear.

Her dark eyes misting with tears, Bobbi pulled Gayle in for a hug. "Just be careful, all right?"

"You too," she said.

"Half an hour to Cardiff. You'll have the cavalry with you within the hour."

"Remind Aled to tell them not to have any cars anywhere they'll be seen from the road."

"You can count on me."

"You'd better get going, before I lose my bottle completely."

"Stay safe, sis," Bobbi said and kissed her cheek. She climbed into the passenger seat and, with pursed lips, gave a small wave as the Land Rover began to move.

In the darkness of the backseat, she saw Finn's face close to the glass. His lip trembled.

Gayle blew him a kiss and mouthed *"I love you,"* hoping she didn't look as terrified as she felt. She crossed her arms across her breasts, shivering in the cold, as the Land Rover rocked along the uneven gravel path. At the turn-out, the brake-lights flashed, then it turned right and made its way down the lane, the sound of the engine swallowed by the wind.

She watched them go, until the Land Rover disappeared

out of sight behind the hedgerow. Eyes burning, she turned back to the front door, then saw the headlights of a car approaching from the left out on the lane. Her breath locked in her lungs and a jolt of adrenaline rushed through her legs. The car was barely audible above the keening wind. It didn't approach the farmhouse, however, instead sweeping past the turn-out and continuing on its way, until she lost its lights in the deepening darkness. Every innocent shadow appeared to be threatening, like some kind of bad omen.

Gayle sniffed, wiping at her nose, and headed back inside. She closed the door on the darkness and the cold.

The house was still and silent but for the crackling of the fire in the living room.

On the floor, the Scalextric remained where Finn had left it.

Gayle looked away, chest tightening.

She took her phone out of her pocket.

Currently, she had one bar.

Thirty minutes until they're in Cardiff, she thought. If the reception dropped, she would get in the Fiat and drive until she had some bars, then return to wait for the police.

And wait for Jax.

In his place on the rug, Max dozed, his forepaws twitching.

"It's going to be all right," she said, unsure as to whether she spoke to the dog or herself. "There's no other way. And I'm not running from that bastard any more."

Max let out a soft snore and a whistle in his nose.

The wind groaned against the cold windowpane.

Gayle felt as though the darkness beyond were a living thing, surrounding the farmhouse, looking in at her.

Not knowing what else to do, Gayle went into the

kitchen to boil the kettle, trying not to think that she may have said goodbye to her son for the last time.

The drive gave Jax a lot of time to think, and while introspection was not really his style, he understood that he was at a fork in the road.

His uncle Felix wanted things cleaned up but only to ensure that he continued to be the ocean to which the rivers of drug money flowed. In that way, Jax himself served only as middle management. He might be a Captain, but what did that really mean? He still got his hands dirty and he lived in a small flat in the city, scarcely a mile from where he had been born. Jax didn't have a stake in a race horse; he didn't own a Porsche; and the only swimming pool he had been in was a public one almost ten years ago.

He didn't know yet how he was going to kill Felix. He wanted to simply walk up and shoot him – and his silly Botox bitch. But Jax wasn't going to give in to that particular impulse. For one thing, he would be a suspect, though he was confident he could avoid prosecution if he was clever. The worst thing would be the power vacuum his uncle's death would create. Jax figured that it would be Felix's sometime business partner, the Birmingham-born gangster Wyman Cross, who would fill the void. In doing so, the branches of the *WEC* would have mini wars of their own as the members decided their loyalties. The gang and the business may not survive.

Jax had to be smarter than that. As satisfying as it would be to put a bullet into the leathery head of the doddery old bastard, Jax had to exhibit some self-control. He could survive and even thrive by striking first, but only if he was systematic.

Felix, he knew, was firing blanks. He had no children of his own and Jax had no siblings. If the old snake was true to his venomous nature, Belinda had been made to sign a prenup. When the old man was gone, Jax doubted that she would inherit everything, and equally Jax himself would receive a pittance – if he got anything at all. Who knew where all those ill-gotten gains would end up?

As the miles passed beneath his wheels, a plan had galvanised in his mind. He didn't have everything worked out – not yet – but he figured he could go to his uncle under the pretext of handing over the cash. With his defences down, Jax could take out Belinda then and there; she wasn't integral to his plan. Felix, however, would have to be taken alive. He would force his uncle to update his will, leaving himself as the legitimate inheritor as the old man's only living relative.

He would take his time with this, of course. He would make it look like a kidnapping. Then, a week or even two weeks later, the bodies would turn up. It made sense to Jax that he ought to concoct a way to implicate Wyman Cross. Why not? Take out a couple of snakes in one fell swoop. But kidnapping Felix would be too bold a move even for Cross, so Jax would need to give the bastard a motive. Perhaps he could shoot one of Cross's guys first when he returned from Wales: perhaps his bodyguard, that fat fuck Femi. He would need to unload the clip into him, to make sure he got through all the flab.

Jax smiled at that thought.

The cops would believe that. They would surround Cross and even if they couldn't pin the kidnapping and murder on him, they would get him for one of the numerous other crimes he and his boys committed daily.

To avoid suspicion, Jax decided not to force the old prick to leave him *everything* in his will. That would be too obvious. A lot of his estate would go to charity, even some to Belinda's family just to allay suspicion. More important than the money he received – which would still be considerable – was the power over the gang. A few wannabes would stand up to him, sure, but Jax wasn't afraid of them.

As General – and with Cross out of the way – the entire city would essentially be his. The few that might conceivably stand against him could be cut down with no trouble.

Jesus Christ, he could be a bigger name than the Kray twins. His mind was on fire with the possibilities.

A short while later, he had stopped on the M5 to eat at a Burger King. He bought some food to take with him – crisps, chocolate bars, a couple of Cokes – and wondered what other supplies he might need. Jax had already dressed for the cold in a sturdy pair of Timbalands, so didn't have to worry about clothes. When he couldn't think of anything, he got back in the car and continued driving.

In Wales, the rain had moved on and the cloud cover had begun to break up. He followed the directions on his phone to Aled Gowan's farm.

It was getting dark as he approached. As he wound along the country lane, the property came back into view beyond the hedgerow.

Jax killed his headlights and slowed to little more than a crawl. He brought the car to a stop on the right side of the lane, the driver's-side wheels up on the mushy grass verge. From here, the land sloped downward, and he saw the entrance to the farm a hundred yards ahead.

He opened the window and the cold air sucked out the

heat. He looked through the dark, tangled hedgerow at the farmhouse, its windows well-lit in the deepening gloom.

"What do we do now?" the voice beside him asked.

Jax looked away from the farm and gave Scotty an annoyed look. "Now," he said, "we fuckin' *wait*."

Scotty looked away, sitting with his knees drawn up and his arms wrapped across his chest. He fingered a budding whitehead on his chin.

Later, Jax saw the door open. He watched a tall man and Gayle Stillwater's kid take a walk across the field, following behind some breed of midsize dog. A moment later, the bitch herself appeared in the doorway, standing beside her neighbour, Bobbi Okoye, before heading inside.

"Do we go now?" Scotty asked.

Jax was tempted, but shook his head. He wanted to be sure that he could get onto the farm without alerting them. The dog made that difficult. And he was sure that he could see Gowan's uncle carrying a shotgun slung over his shoulder.

Later still, as he worried over the problem, he watched the farmer bring an old Land Rover around to the front of the house, then Gayle and Okoye loaded up the boot. Gayle got into her own car, but killed the engine and got out just as Jax thought she might drive away.

"What the hell is she up to?" he muttered.

Scotty didn't say anything.

A few moments later, the boy and the three adults came outside again; everyone but Gayle got into the waiting Land Rover.

"Where are they going?" Scotty asked, leaning across the dashboard, his forehead almost touching the windscreen.

"Wherever it is," Jax said, "she's not going with them."

"But why not?"

Jax didn't know and didn't care. All he knew was that this was his chance.

He reached into the glove compartment and grabbed the Smith & Wesson revolver. He shook an additional six bullets out of the box of ammo and slipped everything into the pocket of his bomber jacket.

Jax elbowed Scotty in the upper arm. "Right," he said, "here's what you're gonna do..."

CHAPTER 31

The Land Rover was old and though not the most comfortable ride, it took the winding country lanes well. In ten minutes, they were on the A470, past Pontypridd, travelling south towards Cardiff.

"How far now?" Bobbi asked.

"About ten or twelve miles," Aled said.

As the Land Rover picked up speed, Bobbi began to feel more and more nervous. She looked out the window at the dark treeline whipping by. In the mirror, she saw headlights.

Aled muttered, "He wasn't a bad boy, you know. Danny, I mean. Least, not when he was little. I didn't see much of him or Lorraine after I moved out this way with the missus."

Trying to shake off the unease, Bobbi said, "Gayle didn't mention you were married."

"She's been passed four years this April."

"I'm sorry."

"Me too. She wanted kids, but... well. She would have loved young Finn." For almost another mile, he retreated into silence again.

From his place in the back, Finn said, "Is my mummy gonna be okay?"

Bobbi turned at the waist and gave him a smile. "Of course she is. Don't worry. It's gonna be better really soon." Bobbi's eyes drifted away from his sullen face to the car behind them. It kept closing the distance to twenty yards or so before falling back to more than sixty. She squinted her eyes, looking away from the starburst-effect its headlights created in the rear window.

She sat facing forwards once more. The road was empty but for themselves and the vehicle behind. She watched in the side mirror as it fell back again.

"Something wrong?" Aled asked, keeping his voice low, his brow knotted with a frown.

"I don't know," she whispered. "Probably not. Just feeling... edgy, I suppose."

Aled adjusted his rear-view mirror. "Are we being followed?"

"I don't know."

She felt the car begin to slow as Aled eased off the accelerator.

"What are you doing?" she asked.

"Seeing if it passes," Aled said, eyes on the mirror. He reached for the shotgun by his left leg, aimed with the barrel pointed to the floor. He drew the stock in against his thigh.

Bobbi looked over her shoulder. The headlights grew bigger and brighter.

* * *

As she set the kettle on the stove to boil, Max joined Gayle in the kitchen. He approached the back door, his tail swishing, issuing a soft whine.

"Full bladder, mate?" she asked, opening the door. "Me too, actually."

Gayle had no sooner drawn the door in than he hurried through it and trotted out onto the dark fields. She eased the door closed behind the dog, certain she could be back to let him in before he got distressed.

She climbed the stairs, gripping the banister to spare her injured ankle. Letting herself into the small bathroom, the landing light illuminated all but the bath, so she left the door open and the light off. She sat down to pee and withdrew her phone. Once again, she was without reception. The battery was at seventy-six percent.

In less than twenty minutes, Bobbi should be calling to say that they had arrived in Cardiff, where she would leave Aled and take Finn somewhere safe in the Land Rover. With reception this spotty, Gayle figured she would have to drive towards Pontypridd to take the call and then get in touch with Jax, but that didn't worry her: she was confident that she would be back to wait for the police with plenty of time to spare.

She wiped and flushed and stood in front of the small shaving mirror, washing her hands in the sink. There were no curtains or blinds and, unlike most new bathroom windows, the old glass pane was clear instead of frosted. The approaching night was inky black and the cold face of the moon was obscured behind a mask of thick clouds. The distant hills, country lanes and hedgerows were barely-differentiated gradients of black-grey. The only details that Gayle could discern were the Fiat parked by the tree and its pile of machine parts, caught in the wash of light from the downstairs windows, and the snaking gravel path, only a few shades paler than the muddy earth through which it wove.

Just then, movement caught her eye.

Gayle ducked, bending at the waist, until her chin almost touched the sill. She stopped breathing.

Amongst the shadows, she saw only blackness.

She narrowed her eyes, scanning left and right.

Nothing.

Just Max sniffing around, she thought. *Or grass moving in the wind.*

But the fine hairs on her arms tingled as though themselves stirred by an icy draught.

Then she saw it again; movement, thirty feet back from the Fiat. A dark shape in the pools of blackness. Much bigger than the old Irish Setter. And coming slowly towards the house.

Jax.

She drew back, not wanting to be seen, but couldn't let him out of her sight completely.

How could he have found her already? Nobody knew she was here. It was too soon; she was unprepared.

Gayle patted her pockets, forgetting for a moment where she had put the switchblade, before finding it and thumbing the button. Its blade glistened in the light from the landing.

Out on the lawn, Jax's dark shape circled around the tree, moving to her left, away from the panel of light coming from the downstairs window.

Gayle inched to her right until her thigh bumped the side of the bath and arrested her movement. She craned her neck.

Down below her, she saw him circle back towards the front door, moving faster.

She backed up, almost crying out in fear when her shoulder struck the doorframe. She stepped out of the bathroom, moving to the head of the stairs, switchblade held down by her thigh. Her palm had gone slick, and she transferred it to her left while she wiped her hand dry on her jeans.

She stood in a half-crouch, back against the wall, looking down the stairs at the front door. It was closed but unlocked.

Gayle hesitated. If he came in before she was all the way down, she'd be trapped.

She listened for the sound of the knob turning or the rasp of the latch bolt, but above the thudding of her heart, all she heard was a whistle, growing louder; the kettle on the stove beginning to boil. The sound of it rose to a deafening, nerve-shredding shriek.

Through the clamour, she strained to hear something of Jax's approach, but there was nothing, until she saw a sliver of light glimmer on the burnished brass doorknob. The door moved in the frame.

Gayle stepped back, away from the stairs, hoping the screeching kettle would conceal her movements from him as much as it did his from her.

The rooms at the back of the house offered no safety: with no way down but the window, she knew she couldn't hope to climb down without further injury to her ankle. She was trapped up here—

The wood-store, she thought.

Orienting herself quickly, she hurried to her left, through a bedroom door, easing it shut behind her. The room housed large cardboard boxes, suitcases and packing chests, which she hurried past and pulled open the dusty curtains.

She looked out onto the front of the property. The long, slender fingers of the tree ticked and rattled against the dark glass. Forehead pressed to the glass, she looked down and made out the sloped roof protecting firewood from the elements.

The casement frames on the old windows were opened by a bar on the bottom edge, but when Gayle tried it, the wooden fixture creaked and groaned but would not open. Sweat beading her forehead, she shoved again with her palm against the flat panel, but it still did not budge.

"Come on," she whispered, laying the switchblade down on the sill. She pressed both hands against the panel and shoved, locking her arms. She heard a *crack* from the weathered wooden frame.

She looked over her shoulder, certain that he would be standing there, but she was alone – for now.

Hurry!

She tried again, shoving at the window with everything she had. Sweat sprang up on the back of her neck. The warped wood rasped and grated before finally coming open with a loud *bang* and a confetti of paint chips. The wind pulled the window out and it slapped hard against the outside wall. Glass shattered and rained down on the tiles.

"Fuck!" she hissed, whipping her head again to look back: still alone, but if Jax had heard the noise, he would be bounding up the stairs even now.

Moving fast, Gayle slipped the blade back into the handle and returned the knife to her pocket. Bracing herself with both hands on the window-frame, she kicked her left leg up and out into the icy wind. She slipped her other leg through, turning to back out an inch at a time. She looked down over her shoulder, judging the distance between the roof-tiles and her swinging feet.

She adjusted her grip on the frame, easing her torso over the wood. Her jumper and T-shirt hiked up, scraping her belly on the rough outer sill. As she pushed herself further out, her woollen jumper caught on the stubby bolt that protruded from the bottom of the frame.

Shit! She felt the garment slip up and bunch under her armpits, tightening across her shoulders. She flailed her feet, hoping to feel the roof of the wood-store, but there was nothing. Gayle tried to haul herself back in so that she could free her jumper, but her biceps and shoulders burned. Then her left hand slipped off the frame. She tried to hang on with just her right but she lost her grip and fell.

The jumper cinched tight around her upper back, burning and biting into her armpits. Momentum slammed her into the façade, bumping her chin hard and ringing her teeth. Before she could react to the pain, she felt the fabric give and she was falling again, arms yanked up over her head. Her feet slapped hard on the tiles of the wood-store but slipped out from under her. She landed hard on her right hip, bounced, then fell back and off the sloped roof, landing in a heap on her left side. The impact blasted the air from her lungs. She felt broken glass beneath her shoulder, which burned against the cold ground and the frigid wind that bit her bared midriff and lower back. Looking up, she saw her royal-blue jumper fluttering like a flag from the window-frame.

Gayle shoved herself first to her knees then her feet. She tottered for a moment, almost fell, but kept her balance and hurried against the wall. She reached for her back pocket, afraid that she had lost the switchblade, but it was still there. With the wood-store at her side, she reached down and snatched up a small piece of firewood that had been cut in half length-ways. At almost ten inches long, it had sufficient heft that she could throw it or use it as a club.

From inside the house, she heard the shriek from the kettle, dulled by the walls and the keening of the wind.

She thumbed the button to draw the blade, then rounded the house, keeping her back to the wall, stepping one foot over the other. She moved to the rear of the farmhouse, peering back but seeing nothing. At the corner, she switched both weapons to the other hand, all the better to launch the log at Jax, but she saw only fields sloping off into the distance.

Gayle slid along the rough wall, staying low to pass below the kitchen window, moving to the back door. Inside, she heard a soft clatter, then the ear-splitting shriek from the kettle seemed to change its harsh note before growing quieter. He had taken it off the stove; all the better to hear where she had gone.

With the shrill squeal silenced, Gayle noticed another sound in the sombre drone of the October wind: the long, low, throaty growl and high, excited barks of a dog.

Max.

Gayle looked out onto the fields, but saw no sign of the Irish Setter.

From the kitchen, footsteps.

The door squeaked open.

Gayle shrank down, pressed her back hard into the wall. She raised the log in her trembling hand.

No more than six feet away, dressed in a black jacket and baseball cap, Jax stepped down and onto the grass. He moved off in front of her a couple of steps, looking from side to side.

Max came into view twenty feet away. His head was hung low, front legs bent, chest almost touching the dirt. He growled again before issuing five sharp barks that hurt Gayle's ears.

"What is—" Jax started to say, and Gayle launched the log, striking him high on the back of the neck and he cried out. Even as it arced through the air, Gayle was hurrying forwards, pushing off with her right foot, moving the knife to her strong hand.

Hearing her, Jax turned, but she slammed against him before they were facing. His feet tangled and he went down, she atop him, right knee driving into the meat of his inner thigh. Even as they landed in the mud, Max was on him, fangs clasping the sleeve of his jacket, head whipping from side to side. Gayle angled the knife, ready to drive it into his belly.

But she saw that it wasn't Jax. He was a teenager, white, with his pale face littered with acne.

"Who the hell are you?" she asked.

Eyes wild, the kid squealed, trying to pull away from Max, who at last stopped thrashing but instead growled and yanked every few seconds at the kid's sleeve.

"I said, who are you?" she demanded.

"S-Scotty," he stuttered.

Scotty? she thought, lowering the knife. She eased back but didn't release him.

"What are you doing here?" she asked.

"Please, get this dog off me."

Gayle slapped his cheek hard enough to hurt her left hand. "Why are you here?"

"Fuck you, bitch," he squealed, *"just get this fucking dog off me!"*

"I said, what are you doing here? Where's Jax?"

"I'm not telling you shit."

Gayle grabbed him by the hair, twisting hard. "We'll see."

* * *

Behind Bobbi, Finn had turned around to kneel on the seat beside the Nike backpack. He looked over the headrest through the rear window.

"Why are we slowing down?" he asked.

"I want to be sure," Aled said. He drew the shotgun out from the foot-well and laid it across his lap, the muzzle aimed at the driver's-side door panel. As he came off the accelerator, Bobbi saw the speedometer begin to drop.

Fifty-five.

Fifty.

Forty-five.

He thumbed on his hazard lights and toggled the switch to lower the side window. The noise of the biting wind and grumbling engine filled the cabin.

Aled reached his arm out the window and gestured for the car behind to pass.

Their pursuer had closed the gap again, and tailed them at a distance of less than ten yards.

"Come on," Aled urged, waving his arm.

Their speed had dropped to forty miles per hour.

"He's not going to over-take," Bobbi said. "Speed back up."

Aled turned off the hazards and nudged the accelerator. As the needle climbed, the car behind them slipped further and further back.

Bobbi looked at Finn. He was visibly shaking.

"It's okay, honey," she said.

Looking at the speedometer, Bobbi saw they were doing sixty again.

Aled raised the window.

"What was all that?" she asked.

"I don't know," he said. "Probably just someone who had a few too many pints." But the shotgun across his lap suggested that he didn't really believe that.

As she was about to ask how long before they reached Cardiff, the headlights dazzled her in the mirror once more. Even over the sound of the Land Rover, she heard the other car's racing engine. She looked over her shoulder and saw it whip over into the oncoming lane and draw up alongside them.

She looked past Aled, peering through the window at the driver, who could not be seen through their pursuer's heavily-tinted windows.

"Now what?" Aled muttered. In the glow from the dashboard, Bobbi saw that his lined forehead was sheathed in sweat.

Behind them, Finn began to cry.

Then, with a sudden bark of its rubber tyres on the road, the other car swerved and slammed into them hard.

CHAPTER 32

With the dog snapping at his heels, Gayle dragged Scotty by the back of his jacket into the kitchen, where she noticed a JD Sports bag that hadn't been there before. She shoved the kid against the table and chairs. In the light, she now saw that he was barely seventeen.

Still holding the switchblade, she rifled through his bag while Max kept the kid where he was. Inside it, she found disposable gloves, a roll of duct tape and a small axe handle.

"Don't need to ask what you were planning on doing with this," she said, snatching up the tape. "Get on the fucking chair."

His eyes darted from hers to the knife and back again. Moving slowly, he rose and pulled out the nearest seat. A trickle of blood oozed down the back of his neck from a wound hidden in his matted hair. Gayle realised that she must have hit him harder than she first thought.

Max ensured Scotty's obedience with menacing growls, fierce barks and a snapping of his jaws, coming up short only by inches. Gayle pocketed the switchblade long enough to tape the kid's wrists behind the chair. She looped a strip twice around his chest then threw the roll aside.

She reached down, taking Max by the collar. The aggressive change in him was surprising and it took almost all her strength to keep the snarling dog back.

Bending at the waist, Gayle leaned into the kid's face and said, "Where's Jax?"

His eyes wide with fear, the idiot still resisted: "Go fuck yourself."

Without releasing the collar, Gayle gave the dog room to move and he lunged again, snatching a mouthful of Scotty's baggy jeans. He tugged and shook his head from side to side. The fabric tore before Gayle pulled him back.

Scotty screamed, wailed, thrashed against his bonds, as tears of fear and frustration sprang up in his bulging eyes.

"Answer me," Gayle warned him, "or I swear to God, I'll feed him your bollocks. Where's Jax?"

"In the car," Scotty blubbered.

"Outside?"

"No, no," he said, eyes not leaving the snarling dog. "Please, keep him back."

"Then where is he?"

"He's following the Land Rover."

Gayle straightened up, a cold chill of fear coursing along the length of her spine. "He's...? What did you say?"

"He's following the Land Rover!" Scotty screamed, but Gayle was already turning, pulling Max with her.

She hurried into the living room and slammed the kitchen door. Max sniffed and snorted at the space beneath, pacing, his flanks quivering as he continued to growl.

There was no time to take the dog with her. Gayle closed the front door and limped to the Fiat, turning over the engine before she even had it shut. She stomped on the

accelerator, wheels spinning in the gravel, before finding
purchase and rocketing her to the country lane. She turned
right and moved up through the gears, hunched over the
wheel, shaking.

She checked her watch. Fifteen minutes had elapsed
since Bobbi, Finn and Aled had left.

When the winding lane allowed, she grabbed her phone
and held it against the steering wheel, stealing glances at the
screen.

No reception.

She urged more speed from the Fiat and hit the high-
beams. The dark green-brown hedgerows whipped by the
windows. The narrow road was a serpentine strip of
asphalt, unlined by road markings.

In spite of the blowing heaters and the sweat trickling
down her temples, Gayle was chilled to the core.

She continued along the road, desperate to keep moving
but terrified that every mile on the unfamiliar road could be
taking her further away from her son. The phone in her
hand only briefly regained reception.

Out in the darkness, she saw a green road sign
coming up.

"Thank God," she rasped through her dry throat.

She slowed to give herself enough time to read it.

Cardiff, next left.

Without indicating, Gayle took the turn and jammed
the accelerator to the floor.

Aled wrestled with the steering wheel as the cabin filled
with the tortured screech of metal on metal; a fierce shriek
that was deafening in the confines.

Bobbi braced herself with one hand against the dashboard, the other gripping Aled's headrest. Glancing over her shoulder, she saw Finn huddled on the seat, eyes closed tight with his hands clasped over his ears.

A hard jolt blasted through the Land Rover, rocking it from side to side, pitching Bobbi against the side window. She rapped her head hard on the glass, then was at once thrown to the opposite side as the tyres skimmed and finally mounted the kerb.

With a mighty wrench of the wheel, Aled shoved the smaller car back. When the Focus swerved away, he quickly corrected his angle to keep them in lane, then toed the accelerator and the Land Rover sprang forwards once more. The shotgun in his lap slipped off his thighs, the butt coming to rest between his legs, muzzle pointing straight up.

The Focus poured on the speed, keeping pace at their side, darting left and right, preparing to ram them again, but this time Aled beat him to it.

He yanked the wheel hard, smashing into the passenger door of the Focus, bending the sheet metal in. The tinted window webbed but did not shatter.

Bobbi grasped the headrest tighter, planting her feet far apart in the foot-well and dug in. Finn was screaming now for his mother.

Aled turned them away from the other car and Bobbi saw that only the passenger-side headlight cleaved the gloom in front of them. The Focus fell back to a single car-length, as if to manoeuvre behind them and ram their tail, but then Bobbi realised their pursuer's true intention even as he attempted to PIT them.

The impact snapped Bobbi's head back against the rest. The Land Rover fishtailed on the tarmac as Aled fought the wheel, weaving in and out of lane, but he didn't lose complete control and soon had the big car righted again.

Between his thighs, the shotgun had continued to slip. Both barrels now pointed straight at Bobbi's face.

Sensing it at the same time, Aled reached for the gun with his left hand, pulling it up. She ducked her head to the left as he struggled with its length in the confines. "Grab it," he urged.

Shaking, she reached for it with both hands, gripping the weapon by the butt and barrel, careful to stay clear of the triggers. She pointed it straight up, the muzzle brushing the roof above her head.

Its engine racing, the Focus drew up alongside them once more.

"What are we going to do?" Bobbi shouted above the noise of the Land Rover's own motor.

All at once, she watched the tinted window of the Focus explode; the sound of the blast lost in the night as Aled instinctively ducked when the bullet struck the pillar, issuing a high-pitched screech and showering the wind-screen with a brief cascade of sparks.

"He shot at us!" he cried, hunched down over the wheel.

Looking across his back, she saw the revolver pointed at them from the Focus's cabin. The man aiming at them stole glances at the road as he tried to train the sights on them for a second shot.

She had never seen Jax Knox before but knew that it could be no one else. Alternating his attention from the road to the gun, she saw his face.

The bastard was laughing. In his hand, the gun bucked as he fired once more, but the shot went wide, missing the Rover.

"Christ!" Aled shouted. His foot was shoved hard

against the accelerator. The old engine roared but it was already giving them everything it had.

Ahead, Bobbi saw only a straight road; no turns, no other vehicles, no safety.

"What are we gonna do?" she asked.

"Shoot him," Aled said.

"What?"

"Shoot the bastard!"

Before Bobbi could make sense of what she was being asked to do, the window imploded, showering Aled with fragments of glass. She screamed as pieces rained down on her, closing her eyes tight, face buried in her right elbow. When she dared look up, she saw Aled slumped towards her, holding the wheel in a one-handed grip, his left clamped over his right shoulder. When he lifted it away, she saw his fingers stained with blood.

In the other car, Knox bobbed his head in excitement, a sick smile stretched across his broad face. He waved the revolver like a rodeo cowboy.

Through gritted teeth, Aled hissed, *"Shoot him!"*

Bobbi pointed the shotgun through the broken window, its barrel bouncing against the frame both with the movement of the car and the violent tremors that racked her entire body.

"Do it, Auntie Bobbi," Finn pleaded from the backseat.

She took a hold of the grip and let her finger fall on the trigger. She squeezed and the *boom* filled the car. Her ears rang in the wake of the blast, blocking out the fury of the wind blowing through the broken window.

Pellets from the shot struck the Focus's bonnet and blew out the passenger-side headlight, sending a firework of hot steel up into the night. Surprised by the blast, Knox pulled

the car away but returned fire with a shot that hit the Land
Rover's flank somewhere behind her.

"Finn!" she cried. *"Are you okay?"*

He was curled into a ball, nodding, unhurt though his
face was leeched of all colour.

She trained the shotgun again, seeing Aled bracing
himself from the corner of her eye.

She pulled the trigger.

And missed.

She took a third shot but nothing happened.

"Empty," Aled told her. As he spoke, Knox fell back
again.

In spite of the cold wind, his face was sheathed in
sweat. His right hand fell into his lap and he snatched at the
wheel with his bloodied left, forcing himself to straighten
up with great effort.

"My pocket," he said. "Only got two more."

Before Bobbi could draw the gun back and reach into
Aled's jacket pocket for the spare ammo, the rear window
imploded and Finn screamed.

Gayle made it to the dual-carriageway and floored the
accelerator, nudging the little Fiat to ninety, a hundred,
until it felt that it was going to rattle apart.

Though the heaters were turned up full-blast, she
couldn't stop shaking. The wheel in her hand was slippery
with sweat.

She squinted through the darkness, desperate to catch
sight of the Land Rover's tail-lights, but saw only empty,
dark road.

"I'll kill you," she said aloud. "I swear, if you've hurt

them, if you've hurt my little boy... I swear to God, I'll kill you."

She glanced at the speedometer. The needle was stuck at just over a hundred. The steering wheel shuddered.

In her mind's eye, she saw the Land Rover on its side, exhaust pluming in the cold air, in a ditch by the side of the road. Inside, Finn was dangling over his restraining seatbelt, hair hanging down in his bloodied face, chips of glass stuck in his cheeks and forehead, unable to move. She could see Bobbi, slumped off the seat, her head set at an unnatural angle on her broken neck. Aled was pinned in place with the steering column pushed back into his chest, blood drying across his chin and beneath both ears. And she saw Jax pulling open the crumpled rear door, levelling an enormous gun into Finn's terrified, upturned face.

Don't, she told herself, *don't even think it. He's okay. They're all going to be okay.*

She checked her watch. They left twenty-three minutes ago.

Gayle prayed that Aled had been driving the speed limit; that Jax hadn't caught sight of them, or had lost them on the twisting roads; that she would soon see the old Land Rover emerge through the evening gloom in the wash of her headlights.

But she kept looking off into the hedgerows and ditches she passed, full of a superstitious terror that she would see the car as she had envisioned it: flipped onto its side, exhaust smoking, tyres still spinning, and her only child executed in the backseat.

CHAPTER 33

Fragments of window glass rained down on Finn. The boy shrieked and tried to wriggle deeper into his seat, until the diagonal band of the belt slipped over his head, leaving only the part across his lap to restrain him.

Bobbi had ducked low when the window imploded, but now sat up straighter, crying Finn's name.

He looked left and right, frantic, eyes bulging, looking to see from where the next threat would come — scared, but alive.

Beside her, Aled groaned in pain, blinking his eyes in an effort to focus on the road. "My pocket," he said. "Hurry."

Holding the weapon upright, Bobbi dug inside and found the pair of shotgun shells. He directed her to thumb a switch and the shotgun snapped open, ejecting the spent casings. She jabbed the first of the fresh shells at the open breach, hand trembling, and she missed again and again before finally sliding it home.

Bobbi changed her grip on the final shell, guiding it in, when the car was rocked hard, jolting forwards and began to fishtail once more. With only one hand with which to grip the wheel, Aled seesawed at it to straighten out the swerve, but in vain. She threw out her hand to snatch the wheel and right them, dropping the last shotgun shell into the darkness of the foot-well.

Together, they wrestled control of the Rover before being struck again from behind, though less violently than before.

"Ahead," Aled grunted, his breathing coming in pained gasps now, "that left turn."

Bobbi saw it. They had left hedgerows and open fields for an industrial park. On either side of the wide road were factories and warehouses, many with lights glowing from within. As they passed an unmanned lorry trailer, she saw the turn. The road was too narrow to take at speed, but Aled hit the brake hard and began to turn the wheel. She held it tight, feeling the inertia pulling her to the right and the seatbelt dug into her neck.

"Don't let go," he said, releasing the wheel to shift into third gear.

Bobbi strained to hold on and forced her weight to the left, against the body-roll. The engine roared as Aled came off the clutch and flattened his foot on the accelerator once more. The tyres squealed and shuddered on the tarmac. At the apex of the turn, nearing the far-side kerb, the interior of the Land Rover filled with light. Before she could look back, they were struck from behind and she was thrust back in her seat, losing her grip on both the steering wheel and the shotgun.

Though Aled snatched for the controls, he was too slow and their front wheels hit the kerb at the same time with a harsh *bang*, ploughing them across the wide pavement and towards a low, iron-fenced wall.

Bobbi tried to brace herself against the dashboard, but

they struck the brick barrier even as the wheels made contact with the ground. She saw the flash from the driver's airbag out the corner of her eye, then the iron bars break away from the concrete, before everything went black.

* * *

Jax brought the Focus to a stop before he mounted the kerb, sitting almost broadside across the unlined road. Through the hazy vapours from his ruptured radiator, he saw the tail-lights of the Land Rover across his scarred and buckled bonnet.

As he took in his surroundings, he realised that the engine had stalled and he had lost the revolver. He spotted it in the passenger foot-well and snapped off his seatbelt to pick it up. He felt a dull ache in his upper chest and shoulder from where the belt had cinched tight, but he wasn't hurt. Armed again, Jax opened the revolver's cylinder and flicked out the three expended cartridges.

Keeping his eyes on the stricken Land Rover, he hurried to reload from the bullets in his pocket.

Seconds passed but nobody tried to get out of the other car. Pitched slightly to the right, it had beached itself on the smashed brick wall. The iron railings had caved in, their spiky ends penetrating the windscreen, holding it like a small fish in a massive pair of jaws.

Jax rolled the soreness out of his neck, then got out and moved around the front end, shielding his face from the hot steam with his free hand. The revolver hung down by his thigh, shielded from sight.

He looked along the street for anyone who might have seen the accident, but there were only a handful of untenanted cars parked with their wheels up on the pavement. Beyond the broken wall, mangled railings and sixty-foot expanse of tarmac, Jax saw trailers left abandoned in the sloping loading bays of the warehouse, eight or more of them. Above the shuttered doors, weak amber lights revealed no employees. He was alone in the relative silence following the crash, only a mild ringing in his ears from the gunfire.

He smiled to himself as he made it around the front of the Focus, bending at the waist and squinting, looking for movement in the stranded car. The nearest streetlight was fifteen or twenty feet too far to reveal the interior, but then Jax heard a noise. Over the hiss of the radiator and the tinnitus-like bell in his ear, he heard the sound of a child weeping.

Think I'd fall for some stupid set-up? he thought. *Your kid's gonna pay the price for it.*

Still ten feet back from the crumpled rear of the Land Rover, he froze and sunk low when he heard a noise. Something metallic. A screech and a scrape.

He gazed over at the warehouse, expecting to see a roller-shutter begin to clatter upwards, then realised it was the warped passenger door being forced open.

It was the Okoye bitch. First her foot emerged, then her head, blood painting one side of her face from a gash in her forehead. She had gotten herself turned around somehow, perhaps by the impact, because she was half-facing him when she exited on wobbly legs.

Their eyes locked. Jax began to smile, then saw she had something in her hand and he stopped moving. Even as he realised that she held the shotgun, he lifted his revolver, but though she was weaving on weak legs, she already had the damn thing levelled at him.

He threw himself back, landing hard on his arse as the

shot sailed past his head; wide, the blast riddled the front of the Focus and blew in the windscreen. He rolled away to his right, putting the rear-end of the Land Rover between him and the bitch. The tarmac took nips out of his cold hands. Flat on his belly, he risked a look, the revolver out in front of him. He fired a shot that missed the Land Rover by a mile, then hesitated, looking for movement.

Jax expected to see her come around the back, so trained the stubby .38 in that direction, but she surprised him again. Instead of coming for him with the shotgun, she had ducked inside for something and now retreated over the ruined fence.

He shoved himself upright in time to see that she dragged the kid behind her, limping through pools of shadow, across the sloping concrete towards the warehouse. Frantic, she screamed for help.

Jax rushed after her, firing another shot that ricocheted off the concrete floor.

He wouldn't miss again.

Gayle raced along the road, going far too fast. Less than a mile back, she had been forced to swerve to avoid colliding with something left in the middle of the road.

A bumper, she thought, sneaking glances in the rear-view mirror, but the object - whatever it had been - was swallowed by distance and darkness.

More than once, she had seen the twinkling of glass on the road surface.

From the Land Rover? she thought.

Gayle swallowed hard, her mouth arid, as sweat made her neck and chest itch in the stuffy car. She thumbed the control to clear her fogging windscreen, straining so hard to see that she had a headache.

She was forced to slow when she entered an industrial park, surrounded on all sides by the dark fronts of factories and warehouses. Gayle let her speed drop to only twenty miles per hour to give herself a chance to look between the cars and trailers parked on both sides of the road.

Further along, a street bisected this one from the left. When the nose of the Fiat was almost level with it, she saw first a dark red or brown car angled across the road, then Aled Gowan's Land Rover lying halfway over a broken wall.

She slammed her foot on the brake, swinging the wheel. Ten or twelve feet after the turn, she got out without turning off the engine. She hurried for the Land Rover, ignoring the pain from her twisted ankle.

She looked for Finn through the broken-out windows, but he wasn't there. Bobbi was also gone. Aled was pinned in his seat by two pointed iron railings buried in his chest below the collarbone.

His skin looked waxy and pale in what little light reached him through the shattered window. He looked at Gayle without lifting his head up off his chest, his eyes swimming in and out of focus. He tried to say her name but only gurgled.

"Where are they?" she asked him. "Did you see where they went?"

Aled turned away from her, facing the long depot beyond the fence that pinned him. "There," he managed to say. "Ran. He has a... has a gun."

"Hold on," she begged. "I'll get help. *Just hold on.*"

"Don't let... don't let him..." Spit bubbled on his quivering lip. "Don't..." Aled's eyes closed and he sat silent.

She reached in, trying to feel his breath on the back of her hand, but felt nothing.

From beyond the fence, Gayle heard the *crack* of a gunshot.

She tore open the back door, looking for the Nike backpack. For a moment, she feared it was gone, but found it tucked beneath the driver's seat. She unzipped it, ripped at the lid of the shoebox, and took up the Glock. Slinging the bag over her shoulder, she hurried over the broken-down wall, smearing whatever fingerprints the gun might still hold with her sweaty palm.

* * *

Jax hurried after, angling the revolver down in front of him, holding it with both hands.

He came to one of the abandoned trailers and sank to a crouch, sweeping the gun back and forth as he peered beneath it. Not finding them in the shadows there, he rounded the end, following along its flank along the sloping loading bay. When he reached the wall beneath the shutter doors, he crept forwards with his shoulder against the concrete.

Approaching another trailer, he pointed the revolver in front as he passed the large tyre, but again, he was alone. Now that his ears had stopped ringing, Jax waited for a moment, listening.

Somewhere in the distance of the depot complex, he heard the rattle and hum of ventilation and heating units. Beyond the steel shutters, he caught the sound of machinery and faint, muffled speech.

Then, further ahead, he heard scuffed footsteps. A woman's voice whispered, *"This way."*

Moving on the balls of his feet, he hurried after, hardly making a sound. He passed the final trailer and came to the end of the wall. Opposite was a second warehouse, three-storeys tall, leaving a damp, narrow alleyway between the two buildings. Dingy, yellowed windows cast piss-coloured pools of faint light along its length that could not dispel all the shadows.

Jax peered around the corner.

Doorways from fire exits were spaced every thirty or forty feet on both sides. Above his head, dangling wires and power cables swung in the cold night wind. Puddles, crushed drinks cans and other refuse lay scattered across the concrete. Halfway along its two-hundred foot length, a rank of three industrial bins lined the right side of the alley. Opposite them, another smaller alley bisected this one.

The Okoye woman was there, pulling Finn Gowan, still holding the shotgun in her left hand. Together, they hurried towards the smaller alley.

Jax stepped out, steadied his aim and fired twice.

One or both of the shots seemed to take the bitch in the back and she went down to all fours, almost pulling the screaming kid with her.

He started to hurry, but somehow Okoye struggled up to her feet, panting and whining. She hitched along, unsteady, thrusting the boy in front of her, then followed him into the alley.

Jax smirked to himself. At the corner himself, he pointed the stubby barrel ahead of him as he looked in, careful to keep his body back behind the bricks.

The alleyway was actually a deep, recessed fire-door with no outside access, set fifteen feet into the wall and lit by a single, fizzing bulb in a wire cage.

Hunkered down in the corner, the bitch slumped facing

him, shielding the brat behind her. With her left hand, she covered the wound in her side, beneath her right breast. Blood stained her fingers and darkened the denim of her hip. Her eyes were wide and terrified. She still held the shotgun in her blood-stained right hand but struggled to lift it, though she tried. She squeezed the trigger and the blast was deafening; echoing along the canyon-like alley, but only tore a chunk from the wall opposite Jax.

He stepped out of cover and thumbed back the revolver's hammer.

"Nice try," he told her.

A second, smaller *bang* split the night, then a third, a fourth. Jax flinched as something exploded on the wall beside his head, showering him with dust and chips of brick. He had less than a second to register it when something struck him in the left thigh like a heavy kick.

He staggered back, reaching out for the wall to steady himself, but his left leg wouldn't hold him. He collapsed in a heap, reaching for his injury, shocked when he felt a ragged hole that burned when he touched it.

He looked down at his hand in disbelief. Blood oozed between his fingers.

Looking back along the alley, Gayle Stillwater limped towards him, eyes cold in the faint light from the windows she passed. Held in both hands, she pointed his own Glock straight at him.

"You fucking bitch," he groaned.

She closed the distance.

In shock after the shot, Jax looked around for where he might have dropped the revolver. He hadn't dropped it: he still held it tight in his hand, but couldn't feel it. He swung it towards Gayle.

Before he could squeeze off a shot, she fired, sending

strobes of light rippling across the walls. Two bullets missed their mark, but a third struck him in the gut, knocking out his breath, then another took him high in the left side of his chest. Jax realised he was looking up at the night sky with no memory of having fallen back.

Thick, black darkness seemed to creep in from the edges of his vision. He was cold, numb and losing the sense from his extremities. He felt small, panicked, like a rabbit in a snare, like a wounded mouse watching a hungry cat approach, licking its chops.

Jax wondered if this was what dying felt like. The experience of it was nothing like it looked from the other side of things. The feeling of running out of time, of being down to his final seconds, was gut-churning. He had so much left to do; his future had been almost close enough to touch but was now receding like fragments of a dream fading from memory. For the first time perhaps ever in his life, Jax Knox was scared — terrified, petrified by fear.

He watched Gayle Stillwater's mouth move but her voice sounded far away.

Jax tried to wet his lips to speak but could not work up the saliva. Voice weak and croaky, he managed to say, "You won't do it, you bitch. I fucking know you... and you ain't got it in you."

Gayle didn't say a word. She aimed for his head and pulled the trigger.

CHAPTER 34

Despite the gunfire and screaming, the staff at the haulage depot were only alerted when a middle-aged man in overalls came out for a smoke break and heard Gayle pounding on the fire-door, screaming for help.

Bobbi had lost a lot of blood. Someone called for a first-aider; a thin, lanky man with a bristly moustache, who put pressure on the entrance and exit wounds and tried to keep her conscious. Someone used their mobile phone to call an ambulance.

Gayle knew that the police would arrive with them, if not sooner.

In the buzz of activity that followed, she kept the Glock out of sight until she could slip it into the Nike backpack.

"Here," she said, handing it to Finn, who put it on his back. She held him close, shushing him as she hadn't done since he was a baby, while watching over Bobbi. The shock had worn off and her face was twisted in pain.

As workmen hurried back and forth, and others gawked from the doorways set along the alley, Gayle heard chatter about the Land Rover that had mounted the wall.

They confirmed what she already knew: Aled Gowan was dead.

As the loss of him settled in, Gayle's eyes misted with tears. It was her fault. She should have known better than to stay; known better than to involve them all in this. Aled was gone, and now Bobbi... She wouldn't be able to forgive herself if Bobbi died too.

Within minutes, the alleyway was a buzz of activity with paramedics rushing in. Gayle ushered Finn out of the way. He buried his face in her side and clung to her, no longer sobbing, but shaking all over.

One female paramedic came to check on Gayle then Finn, shining a penlight in his eyes and checking his neck for signs of fracture. When she determined he was unhurt, Gayle asked about Bobbi.

"The bullet passed through," she said. "We're taking her to the hospital now."

"Which?"

"UHW," she said, "University Hospital. They have experience with injuries like these."

Policemen in uniform arrived to secure the scene and interview witnesses. As they worked out what happened, she heard them asking about CCTV footage. An employee offered to take an officer to review it and burn a copy for evidence.

Gayle knew she only had a couple of minutes left.

While other police officers moved in to photograph and bag evidence, medics were busy loading Bobbi onto a gurney. When an officer came and asked Gayle's name and residence, instinctually, she said, "Jess Slater," and gave a fake address.

Finn looked at her, confusion lining his face, and she gave him a reassuring smile.

Bending to Finn's height, the cop asked, "And what's your name, young lad?"

Finn shrank back, tightening his grip on Gayle.

"Andy," she answered for him.

"And how old are you, Andy?"

"He's six."

"Do you want to come and sit with me in the car?" he asked. "It's nice and warm and I think I have a Snickers. I'll let you look at my radio. See? It's pretty cool, right?" He offered the radio to Finn. "What do you say?"

"He stays with me," Gayle said.

"Detectives are en route," he said, standing up to his full height, five inches taller than Gayle. "They're going to need a statement, Miss Slater. Don't worry, we have social workers and people to keep an eye on young Andy while we talk, there's nothing to worry about." He offered a smile that didn't work to reassure her.

Nonetheless, Gayle nodded. "Are they here now?"

"Soon," he said, then thumbed the switch on his lapel mic. "Rodgers at the scene at Ridley Haulage, do you have an ETA on Detective Lowell?"

Gayle looked back along the alleyway. Bobbi was already on the gurney, being tended to by three paramedics who began to usher her this way towards the waiting ambulance. Its beacons spun and lit the night, so bright that she was forced to look down.

She looked at the officer and gestured to Bobbi, mouthing the words, *"We're just going to say goodbye."*

He nodded but rose a finger, as if asking for one minute. Gayle pretended not to understand and turned to lead Finn away.

Over her shoulder, the officer's words were fading, but she heard, "Yes, and one deceased male — Knox, Jackson, also from Leicester. Detective Graff? Yes, I'll let Detective Lowell know."

Graff? she thought. She didn't know the name but wondered if he was one of Felix's men on the inside. Perhaps not, but she couldn't risk it.

"What's happening, Mummy?" Finn asked.

She leant down as she walked, whispering close to his ear, "If I tell you to run, baby, you run. Okay?" As she neared the approaching gurney, Gayle saw Bobbi's eyes find her above the oxygen mask. She raised one arm, reaching out from under the blanket across her chest.

"Do you have just one minute?" Gayle asked the first paramedic.

They all exchanged a look before he relented and nodded, "Sure. Very, *very* quick though."

Using the same hand with which she'd reached for them, Bobbi pulled the oxygen mask from her nose and mouth. She looked weak and her eyes were sunken, surrounded by dark rings.

Leaning in close, Gayle kissed her friend's forehead. Her skin was clammy and ice-cold. "You're gonna be okay," she said.

Bobbi tried to force a smile but it looked more like a grimace. She took Gayle's hand and had not enough strength to squeeze.

"Don't try to talk," Gayle said, voice hardly more than a whisper. "We can't stay. But I'll find you. Somehow, I'll get in touch."

Bobbi's eyelids fluttered for a moment. Her vision swam, then found Gayle's eyes. She tried to moisten her chapped lips, but to no avail. *"Michael,"* she rasped. *"Through... Michael."*

Gayle gave her a gentle smile and knew that she understood what was happening. "I'm so sorry, Bobbi. It's all my fault."

"It's... okay. Deep water... both feet."

Gayle kissed her forehead again before a paramedic leaned in to place the mask over Bobbi's face.

"We have to go," he said. "You'll be able to talk again soon." As they led Bobbi to the ambulance, Gayle walked with Finn in step with her behind them, head down.

In her periphery, she saw Rodgers still talking on his radio.

She passed him and leaned in to Finn. "This way," she whispered, and pulled him to the left. At the corner of the building, the floor of the loading bays fell away beyond a steel railing. She slipped beneath the bars, guiding Finn with her, then lowered him down. She followed after, pulling him in close, ducking out of sight and moving past the trailers. She looked over her shoulder to check if they had been seen, but for now, they were alone.

As they passed beneath the third trailer, Gayle could see the ruined fence and the Land Rover, its one remaining headlight still blazing in the gloom. Fifteen feet to its right, a police car sat with its beacons aglow. She couldn't see anyone surrounding the stricken Land Rover, so figured if officers weren't in the police car, they had joined their colleagues back at the alleyway.

More cars would turn up soon if they didn't go now, setting up barricades at both ends of the road, keeping back onlookers and media, whom she knew must also be on their way.

"Quickly now," she told Finn, pulling him out of cover, crossing the open expanse of concrete to duck behind the broken wall.

She got behind him and raised him over the sagging railings, telling him not to look at the Land Rover, and gave him a gentle push. He clambered over the fence and Gayle followed. On the other side, she took his hand again. The Fiat was where she had left it, engine still running.

They hurried to it and she pulled open the driver's door, pushing Finn in first. As the boy climbed over the console, she looked back. She saw no one giving chase but the ambulance was starting to move. She heard the sound of other sirens too, growing closer.

She jumped in beside Finn, slammed the door, put the car into reverse and did a one-eighty. She struggled to depress the clutch with the pain in her ankle; grinding gears until she got the little car into first. She pulled out and turned right, heading back the way she had come, sweat sheathing her brow.

"Where are we going?" Finn asked.

"Not sure," she said, "but we're not safe with the police here. We have to hide until we can figure this out."

"Won't the police help?"

"No," she said, "not this time. They'll take me away. But I'm not leaving you, okay? Not ever again."

Gayle looked up in the rear-view mirror. At the T-junction, she saw headlights and emergency beacons, their shrill sirens splitting the night.

Oh God, she thought. She couldn't hope to outrun them, not in the old Fiat 500.

She watched closely as they drew nearer, nearer, telling herself not to panic, not to floor it and draw attention to herself.

Beside her, Finn twisted around and climbed up onto his seat. He looked through the rear window. "Are they coming after us?" he asked.

Gayle didn't answer. She checked the mirror again.

Back there, at the junction, she watched them turn right until their lights were gone behind a bend in the road and the sound of their sirens faded into nothing.

But they still weren't safe. She chewed her lip, wondering if they ever would be again.

With Jax dead and the immediate threat over, she ought to feel some measure of relief, but there was none. She knew that she now had a much larger problem than just one man, more than even the whole of the *West-End* gunning for her. She had nowhere to go and no one who could help her. The enormity of the forces against her was overwhelming; too much to think about. Right now, she just had to get away.

She looked over at her little boy — the only thing she had left. *Whoever it is*, she promised him in her mind, *whoever tries to hurt us, they better be ready for a fight. I won't let anything happen to you. If I have to kill them all like I did Jax, I won't think twice. I'll keep you safe. They'll have to kill me first.*

With her son at her side, Gayle drove into the night, wondering who would come for them next.

THE END

ABOUT THE AUTHOR

James Dunn was born and raised in Leicester, England. Over the years, he has worked as a chef and supermarket manager. In his spare time, he draws and plays guitar.

Cut All Ties is his first published novel.

www.jamesdunnwrites.com

Printed in Great Britain
by Amazon